I0827172

The Ruins of Evermore

BOOK TWO

Maiden of a Darkness Shining

Part Three

A Nearling Arises

A NOVEL BY

DAVID J. SACCHERI

BOOK TWO

Maiden of a Darkness Shining

Part Three

A Nearling Arises

A NOVEL BY

David J. Sacchert

A GOLDEN HOUR™ PUBLICATION

A GOLDEN HOUR™ PUBLICATION

First Edition

This novel is a work of fiction. Names, characters, places, events, organizations, businesses, and incidents are either a product of the author's imagination or are used fictitiously. Any resemblance to actual persons, living or dead, events, or locations is entirely coincidental.

www.theruinsofevermore.com

ISBN-13: 978-0692824870
ISBN-10: 0692824871

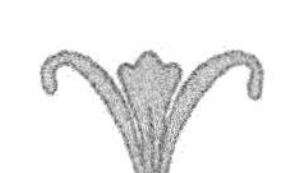

Part Three

The Evermorian Schedule of Events

IN COOPERATION WITH
THE BRISTOL HOUSE

BOOK TWO

Maiden of a Darkness Shining

Part Three

A Nearling Arises

A NOVEL BY

David J. Saccheri

   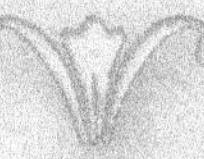  

Life is comprised of many things, some of which
leave us empty.
And in that emptiness exist the many things that
fill us up.

- A wall plaque located somewhere in
The Bristol House Library

Prelude

A Surprising Discovery and Introduction

Having traveled for hours on end with only a brief stop, Starbrill and his band of six finally halted near a small ravine. As the party rested, snacked, and drank, Heather went over to Archie. She ran her hand through his furry flank, over his muscular ribs.

How're you doing?

I'm well, StaLia. And you?

Great.

Good. I can't help but notice your MindSpeake is improving. Any thoughts to share?

Heather shrugged. *Oh, you know…the usual…just wondering…* She found and removed a couple of stickers from Archie's fur, then ran her hand through his coat to smooth it out.

Wondering what?

Just thinking, that's all, wondering about everything going on in Evermore.

Like?

"Like a *lot.*" Heather deftly untangled a burr.

And more specifically?

"Well, things like: Am I here doing what I'm supposed to be doing right now? And if I really am the green-eyed Maiden, shouldn't I be looking for Maidens to join in with instead of looking for my grandmother? And how am I supposed to know what *is* the right thing to do? Or the next right thing after that? I mean, it'd be great if the Portent Prophesies came with a manual and a bunch of directions.

"And am I even in the right place—after all, didn't Sedgwar and I choose the wrong FluxPortal? I guess what I'm getting at is, without knowing it, am I watching a great old movie in the Art Deco theatre when I should really be doing my homework in the Bristol House library? Know what I mean?"

My suggestion is, at this point, you should just let the Universe have its way directing your life, knowing that wherever you find yourself is where you're supposed to be.

"When I came back to Evermore this time, that's exactly what I planned to do—you know, not having a plan, letting the Universe direct me and stuff." Heather patted Archie gently, feeling the brushy give of fur. *But now I'm with you—with an AniMate, I mean—and I know there are supposed to be Maidens around somewhere, so shouldn't I get started doing something more Maiden Portent-like?*

Simply by standing here, you are doing something very Maiden Portent-like. You're being. And if you need to do something else Maiden Portent-like, you could always try being patient.

But what if I miss the Maiden bus? Know what I mean? What if they want my help, come to get me, but I'm not where I'm supposed to be. And then they go wherever they're going, doing whatever they're supposed to do for Evermore, but without me.

You're doing exactly what you need to be doing simply because you're here and doing it. Now trust. You already know that you'd like to get to Wisenhope. The next step sounds like a very logical one for reasons of safety and practicality, and that is to get your TravelTaggs. Especially since what you intend to do is travel without hindrance.

**If* Grandma Dawn is in Wisenhope, yeah, I'd like to go there with some TravelTaggs.* Heather drew deeply. "But, Archie, what if she's not?"

Try not to think too much, StaLia. Choose a path. Let life play out as it will. You can change course any time you deem necessary.

Heather nodded, inclining her head against her AniMate.

Let your mind rest easy, StaLia. Nothing needs to be decided on the instant. The Maidens say to let time give with time. I think it wise. Don't you?

Heather nodded. *I've heard that.*

Then, as the possible Maiden Portent, believe it. Practice it. Faith and impatience don't always make amicable companions. Rest assured, you'll act when necessary, for when have you not? Now, if you'll excuse me, StaLia, I've some things I'd like to attend to. We can talk more at the later, should you wish.

Okay.

Heather watched Archie depart through the foliage, not wanting him to leave, and yet, at the very same time, feeling more than content to be solely on her own. Seeing Molly immersed in lively banter with Starbrill and Toya, and with Sedgwar nowhere to be found, she chose a path in Archie's direction, but not quite.

Awash in inexplicable blue as she had become, Heather simply felt the overwhelming desire to be sequestered with the quiet of day and its welcoming aloneness. She could never really explain why she sank into herself as she did, putting up a shell. Heather only knew that, when feeling this way, it was a time when everything around her spoke to her by just being there for her to see. And she didn't want anyone to disturb their most secret encounters, their secret conversations and revelations.

For a while, she walked silently through the knee-high growth of greenery, in and among the sturdy and comforting presence of trees. She took into account the buoyant, spirited chatter of the birds and was able to see that the sun had penetrated the cloud cover, its rays filtering through the boughs in splashes of contrasting light. Their careless, slapdash appearance lifted her spirit somewhat, making brighter, warmer, happier, whatever lay favorably touched with sun gold.

As the trees thinned, she was surprised to find a small ruin, a circular building of white stone that, at first glance, appeared to have collapsed in on itself. Along the roofline—what Heather could see of it—the statues lining the perimeter had all busted loose, the draped figures scattered in pieces on the ground, amid the strewn discard of columns.

Maidens, thought Heather. These are Maiden statues.

Going to a knee in the grass, she wiped away the dirt on one of the upturned faces, the figure broken in a diagonal across the chest and upper arms.

"She's beautiful," the girl murmured.

When Heather started to set the partial Maiden upright, she spun at the subtle disturbance of bush and grass.

"Well, well, and what have we here, but a child for our growing collection," said a man standing among the many. "Pray tell, youngling, are you in possession of your TravelTaggs? If so, I'll have a look at them straight away."

On the opposite side of the tree-spotted clearing, past the ruin, Heather was surprised to see that such a large group of people had been able to approach from out of the thickness of forest with so little sound, their bindings made of a material that didn't clink in giveaway, of something other than metal. At a glance, there appeared to be thirty to forty men, women, and mostly children, all bunched together and herded by the slavers in command.

Slowly, Heather stood. "Who are you?"

"I am what is known as a SlaveTrader, but have been called far worse in name and presence. Once again, I am requesting a show of your TravelTaggs forthwith."

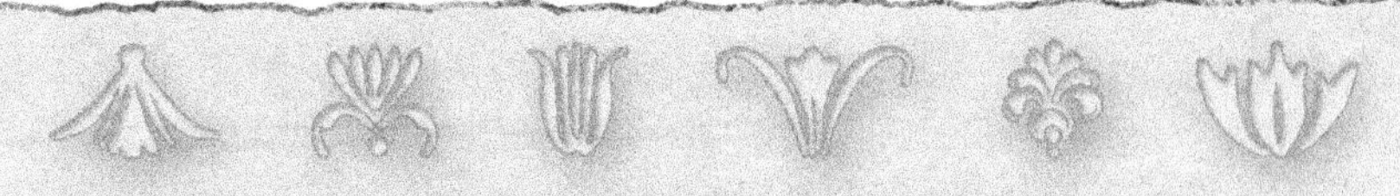

Part Three

Maiden of a Darkness Shining

chapter one

A Battle, a Lesson, and a Riddle

Heather remained cool, observant. By swift count, she could see that trailing up the rear and to the sides were seven or more imposing men assigned the task of keeping the prisoners coalesced and under close supervision, their auras surging sharply in overbearing, garish yellows interspersed with malicious red intent. She hadn't noticed the two other slavers that had broken away previously when first sighting her. Presently, they were sneaking around in surprise, and, obligingly, she backed directly into one.

"Got her!" Embracing Heather roughly across the upper chest, attempting to get a view of her face, the thickset man sneered through twisted lips and missing teeth, "Isn't she a pretty little keeper, Jertsie? Got green eyes, too. That'll fetch a handsome fleuren. Seems we caught ourselves the grand prize, here."

Archie, wherever you are, Heather MindSpoke, *I'm going to need your help right away! Hurry!*

With the slaver's meaty, sweaty arms locked in tight embrace beneath her chin, Heather stared at the grim faces of those captured children at the front of the pack and, focusing there, she seemed to swell with rage. Feeling every bit her Nearling Maiden power, she stomped on the instep of her captor, and with a sharp half-twist, slammed an elbow into his ribs. Set loose, she dipped straight down and, spinning, delivered a blazing uppercut to the groin. With the attacker's anguished face now fully exposed, she pounded a wicked fist squarely into its midst, followed by rapid-fire second and third jolts. Seeing it did nothing more than to stand him upright in a loutish daze, Heather quickly dropped to a forearm. Her side to the ground, she drew in her knees.

"Just go…" from a gathered ball, she thrust her feet upward, full force, "*…down,* already!" Her kick connecting explosively to the chin, the brute spilled over backward, Heather bouncing brightly to her feet.

From over her shoulder, Heather glimpsed a second slaver nearly upon her and so spun in confrontation. Meanwhile, the girl could hear the others rushing her from beyond the building, rustling through the low dense growth.

StaLia? Did you call me? said Archie, from someplace in the trees.

Help! was all the girl had time to MindSpeake.

Ducking her attacker's flying fist, Heather seized his upper arm and elbow on follow-through, and ramming it into his chest while driving him rearward, tripped him ankle-to-heel. Her momentum carrying her forward, her knees landed on his chest and throat, effectively crushing his windpipe. At that, Heather rose swiftly, leaving the slaver to writhe.

Just as six or seven more swarmed in an attempt to wrestle her down, Archie crashed into the clearing, driving through the group, sending them reeling. Snaring one in his mouth, the Archmount shook him fiercely side-to-side, tearing the man open at the midsection. Then he bit clean through him in discard. Blood-muzzled, the beast gathered himself on the pivot and lunged headlong into another. The ill-prepared slaver hadn't time to raise his newly drawn sword, and the savage creature was quick to end his life.

Archie, look out! 'Spoke Heather, on the charge.

Sprinting up behind the Archmount was another slaver, this time with his sword poised high, intending to deliver a decisive blow.

"No-o-o-o!" screamed Heather, cutting him off in pursuit.

Lightning quick, in one slick sweep, Heather snatched up the downed slaver's abandoned sword, and in all her unbridled vehemence, in all her surging, storming momentum, lanced it straight through the aggressor's exposed chest. With the enemy skewered and riding on the weapon's hilt, without breaking stride, she then drove the pointed tip deep into a tree several paces behind him.

Wickedly out of control, Heather was pounding blisteringly on the pinned man's face, now his stomach and ribs, whomp!, whomp!, whomp!, whomp!, dull thuds, all.

He's dead, StaLia. Leave him!

But blinded by fury at anyone attempting to harm her AniMate, Archie's words refused to penetrate, leaving Heather to impotently pound away.

StaLia, behind you!

The Archmount's words finally registering, Heather whirled. Rumbling toward her, sword drawn in glints of steely light, was one of the taller, more muscular SlaveTraders. Beyond was a snarling Archie, engaged in a tangle with three attackers.

Reaching in a desperate half-turn, grasping the haft of the weighted tree-bound sword, Heather pulled and pulled, but the lodged weapon refused to slide free. Now the assailant was upon her. Stepping forward to engage him, grasping for her dagger, she was late in releasing its razor-edged potential. In a flash of steel, she was disarmed at the scabbard, her blade clacking metal-to-metal, her smaller weapon flying freely out of reach. Heather backed and, from behind, felt the hilt of tree's implanted sword dig into her cloak, impeding further retreat.

"Heather, catch!" It was Sedgwar, bursting into the clearing, throwing his trusted and well-used steel her way before turning to do battle.

Instinctively, she grabbed at its hilt in flyby, but missed, the weapon falling aimlessly to earth. That's when the powerful SlaveTrader unleashed his streaking blow. Twisting, turning, deftly dodging the attempt, Heather tripped over his unconscious slaver companion and watched as her attacker's errant, cleaving blade found the recumbent body in full, effectively ending his life.

Meanwhile, Heather, off balance, seeking in vain to keep her footing, fell face first to the ground. Quick to spin belly up, she scrambled rearward in a crabwalk. Hotly, the slaver kept pace in pursuit, his weapon dangerously poised at the ready, its tip gliding ominously overground with every closing step.

Her arm tangling with a clump of foliage, Heather fell flat to her back. Ugh! Recovering, rearing her head to once more fix on her towering aggressor as he raised his sword, she was surprised to witness a blur of flashing silver that whistled by overhead, originating from a source out of sight. Hearing the slaver cry out, seeing him recoil and then pitch toward her, Heather rolled away in time to avoid his toppling body and once more gain her feet.

Recovering her dagger, she raced to assist Archie, but slowed when she saw Sedgwar, his hands in a lethal blur, succinctly making quick work of the lone swordsman who remained.

Only after a reassuring scan of the area did she sheath her weapon.

Are you okay, Archie?

Fine. How are you?

Good. Great. Couldn't be better.

At Heather's sarcastic response, Archie asked, *What came over you?*

I don't know what you mean.

Your anger? The slaver? The sword and tree? What came over you?

Heather turned away, MindSpeaking curtly, *Lots, I guess.*

StaLia?

I don't know, okay? I don't know.

She regarded the slaves who were milling about, looking on in silence. She didn't want to know what they were thinking, what their expressions or auras were saying to her. Stepping over a few dead slavers, she wearily retrieved Sedgwar's sword and brought it to him, handing it over.

"Heather?"

"What?" She chose not to face him.

"Look at me."

Heather scarcely shook her head.

"Look at me."

Annoyed, restless, she burned. Her gaze stayed focused elsewhere. "What?"

"Are you all right?"

"What's with you guys, anyway?" she grumbled. Her brow furrowed, her head shaking side-to-side, her words came out softly, "Sure, I'm all right. Why wouldn't I be?"

Sedgwar held her gently by the shoulders, thwarting Heather's attempt to turn away. He raised her chin, and she reluctantly met his eyes. The two stared, Heather defiant, struggling to calm her inner warrior.

The girl drew a deep breath. She softened, saying, "Yeah, I know. I killed someone, okay? It was bound to happen. And I don't know why, but I *still* want to kill him over and over and over again." Heather pulled away, perturbed, on the brink of tears. Collecting herself, she asked, "What do we do with all those people?"

"Free them and—" At the sound of another's approach, Sedgwar cut himself short, his hand flashing to hilt.

"What did I miss?" said a less than enthusiastic Starbrill upon appearance, his sword bared.

"Slavers," said Sedgwar. "And their bound slaves. Over there. Why don't you talk to them and piece together a narrative." Then to Heather, "Let's find the keys and release these people from their bindings."

"What about some of the slavers, Sedgwar? They might not be totally…" she forced the word, "…dead." Unsure of why, she felt even more rankled.

"I'll see to them. Only, before I do, there's one slaver in particular that I want to inspect more closely." Before doing so, Sedgwar asked, "Starbrill, where are Toya and Molly?"

"I expect they'll be stumbling onto us at any moment now. A bit worried, we all set out to look for you."

"Better they didn't find us then." Turning, he mumbled, "Might have complicated matters."

Sedgwar now strode toward the trees, Heather alongside—but not too near. She required space. Behind them, each could faintly hear the newly liberated slaves collectively shuffling their way, hindered at the ankle. Starbrill soon engaged them, and a spattering of hushed conversation ensued.

Near the feet of the slaver that Heather had lanced to the tree lay her impressively built attacker, his face to the ground. Going to his haunches, Sedgwar hesitated turning him onto his back. "You may not want to see this—"

"Just go ahead," said Heather. "Really. This stuff doesn't bug me."

Sedgwar nodded and rolled him. Then he ripped loose the jeweled axe that was embedded in the SlaveTrader's blood-soaked forehead. Briefly, he examined its elegantly shaped handle, its exquisite scroll and lapidary work before handing it to Heather. He felt Heather take it while his gaze remained concentrated on the perfect pitch—where and how the axe accurately struck its intended target and the damage inflicted. Sedgwar also inspected the direction and possible distance from whence the hurled weapon came.

"A Maiden axe?"

"Looks that way."

"I don't get it, Sedgwar. Why don't they just show themselves?"

"Maybe, these days, like someone I know, they're looking to find distance."

"Archie thinks that the less people see Maidens, the better.

That way, they can't talk about what they never saw." At the mention, she regarded her AniMate, seeing he had taken to lying down to clean himself, his muzzle moistly red.

"Could be their reason. And maybe the Maidens only step in now and again to save their Maiden Portent." Sedgwar waited for Heather's reaction.

The girl gave none. "Maybe." She returned the axe.

Upon taking it, Sedgwar stood, and with a flick of the wrist, he wedged the elegant yet deadly weapon into a large branch just within reach above. Afterward, he began rifling the slain man's pockets.

Avoiding her victim affixed to the tree, Heather focused her attention elsewhere, wandering off to search the pockets of the downed slavers.

"I found them," she announced, successful in her very first attempt. When Sedgwar looked her way, she held up the collection, adding, "The keys for the handcuffs. They were here, in this guy's pocket."

At the girl's words, the prisoners restlessly ventured closer, Heather tossing the small but weighty ring to Starbrill. In turn, he started searching for the key among keys that would release the group from bondage.

Now hunched above the slaver with the busted windpipe, Sedgwar could see the man was near death, suffering as he labored to breathe. He looked up at Heather, offering his blade, saying, "Someone has to end this."

"Show me."

The girl observed while, with a slip of his stiletto, Sedgwar finished the job. He moved on.

"Sedgwar?" said Heather.

"Hmm?" Positioning himself over the next disabled slaver, he was feeling for a pulse. None could be found.

"Sedgwar."

"What's that, Heather?"

When the warrior looked up from his task, the girl nodded to the branch overhead. Sedgwar peered. The Maiden axe was gone.

Chapter Two

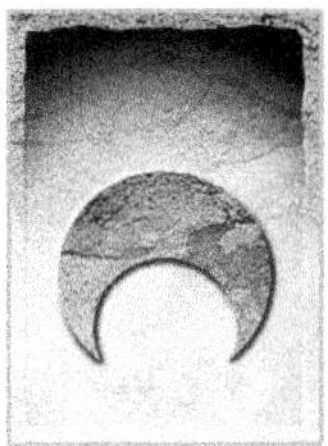

Once upon a Sedgwar

"They're coming with us."

"The slaves?" asked Sedgwar, giving the young man an inquisitive onceover. "As you wish, Starbrill. Truly, I have no issue."

"They can join us for the remainder of our journey to TiaraReign, and afterward decide if they want to return with us to HomeBase. If not, we can find them a Portal to SummersBreath Still on our way back."

"A large group like that, they could prove cumbersome in the handling."

"And, yet, we can't just leave them here alone."

Sedgwar nodded his understanding.

As Starbrill had predicted, it wasn't too much longer until Molly and Toya meandered onto the shocking scene that had unfolded around the derelict structure.

"What happened here?"

"I arrived late, Toya," said Starbrill, "so you'll have to ask Heather and Sedgwar—or Archie, if you can get him to talk."

The girls joined Heather in heartfelt greetings and, afterward, awkward idleness, the Nearling very much withdrawn.

Starbrill, having eventually located the correct key on the ring, released one slave and then left her to unshackle the remainder. He joined Sedgwar and Archie in dragging and laying the bodies of the SlaveTraders near to one another.

"Why bother, I wonder?" asked Molly.

A subdued Heather just shook her head.

Toya, noticing the slaver affixed to the tree, said, "How did *that* happen?"

"You guys want to come?" asked Heather. "I'm going to find out what's going on with those slaves over there." Detaching, she headed toward the partially freed party who mingled about, talking among themselves.

"What's with her?" asked Toya.

I have a sneaking suspicion *he* is, thought Molly, grimacing in glance at the impaled slaver. Instead, she shrugged and said, "I think I'll join her. Feel like coming?"

By the time they walked up, Heather had engaged a short, bespectacled man of later years. Standing alongside his TrueMaite, he was explaining their predicament. "A majority of these people here have been turned over to the SlaveTraders by collectors, with a great many having been kidnapped, others being strays and orphans. Some were found wandering with or without 'Taggs—it didn't matter to this bunch of hooligans. They just threw away their identification and forced them to join the pack.

"And then there are those of us, like Lissi and me, who're illegals—Loyalists, if you have to ask. We're wanted by the KA and so were unable to apply for TravelTaggs. Anyway, as the hatred for Loyalists and the harassment by Rogues intensified, in fear for our lives, we abandoned our home in CloudBorne CityHeights, leaving our relatives and friends behind. We found a shunneler who said he knew the whereabouts of the LostPortals to Autumnsloe—"

"He made lots of promises, this man," interposed Lissi. "Only, he ended up betraying us, forcing Hanin and me into the hands of those SlaveTraders."

The old man added, "But not before taking our money."

"And jewelry. Other belongings, too, mostly sentimental. We lost everything, what little we had."

"Where are you headed?" asked Molly.

"Lissi and I had originally planned on getting to Autumnsloe—"

"Wisenhope," said his TrueMaite. "Everyone wants to find Wisenhope. Right? Right, Hanin?"

"Yes, but now that we're a part of this bunch, here, it looks like we'll be traveling with you for a while."

The TrueMaite added, "At least until you return from TiaraReign."

"Safer that way," said another in their party, overhearing. The lanky man struck Heather as odd-looking, one ear on his otherwise normal head being noticeably higher and larger than the other. He had one eye closed in a perpetual squint.

"Oh, it is, it is. Much safer, Kaggal," said the woman, "especially when we're not as spry as we once were."

"Glad to have all of you along," said Toya, although concerned for the potential liabilities involved when attempting to oversee so many on what may prove to be a long slog.

Somewhere in the midst of conversation, their task complete, Starbrill and Sedgwar had joined them, the entire group loitering close to the structure and its remnants. At that point, Heather drifted over to Sedgwar, who stood isolated from the gathering.

"What do you think happened to this little building?"

Sedgwar studied the maligned structure, the collapsed roof and its pieces. "My guess is that it was destroyed, probably by HumanKinders during or after the Bloodlet Overthrow."

"What do you think it used to be?"

"Maiden influenced, I'd say it was a Portal, perhaps to their home near the DiamondSpark River, in the ShadowSlip Wood."

"Not Wisenhope?"

"Probably not, but who's to say? It's obviously nonfunctioning now—sealed by the Maidens, themselves, I'm sure, in their defense. And since it once belonged to a better time and day, I guess we'll never truly know what destination awaited us on the other side."

"Unless things change."

"Yes. Unless things change."

For several moments, the two stood side-by-side in quiet retreat.

Her eyes coming to rest on the carved Maiden face she had brushed free of dirt, Heather asked, "They're watching us, aren't they?"

"The Maidens?"

"Yeah. All around. This very minute."

Sedgwar scanned the impenetrable denseness of the trees, before refocusing on the mysterious and moody girl with an Archmount, on the tall and slender TimeLight Traveler who possessed green eyes, implausible strength, and carried a Maiden's jewel-encrusted dagger.

"Yes," concluded the man, despite himself. "I'm more than

certain they are."

Covering the oval-shaped WhisperEye Mirror with blue satin cloth, the inspired figure that had listened in darkness stood and called another near. Whispers were exchanged and, in turn, more were generated, person-to-person, room-to-room, and then courier-to-courier. Hands finding shoulders, lips finding ears, hushed tones met with bobbing heads, and as a result, more secretive words brushed the thinly veiled air, all causing deep concern, pressing a necessary spur for action.

And with heads atilt and chins inclined—each expressing their pondering and passion—grave meetings convened, all swiftly to the point. Brows were raised and noses pulled, and when an accord was struck, decisiveness followed on the dispatch. Then, clandestinely and as one, within the continental spread of forest, daring riders set their course, their intentions hellbent for Evermore, cemented hand to hilt and heart to mind.

Empress Insensatia, having left the Castle Grimmivid, was sitting back sedately in her air-conditioned Hover°Carriage. Scenes drifting by on either side, the vehicle floated easily as she progressed through the immense TentCity of Glun DunnArray, past the whitewashed market stalls and the sun-baked plazas, past the pitched-and-pointed rooftops and glum, slumping faces of the rotted row houses. Worn down laggard since the Bloodlet Overthrow, the once proud city wasn't what it once was, but none in Evermore were. Under the Dahklarr, they weren't meant to be. And while the swell of people lining the slovenly streets of radiant heat parted at the passing of the Royal Carriage, the Empress found herself unable to care about any of it—or them.

Not a shred.

What fully occupied her thoughts was her upcoming rendezvous with SpringShoot Green's King Raptillion, and how to keep him unsuspectingly under her spell as they continued to plot their incursion—and, furthermore, how to position herself with both he and Rasparr of Autumnsloe, two ruthless, cunning, and power-hungry men with their lustful eyes on Winterspire.

As it stood, she was convinced that one of her two lovers would have to die by the time the invasion was complete. There simply would no longer be room or need for both men in her life.

Having treaded through the rainforest for hours with only brief respites, Starbrill's inflated party finally had no choice but to halt, the older travelers unable to progress any farther without rest. Noticing their need for a lengthy break, Starbrill removed his pack and told everyone to take some time. He recruited Toya, Molly, and a few of the younger former slaves in close proximity, and together they left to gather fruit, berries, and other edibles for the group.

Afforded the opportunity, Sedgwar approached Heather.

"Have a moment?"

"Yeah. Yeah, sure." Heather's mind was far away. "What's up?"

"Nothing urgent. I just wanted to talk, that's all." Sedgwar felt hemmed in by the crowd. "Feel like walking?"

Not really wanting to spend time in the tangled, sticky presence of the others, Heather welcomed the offer.

When they were out of earshot, Sedgwar seemed to ruminate before saying, "That was quite a battle back there."

When all he received was barely a nod, the warrior realized the conversation he had imagined taking place would not unfold as scripted in mind, the girl apparently prickly and sensitive to the touch.

In return, Heather offered, "I think I know what you're trying to do, Sedgwar. And you don't need to. I'm okay. Really, I am."

"Good. I'm pleased to hear that. You see, I couldn't help but notice a few things—

"You mean how angry I got."

He looked over to see Heather's gaze fastened before her. "Yes. How your anger overcame you, getting the best of you in battle."

"You're talking about the guy and the tree."

"Yes. I witnessed most of the confrontation on my approach."

"Yeah, okay…" Her words were soft, the silence short. "I, um, I sorta lost my temper, there, didn't I?"

"Mmm." Sedgwar hid his amusement at the girl's understatement. "I suppose it wouldn't have mattered much, if you weren't almost killed because of it."

"I know, and I, uh…I know, that's all."

"I would have missed you, too, just getting to know you as I have…" Sedgwar didn't even want to think about having to clean up the youngling's remains, imagining how such an act would affect him.

Her face in a squint, Heather glanced up at her warrior companion, and the pair retreated into uneven silence. Finally, she said, "I've been watching you, and I saw how you fight."

"And how is that exactly?"

"Honestly?"

"Always."

"Okay, then. And I mean this in a good way. You remind me of the small fish I see sometimes in Whisper Creek—you know, when I'm looking down into the water from on top of a rock. And it's like you're flowing in some liquidy world with everything around you floating by, and you're doing stuff like it all doesn't matter and belongs to someone else. I mean, you seem totally far away, like you could care less, and then, when a mosquito or fly comes by, suddenly, wham!, you attack and leap to catch it. And then the next second, you're back floating again like you hadn't moved at all. Only, now, the bug is dead, and you're waiting for the next one to come around."

At Heather's description, Sedgwar was unable to help himself and a reluctant smile stole over his solemn face, softening his handsome features.

"I'm kind of afraid to ask, Sedgwar, but what does *my* fighting remind you of?"

"Heather, really, I'm not so sure—"

"And you have to be honest."

"You're serious, I see. Well, then, all right. Let me think." Sedgwar pursed his lips, drew a breath through his finely ridged nose. "I suppose, if I can use the same analogy, you definitely have the fish part working, the part where it leaps to snare the bug. You're very impressive that way, especially for one so young. But then there are times when you completely forget the bug and go after the girl on the rock." Sheepishly, Heather chuckled, and Sedgwar continued. "What I mean is that you completely forget your purpose, becoming overwhelmed with anger that way. It's self-defeating."

"I know, you're right…"

"I think you'd also agree, if you have to fight, that being detached is the best way to engage in battle."

Heather stopped to face the broad shouldered man. "You think I should fight like you?"

"No, not if you don't want to. But I think it's important that I speak bluntly, here, for your sake and for those who care about you—"

"And you want to show me how."

The pair resumed walking.

"If you want to learn, yes. Yes, I do. I have a sneaking suspicion that in your role, and with what you may have yet to accomplish, knowing how to fight properly will be imperative. *And* in the future it'll prevent you from having to suddenly rely on your dagger, because, only moments before, you just angrily stuck your sword through a tree."

Heather's face elicited a dim spark of humor. She reddened. "Goof."

At the sound of water, the pair headed in its direction. When they came upon a large rock near a small pond and its impoverished falls, Sedgwar sat on the smooth stone with the girl lowering herself to the ground. Past the water, the flatter areas sloped away to give a distant view of the hills.

Heather took the opportunity to ask, "Where did you learn to fight that way?"

"As a soldier for my kingdom, it was necessary. I had to learn as a matter of basic survival. In earnest, it began there and then, later, became something more."

"What do you mean?"

"I mean that when you *fight,* it's not just about the fighting..." Sedgwar leaned back, uncomfortably. "It never is just about the fighting. But at the time, it only seems that way."

The girl waited for more.

"I'm sorry, Heather. Truly, I'm not sure what I'm trying to say here. Or even where to start if I knew, exactly."

"Just pick a spot."

"Pick a spot?" Sedgwar chuckled. "It's not like I'm about to clean the barn, and to start I simply need to choose a stall. To try and explain fighting, I suppose I would need to explain myself, in part."

"So, then, go right ahead."

"You seem eager."

"Well..." She shrugged.

Silently reminiscent of AstarraAporra, Heather waited openly, Sedgwar's frown not at all serving as a deterrent. He started to speak, but then shut down on a headshake, remaining solitary and to himself.

However reluctant, Sedgwar began to tunnel, seeking a point of appropriate consequence, a starting place located deep within himself, looking to delicately probe and uncover the remains of a fossilized lifetime buried under thick layers of smothering sediment.

Having been inwardly adrift on the rock, Sedgwar finally

surfaced. Then, feeling like his every word was a chafing of the skin—the wearing away of a hardened, protective, insulating crust—he began to recount the time when, as an experienced soldier of the Realm, he had found himself on a mission to the Northwest Territories of Winterspire, leading his troops to interpose in a conflict between tribes in an attempt to restore peace. Gone for several months to the remote area, he returned to find Evermore in shambles, a result of the Bloodlet Overthrow that had occurred in his absence.

Curfews in place, martial law had been imposed on an unruly populace, and his garrison had been summoned once more and pressed into crucial duty. But Sedgwar refused, and leaving the troops under the charge of his second in command, he had instead returned home to see to the welfare of his family.

Upon arrival, he discovered his farmstead had been laid to waste, with his wife and three children dead inside their home, lying bloodied upon the floor. Consumed with grief, forcing himself to act, he numbly located a site high upon a hill, a place of serenity, he felt, with a view overlooking the valley. There, Sedgwar dug graves and, one-by-one, he carried their lifeless bodies—first his wife, then his girls, and finally his young son—and laid them preciously to rest. And, always near, he stayed with them for several nights, unable to find sleep or appetite to eat. Intermittently, against the stars, he spoke softly to each.

Returning to the house one morning, Sedgwar declined all visitors, including the Emperor's men and their offerings. Shortly thereafter, gathering what little he needed, Sedgwar set his home ablaze and, climbing the hill, stood and briefly watched it burn. Then he turned his back, promising never to return, vowing never to have anything further to do with HumanKind and its plots, woes, misdeeds, and fortunes—what he felt was its wretched existence.

Afterward, Sedgwar wandered Evermore's uncharted Outer Reaches, and the days turned to weeks, and those to months. Exhausted and ragged, dirty and starving—empty in spirit—he found himself one morning outside the great gates of the Monastery of Hiberius. Allowing himself in, he looked upon its main house and surrounding fields. Spotting what struck him as a peaceful patch of grass near a tree and small bridge, he staggered their way and lowered his weary frame to ground. Then, still in his warring breastplate, he slept.

Sedgwar didn't stir when the monks passed him as they set out for the fields to work their day. Nor did he stir when they returned that evening. Yet, when the warrior finally awakened, he found food and water had been placed nearby. He turned away and slept some more.

This routine lasted days, Sedgwar growing weaker and approaching death. Still, he ignored the repeated offerings. And, finally, when the monks found their visitor to be unconscious, the Abbot sat and assisted him with drink. Aware of the stranger's impoverished state, he took to feeding him broth daily.

Slowly recovering strength, Sedgwar began to eat on his own. And when he was first able, without seeking permission, he joined the ranks of monks laboring in the fields. Not a word passed among them as he toiled in his boiling armored shell, his belt and weapons awkward and weighing him down. And when the day had run its course, the mute stranger went back to his place beneath the tree and near the bridge, nodding his thanks whenever the Abbot brought him a plate and glassful.

When the season grew weary and the skies turned cold, Sedgwar ignored the blanket placed next to his daily servings. And when the nights grew all the colder still, the monks found and carried a shivering, fevered Sedgwar into the monastery. Later, he would awaken on a mat in front of the fire, a blanket over his lean and naked body. Near at hand, he found nourishment, and a monk's attire alongside his washed and worn battle gear. When feeling well enough to return to the fields, he adopted the monks' dun-colored wear and again set to work, the days bleeding blearily in passing.

Winter soon descended in all its snowbound fury, and Sedgwar was given a small, barren room in the dormitory, and into a corner he propped the armor, along with the swords, knives, and clothing from his previous life. Everyday thereafter, he dressed in dullish brown and immersed himself in a monk's existence, his tasks varying to change, as did his seasons. He took up meditation and, when troubled, long hours of prayer, and in time he felt he was able to successfully push away all that attempted to intrude from the outside world.

Months turned to years. One day in early spring, when bathing in a mountain lake among his brethren, Sedgwar glimpsed the scars covering the much older Abbot, scars similar to ones he, himself, had acquired in battle.

Having spoken very little to this point in his stay, he approached and asked, "The wounds, Abbot, do they ever heal?"

To which he replied, "Only when the child who received them has forgiven those who inflicted their pain."

With those words, the older man dove from the rocks and into the clear water, leaving Sedgwar to linger on his own. Later, upon their return to the monastery, he sought out the Abbot and inquired about his time as a soldier, to which the older man offered little in response. When Sedgwar pressed him, the Abbot confided that he had once been considered a great warrior, but had reached a point where conflict no longer drew his interest.

"Why was that?" asked Sedgwar.

"I'm saddened you find the need to ask."

Later that spring, when Sedgwar awakened and reached for his monk's garb, he found his armor and battle gear instead. Perturbed, he searched for and discovered the Abbot in meditation. When in the morning air Sedgwar confronted the older man, asking the meaning of having him leave when he sought only a life of peace, the leader of monks rose and stood quietly before him.

Peering into Sedgwar's eyes, the Abbot suddenly slapped him. Caught off guard, Sedgwar stood completely dumbfounded. The Abbot slapped him again. As a result, Sedgwar angrily lashed out, and calmly, the older man deflected his blow. When he tried again, after brushing aside the attempt, the Abbot boldly stepped forward to touch him lightly on the cheek. Enraged, Sedgwar struck out in counterpunch. Same result. Once more he cast a blow, then another and another, only to encounter similar deflections and conclusions.

Sedgwar, the proud and proven warrior swelled with indignation, with rage. The Abbot, meanwhile, remained distant, awaiting Sedgwar's next move. When it came—a kick—once more, the older warrior sedately deflected the blow, but this time he laid Sedgwar down easily on the ground, no harm done. And incensed, Sedgwar attacked again and again, with blows swift and swifter, harder and hardest, and each time was thwarted and graciously laid to earth.

"Throw me!" screamed Sedgwar, his hot breath mingling as cool clouds in air, his raucous words echoing amid the placid mountain faces. "I'm a warrior! I'm a *man! You throw me!*"

But, impassive, the Abbot would have nothing to do with Sedgwar's request. And so the warrior intensified his attack, to which the Abbot turned away every attempted thrust, slice, and kick, only to counter with a gently placed touch or kindly landing. Finally, the muscular man fell to his knees before the Abbot.

Head down, Sedgwar said, "Abbot, if you will not throw me like a man, then I ask that you teach me as one. I wish to no longer be that child."

To which the Abbot replied, "Rise. What animal does not fall victim to its own power? And who doesn't want to slay that very beast?" Sedgwar rose, but was no longer in possession of the boldness that once cloaked him. Aware, the Abbot said, "Before me, happily, I see the makings of a man."

Throughout the winter, Sedgwar was to meet regularly with the Abbot. Under his tutelage, the older master demonstrated and explained to the younger student the Art that accompanied the craft, the mind that complemented the skill. He taught Sedgwar how to be closer to oneness with the universe, to seek that place where there existed no separation from inside and out, where there was no need to think, only to react, instinctively, dispassionately, and with purpose. He instructed him when fighting not to act out of fear or anger, but to control by slowing down time, and how, from the eye of the storm, to control the storm itself as it raged around him. And in this process, Sedgwar was able to achieve a certain tranquility.

And when the pupil had shown his learning complete from the master, upon awakening one morning in spring, Sedgwar once more found his armor and weaponry at his bedside.

Locating the Abbot, Sedgwar bowed his head and asked him, "Why do you wish that I leave the monastery?"

"Because your time here is finished. We are settled here. You are not. You've a demon, a dragon, to slay, and he is to be found outside our gates."

"In what land does this dragon reside? There are many such creatures in Evermore, in so many forms, such as winged thunder lizards, demon serpents, or those that conquer with fire. Tell me and I will seek and slay him forthright."

"Of the many that exist, you must identify and conquer him yourself. And only if you desire to embark on such a journey."

Sedgwar looked troubled. "A dragon?" He laughed, bitterly. "Must I truly be a part of Evermore's tired fascination with dragons?"

"The dragon you seek is no mere dragon, of which there are many, and many who never die."

"Riddles, Father Abbot. Can you not be precise? Where to start? How to seek?"

The wise man shook his head. "Only you will know him, and know when he's no more."

"But why this, why him? Why *me?* I am no hero, no legendary conqueror or mythological leader. Me?" Sedgwar scoffed, "I'm lost…I'm only a lost warrior."

"Consider yourself fortunate. It is only the lost who can find themselves, and by doing so stand to discover their own true hearts. You, you are a warrior who suffers much, who cannot find rest due to his conflict with the outer world—due to the conflict with his inner world. Sedgwar, go and make your peace for the sake of your life. This is my advice at your leaving."

Dispirited, at a loss, Sedgwar silently agreed.

"And until such time as you return, if you ever do," continued the Abbot, "you have taken me to heart, and I, you. Such are our lasting gifts to one another. If time and circumstance allow, I will embrace you and the day when we shall see each other once more."

"And I shall rejoice in that moment..."

Having reemerged in the present, the sound of the falls trickling into the nearby pond became once more apparent to Sedgwar. His eyes no longer focused within, the warrior didn't speak right away, but instead kept his attention fixed on the distant horizon. Finally, he turned to Heather.

"And, that, young Heather," he concluded, "is when I left the Abbot and his monastery and later encountered you on the road. In search of this supposed Evermorian dragon, I had no idea really of where I was headed or where to begin my quest."

"Kind of like me."

"Very much so."

"Even though Grandma Dawn is hardly a dragon."

"Of course." Humor lit his features, but the glints quickly faded. "Where this dragon is, if it exists at all, I must seek him out. The Abbot, he is a wise man, one who saw me completely, and who fully understood my soul. I also believe he recognized the warrior in me as he recognized himself. And if I am honest, it is true that I am not settled like he claimed."

Wearing a soft grimace, Heather was staring into the distance. "I never thought about it before, Sedgwar—and don't laugh, okay?—but I don't think I've ever been settled, either. I mean, when I was with my grandmother, I always thought I wanted to meet my mother, my father. I felt left out, like I was missing something that made me different from nearly everyone else." Heather turned briefly to Sedgwar. "I found out later that I felt different only because I *was* different, and it was okay, that it made me special in my way.

"Anyway, when Grandma Dawn went away, well, I also figured out how really special *she* was, too, and how much she meant to me. I guess I knew it all along, but never more than when she wasn't around any longer. That's why I have to find her, before something happens to her or maybe even me." Heather's face displayed her struggle, and seeing this, at a loss for words, Sedgwar found need to look away. "I can't just not see her again, you know? I just can't."

"Unfortunately, sometimes the choice isn't ours to make."

Heather's words were soft. "Well, until I have to bury her on a hillside, I'm not giving up, ever, never, ever."

The two shared a comfortable gaze, Sedgwar being the first to break it. Looking past the hem of his OverRobe, near his boots, he said, "If you don't mind, like the Abbot in my life, I have decided I will be a part of yours until I'm no longer able. In that span, you can quit or leave me anytime you'd like. Yet, if you stay and learn, I want to share with you what I know, including what he taught me. You can look at it as a way that helps to ensure you see your grandmother again."

"So, what about you? I mean, won't it ensure anything for you?"

"It will."

"What's that?"

Sedgwar shook her off.

"What?" She waited. "Sedgwar?"

His grumbled words were reluctant and tumbled out like weighty stones. "It ensures that I see my daughter AstarraAporra again."

"Oh, okay. All right. But I thought you said she was..." Heather went quiet. On a sudden realization, the girl let the moment drift. "Well," she resumed, perhaps a bit too enthusiastically, "I've always been super athletic. I'll probably learn what you have to teach me really fast."

The warrior could tell Heather wasn't boasting, but simply confident in her abilities. "Then you should be a quick study. We've not a lot of time today, but you can learn about two important fundamentals that I see as necessary for survival. And we can begin immediately."

At home in her Castle Densearling, S'ilKuSheere walked into the encompassing drear of her study. Dennunciating, she cast eight swirling ShimmerBalls into the vagueness, and, upon contact all around, the freestanding candelabras burst into tall narrow flame. Then she threw another ShimmerBall against the wall, and it exploded and spread to form a ragged-edged screen of great breadth upon the stonework.

Standing stiffly and powerfully erect, she spread her hands outwardly from her face. “Show me the progress of my winged soldiers,” she commanded.

Starting at a point towards the center, and then rippling outward and into sharp focus upon the screen, S’ilKuSheere was able to look upon vast numbers of ominous dark moths that clouded the skies, the snowy white lands of Winterspire visible in the distance.

“Superb. Excellent, in fact. And now, with the second ‘Door of the DualPortal soon to align, my beautiful warriors of the night shall be able to carry out and complete their mission of death and devastation. And to think, I’ll be able to watch the entire massacre in the privacy and comfort of my own home. And all without commercial interruption.”

Chapter Three

The Art of the Fight

"Good! Good, Heather!" said Sedgwar, encouraging the Nearling in her lightning swift attack, although warding off her intended blows. "Reaction is the most important thing. Don't watch my hands—don't anticipate. You're more than quick enough, so there's no need. Many warriors have strength, others speed. You're among the few who possess both. Remember: speed overcomes power, and timing overcomes speed. You must learn when to utilize each to your advantage."

Sedgwar was quick to counter Heather's moves by parrying, and ended by halting a devastating thrust of his massive fist within an inch or two of her face and, then, in the very next instant, producing his index finger to touch her spritely on the tip of the nose. Heather laughed.

"How did you do that?"

"Practice. Years of it." Sedgwar again pressed his attack. "Heather, move a bit so you can counter. Like this. That's it. Good. Slip easily. Now, maintain that flow while staying relaxed, just as you're doing. That's right. You're a natural that way. At some point, you'll reach a state where you're at one with all that exists outside of you, whereby there's no barrier, and inside becomes outside and outside, in. And from that calm center is where you'll generate power—not from tenseness, mind you, but from a point of peaceful centeredness."

Sedgwar stopped to demonstrate, rotating his torso as he did so. "You see, you explode with acceleration, generating heel to hip to shoulder to elbow to fist: wham! Then you'll 'strike like lightning out of a clear blue sky,' as the Abbot used to say, as did his master before him."

Heather practiced, twisting at the hip. "That's probably why that slaver wouldn't go down when I kept punching him in the face. Not enough oomph."

Back in their fighting stances, Sedgwar scored by moving swiftly, again touching the girl on the tip of her nose. The next moment, however, had him deflecting a volley of shots as Heather was able to deftly slip inside. When she backed off, he said, "Very good. Now, I can certainly tell you all about technique, but you have to practice any move hundreds to thousands of times before its absorbed entirely into muscle memory."

Swift to dip his head, Sedgwar barely avoided Heather's kick. "Then again, I see it may not take you as long to learn as most."

When Sedgwar countered Heather's next attack and took the offensive, he again moved in and lightly touched her, fingertip to nose. Bink.

This time Heather didn't laugh, her teacher sensing her frustration. "Don't do it, Heather. Don't go there. Clear your mind of darkness."

Heather stopped and took a deep breath.

"Now, I want you to feel my hands, Heather, as if yours are connected to them. All the time, *feel* them, their whereabouts, sensing their presence. Then you're always ready to react wherever they happen to be when I attack. You feel, all right? No thinking. Understand? No anticipation. Excellent! That's it."

"Oh, sorry!" said Heather, her potent blow glancing off the side of Sedgwar's cheek.

Startled at its power in just the near miss, the warrior shook it off. "Don't stop. Keep coming. Good! Very good!"

Sedgwar lashed out with a series of shots, Heather ducking many, blocking the rest.

"Don't block them too close to my body," he said, stopping the match. "See here. Extend your arm to my chin. That's right. Can you understand how easy it is for me to deflect the blow when you're extended that way? See? Just a little push and your punch goes awry. It takes only two fingers. Now, if your arm is close to your body, and I try to block it, you have power there. It takes more effort, more exertion on my part to turn aside your strike when it's completely unnecessary and doesn't serve me as well. And if you're in a long battle, you'll lose strength and become fatigued faster. Understand?"

"So, I should let you throw the punches."

"Let me commit, Heather, and you can brush me aside and react to the opening."

"Got it."

"One more thing. Lacking weight and bulk as you do—no matter how strong or quick—you must never let your opponent tackle you. You don't want to brawl. You want to retain your distance so you can unleash those potent weapons of yours. Am I clear?"

Heather nodded and Sedgwar pressed in with a series of thrusts, and displaying little effort she deflected them and then countered in return. Sedgwar was impressed, continually marveling at her speed, her agility, and how quickly she picked up what he had just demonstrated. And when Heather slipped inside to touch him on the nose, he burst out laughing.

"Where did you learn to fight this way when no one has taught you technique, Heather?"

Both participants sweating profusely, Heather dropped their hands. "This probably sounds like a stupid question, but do you have movies here in Evermore?"

"Of course."

"Well, it's hard to explain, but when I was alone in the Art Deco theatre of the Bristol House, I watched a lot of movies, you know. Not great art movies like Seven Samurai that I watched with Molly, but fighting movies. When I saw what those guys were doing on the huge screen, I sort of became them, you know, and then *I* was doing their stuff, memorizing it from inside of their heads while we did it together. So, by watching those movies over and over, I kind of learned what they did while adding some of my own touches to it. And there's a sort of gymnasium in the Bristol House basement where I practiced a lot, as much as I could. I guess I just have a way of getting this stuff really quick-like—honestly, Sedgwar, it's like I already know it, but just haven't done it in a long, long time."

"Well, it's paid off, youngling." Though he had encountered many an opponent with Heather's strength, Sedgwar had never met one with her incredible degree of swiftness. "And you're right, you do learn quickly. So, come again."

Once more in their fighting stances, Sedgwar was temporarily distracted when he heard a rustle behind him. He turned.

"There you are!" said Starbrill, emerging from the trees. "We've been looking all over—watch out!"

Having already launched into a roundhouse kick, Heather was unable to halt its blurring flight. Sedgwar, however, without displaying the slightest flinch or hesitation, caught and held her foot in a stab of nonchalance.

"Are we getting ready to leave, Starbrill?"

"Yes, very soon," said the young man, looking upon the scene with curiosity, Heather's leg remaining hoisted in air. "It looks like everyone's rested and ready to go."

"Hello? Yoo-hoo. Hey, Sedgwar, remember me?" said Heather. "Can I have my foot back, please?"

Sedgwar released it. "Give us a few minutes, if you could, and then we'll join you shortly."

Nodding, Starbrill withdrew, but not without another curious glance between the pair.

"All right, one more thing—and this is so very important."

"My anger?"

"You know, then, don't you?"

Barely a nod.

"What you must learn, what you must practice most is temperance, Heather. This was the Abbot's greatest gift to me, the man a warrior who became so accomplished at his craft, so at one with his skill that he surpassed it, transcending in power beyond the fight, beyond the battle. Regardless of your opponent, to lose your anger is to lose the war against yourself.

"When angry, your anger controls you. You don't see your opponent clearly; you only see what you want to do to them, causing you to become blind. And in turn, this blindness makes you vulnerable and, so, in the end, doesn't serve you in battle.

"When you're calm, Heather, you can control the situation like an open child, seeing the field clearly while being aware of what is transpiring around you. Free the mind and unleash the will, work from instinct, and not only will you control your anger, but also conserve your energy. You'll ebb and flow at one with the universe, like that fish you described in the creek."

"I see what you're saying, Sedgwar, and I'll try. I promise I will."

"You do that, Heather. Your life truly may come to depend on it."

Heather nodded in contemplation. "Can I ask you something, Sedgwar?"

"Of course."

"After we fought, why did you and Starbrill sort of organize those bodies of the dead slavers, putting them all tidy-like in one place?"

Preparing to head back into the forest to join the others, Sedgwar motioned Heather to join him. He wiped his wet face on a sleeve.

"Reverence for the dead, Heather. Respect yourself and your opponent, respect the Art of the fight. I could probably tell you it's a practice you must learn, but something tells me you've recently come to know it."

"Does it have something to do with 'life giving unto life in death'? Or maybe 'giving due to what another has sacrificed in your honor that you may live on?'"

"It could, yes. Perhaps more to the latter. Where did you learn of such things? Your movies?"

"No. From a special visitor who came out of nowhere one day. And, I think, Sedgwar, she came just in the nick of time."

"Like that Maiden and her axe."

"Yeah. A *lot* like her, I'm sure."

Once more on the move, the group intentionally lost and found the crowded road to TiaraReign CityHeights, loosely paralleling its course from the forest. With Starbrill again taking the lead, Heather dropped to the back of the pack, and Molly soon joined her, the trail widening.

"Hey, there!" she said. "What have you been up to?"

"I was hanging with Sedgwar, talking about fighting and stuff. How about you?"

"We collected fruit and other things for the newcomers." Heather liked the fact that Molly no longer referred to them as slaves. "Here. I brought you some sweetstalks."

"Hey, thanks, Molly!" Accepting the piece of red and green fruit, Heather said, "It kind of looks like some celery cozied up to a bunch of strawberry-grapes. Are they good?"

"I thought so. You eat the cluster of small round plump parts at the top right away, and then the stalks you take your time with, chewing on them before you swallow. Like candy, it takes a while before they melt in your mouth. Toya says sweetstalks give you lots of energy. Try it."

Heather did, mumbling with her mouthful, "Hey, the top part is really good, sorta burst in your mouth squishy, juicy and sweet."

The girls continued to walk, side-by-side.

"Boy, Heather, the newcomers have very little to eat. I can't imagine how they're all going to get to TiaraReign and back again without food."

"I bet Starbrill and Toya will pick something up for them in the CityHeights," said Heather. "Maybe while we're getting our TravelTaggs."

"Maybe." Molly lowered her voice even more. "We're behind schedule, and Toya thinks we won't be getting to TiaraReign until after nightfall, later than we had hoped."

"Whatever. As long as there's no time limit for getting stuff done, I figure we're doing all right."

The group temporarily clotting in front of them on the path, the girls slowed.

"I haven't seen Archie. Is he around?"

Archie, we're on the move again, Heather MindSpoke.

I'm not far away, StaLia.

Great. "He's out there, Molly."

The girl looked around. "How do you know?"

"Archie just said so." When Heather saw Molly's perplexed look, she added, "Don't forget, we can MindSpeake with each other now. It's pretty great because—okay, Molly, *what?*"

"What?"

"What's that look for?"

"What do you mean?"

"I mean, Molly, your face is getting all goofy and smiley and dancey and stuff, like you know a secret you're not telling me."

Molly laughed. "No secret."

"No secret? Are you sure?" Heather snapped off a juicy piece of sweetstalk and shared it with her. "Is it about *you-know-who?*"

"Who?"

Heather gestured with her eyebrows and then tapped her fingers palpitatingly over her heart. "You know: you-know-who."

"*No!*" Molly's cheeks reddened. Then she gushed, "No! It's *not!*"

Heather joined her in laughter. "Sure?"

"I'm sure."

"You know, right now, you sort of look the color of some of

these sweetstalk dingle-balls."

Molly slapped her friend playfully on the shoulder. "Heather Nighborne, you stop that." Truth be known, Molly would have loved to lean around the newcomers crowding the trail to get a glimpse of Starbrill, but didn't dare. "He's very special, though, don't you think?"

"Very," said Heather, with a wink and a smirk. "Yep, I can see it now, you and you-know-who with forty-seven kiddos, and you guys living in a big ol' shoe, just like in that nursery rhyme."

"Oh, stop…" Hotly flushed, Molly was grinning.

Heather brightened. "By the looks of it, I think that sweetstalk dingle-ball just turned into a bright red tomato."

"Heather, will you *stop* already," said a squeamish Molly, riding a laugh.

"Okay, okay."

"So, what did you and Sedgwar do?"

"He was talking about fighting, showing me moves and stuff. You know, Molly, I wonder how long before we have to go back to Noble."

"Probably depends on when the Bristol House wants us to return home. Why?"

The trail narrowed, and, traveling single file, Heather waited until it widened before answering.

"Well, Sedgwar wants to teach me a bunch about fighting, and if I'm not around, I can't learn it. So—"

"So, you were wondering."

"Yeah." Heather did a double take. "Molly, there you go again! See? You're giving me that look."

"What? There's no look."

"There is, too. And it's right *there.*" Heather pointed directly into Molly's face. "There's no denying it. I'm looking at your 'look' right now, and it's making me laugh. So, what gives? What are you thinking?"

"Honestly?"

"Yeah, honestly."

"All right, then, I'll tell you," said Molly, waggling her brows. "I'm thinking you, Archie, and a litter-full of ArchHeathers running around your big ol' Evermorian doghouse."

Heather roared with laughter and was shushed by others on the trail. "Oh, man, Molly." She chuckled, wiping her eyes. "*That* was a good one. Okay, so, come on. Be serious. Why the look?"

"All right. Here's what I'm thinking. And before I tell you, I have to say that I think it's all pretty astonishing, really."

"Molly, you're killing me. *What's* pretty astonishing?"

"The synchronicity of it all, how this entire scenario is coming together. And to think you were so worried! Heather, you do realize you're becoming more and more like the green-eyed Maiden in so many ways. Everyday, it seems something new is happening, making you exactly like that person mentioned in the Portent Prophesies: you've returned to Evermore older, taller, and more like a Maiden than ever; you've got an Archmount that you MindSpeake with; it seems you've got Maidens guiding and protecting you; you look so, *so* beautiful in your new Evermorian clothes and MaidenBraid; we're hanging around with Starbrill, Toya, and the Savages on our way to get TravelTaggs; and now Sedgwar wants to teach you to fight better. It's all very surprising, *and* stunningly coincidental, if you ask me."

"Yeah, I know. It is. It really is. Pretty wild, huh?"

"Yes."

"So, how will we know when it's time to return to Noble?"

Molly's face once more wore her look. "Heather, after all I just mentioned, do you really have to ask?"

S'ilKuSheere was sipping her icy black Concoction, sitting alone in her castle room, the large widescreen gone dark. The candles burning low, dennunciating, she magically had them grow taller and fill out without inducing a single flicker. She then lowered their flames.

Comfortably blending with the dimness, she gave thought to the possible invasion between kingdoms and the resulting implications, first and foremost among them being: could a power struggle eventually ensue where one or more of her surviving sisters would rise up in an attempt to overthrow *her* in her superior position as Majestic Sorceress? She realized that such an attempt would not be so farfetched, never out of the realm of possibility. After all, between this murky, greedy bunch, could there ever be enough wealth, ever enough power, ever enough Realms over which to rule?

To kill them all to ensure her own safety would be foolhardy. S'ilKuSheere couldn't rule without their assistance. And, yet, to sit and do nothing, allowing them to kill one another would achieve much the same result, ultimately securing her downfall.

S'ilKuSheere assumed that her sole superior, ShakkGôn Sul, wouldn't intervene in their infighting so long as the Dahklarr Herth retained its hold over Evermore, although she could never say for certain.

So, if Brutessa and Rendskorra attempted to invade Winterspire, killing Drakiera in the process, what would become of Mistraya? Would she be isolated and killed also? And foreseeing such a possibility, whom would the Autumnsloe sorceress ally herself with beforehand? Would she even have a choice? Earlier at the Castle Grimmivid, Mistraya didn't seem to be in the confidence of either sister. And, yet, if an alliance *were* formed among those three and then pitted against Drakiera, could Mistraya really trust the remaining two after a successful invasion?

Mistraya's power and self-possession only serves to create insecurity among her peers—at least in Brutessa and Rendskorra's cases, Drakiera not so much, if at all.

Sipping, feeling the intoxicating pain offered by the beverage, the Majestic Sorceress arose in restlessness. She felt certain that any plot for invasion originated in SpringShoot Green with the power-hungry King Raptillion colluding with Rendskorra, the pair eventually approaching Brutessa with the plan. With Brutessa in accord, Insensatia would have had no choice but to join in league with the conspiracy, as she did by agreeing to turn her kingdom into the Slave Planet at the KA's request—although, ultimately, she had no say in the matter. This Insensatia wisely surmised.

To retain her power, that poor Empress has really learned to dance the Duck-And-Dodge Sidestep. But what do you expect? Power comes with all its trappings, and achieving it is one thing, sustaining it another. Just ask the missing Emperor who formulated the Bloodlet Overthrow that brought *us* to power—*if* anyone is ever able to locate that repugnant and rapacious schemer.

So, what do I do about my own survival? wondered S'ilKuSheere, sipping once more her exotically conniving mixture, again welcoming its rush of prickly pain. To retain my power, surely I must carefully monitor the course of events, the buildup to any foreseeable invasion, while weighing the consequences of each and every one of my actions, interceding swiftly and shrewdly when necessary and as each new situation dictates. And, of course, I must *never* trust a single one of my nefarious sisters, even as a promised ally.

But from the outset, since our turn from the Light, when have I ever? And how could I, knowing they're Dark like me at the heart? After all, didn't I murder my youngest sister Quillaria and scheme to do the same to my eldest, Lunaria? Wouldn't that leave my remaining sisters forever leery of *me?*

Ah, concluded S'ilKuSheere, these sibling rivalries, I tell you. Is it really so surprising that I find this thing called family so vastly overrated?

The hour had grown late, the skyline ahead through the trees seeming to swell in brilliance only to have waned, giving way to the creeping lull of twilight. Starbrill had thought it wise to set up camp far enough from TiaraReign and the road so that few if any unexpected travelers might stumble onto them.

Meanwhile, Archie had assisted in hunting prey for their evening meals. And as the party ate catches of forest prattels, skinnelins, and brush-headed mellbirds freshly cooked on the small and cautious campfires, Starbrill talked in front of the group about their plans for the upcoming evening.

"So, I've decided it's best that, due to the risks and dangers involved, only our original small party of six shall continue on to TiaraReign, leaving the newcomers to rest in preparation for our return journey home. Once our business is finished in the CityHeights—as I discussed with some of you earlier—we will be returning to TreeLoft where you are welcome to join our group who live in reasonable comfort there in the forest. If you should decide otherwise, there's a PortalDoor to SummersBreath Still that we know of on our way home, and we'd be happy to deliver you there and see you off. That's for you to talk about and decide among yourselves. Any questions?"

Starbrill answered the few questions posed of him, and then stepped aside to set about eating his meal. Exerting himself as he had throughout the day, the young man was famished and eager to indulge. As the group eased into their comforts and talked among themselves, some found need to venture out on their own. When doing so, none wandered too far from camp save one, and this for good reason. Kaggal felt it was imperative that, when rendezvousing for a prearranged meeting, not a soul among the group should be on hand to see him imparting valuable information about their movements to the face of the sorceress Rendskorra in a small and silver, handheld flame.

Such a long way to go. Yet, the stalwart riders charged full stride to engage completely the weary hours, making haste through the brush and encompassing green of forest. And when the WhisperEye murmurs found additional ears, and ears found hand and pen and script, and messages took to the wing to precede their course, more riders were waiting in the ready to journey along, meeting up in stealth along their route. Growing in strength and number, stirring path and plain and far plateau, these riders pressed onward, bearing a perilous destination in mind, and a rallied resolve to persevere.

"Ready?"

Molly nodded in answer to Starbrill's question, and Heather drew alongside. Having helped Toya on with her pack, Sedgwar fell in line. And with Archie drawing up the rear, the sextet started out amid waves of sentiment and see you soons.

Leaving the greater group in camp, no one spoke, the six stringing out along the tardy trail. With the stain of darkness setting in, Starbrill and Toya's LuminTorches were produced, casting their beams about to light the way. When Archie took off on his own, Heather felt as if something had gone missing. She told him so.

StaLia, I'm right here. I've not gone far.

Doesn't matter. I miss you, anyway.

S'ilKuSheere looked over the street scene visible before her on the big screen. The intoxicant that she had imbibed had produced its desired effect, and she felt painfully sedate, the sensation pointedly underwhelming to her system. Later, she would pleasure herself with more.

Her WallScreen able to SightShare with some surveillance moths sent earlier to TiaraReign, the Majestic Sorceress of the Dahklarr Herth looked to insure all was in place and ready for Starbrill, Heather Nighborne, and their companions when they arrived. Having just spoken to Rendskorra, her sister claimed her funny-eared spy, in place among the freed slaves, had informed her that the six were now on their way. She further opined that, vastly outnumbered, the small party should be easily exterminated.

And if they weren't, just in case, S'ilKuSheere had a backup plan.

chapter four

Battle at TiaraReign CityHeights

"Oh, Toya, it's more than magnificent."

Cresting the forested hill, Molly could see on the distant rise the immense arcing swath of lights known as TiaraReign CityHeights.

At her side, Toya said, "It used to be something a whole lot more. From a distance, it looks impressive, but when you're inside its limits, you'll see it's become so horribly run down. Like all our Evermorian cities, every one of them once infused with Light Magic, they stood out so beautifully. Now, overcome by Darkness, they've become every bit that in their outward appearance, reflecting what they are at the heart. It's a pity really."

"I remember when Heather and I first saw Elderraine on Parade Day. It was so beautiful, the design of their buildings, the colorful rooftops, the way that the buildings looked like they were really a part of nature—and nature a part of them. It was something very, very special."

"Then you wouldn't want to see Elderraine presently. It's been renamed after the Bloodlet Overthrow, and it's now called Brakkenslew Mith. With Dark Magic having replaced the Light, it's turned into something morose and dreadful."

"I'm sorry for Evermore, Toya, so sorry for its people."

"For its everything. It's crumbling in ruin and chaos. It seems the KA and Crown would rather invest in wars than in its own infrastructure. Come on, we better hurry and catch up to the others. We don't want to get too far behind."

With Starbrill and his LuminTorch leading the way, the six continued their course through the darkness, the scent of the Archmount keeping at bay many of the night predators that might otherwise drift in for closer inspection and, perhaps, confrontation.

As they pressed onward, when the forest would periodically quieten, Molly was able to hear through her own noisy step how silently Heather traveled, how natural such stealthy movement seemed to be for her. In comparison, only the Archmount proved to be in her companion's league—with his nose to the ground, he slinked among them only to suddenly be gone, and after an interval, to surprisingly be spotted once more moving within their ranks. When in the occasional open, overhead, Molly could sometimes hear the sound of some nocturnal flyer, the whisper of its wings distinguishable in passing, though barely.

Nearer to the CityHeights, the road they would sometimes parallel wasn't completely deserted, with many travelers sleeping right out in the open, along its bushy fringes. Most of them would eventually bypass the CityHeights, sticking to the main routes that would lead them to some undiscovered elsewhere. Due to the upsurge in robberies after dark, coaches and °Carriages mostly traveled during the daylight hours and rarely late at night.

The closer they progressed toward TiaraReign, Molly could see how spectacular the place truly was, stretching on for what seemed like forever, situated high up in the trees. She would have loved the chance to see it during the morning or afternoon hours, wondering how it would have appeared to her when viewed under the sobering strains of daylight. No matter. Here, at night, TiaraReign struck her like the interlacing of thousands of glorious, glowing, harp-inspired bridges.

When they neared the CityHeight limits, Starbrill took them on a route far from the major thoroughfare and away from the many good-sized smaller approaches. They dipped into a hollow near a ravine to find a concealed cave, and it was there at its entrance that they left Archie. Following the course of its extensive tunnel, the group emerged in an area surrounded by heavy bush and several effusive trees—and directly beneath the vast sprawl of TiaraReign itself. Looking up, they could see stupendously thick trees rising to pierce the undersides of the unseen buildings and streets, waterways and bridges, the density and extreme girth of the old growth of forest important to the sturdiness of the CityHeights foundation.

Heather thought it was like looking up at the immense belly of some fantastical starship that stretched off into infinity, impressive in its circuit board complexity comprised of protruding and recessed channels, of pipes, drains, shafts, and ducts. Where the multitude of trees rose to intersect with the underside of the massive city far above ground, reinforcements of support were added in a girdered, fluted framework, and these were covered with a mesh of muted lights in reds, yellow-greens, and whites.

Cutting into the CityHeight undercarriage, rectangular holes of various widths and lengths broke up the minutia, and beyond could be seen stairways and doorways, ventilation shafts and open space that allowed glimpses of CityHeight street scenes, as well as the distribution of moonlight in long-armed reaches to touch down on the forest floor.

Dropping from geometric openings of various size were platforms supporting seating areas with tables for dining, drinking, and gazing amid the elevated lights and heights. These sunken additions belonged to upper-storied parks or restaurants, hotel coffee shops or residences, transportation or relaxation stations, all providing a striking view of the forested landscape below.

Visible now and again, snaking between manmade and natural obstacles was a sub-street transit system, the string of seemingly predatory cars speeding by overhead to the sound of a slippery hiss. On hand in the lighted windows, a spattering of late hour passengers could be glimpsed in tiny silhouette, before the metallic serpents which ingested them had once more sleekly skimmed out of sight.

Down on the forest floor, few pedestrians could be seen in the warm late hour air, but armed soldiers of the Crown could be openly detected routinely making their hard-nosed rounds. They walked beneath the streetlights that punctuated at intervals the grid of intersecting streets and lanes, the roadway closely mimicking those directly above in the CityHeights layout.

Lining the flat roadsides were °Carriage houses and coach garages, storage sheds and elaborate stables, the latter used to lodge the many animals that provided transport or were hitched to draw vehicles.

Situated amid the overflow of greenery were strategically placed elevator depots, each possessing a series of lifts to take people, their vehicles and belongings, to street level above. A few could be seen rising or descending, but most hoists were inactive, due to a lack of traffic at the impending curfew hour. Encircling many of the larger trees were wide, elaborate staircases climbing to disappear into the floating

CityHeights' substructure above.

Domineering and solid, lost to the intervening trees, were the repetitious rise of immense towers. Encased within, surrounding the corded bulk of plumbing and drainage shafts, were a series of stairwells. Lacing back and forth, they wound upward from the floor of the forest to plug into the substrata planking of TiaraReign. These towers were useful not only for housing pedestrian travel, for concealing water and sewage lines, but also for lending support to the vast citywide infrastructure perched ponderously above.

Sedgwar had seen pictures of SpringShoot Green's many CityHeights before, and had even visited a few in his youth, but to see such a sight firsthand once more provided an overwhelming sense of awe to the normally unsusceptible warrior.

Starbrill said, "To use one of the lifts means we'll have to present our TravelTaggs—which some of us don't possess at the moment. With this in mind, it's good to know there's no need to climb one of the enclosed stairways leading up into the CityHeights."

"Whew," said Heather, looking up at the breadth of the support column, imagining the run of stairs inside. "I was wondering how long it would take us to get to the top."

"Depends on how fast you can climb," said Starbrill, amused. "Nevertheless, thank the Universe for ScatterPortals. I have to say, I truly don't know where we'd be without them. Sedgwar, from here on out, you and I will take the lead. Toya, you'll fall back and position yourself as rear guard. The last to exit, you'll use your MindKey to see to the closing and securing of all doors behind you. Any questions?" When no one spoke up, Starbrill added, "All right, then. Follow me."

Departing the concealment provided by the abundant bushes and low-hanging limbs, crossing an unkempt green, the five resumed their course in stealth.

Having read in stern silence the message of severe magnitude and implication originating from the WhisperEye Mirror, at once sturdy BracchaBeasts were untethered, saddled, and sent skyward from lodgings in the Undulant Valley. Their riders had a giant score to settle, both with themselves and on behalf of Evermore. To accomplish this, it was imperative they weren't too late to encounter the DualPortal in necessary alignment.

When riding out late on the wing this way, in sacrifice and

assistance, the once highly regarded race of people hoped to overcome their recent past, a shameful and monumental deviation toward the Dark. In times as these, riders of such immense proportions were welcome allies, both in need and in deed.

Having evaded the eye and inquiry of patrolling soldiers, seeing to it they avoided all pedestrians along their route, the band of five slowly progressed from the rough patch of forest through an open, neglected park. Approaching a life-sized statue of several HumanKinders posed with climbing ropes at the rooted base of a truncated, mammoth tree, Starbrill's group slowed to a stop.

Ever on the alert, he crossed an overgrown path and slipped behind a hedge that surrounded the statue's massive pedestal. Once there, after inspection, he signaled all was clear and waved the rest over, and one-by-one they disappeared from sight behind the tall row of greenery. Above them, pointing upward, insufficient lighting sputtered in its attempt to bath the statue, the meager spillage allowing the small party to follow alongside the marble base without the aid of their 'Torches.

Concealed completely from sight, they walked upon the rectangular steppingstones that marked the perimeter. Reaching the statue's backside, Starbrill brushed his hand over a spot on the smooth pedestal wall. With the motion, a faint hum could be heard and momentarily visible was the illuminated, interwoven design of the ClearWeave. Exchanging looks, Heather and Molly watched with fascination as directly before Starbrill a narrow patch of ground sank at an angle and steps were formed, their planking comprised of the steppingstones that once spotted the soil above. The girls exchanged looks once more.

On Starbrill's heels, the group descended the stairs. Along one side, now serving as a wall, was the deeply sunken base of the pedestal itself. Reaching the bottom step, again placing his hand over an appropriate spot on the stone, the sign of the ClearWeave was once more displayed in light. An instant later, the outline of a door could be seen. Set ajar, it opened inward, and Starbrill motioned for his companions to follow.

An excited Heather thought, So, *that's* a MindKey.

Once inside, the room brightened and Starbrill pointed to Toya, the last to enter, a reminder to seal the door behind her. This she did with a passing of her hand, the fraternal sign of the ClearWeave once more evident, briefly coming to light before fading. Outside, the stairway rose to meld seamlessly at ground level.

And now, the group found themselves directly below the statue, within the confines of its base. Walking the length of the dimly lit room, Starbrill stopped before a wall. On it were the vaguest indications of a door. He turned to address the others, his voice low.

"The door before me is the ScatterPortal. When it's opened and we walk through, instantly we will be transported, exiting from a similar door located in the base of a statue above in the CityHeights. In TiaraReign, they're currently approaching the curfew hour. This means we'll have to move quickly and be on guard the entire way. Unless necessity indicates we do otherwise, we'll stick reasonably close together.

"If for any reason we're stopped, we'll have to act casually, our story being we've just returned from an extensive trip to the Ancient Rainforests of Tabeer, trying to get home before curfew." Starbrill looked at Sedgwar. "If they ask for TravelTaggs, and most certainly they will, then we'll have to position ourselves to overcome the soldiers as quickly and quietly as possible. I think you know, we mustn't draw attention to ourselves. The idea is to get in and out of here as fast as we can without rousing interest, first getting TravelTaggs on the way to exchanging our goods with the shopkeepers. That's the plan before heading home. Sedgwar?"

The warrior gave a brief nod. "Fine."

"Anyone else?"

More shrugs and head bobs.

With that, Starbrill waved his hand, the sign of the ClearWeave fleetingly shone, the overhead lights went dark, and the door opened a crack. He peered out, his form softly lit by the filtering light from above, its muted influence infiltrating inside the doorway.

When he saw no other souls, Starbrill turned, his voice just above a hush: "One at a time. Follow my lead. Remember, the soldiers have Vigen°Darr weaponry. From a distance, their guns overmatch any hope we have with our swordplay. If they open up on us, we won't stand a chance. And should they use their weapons, their magic is detectable, so it may bring Rendskorra or her RedSuits—at the least, it will definitely alert them. So, again, if we're approached, play innocent until you're no longer able. Remember, the idea is to get in reasonably close to the soldiers, and from there we'll do what's necessary to disable them."

From an overly large pocket of his OverRobe, in the lowlight, Heather watched as Sedgwar produced the DartBow that he had taken from KArtelMaster Slyope. From another, he carefully removed the accompanying SharpDart and threaded it into place. Armed and ready, he activated the safety mechanism and placed it once more into his pocket.

Waiting until the warrior finished, Starbrill again pointed, this time counting off first to last the party's sequence upon exiting. And following a lean through the doorway, after once more casting a discriminate eye about for immediate threats, he left the seclusion and safety of the pedestal.

Monitoring the TiaraReign streets, S'ilKuSheere followed the progress of one of her moths. SightSharing on her magical widescreen, she was able to manifest the insect's vision, its point of view. She could see people on the run here, worried and glancing about while scurrying there, the CityHeights inhabitants trying to finish whatever activities they had planned by curfew's strict commencement hour. As far as the sorceress could tell, all appeared to be as normal.

S'ilKuSheere sat back and conjured up a refill of her dark concoction, the liquid rising, brimming in her fluted glass. She felt tense, watching while the moth passed over the rooftops, above the dingy alleyways, porches, and yards, to settle where the streets darkened and narrowed. It was there she detected movement—a lot of aggressive movement—perceivable in the shadows.

She sipped her drink, her eyes never leaving the WallScreen.

Recognizable to the knowing, Rendskorra's RedSuits were fanning out to take up their predetermined positions in the artisan district. The noose was tightening. The ambush, it was beginning.

Inside TiaraReign's This 'n That Gift & Thrift, Greesha and Mastow Stomminam were getting ready to close up shop come the end of what felt to be an emotionally exhausting day. They had a lot on their minds, some transactions to see to, some items to hurry and set aside before Starbrill's scheduled arrival later that evening—necessities that the young man and his sister were to take back with them to TreeLoft.

Greesha worked the counter and till while her TrueMate Mastow made hurried advances to the back room, bringing out new stock to replenish the emptied shelves. Most were giveaways, knowing the people who stopped in hadn't always the means to make a purchase, but needed new or second hand tools and supplies to fix a leaky roof or repair a broken window, drainpipe, or door. Some had want for shoes or clothing, having worn through or outgrown the old. A few visitors had news of import to share, secretive news for their ears only—Maiden or ClearWeave news.

A lot happened in that small thriftshop. Hahlbee Starkow, the overly observant proprietor of the Hidden Facet jeweler's shop nextdoor had become aware of that fact. That's why he reported them.

Like many family-owned shops in the old quarters, Mastow and Greesha had stubbornly refused to sell out to the Crown. Not so for Hahlbee. In fact, he did just the opposite, taking advantage of the opportunity to seize the business reins of a Crown repossession. Leasing his new jewelry shop from the KA, he intended to seek approval and draw upon their favor, and knew there was no better way to do so than to become an informant. It paid dividends. It offered rewards. It brought recognition and importance.

Besides, all of these longtime shop owners wanted little to do with Hahlbee, being cordial but distant to the Starkow's in general, his family running the shop once belonging to old friends who had been arrested and sent to a Loyalist KAmpound. But he, Hahlbee, would show these proud and uppish owners. All of them! His family bled in their way, let the Stomminam's and the rest bleed in theirs.

So, as Greesha walked the last of the remaining patrons to the door of their Gift & Thrift, closing up for the night, she heard her TrueMate say, "We've been asked not to lock it."

"Not lock the front door?" She reached and with a small pull of its chain turned off the glowing sign. "Why in Evermore's name would we not lock the door?"

The woman turned to find her 'Mate standing at the end of a nearby aisle, surrounded by several RedSuits. One had his Råd°Emission pistol drawn.

"Oh," she said, under her breath. "I see..."

Heather took a definitive aura scan of the grassy commons, and it revealed nothing of consequence. Having exited the statue in the

Tiara Reign CityHeights, she was now standing alongside an anxious Molly near the gated entryway, near to Starbrill and Sedgwar. The four were waiting for Toya to seal the doorway and vacate the hedge in her turn, hastening through the sporadic lighting of a park in darkness, joining them in its thickness of shadows.

Having observed Starbrill and Toya's actions when entering and exiting the statue's secretive doorways, it became apparent to Heather that she, too, was in possession of a MindKey, inadvertently putting its power to use while in Evermore on her very first visit. She could only guess that it was the Matron who had given her the ability upon their initial encounter, although at the time she was unaware of its implementation. And she liked knowing that, if ever needed, she would be able to access the ClearWeave's vast network of unexpected and deftly concealed doors. Of course, she'd have to first learn of their hidden whereabouts, but, nevertheless, the girl was keen on the prospect of doing so, while titillated by the intriguing secrecy of it all.

Heather's wary eyes never at rest, they finally landed on the statue from whose pedestal the group had just emerged, having used its ScatterPortal like an elevator to the penthouse. Similar to its bronze counterpart below on the forest floor, this version of the statue depicted those same life-sized HumanKinders—or ones like them—posed aloft in the sculpted trees, laying out planks, beginning to build. The founders of TiaraReign? Most likely. Flooded with lighting from below, the statue's figures were dramatically enhanced for few to see.

With Toya finally at their sides, the party took to the street, stringing out so as not to look self-conscious and conspicuous. Heather found herself near to Molly and Toya, with Sedgwar and Starbrill steps ahead. They set for themselves a pace similar to most citizens they saw coming and going, Molly remarking in low tones how dreary and unclean the city seemed.

"And this," said Toya, "is one of the better areas of TiaraReign. Just wait until you see where we're going."

Taking in her surroundings, envisioning what it could be—or once was—only caused Molly to feel a sense of disappointment—or maybe even sorrow. She loved the boughs swaying high above and the scent of enveloping woodland, but periodically found herself being put off, catching wind of a patch of rotting garbage or glut of open sewage.

On either side, rising up blank-faced and hollow-eyed, the once immaculate multistoried homes were set back, situated behind assertive fencing with the constant interloping of trees protruding from below. Piercing TiaraReign's rooftops and yards, interrupting its walks, walls, and gardens, all trunks were willingly accommodated for with decorative planters, borders, and trimmings, giving the CityHeights an inclusiveness with nature and an ambiance all its own.

Mostly overgrown and occasionally sagging, lamplit walks stretched over their heads at differing directions and heights. Laced tree-to-tree, they began near one building and concluded with a ramp or stairway at another.

At street level, branches of the great trees went unattended, no longer trimmed back to make certain that vehicles and pedestrians alike had ample clearance. Also adding to the overall miasma of dereliction was the overabundance of plant life that ran rampant throughout, fighting for dominance and light. Like unruly invaders, the vines and creepers smothered the gates and walls, the terraces and rooftops, overrunning other plants that strove vainly to grow free of their clutches.

When asked by Molly, Toya explained that there were many reasons why TiaraReign's infrastructure was implicitly ignored, most due to the CityHeight Dwellers being distracted by greater and graver concerns, the self-serving privatization of the Parks system, and the governing body caring little to spend the money in hiring workers to remedy what ailed it. As well, so many of the TiaraReign houses now stood abandoned, the citizenry having departed following the Overthrow and its fallout, with more and more people seeing fit to leave every warring, rodent-infested day.

Through the trees, pedestrians could be seen intermittently on the wide avenue, at times crossing it at a fast-paced angle, not waiting for a crosswalk or corner where soldiers might be stationed. A lot wore hats or hoods, their features covered, their collars up. It gave the air a sinister feel. No carriages or vehicles of any kind disturbed the pitted roadways.

Often, in what were once the more affluent areas, the KA's excessively brilliant ground level searchlights augmented the dimmer lamps located overhead on higher posts. Come curfew, with their furious bore of white light glaring stridently down the main and side streets, many silhouettes of the passersby were thrown monstrously large and distorted upon the walls, the highlighted shapes seen to crawl over windows, walks, and doorways. Manned by soldiers, the searchlights swiveled to sweep the shadows, later looking to expose those violators stealing through the KA's forbidden hours.

Now approaching a corner, Starbrill and Sedgwar slowed, allowing a middle-aged foursome to proceed before them. And there, unforeseen, stepping from the shadows of a landing, three soldiers were on hand to intercept and confront the quartet, demanding identification. Greeted with a pelting of rocks from an unseen source, one of the soldiers broke away to pursue the hidden enemy. Pulses from his Hemorrhage°Ray were soon heard agitating the night's uneasy calm.

Sedgwar and Starbrill gave the encounter wide berth before quickly turning the corner, heading down a side street of equal width but darker shadow. Drawing up the rear, Heather, Molly, and Toya hurried past the soldiers, too—but not at too great a clip—discreetly watching as the four late hour walkers nervously dug about to produce their TravelTaggs.

Lagging until they saw that the girls had turned the corner in their wake, Starbrill and Sedgwar maintained their slower pace, waiting for the three to join them in tandem.

Noticing the signs in windows and on walls, signs she had glimpsed earlier in Mustiffaire, Heather asked, "Starbrill, what does that mean, We Need To Bleed?"

In response, Starbrill's countenance darkened, growing as cheerless as the CityHeights around them. He lowered his voice, his hands tightening on the straps of his backpack, his distrustful eyes darting between windows, scanning beneath overhangs. "Heather, having visited Elderraine before the Overthrow, you were able to see Evermore in some of its finest hours, at a time when Light Magic was intricately at balance within the environment, woven into all things, a part of HumanKind and nature."

"I remember, Starbrill. Evermore was a different place totally. Back then, they even liked Maidens—maybe all except Borray and his RogueTag buddies."

"There are those who still like Maidens," said Toya.

"True, although at their peril." After a pause and a hitch of his backpack, Starbrill resumed his walk and talk. "Come the Overthrow, when Light Magic was banished from Evermore, the magical connecters that were both catalyst and bond between all things natural and manmade were expelled. As a result, it left magical gaps where that interdependence had once existed. So, deprived, all the structures reliant on Light Magic started collapsing in decay. As a consequence, the trolleys no longer ran, water systems didn't flow as they once did, structures began to atrophy, and utilities were left inoperable and unfixable. Am I making sense?"

"So far. Molly?"

"Yes."

"So, the KA realized they needed something to replace the Light Magic. They needed a substitute." Starbrill went quiet, waiting for a passing pedestrian to hurry out of earshot. He picked up again. "They realized they needed something that, in its purest form, resembled Light Magic, that had all the properties of Light Magic, but, obviously, hadn't the qualities of the Light itself."

"What about Dark Magic? I mean, couldn't they just use that, and with a couple of spells, you know, just pump it in there and get everything working again?"

"They tried, Heather, only to find it didn't work when used directly. It was too coarse at its heart, too unrefined, the core systems continually breaking down under its corrosive Influence, rejecting its Dark essence. And while desperately searching to find a substitute, the cities, CityStates, and towns continued to become all the more dilapidated, collapsing in on themselves, drifting toward total ruination. And the KA and its Darkness, they obviously had no intention of bringing back the Light Magic to remedy the situation."

"So, what did they do?" asked Molly.

"By experimentation, in consultation with Evermore's sorceresses, the KA sought to develop an acceptable form of Dark Magic, magic that wouldn't disrupt or disable the Realm's fine-tuned *circuitry*—for lack of a better term. So, after consulting with the WhisperEye Mirror network, they learned of an ore substitute that could be mined in the TribalLands, and that by digging up and drawing out the irradiation from GlissenStones, and then converting *that* to Darkness, to a degree they would be able to start replacing the Light Magic."

Molly exclaimed, "And what better way to replace the Light in Light Magic than with Light that has been converted to Dark."

"Did it work?"

"It worked, Heather. Boy, did it work. It's working now," said Toya. "Refined Darkness. But as Starbrill will tell you, the GlissenStone wasn't enough."

"No, it wasn't, in many, many ways. You see, throughout the Realm, when substituting the Light Magic with refined Dark, there's a change that takes place in the intrinsic characteristics of those things under its Influence. What was once beautiful is now ugly, what was once shapely is now shriveled, what was once elegantly smooth is now rigidly serrated. As the pure white Light of the Universe—the Glissen Sohlarr—is being replaced and the Realm reinforced with Dark Glissening, the world around us is taking on the hideous qualities of the

Dahklarr Herth."

"So, everything is slowly becoming Darkly beautiful," said Molly.

"I suppose, if you want to call it that."

"Hey, Starbrill. This Glissening. Isn't that the stuff Toya said was in our souls?"

"Yes. And, yet, what these rocks possess is not true Glissening. It's a viable substitute that contains some of its purer, radiant qualities—star matter as opposed to true Universal matter. As well, GlissenStone is rare, deadly to handle, difficult to find and excavate, and expensive to refine and convert—and never mind the problems with the resulting waste. And if those weren't reasons enough, long term, GlissenStone is a finite resource and so, with our reliance upon it, there will never be enough to sustain us for the long term. So, now, the KA discovered a way of getting pure Glissening directly from another source."

"So, 'We Need To Bleed.' No way," said Heather, hitting upon a realization. "You mean, they're draining Glissening directly from people's souls?"

"They are. They've found a way. And the signs you see posted mean that the KA and its perpetrators need Glissening on behalf of the Realm in Darkness, and its people are asked to sacrifice their Light as a matter of duty. Hence, they need to bleed."

Sedgwar muttered, "As if we haven't bled enough."

Reaching an alleyway entrance, Starbrill slowed. Seeing no other people, he turned and headed in a new direction, beckoning the rest to follow. On either side, the sheds, fences, and garages appeared squalid and in desperate need of repair. At times, they found it necessary to step over bodies that they found lying in their path, the people either sleeping, disabled, or drunk on extract. Nearing overturned cans, the passersby caught whiffs of pungent trash that lay rotting in the open, the rodents having their way with it, squeaking and scattering. Although feeling squeamish, Molly bravely held her own, the five maintaining their course.

"So," continued Starbrill, picking up the thread in his low tone, "as a requirement of being employed by the KA, by the KArtels and their KAnglomerates, all Evermorians have to give up part of their soul every working day. You're bled. It's expected or termination results for what they call unpatriotic nonperformance. And consistently depleted of Glissening, it runs down their spirits, robbing their souls of inspiration and the will to persevere, making them susceptible to the

Dark and its Influence."

Heather asked, "Is that why all the people I saw walking around Mustiffaire looked so dead-like?"

"Yes. Evermorians everywhere, ruled by the KA, reliant on the KArtels, they've become depraved, deprived of the Light in their souls. They've lost their way, dependent upon the selfish, self-sustaining practices of the KA for survival."

"And sucked dry that way," added Toya, "we're giving up our HumanKinder identity, our individuality, our link to one another and our planet kingdoms, to feed the faceless KAnglomerates that, in turn, need to perpetually feed on us for *their* survival."

"I never realized. Wow. Evermore...what's happened to this amazing place? It used to be so special. No wonder there's no hope."

Sedgwar glanced Heather's way, realizing the youngling was thinking of Evermore's people, why a Maiden Portent was so desperately needed, and the magnitude of the task confronting her.

Molly asked, "Our Glissening, does it replenish itself? And who converts it to Dark Magic?"

"Thankfully, Molly, Glissening *does* replenish itself. And they can only bleed a portion at a time without killing the host in a shock to its innermost system. So, all is not lost. A soul *can* recover and return from the Darkness—if it desires. As for the conversion, it's done by a Dahklarrian chemist—or Dahklemist—through a complex process, utilizing what's come to be known as a Converter, a spell-enhanced piece of machinery, a reactor of sorts."

"Makes sense," said Heather. "So, first you see a bleeder—"

"Extractor."

"—and then your Glissening is sent off to the Converter. They change its, its—"

"Essence."

"—essence from Light to Dark, and that's thrown around and let loose everywhere—"

"By our sorceresses."

"—by sorceresses. And using a bunch of Dahklarr spells, they replace the Light that's gone from Evermore by putting Dark in there instead. And that goes into the balance between HumanKind and nature and all those things that are Evermorian."

"I think that pretty well sums it up. Simplified, but appropriate, nevertheless. And, thankfully, the Dahklarr Herth still has a long way to go yet, a lot of Glissening and GlissenStone to convert and replace before the Realm is totally under its Influence."

Sedgwar added, "Meanwhile, wholly corrupt, Evermore continues to rot."

Starbrill stopped suddenly and cocked his head. Visibly ill at ease, he scanned the area.

"Something bothering you, Starbrill?" asked Toya.

"No. It's nothing." He started walking again, still wearing his concern. "This way. We turn here."

Proceeding down a dingy lane with its lining of trees, Starbrill ducked into the shadows at the side of a building, bidding the others to hurry and do the same.

Hustling alongside, Sedgwar asked, "Is there a problem?"

"Might be. On that building directly ahead, there's no light—they haven't turned on their light. It could very well be a warning."

"What do you mean?"

"The place where we get our falsified TravelTaggs? This street provides a clear view of the building's rear entrance. There you can see it ahead of you. By the back door, the green invitation light isn't on. It tells me something's amiss, and we need to get out of here." He whispered, "Everyone, follow me."

"You mean we won't be able to get our TravelTaggs?" asked Heather.

"Looks that way."

"Well, that's a stinker…"

Starbrill began their retreat, this time leading the group a different way, and back once more into another seamy alley.

Encountering not another soul in passing, the small band slipped among the squalor and through its rubble, most of it consumed in an enveloping sprawl of shadow. To Molly, the darkness seemed to lie in wait, ready to swell and strike, and she began to secretly want to leave the CityHeights, finding it increasingly repulsive and frightening.

Emerging onto a wide dimly lit avenue once more, to a person, the group seemed to breathe the easier for it, although Starbrill stuck to the shadows. Gone were the glowering searchlights that were all too evident upon their arrival, the avenue's lamplights above them weak, overgrown with green, and hardly penetrating. When the young man paused overlong once more, Sedgwar moved in alongside, a hand to his upper arm to waylay further advance.

"If something is bothering you, Starbrill, it's best to acknowledge it, even if it's scant intuition."

"All right, then. I'll do more than that. I'll share. *So,* doesn't it strike you as odd that we've at least an hour before curfew, and have only encountered one person since we first turned the corner near those soldiers?"

"Happenstance?" asked Sedgwar.

Starbrill shook his head, thoughtfully. He reflected on KAngressman Marmenside's warning, of the KA possibly having uncovered a "vital something" in their operation that would put an end to the Savages. "I don't think so, but, of course, can't be certain. Usually at this time, there are people rushing around, hurrying to be indoors to beat the hour. Add to that the fact that the light was off back there at the counterfeiter's, and it lends itself to greater concern still."

Toya said, "Maybe Sedgwar is right. Maybe it's just coincidence that no one is bothering to walk down this particular street at this particular time."

"That. Or maybe the KA has cleared the streets and we're heading straight into a trap."

Having spent an extra day at his friend Zilhenny's house, Gerlin had departed the subway station along his customary route towards home. Surprised not to see his older sister awaiting him upon his arrival as she usually did, the thirteen year old walked on past the shadowy shops and houses with their overgrown rooftops, drunken doorways, and reclusive windows and porches.

Uncomfortable at the lack of people on the streets—although knowing the curfew hour still lay ahead—he produced a small rubber ball from his coat pocket. As he walked, he began tossing it to the ground in front of him before catching it on the rebound: choog waddup...choog waddup. It was the sound of the carom off the slatting at his feet that he found comforting, the ensuing slap against his palm sharp and reassuring.

When on the next toss the ball hit the tip of his shoe and dribbled away into the roadside darkness, Gerlin hesitated before giving chase down the junk-filled alley. He trailed the hand-sized sphere to where it disappeared behind some rubbish bins and discards. Dodging about at a scamper, he finally overtook it and employing a swipe, missed. The ball rolled harmlessly onward. In its wake, he pursued and watched as it bounced off of a pair of heavy-duty military boots.

Crouching to grasp the errant sphere, he paused. Slowly raising his head, his eyes traveled up the uniformed legs, past the torso to the slotted mask of the RedSuit soldier standing rigidly before him in the darkness. Peering upward, mouth open, Gerlin rose to his feet.

Initially gazing straight ahead, the masked face suddenly snapped downward to stare at him. Gasping, wheeling, letting loose the ball, the boy took to his heels, his steps echoing off the facing of the buildings. His footfalls fading, Gerlin disappeared into the night.

"So," said the small but lovely face in the silver flame, "are we ready to spring the surprise party on our unsuspecting guests?"

Rendskorra's Soldier One nodded in the darkness of the This 'n That Gift and Thrift. "We are." His words were pure gravel.

"Well, then, I say let the fun begin. May the Darkness guide you in your success, my Number One. You'll hear from me."

Both parties closed their hands on the conversation, the TeleFlame snuffed out in unison.

Listening through the stillness, Soldier One returned to his tense waiting game, biding his time in the back room of the thriftshop. Meanwhile, still at Brutessa's Castle Grimmivid, Rendskorra received a comforting, kneading massage. Afterward, her back still sore and aching, she would take a deviant potion and retire early to bed.

Soldier One, on the other hand, would get very little rest.

Slinking between and behind the dormant buildings, Starbrill led his small circle to a little used stairwell. From there they climbed and moused to the far corner of a balcony overrun with greenery, a strategic spot mostly hidden from prying eyes. From their corner vantage point, to one side they were able to overlook the entire spread of a main avenue and vacant marketplace, and, to the other—beyond an intersecting street—a vast fenced-lined opening that provided gaping views into the depths of the forest below.

Perched on high, the visitors had not only attained a better overall perspective of the once great city, but of its panoramic splendor gone horribly derelict with the infusion of Darkness, perceivable within its vacant dormers and steeply pitched roofs, evident amid the gloom of its sporadically lit spires and upshoot of crumbling chimneystacks.

Intermittently, searchlights combed the nighttime sky. The lack of trees directly above the adjoining streets and marketplace allowed for an unimpeded glimpse of the clear SpringShootorian sky and its stars. Fresh upon their moist-skinned faces, a breeze arose to swell on a moment's notice, stirring the grounds with its gentle but firm insistence.

"Across the street, near the corner," said Starbrill, shedding his backpack with Sedgwar's assistance, "that's the thriftshop where we need to exchange these goods."

Heather helped Toya unburden herself of her load, setting the slightly smaller pack near to Starbrill's, against the wall behind them.

Examining the darkened storefront from between the burgeoning greenery, Sedgwar said, "It looks deserted. Is it supposed to?"

"That's the problem," said Starbrill. "This entire area looks deserted. It's true that normally the small shop does after hours—as do all these shops. But I've never seen it so totally quiet before curfew. And see those burning refuse bins down there? In all of the CityHeights everywhere, it's a criminal offense to leave those refuse bins—or any fire—unattended, even for the shortest interval. It just isn't done."

"You don't usually go in the front door of the shop, I take it?"

"No, there's a door at the back. That's where we enter. And, yet, it's in the front window that they usually turn on a lamp with a green shade. It's their invitation light, letting us know it's safe to conduct after hours business."

"And I see it's not on."

"No."

"Well, if you suspect a trap, it might be wise to abandon this entire errand of yours rather than to risk lives—"

"No, Sedgwar. For all I know, the KA could have changed the curfew hour. Look, I suggest everyone wait here while I go down myself and have a look around. Besides, if something *has* happened to Greesha and Mastow, if they're being held as suspected Loyalists, then I have to get them out of there. They'll be tortured and killed for their information—and they've plenty of information to betray, about our organization, TreeLoft, ScatterPortals, and the shunneling of children, slaves, and arms."

"Starbrill," said Toya, "You can't risk it. There's far too much at stake—"

"There's too much at stake *not* to risk it."

"I'm sorry, brother of mine, but our movement needs you."

Molly was about to offer similar advice, when Heather spoke up.

"Starbrill, if you're a seer like the Matron, can't you just sort of, you know, look into the shop there and see if we're going to get jumped or not?"

Starbrill chuckled on the low. "I'm afraid that this special gift of mine doesn't quite work that way, that it takes its time and reveals things to me of its own accord—surprising things." Oddly, at the mention, his gaze settled on Sedgwar. "So, unfortunately, any second sight occurs not at my bidding, but when it desires and only then with topics not of my choosing—and, of those, most often in fragments."

"Well, then," said Heather, removing her cloak, "I'll go down there instead." Dismissing the hushed protests that ensued, she handed the garment to a distressed Molly.

"Here. Take care of Fallasha until I get back."

"Heather, you're not going down there." It was Starbrill, the girl ignoring him, a mind to her business.

Stripping down to her skin-hugging Adaption°Suit, Heather pulled its head-covering frontispiece over her face and chin. There, it melted into place, conforming to her features. Into her BodyTote, she sequestered her belt and Maiden dagger.

Looking at Heather in the low light, Molly couldn't help but be overcome with admiration, with awe. Older, her friend's physique was curvaceous but sinewy—rippling with muscle and charged with purpose. Over the surface of her newly revealed inner 'Suit, she could see subtle flourishes, especially around the eyes.

Remarkable, she thought. Stunning, really. When and where did Heather find that outfit?

Like her companion's new cloak and clothing, Molly determined that her inner garment had to be Maiden-related. It reminded her of the wounded Avella's formfitting indigo attire, from the scenario that had unfolded once upon a time in the Bristol House basement. "Heather, are you sure you want to do this?"

Heather didn't look up, but continued, looping her MaidenBraid overhead, readjusting the accommodating headpiece of her Adaption°Suit.

"Are you able to breathe in that thing?" asked Toya.

Sedgwar said, "Heather, just because your clothing is more streamlined, it doesn't insure you won't be seen and that the task is any less risky. Let me go down there. I've done reconnaissance work before, and I'll be able to—Heather?"

At the turn of a switch, Heather had vanished from sight.

"Wait here, you guys," said her voice, emanating from the

vacant space before them. "I'll be back as soon as I can."

Unable to relax, S'ilKuSheere had another dark oily drink, a small pool of opaque green floating on its surface. Below, in the translucency of the liquid, the concoction's whitish Evermorian olive could be seen, glowing eerily until eaten.

Setting down her glass, S'ilKuSheere was assisted when donning her new high-collared cape, appraising her immaculately beautiful reflection in her dressing room mirror. She eyed her seamstress in reflection.

"Like it?" she asked the timid creature.

Demurely, the girl nodded.

"Oh, but we sorceresses are a gorgeous set," she said with a spin, now admiring the shorter cape, with her in it, from another angle. "We really are. Although, admittedly, we have our faults, each of us possessing a bit of a Dark side." Slightly intoxicated, she hiccupped and then smiled at her little joke. She watched as her face turned serious.

Why hadn't she heard recently from Rendskorra? She was to report to her.

Head high, distractedly handing off her cape while in passing, S'ilKuSheere breezed through several rooms before finding herself once more before her WallScreen. Waving it to life, SightSharing with her moth in TiaraReign, she saw nothing of further interest. She tried other moths and other scenes. Nothing still.

Perhaps Starbrill and his little group hadn't yet arrived—or maybe they weren't going to come after all. Or—*or!*—maybe, suspecting a trap, they're plotting an alternative course of action. And what if they elude us in the process?

In contemplation, she inclined her head and pursed her lips.

What if we miss out on killing Starbrill *and* the Maiden Portent? This is a chance we can't let slip away.

Brooding with indecision, the Majestic Sorceress turned away from the wall.

She thought, Rendskorra said she would handle it, didn't she? So, relax and let her handle it.

And, yet, with so much at stake, one could never be too sure, never have enough firepower. And although her sister was undoubtedly a deadly sorceress, S'ilKuSheere was well aware of her flighty tendencies.

Waving an arm at the screen, she changed the image. Gone was the picture of the CityHeights. Now the WallScreen was full of moths flying in loose formation, the light of the moon over their wings.

"Ah, my beautiful Turlakk soldiers of the Ravaged Heavens, soon to transform and wreak havoc. Simply upon a whim, I've decided it's strategically necessary that I put my backup plan into motion. It will ruffle some feathers—Rendskorra's to be specific—but flighty birds can be so unpredictable. So undependable. So easily distracted. And that's why they have older sisters. Like me."

Dennunciating, casting her spell with a flick of the fingers, she watched as a sizeable portion of the large swarm broke away and changed direction. The rerouted moths of Darkness set a new course for TiaraReign.

Taking an aura scan before leaving the balcony, Heather was unable to spot anything of immediate concern. If anyone was lurking, both they and their auras were completely hidden from view.

Mindful of her invisibility in the Adaption°Suit, the young Maiden hugged the shadows regardless, sneaking past the intermittent lights thrown at angles upon the building's walls. Around her, the greenery rustled with the wind, and her silent tread was just that should anyone have thought to raise an ear or suspect a presence.

Crossing the street, she could hear the creaking of the shops' signs and weather vanes, perhaps even some upper storied shutters, but saw no one and nothing that could be construed as threatening. Impervious when passing, the windows could only mirror softly their revelations of barren street life, and so, with a final glance in the direction of the balcony and her hidden comrades, she edged around the building's corner.

Stealing along the wall beneath some windows, and now entering yet another alley in disarray, Heather sidestepped the usual clutter, pausing to take a brief aura scan of the vicinity. Again coming up empty, standing invisibly in the open, she looked over the backside of the unkempt structure.

Now and again, driven by the breeze, the lax screen door would drift open only to pause, as if listening hand-to-ear, before slamming and slapping in fits against the jamb. Then it would rest perfectly still. All windows appeared dark and unforthcoming. It was at that moment that Heather wished she could simply walk through walls.

Moving closer, peering into the hollow of the blackened doorway, she noted that the backdoor was more than ajar. While under her gaze, she heard it groan on the wind, retreating to open all the more. Gauging a forthcoming series of gusts, timing her entry to perfection, when the screen blew outward, Heather knifed into the gap created, barely squeezing through the open door just inside.

Engulfed in the darkness of a large back room filled with tables and shelving, boxes and merchandise, she scanned for lurking shines of any kind. Momentarily taken aback, she observed the sharply pulsing hues of many RedSuits stationed at the ready, poised to pounce on the instant. On the glide, she moved through the doorway and into a short throw of hallway.

Slowing before the entrance to the front room of the thriftshop, Heather browsed the shaded jumble of fore and midground objects, of counters, shelves, and flooring, before glimpsing out the window and into the lifeless face of the dim street beyond. All appeared perfectly calm. An aura scan, however, revealed differing results. At various locations hidden throughout the store, deadly auras glowed treacherously violet, the RedSuit soldiers sheathed in stealth while awaiting an unsuspecting entrant.

Retreating, feeling every bit ghostly in presence, Heather scanned the confines of the next room she encountered, its space smaller and more cramped. Within were a table, a couch, and an assortment of chairs, with a sink, cupboard, and washroom. Seated in two of the chairs facing the door were the shop's owners, tied up and gagged, their auras agitated, blaring in frightened yellows and frantic greens and oranges.

Popping her head into the last room at the end of the hall, the girl wasn't in the least bit surprised to find it contained more RedSuits in reinforcement, and so swiftly withdrew.

Heather wondered, With these soldiers all over the place, how am I supposed to get Starbrill's friends out of here without being seen? Or killed?

The task seemed impossible.

And, then again, like Fallasha, maybe she would have to kill *them* to prevent the pair from divulging vital information and secrets when tortured. If necessary, she knew she would do it. She'd have to. For the moment, she set the hard-hearted thought aside.

Navigating into the room that held the two bound shopkeepers, Greesha and Mastow, Heather stood before them. With a finger placed to her lips, she stepped forth from the shadows and into visibility. She watched their eyes grow wide, glad she had left their gags in place in case they cried out.

On a hunch, she whispered, "Four the Four."

If part of the ClearWeave as she strongly suspected—what Starbrill had termed their *organization*—they needn't complete the secretive phrase. Heather's simple intention was to infer that she was friend and not foe—moreover, that she was one of them. Their surging, hopeful auras told her all she needed to know.

Following a glance toward the door, she leaned in and spoke softly, "Starbrill is my friend. I'd like to get you two out of here, but I don't know how. Those guys are all over the place, in every room I saw." She watched the pair exchange troubled glances.

Swift to remove her dagger from a BodyTote pocket, Heather swooped in and cut their bindings, the TrueMate first, then the 'Maite. They pulled their gags free, down over their chins.

"There's a tunnel right nearby, hey," Mastow whispered. "It's over there, in front of the fireplace, below the hearthstone."

Another ClearWeave door? At the mention, she felt a vague sense of relief wash up and recede.

Finger to her lips once again, Heather encouraged them to rise. When faint steps could be heard from the hall, she heatedly motioned them back into their seats, the middle-aged couple quick to work their gags into place before hiding their hands from sight. Heather went invisible.

Stepping into the vagueness of the room, something about the character of the prisoners or the environment struck the RedSuit as suspicious—exactly what, he couldn't determine—and he freed up his Råd°Emitter. It would be against orders to turn on the light. When he began to walk toward them, his eyes slowly scanning the content and corners, without a sound Heather ever so slowly closed the door behind him.

Knowing they were about to be discovered, the invisible young girl walked up behind the soldier. She tapped him on the shoulder. Spinning, he saw no one. An instant later, he saw Heather.

"Surprise," she whispered on a pivot, the girl already in motion.

Before he could cry out, she knocked his gun aside while her wicked upper-thrust connected squarely under the jaw. Head snapping sharply, he flew backward where Mastow caught him under the arms and laid the unconscious RedSuit to rest quietly in his chair. Then, using his loosened gag, he strangled him from behind, insuring silence.

"Go to the tunnel," said Heather, motioning with her head.

"I'll be there in a second. Before we leave, I think it might be a good idea to open the bathroom window, so they'll think you escaped that way. When I finish, I'll follow you."

But first things first, thought Heather.

In soundless haste, she grabbed up and delicately propped a chair beneath the door's knob, and only afterward moved with intentness toward the small washroom. As coolly and quietly as possible, the girl slid the window up, scanning to be certain that she wasn't observed from outside the shop. Gratefully, there wasn't a screen and so no need for its noisy removal.

Completing her small diversion, Heather strode back into the room. She saw where a small portion of the hearth had slid aside, revealing a hidden tunnel below the floor, the TrueMate and his 'Maite having already descended. On impulse, she decided to recover the RedSuit's weapon located somewhere on the muffling carpet. Startled, the girl froze mid-step at the sound of a discreet knock at the door.

"Ruhnster?" came the hushed voice of the RedSuit. There was a pause. "Yay, Ruhnster?" Another light knuckle-knock.

Abandoning her quest, Heather began to navigate nimbly across the room, between chairs, past the table, and towards the hearth.

"Everything all right in there?" Yet another cautious knock by the RedSuit. "Ruhnster, open up."

Mastow's head protruding, he awaited Heather at the top of a short ladder, assertively waving her onward. *"Hurry!"* he whispered. "I can close the tunnel from below."

Yet, even in the dimness, Heather could see he was no longer attentive to her approach. Rather, his anxious eyes were now permanently affixed to the door. Unable to refrain, she glimpsed behind her.

The knob jiggled irritably and, briefly, muffled voices could be heard. That's when the pounding started.

"Ruhnster! Open this door!" *Wham!* slammed a fist. *"Now!"*

"Something is happening." Sedgwar nodded his certainty. "Something is happening down there." He spoke his words calmly, although wanting to act, his eyes never leaving the thriftshop.

"I see it," said Starbrill, Toya concurring, watching as lights flicked on inside the premises.

Immediately, RedSuits hustled from the front of the shop.

Their Råd°Emitters drawn, they alertly positioned themselves to either side of the doorway.

"Oh, no…" Molly murmured to herself, watching with fear and fascination. She knew that invisible was *not* invincible, that even unseen, Heather was susceptible to an errant shot of a gun or rip of a RazorSlicer. And what was happening with the shopkeepers? Were they even in there? "Come on, Heather," she urged in the same low tone. "You can do it. Get out of there safely. Come back to us."

"Look out, you two. I'm coming down."

Heather wasn't completely within the confines of the tunnel before she saw Mastow pass his hand over the wall and the ClearWeave symbol reveal itself for an illuminative heartbeat. To one side she glimpsed the displaced slab of hearth beginning to slide its way back into place. Hurrying down the ladder, she ducked just in time to avoid its press, listening as it locked tightly into the base of the fireplace facade. Heather motioned them to hurry along, the TrueMaite in the lead turning on a LuminTorch that had been stashed just inside the tunnel's entrance.

Above them, the impatient pounding turned brutally excessive, Rendskorra's elite troops throwing themselves mercilessly at the old thick door. Finally, a Råd°Emitter shattered the knob, causing it to shimmy and explode. Although muffled, Heather could hear the thumping stampede of footfalls, the sounds of chairs being thrown aside and, afterward, a table's thunderous, slumping collapse on the floorboards overhead.

Meanwhile, the three escapees were coursing swiftly through the long corridor, Heather wondering how far below the floor they were, and, moreover, how far above the very bottom of the CityHeights itself.

When she was sure they were clear of the shop, the girl felt it safe to finally speak. "Where does this tunnel lead?"

"Across the open marketplace, to the other side of the avenue."

"Okay. Good."

Several steps later, Mastow asked, "What's your name, youngling?"

"Heather Nighborne. Starbrill said your names were Mastow and Greesha."

The woman took a moment to point her beam indirectly at

Heather, softly illuminating her face. "Starbrill, he's here in TiaraReign?"

Heather nodded.

"So, the good lad came after all."

"Yeah, he suspected a trap. He and Toya are close by, waiting for me to take you to them." Heather gave a glance back the way they had come, the lightlessness persistent in its pursuit, clinging to their heels. No new lights shone in the distance. "I hope you don't mind, but we should probably only talk when we have to."

"You're not only brave, Heather Nighborne," the woman dared to breathe on a half-turn, "but you're smart, too."

Feeling her face redden, self-conscious even in darkness, Heather followed after the fleeing pair.

Staring with heightened anticipation from the balcony across the avenue, Starbrill and his band watched as even more lights began blinking to life in the thriftshop. Across the upper story dormers, too, blink, blink, blink. At that point, a siren alarm went off and from concealed positions along the street, searchlights abruptly slapped the face of the storefront, harshly detailing its haggard features.

Shortly thereafter, RedSuits descended on the building from exterior posts in hiding. They proceeded to surround the shop, more soldiers, still, fanning out of the front door to take up positions near the building's perimeter, up and down the avenue.

Men swiftly at their stations and premises secured, out of the entry door and into the thick night air stepped Rendskorra's battle-seasoned commander, Soldier One.

Riveted, over the wailing siren, Molly said, "Whatever's happening out front, I'm sure there's more action like it taking place behind the shop."

"If we don't hear from Heather shortly," said Starbrill, "I'm not sure how much longer we can wait here, especially if they intend to mount a search."

Molly refused to look his way.

The four dipped behind the railing's overgrowth as a searchlight crawled above their heads, continuing onward, sliding across the buildings' ragged facades, and at times slowing to linger in their hoarding shadows.

Sedgwar said, "Starbrill, why don't you take Molly and Toya and head out of TiaraReign before it heats up all the more."

"Leaving you alone to do what?"

"To go down there. Approach from a different direction to find Heather. No offense, but I operate much better when working alone."

"You heard the hour ring out. It's curfew. If they see you, you'll be shot and killed."

"So will you. So you best hurry and go."

It was obvious to all that Starbrill was struggling to make up his mind, his eyes wandering to focus on the seized shop once more.

"Go on," encouraged Sedgwar. "Take your packs and get out while you're still able."

"I can't," concluded Starbrill. "I'm going with you. Toya, Molly, the two of you get back to camp. If you can't take both packs, stash one. We can claim it on the next trip. Toya, you know where to find the 'Portal to SummersBreath Still. Those newcomers who want to leave the kingdom at that point can go. With those who wish to stay, return to TreeLoft and give them a home. Then, when it's time, shunnel the lot of them *and* the children. You and Molly—"

Molly interjected, "I'm not leaving without Heather."

"This is ridiculous," said Sedgwar, "with the lot of you climbing on their bravery this way, intending to play hero—"

"You're accusing *me* of playing hero?" countered Starbrill.

Sedgwar scoffed softly with a headshake. "Look, you don't understand. You're needed. All of you have vital lives ahead of you, with something to give to Evermore, something to live for."

"What about you? It's not like you're ready to join the geriatric crowd."

Sedgwar became less strident, more subdued. "It's different…for me, all right, it's different."

Starbrill knew all too well he was telling the truth. Disarmed, the young man looked away.

"So, go," encouraged the warrior. "Right now. Go on. I'm not playing the hero, here, and I'm not playing the martyr. You'll just have to trust—"

"What exactly *are* you doing, then?"

"If you have to ask…something about a dragon, I think, all right?" Sedgwar stared challengingly at Starbrill, then picked up the tempo. "So, I want each of you to leave while I try to get to Heather and help her out of trouble. I'll join you afterward."

"I'm not going." It was Molly.

"I'm not, either." Starbrill was dead set.

Toya shrugged. "Sorry, Sedgwar. I can't leave without my brother. He'd tell Mother."

All heads perked up when the siren wound down. Sedgwar briefly turned to the street, checking on the course of events. The warrior returned his attention to where the four stood defiantly in stalemate.

"Then *I'm* going to leave," said Sedgwar. "Please don't follow."

"No. No, you're not going anywhere. And that's because you're all going with *me.*" The sudden voice was unfamiliar, coming from the direction of the stairs. "I insist."

Sedgwar spun. Standing deeper in the shadows and splashed with slips of light, leveling a Råd°Emitter their way, was a RedSuit.

He walked toward them. Molly gasped when the soldier grabbed, twisted, and then held her roughly from behind. Wanting to reactively come to her defense, Starbrill restrained himself, knowing to do so now would only insure death for both of them, perhaps all of them.

"You see, I will be more than happy to resolve your petty little problem," the soldier continued. With his gun, he motioned the parties backward, away from him, all except for Molly. He turned his pistol on her, above the brow. "The slightest move out of the ordinary, any flinch, hiccup, or sneeze—*anything*—and I'll show you how a head expands and explodes." He glanced around and behind him. "Anything. Understand? Now, over there."

Solemnly, they bunched.

"What's in the backpacks?"

"We just returned from a camping trip to the Ancient Rainforests of Tabeer," said Starbrill. His eyes darted to the captive Molly. Other than to discreetly swallow, he showed no visible signs of distress. His tone remained casual. "It looked as though it was past curfew, so, naturally, we thought it best we spend the night on the balcony, out of sight and harm's way. We heard the commotion, so we—"

"Enough," said the RedSuit. "You can explain yourselves to the commander. I'm sure, then, that both of us will think you're lying. For your sakes, you'd better have your TravelTaggs and your stories straight. Oh, and by the way," he added, pointing the gun between them, "which one of you is Starbrill? The younger man? I should think so. Just so you know, we were expecting you."

Partially hidden behind Toya, Sedgwar slipped his hand into his pocket, undoing the safety catch on his DartBow.

"So, let's go," said the RedSuit, gesturing with his weapon. "And keep your hands in sight. May I remind you not to act rashly, or, I promise, it will end in your demise." The soldier released Molly, keeping his weapon trained on her. He gave the girl a push. "Behind you is another set of stairs. If you'd care to march in that direction—*wha—?*"

Molly spun and backed off.

As the four looked on, they saw the upright soldier buckle rearward, his legs giving out at the knees. Immediately, the Hemorrhage°Ray miraculously skipped from his hand, his mask was torn from his head, and an unseen elbow came crashing down on his upturned face. He collapsed into a pile, Heather appearing over him, delivering a series of flashing, punishing blows on his way down.

Sedgwar winced. He was all too aware of the girl's strength, and in that, knew her lightning speed generated even more power from that source. He went to her, collecting the RedSuit's weapon along the way.

Starbrill broke from Toya's side, and Molly rushed to his arms, burying her head in his shirt.

"You're all right?"

She nodded and hung on.

Meanwhile, Heather appeared ready to unleash more savagery, but had calmed to check herself, managing to retain her composure. "You don't hurt my friends," she said, under her breath. "You don't." She rose and backed away, still staring LaserDarts.

Starbrill interrupted her focus. "Mastow and Greesha, where-?"

"I don't know why," said Heather, "but before bringing those guys up here, I left them behind to make sure everything was okay first. They're down at the end of the balcony, waiting on the stairs."

Gently disengaging from Molly, Starbrill left to attend the couple. Toya collected her, and they followed.

Meanwhile, Sedgwar was bending over the unconscious, bloodied soldier, feeling for a pulse. Heather looked on, not knowing what to think, aware of herself and her newfound power, and at times how it seemed to become an uninhibited force all its own. The realization gave her pause.

"He's still breathing, right?" She pulled off her Adaption°Suit hood and facial mask.

Sedgwar nodded, distractedly.

At that, Heather turned away, unsure as to whether she had failed or acted properly when not ending his life. She distinctly remembered what had just taken place in the thriftshop, and how callous Mastow had seemed when taking the RedSuit's life.

Producing some cord from his OverRobe, Sedgwar began to lash the wrists of the RedSuit. His gaze shot upward when he heard Heather say in a stronger than normal tone, "That was some show of force just now, Heather. And I must say, I like our new Vigen°Darr Adaption°Suit." Arms out, she was admiring herself.

"Aria, you're back." Heather's brooding countenance brightened. A smile appeared. "I thought I felt you there."

"Yes, and I'm glad I held off and left you to your handiwork. By the way, some little birdies—and one not so little—informed me of your escapades as of late. You can fill me in on the finer details later."

"Happy to. I've missed you so much. Aria. Hey, I'd like you to meet some friends of mine, starting here with Sedgwar."

Down on the walk in front of the thriftshop, Soldier One was angry, but to his credit he was keeping a clenched fist on it.

Set up perfectly, how could the plan have gone wrong? What happened in that room that allowed the traitors to escape? We had troops watching the rear entrance, the front entrance—*every* entrance! If the prisoners had gotten out through the bathroom window, why didn't we see them running down the alley or climbing onto the roof? We would have heard *something* for Evermore's sake!

So, how did they escape? *How?* Ruhnster must have had an idea that something wasn't right. Good soldier, he was smart, nobody's fool. Walking in on them, he must have been taken by surprise.

Pacing, features drawn, Soldier One continued to fret.

I have to know. And Rendskorra will want to know, too. The traitors didn't just vaporize. If we can't find them, she'll want to vaporize *me,* vaporize my soul, my family—whatever these sorceresses do. I've been to the rallies; it gets gruesome.

The military leader's mind was working frantically while he tried to retain his composure. He couldn't fail. He couldn't. He'd heard the rumors about what happened to Mistraya's Soldier One at the Crown & Scepter. Some claim it was the green-eyed Maiden who had put an end to him in that freakish way. But soldiers say it was really Mistraya who did the deed for failing to capture and kill the Maiden

Portent. And that's the reason she let the costume shop burn to the ground, her GraySuit army with it. The unforgiving punishment of the Purple Flame, they say. That's the rumor, all right, shared not only by officers, but the rank and file, too.

Mistraya. Rendskorra—all these sorceress sisters: succeed and they feed your Mark with that addictive prickly pain; fail, and they'll crush you like a three-toed lippenscutt.

All right, he thought, so, what have we got? So far we've got RedSuits under Soldier Two searching the neighborhoods behind the thriftshop, expanding the perimeter as they go. The escapees couldn't have gone far without being seen. There were RedSuits holding down key positions in the outlying neighborhoods, too, just in case there was a Loyalist ambush. Streets cleared, they would have captured any wanderers. And now, I've ordered men to go house-to-house, building-to-building, checking in all directions, so that's covered. So, what else? What am I missing?

Soldier One ceased to pace. Holding his ground, he reflected, worried that his Mistress might just put in a surprise appearance. Sure, Rendskorra might look a bit dizzy at times, but the commander had nothing but respect for her shrewdness and her ability to kill without a care, anywhere, anytime—over lunch even, and afterward have the servants clear the remains along with the dishes.

And although Soldier One assured his Mistress he could handle the entire operation, it wouldn't be the first time that she checked in with him on the fly. She does that. In person or by TeleFlame, surprise, surprise.

Just don't call on me now, he insisted. I need time to sort this one out.

He took a deep raspy breath. Mind churning, grimacing through the glare, his eyes attempted to pierce the dark overgrown facades across the street. He had sent a few soldiers over there arbitrarily, even though he knew the escapees couldn't have made it that far without being seen. And yet…

"Brattenslag," he growled, "you and your men get over there and help search those buildings across the street, inside and out. If you find anyone, I don't care who they are or what they look like, bring them to me. Understand?

"Right away, Sir."

Rendskorra's lead commander turned towards the large front window of the thriftshop, his hands clasped behind his back.

So, how did they get out?

Thickset, he caught sight of his dark form appearing like a cutout against the reflection of the lighted street scene behind him, his troops jogging toward the far structures. The military man knew that, if the traitors managed to escape the perimeter already in place, chances are they'd be long gone in a couple hours, safely holed up somewhere, or probably even smuggled out of the CityHeights entirely.

On the other hand, they could very well be waiting somewhere close by until the RedSuit traffic died and their search was put to bed. Then they could leave sometime during the night—or in the morning without a worry in the worlds, blending into the CityHeight street crowds.

And that just won't do. It won't. It's imperative that we find them *now.* And find them we will.

Brief introductions having taken place, Sedgwar stood dumbstruck, trying to hide his sudden dismay.

Aria? A second self? Are you joking? Could it be that he, Sedgwar, had allied himself with a young MindSkew? Say it's not so.

Upon their return from the stairwell, Starbrill and Toya, he could tell, were also at a loss and didn't know what to think. The same could be said about Mastow and Greesha. Molly was the only one who seemed comfortable with the fact that Heather was in possession of an alter ego. She even engaged in some brief pleasantries and small talk. Brooding, Sedgwar turned his attention toward the street.

Realistically, there was no way the warrior—or any of them gathered there on the balcony—could be blamed for their discomfort and doubt as to the youngling's sanity. After all, how were they expected to know of or come to terms with the notion of a SoulSylph? As well, in the shadows, it didn't help that they hadn't been able to witness Heather's change in eye color from green to amber during her transition between personalities.

One of the things Sedgwar did happen to notice was that, all the while, during their rushed formalities, this Aria kept looking over the railing, distracted by what appeared to be transpiring below.

And when she remained riveted, her feet firmly in place, saying, "I think we have a problem," is when everyone discreetly found place at the rail.

"It appears they're starting to search this side of the street," observed Sedgwar.

"They're desperate," said Mastow. "Soon they'll figure it out and be turning that small room upside down and inside out."

Heather asked, "Think they'll find the tunnel?"

"Doubt it. Not under that slab, right. And there's a bit of ground between the floorboards and the top of it. But you never know, hey, they could."

"Forget that little room," said Greesha. "If they've gotten to the alley and the stairs behind us, we'll be cut off, unable to get out of here without being seen."

"Unless we lure them elsewhere with a distraction."

At the pronouncement, everyone looked at Aria. And what she did next would make believers of them all.

"Jacktern, have Dakkers give the order to shrink the outlying perimeter," commanded Soldier One, "I want those soldiers moving toward us, choking off any chance of escape. Also, I want all available RedSuit forces on hand joining them in their door-to-door hunt. At some point, they'll meet up with our troops under Soldier Two who're working out from the center. Those escapees, I want them squeezed. Look sharp! Be thorough in your searches and, in your interrogations of the residents, be brutal. And I *want* brutality. I insist on it. Slap these dwellers around. See what shakes loose. Got it? Kindness doesn't win wars."

"Yes, sir."

"If they come up empty," Soldier One continued, "bring the troops over to assist in the searches across the avenue."

"Right."

"Hartle!" barked the RedSuit commander. "I want that room in the thriftshop stripped, and the walls and floors searched for trap doors and hidden panels. Tear out those shelves—the cabinets, too—making sure there's nothing behind them. I want to know if you find anything. *Anything!* Got it? Now, get in there and *stink in it! I want you wearing that room like a swill bath!*"

"Sir!"

Chapter Five

Aria Creates a Fighting Force

Aria was restless, stalking the rail. "Heather, who is Mrs. Dentspire?"

"Mrs. Dentspire? She's some silly woman back home who wrote a really, *really* stupid play based on one of Molly and my favorite movies."

"Is that so?"

"Oh, yeah. Totally. We had to watch that thing, too. Luckily, this guy named LoviL hijacked her play at the end and turned it into something great. Molly says there's nothing worse than a stupid adaptation."

"I couldn't agree more."

"Aria, I have to tell you, this seems like a pretty crazy time to be talking about this stuff with more of those RedSuits coming after us, searching these buildings. So, what's up? Why are you—?"

"Oh, you know, Heather. No reason. Just thinking."

Yet, Heather knew better. "Aria?"

The girl's iMagiNacial counterpart simply laughed, and while Lyricying, employed a magical wave of her hand. Immediately thereafter, like cloudbursts, areas of brilliant light began to flood the nearby roads and empty marketplace at bracketed intervals, first along one stretch of the grand avenue and then back again along the other. It was as if Aria were turning on banks of stadium lighting one set at a time—only minus the very lights themselves and their supporting standards.

On the balcony next to the charismatic Maiden Portent, the six bystanders sheltered their eyes, squinting into the spectacular arena awash with white light. And now Sedgwar was gazing at Heather incredulously, at her green SearEye, his head shaking slowly side-to-side. They all took their turns, in fact, staring in awe at the youngling, knowing she had set the stage, anticipating what would follow as Aria's opening act.

Down on the street, Soldier One and his RedSuits found themselves at a loss. From their low vantage point, they couldn't see through the overgrowth above to catch sight of the iMagiNator and her accomplices. Truly, they wondered at the intention behind what had just occurred, and who could have conceived of such a stunt.

Glancing about, squinting at the crisscross of walks overhead, Soldier One didn't know whether to hope it was Rendskorra appearing on the scene or not. If his Mistress turned up now, she would only catch her lead officer derelict in his duty, the carefully planned ambush having gone inconceivably wrong. Perhaps the commander *should* hope it was some other super power turning on those dazzling lights, so that he and his men could engage and overcome them in an effort bury his blunder and salvage his impeccable standing.

Rousing and asserting himself, pointing this way and that, the RedSuit leader shouted at his troops to hurry and get out of the street, waving at them to take up defensive positions in and around the shops, behind trees, buildings, and other strategically placed obstacles in the area.

At the suddenness of the inexplicable lights, in the ensuing confusion, the soldiers he had previously dispatched across the avenue had initially hesitated in stupefied wonder before diving for cover, their Råd°Emitters in hand. Soldier One, pulling two of his nearby troops in close, gave strict orders to his men on the quiet, before shoving them on their way. He signaled the others to await further orders.

Meanwhile, positioned aloft, Heather said, "Aria, I'm afraid to ask, but what the heck are you doing?"

"Watch, my friend, and you shall see."

After more HandFashioning, below, emanating from the center of the nondescript avenue spread a curl of yellow and red brick. Afterward, smack-dab in the midst of this LightPlay appeared four unusual figures. Wholly out of place, they stood dimwittedly looking about themselves, blinking on the squint.

Heather said, "Aria, you're not—I don't believe this. Have you lost your *mind?*"

"Open fire!" screamed Soldier One from below, and immediately, the Råd°Emission weaponry blazed to life, the bluish, red, and green pulsating, streaking beams finding the four. Surprisingly the deadly rays passed right through them without inflicting harm of any kind.

"The good old Vigen°Darr," said Aria, "inventing and selling weapons to all buyers that prove feckless against iMagiNacia. Now, the RedSuits will have to resort to using their swords, if they want to slay any of my iMagiNaciale soldiers." Head held high, a thumb and curled forefinger in contemplation at her chin, she awaited their next move. "So, this quartet of misfits is from one of your favorite movies?"

"Yeah, and it's a classic, too. One of the all-time greats. 1939. A super year for movies…some say the height of Hollywood's Golden Age."

"I'll take your word for it."

"Aria, there are a whole lot of fighting movies in my head, you know. Why don't you pick one of *those* to work from? Maybe a documentary from D-Day or something. Those guys would get a heck of a lot more done."

"We've no time to find and sort through them. Now, I like the fact that this one features a young girl, but at the moment, I certainly wish she were an older, more experienced warrior."

"Aria, *we're* a young girl. Besides, she can't be all bad. I mean, she's got red sparkly shoes…"

"Perhaps she'll do. But a cowardly lion?"

"He's still a lion. I mean, a lion is a lion, right? Can't you just put him to work tearing into people and stuff?"

"For Evermore's sake, Heather, he has a little red bow in his hair. It hardly instills confidence, I'm afraid, unless you're looking to compete in a pet show. What else do we have here? A scatterbrained scarecrow and a heartless tin woodsman? Hardly reassuring. A little black dog? You're not giving me a lot to work with, here. And you expect this bunch to engage in a battle against a company of RedSuits?"

"Aria, don't blame me. *You're* the one who picked my brain and thought up this mess. Maybe you can come up with a magical tornado. Drop a house or two. That'll sure clear things out."

"We don't effectively possess power for that yet, or trust me I would. All right, so, what are we to do with this ill-equipped bunch? Really, I'm afraid they simply won't suffice."

"Well, then, just get rid of them and do like you did the last time we had trouble in Evermore, shooting all those toppings and stuff around from the Latest Scoop Ice Creamery."

"What? And create yet another remake? Hardly."

"Better than a stupid adaptation."

"Looks like the fun and games are over. Best prepare yourselves for battle," said Sedgwar. Loosening his OverRobe, he allowed himself easier access to his weapons, the experienced warrior recognizing a distant sound that the others hadn't yet discerned or identified. "Aria, Heather, I don't quite know what you have in mind, but despite the curfew, the bright lights are drawing quite a crowd of TiaraReigners up and down the avenues."

"Good," said Aria. "This is my intention. You don't reach Evermorians and instill hope without creating a memorable spectacle worth the effort to pass it along."

"I hate to break the news, Aria," said Heather, "but we're *definitely* not instilling hope. Not with those four. It's more like we're instilling *goof.*"

"So, I say let's indulge ourselves in real life entertainment with real life consequences. If we're lucky, someone here will have a MindsEye Camera to record and share the event, now that the KA has outlawed the many photographic devices once held in the hands of the masses."

"Aria, why anyone would want to film this, I don't know. I say, go watch the original. It comes complete with a wicked witch."

Starbrill grew concerned. "Can you hear that?"

"Yes," said Aria, heartened. "And, actually, it's about time, too. I've been awaiting such a sound. Reinforcements."

Growing louder was a deep rhythmic thrum, a multitude of boots at a distance treading on the roadway's surface.

They waited, and finally Molly said, "You mean, *their* reinforcements. There, at the top of the avenue. Look."

In rigid formation, appearing from out of the dimness, a great many RedSuits had turned the corner. From there, they marched down the wide street, drawing to a snappish halt in front of the Gift & Thrift where Soldier One emerged to join them. From their positions of cover, RazorSlicers at the ready, the other RedSuits angled in, lingering at the fringes. All attention remained focused on the four strange new arrivals.

"If we don't do something soon, the RedSuits are going to get bored and start looking for us again."

"Heather, I'm quite aware of our present situation. Trust me, all right? We have their attention. They're not going anywhere."

At the sight of so many, the small black dog jumped from the girl's arms and scampered off into the seclusion of a nearby lane. Frightened, the cowardly lion was cringing, attempting to hide behind his mates. The scarecrow, meanwhile, along with his tin woodsman companion, had put on an air of bravado, attempting to protect the girl in the blue and white checked dress while threatening to take on all comers.

"Dorothy, the lion—all of them," said Molly. "You can tell. They're frightened half out of their wits."

On the newly designed street, everyone could see and hear the anxious, pigtailed youngster caught up in breathless exclamation. She was glancing about frantically, saying that she was *sick* of traveling to such godforsaken places, that she had never asked for these ruby slippers to begin with, and why there was never a hot air balloon around when you needed one she could never fathom. *And,* the girl continued, indignantly, to hell with it, that the first chance she had she was going to chuck it all in, gather up her sweet little dog and just head straight back to Kansas. She added that putting up with some narcissistic old shrew of a neighbor was certainly a lot easier than putting her life in danger time and again, and that, truly, there *was* no place like home, even if it happened to be some crummy old farm in the middle of nowhere. Why, wherever and *what*ever, she'd make it work.

Heather muttered, "This is embarrassing."

"We've distracted them," said Toya. "Isn't that enough? Can't we sneak out of here now?"

"If you wish. My suggestion, however, is that you wait, that you leave when we're up to speed," said Aria, in response. "It would be the safest time for it."

"Heather is correct in her assessment. An engagement of some sort has to take place soon," said Sedgwar, "or they'll ignore these four, and simply resume their search."

"Aria, will you hurry and do something, already."

Despite her counterpart's grumblings, the SoulSylph remained cool. "Soon, Heather, soon."

"Well, I don't know what you're waiting for. Man, look down there. See that guy scared out of his skull?"

"I assume you're referring the one crying, wiping his eyes with his tail?"

"Yeah, your lion with the red bow. That guy. Any second you're going to see him scram, just head the heck out of here and go hide somewhere with that dog. Then we'll have only three down there against that entire legion of RedSuits. And if the tin man starts crying because the lion left, trust me, he'll rust. He does that. We've seen it. And then you'll *really* be in trouble, because, after that, we'll be stuck with only two.

"Also, I've got to tell you, Aria, Dorothy would never act or talk that way. She'd be up for anything. Just ask Molly."

"It's true. Actually, Heather, she's a lot like you."

"And those other guys, acting scared like that. Well, they *were* scared, all right, but only until they got a little confidence, until they had to rescue Dorothy."

"Heather," said Aria, a terse edge to her voice, "it's called artistic license. Even SoulSylphs have to have their creative fun. Now, with all due respect, my suggestion is that you *stop* acting like a purest snob."

"Whatever..."

"Heather," said Molly, "look how many more spectators have come. There are really a lot."

"I see them, Molly. Aria?"

"It's not yet time to engage. And we want more."

"More people? More soldiers? What?"

"More *everything*. And we're going to get it. Watch."

Below, at Soldier One's command, the RedSuits drew their long swords. From extended forearms grew shields. Then they began a slow march forward, their boots tramping like drumbeats.

Whump...whump...whump...

In between the resounding footfalls, the bystanders could hear the lion rambling, pacing, carrying on, *oh, dear, oh, dear, oh, my,* his fear pouring out in a nonsensical stream of consciousness. He continued to grovel and fret, dabbing his eyes with the puffy end of this tail. The others were cowering, shaking with fear.

Whump...whump...whump...

And now, without further delay, Heather's SoulSylph began to Lyricy, and amazingly down over the yellow and red brick roadway, the four figures transformed. The girl in the dress grew taller, sleeker, her pigtails merging at the back of her head to form a MaidenBraid. Her costume drew tight to her body in elegant and understated flourish. Letting her straw basket of apples drop to the ground, from points at her waist, she freed up her sword and dagger.

Starbrill did a double-take, saying, "She looks like Heather."

Meanwhile, the lion had gone to all fours, transforming into a streamlined, muscular, and wavy-maned Archmount. His red bow altered shape, too, becoming a stylish headpiece accentuating his fierce brow and menacing sneer.

The scarecrow, awakened from his fearful posture, straightened and filled out, while the exposed straw emerging from gaping tears in his clothing became a spiky fringe of design sweeping up his arms, across his back, and down his legs, arriving at a swirling conclusion above his modern, shiny boots. His twined belt thickened to become a sash.

Loosening the short bit of rope at his cuff, he dipped it into Dorothy's discarded basket that, only moments before, he had snatched up at his feet. When he pulled the rope free, the three apples adhering to its fibrous length changed into spiky balls of a medieval mace, each at the end of a short chain. The remaining rope lengthened and went rigid in his grip to form its metal shaft.

In his opposite hand—the scarecrow still ahold of its handle—the basket itself enlarged into a tall, rectangular shield of woven metal. At his neck, the excess material from his head sack formed the beginnings of a cloak unfurling at length down his back, the encircling rope a choker and medallion below neon eye slots and a red triangular nosepiece.

And the tin man, he melded at the joints, reconfiguring into a more finely contoured, windblown version of himself in lustrous silver and bronze. In his hand, his tree-chopping axe shortened into one designed specifically for battle, while his oilcan expanded to form a rounded shield. Upon his head, his hat altered shape, as well, to become smoothened and elegantly swept, its once upright funnel now pointing rearward, while his facial features below turned grave and menacing.

At the transformations, the streets lined with Evermorians cheered their approval, wholly unaware of the foursome's storybook and Hollywood beginnings. Yet, Aria didn't stop there. Once she reshaped her characters into more formidable warriors, the SoulSylph replicated her four stylized creations many hundredfold to fill the expansive marketplace.

And although the spectators roared maniacally at the impressive iMagiNaciale conjurations, the advancing RedSuits didn't raise a brow. No, not a one. Robotically stoic, the steadfast aggressors never even flinched, the Mark of the Silver Bolt tattooed upon their chests resonating with euphoric, mind-numbing pain.

Whump…whump…whump…

"Why are you stopping there, Aria? Can't you make ten times that many?"

"Heather, I can only give life to so many of these creations. To keep them operating draws on magical power of which you and I, together, possess only so much. And it's prudent to keep some in reserve, just in case."

"In case of what?"

"In case of 'you hope you never need to find out.'"

"Well, okay, then, I guess we'll just have to see what happens. I'd say our Ozmonds match up pretty well."

"In number, yes. So, now, let us see how they perform on the battlefield." Intent, Aria muttered, "This, Heather, is where the game becomes serious." She paused on a nod and a breath. "Deathly serious."

Hands on hips, feet spread, Heather and Aria sank into heightened silence, looking on as the RedSuits continued their slow advance up the avenue, the gap between the armed combatants closing.

Whump…whump…whump…

Glued in place along the spread of balcony, the seven conspirators raptly looked on. Stern-faced amid the greenery, Starbrill's fingers clasped and milked the railing. At his side, Sedgwar stood tall, his jaw clenched, his facial muscles faintly a-twitch. Opposite, Molly had her arms crossed tightly before her, lips taut. Withdrawn, a step behind, Toya remained stark still, leaning slightly forward. At her side, Greesha had found a knee, her TrueMate Mastow still standing, pressing into her, his hand choking a corner drainpipe. Ever so softly, Aria cleared her throat. Around her, the breeze lightly brushed the leaves. The crowds below had seized and grown quiet. And the RedSuits marched.

Whump…whump…whump…

Hurtling headlong down the forest road, the swath of riders stayed surprisingly clustered, galloping low, head-to-tail, flank-to-flank, always pushing to the fore, pushing for more. And should a beast happen to falter and tumble in the darkness, the cost would be great to many a life in the roil and spillage. But urgency called upon daring, and there were chances to be taken and moments to be won, the uninterrupted hours succumbing heedlessly to distance, having fallen away long ago to possess any rightful claim to timeliness.

At a junction, more riders joined the surge, their daring just as bold, their demeanors just as urgent.

Overhead, the moon cast off what it could, its delicate light spread over hill and hollow, helping to light the way to the CityHeights. Late, late, late, the riders strove onward; recklessly they drove their trampling hoards, lest the awaiting hours age ever ruthlessly and grow far too dim for deliverance.

Balanced on the glistening edge of a finely honed moment, just waiting...waiting...lulling into an electrified hush...*abrupt!* the bloodcurdling cries cleaved the swollen night and a deafening roar erupted to rend the pent-up air, the RedSuits and Ozmonds charging one another in release, crashing in droves, in heaves and thrusts and clanks and grunts. Shields butted and weapons clashed and smashed and bruised and felled with soldiers scrumming every which way in the armor piercing, bone jarring, flesh-and-fiber bloodletting mêlée. Swings were swung and punches scored and helmeted bells were rung and rung and rung, and point-laced slings were slung, while scores were left to weather wounds or lay unmoving, bleeding out until their shuddering, gasping ends. Surging advances were made and repelled and reclaimed on behalf of their side and our side and your side and mine, with winging, flinging, and stinging metal ringing all about, weaponry a-riot in glints and groans and shouts and a thrashing of steel.

The battle soared and warred and ebbed and raged. At various times, catching snippets of action throughout the swarm of soldiers, the balcony observers grimaced and cheered under their breaths, depending on the outcome of the many hard-fought duels.

Feeling faint, Molly turned away.

"We're winning!" cried Toya, crouching low alongside the spiritless girl at a gap in the greenery.

"With the distraction at its height, now is the time for you to leave," said Aria, speaking above the din. "All of you."

Not one of the six in observation paid her any heed, Molly crawling to sit herself, head bent, against the wall that she thought for sure was sickeningly swaying.

Without comment, the men monitored the confusion, Sedgwar aloof from the proceedings, Starbrill thirstily wanting to partake in the battle against the RedSuited, red-blooded forces of the Dahklarr Herth. Mastow remained unmoved by the dead and dying, Greesha at his feet silently clutching his leg, kneading his flesh, knowing that one of the many fallen could have been him. Or her. Or, perhaps, any of their brave ClearWeave confederates.

Mastow was the first to notice another group in formation advancing upon the well-lit battle site. "On the connecting avenue, hey, across the way, just past the marketplace. Looks to be soldiers of the Crown."

It was indeed, the hostile TiaraReign crowds grudgingly parting before the fighting unit's deliberate, rhythmic progress.

Aria tsked, saying, "Unfortunately, I didn't foresee the involvement of Crown soldiers."

When the force neared the avenue, the CityHeights' youth started pitching objects from the rooftops and alleys, doorways and windows, the Crown soldiers breaking formation to raise their shields. Crouched behind their tilted defenses, they responded to the outburst with °Concussors and Hemorrhage°Rays, the shards of debris exploding from the structures, the flesh erupting from the faces and bodies of the antagonists, the dead young men and women falling from on high. That's when the crowds swarmed them.

"I'm going down there," cried Starbrill. "Toya and Molly, I want you to get back to camp and the newcomers. Now. It's important you're able to show them to the Portal or HomeBase. Take Greesha and Mastow."

No one moved.

"I'm going with you, Starbrill," said Sedgwar.

"And I, hey," said Mastow, watching the Crown soldiers and RedSuits beating down the masses, inflicting on them the worst of the encounter.

"I'm going, too," said Greesha.

"You're not," said her TrueMate. "You're no warrior."

"Neither are they." She motioned with her head toward the street.

"They're not needed for the movement. You are."

"And I'd say to you that they are the movement."

"You're staying." His words were dropped with finality.

Heather watched the backs of the departing men and their weapons as, each in their turn, they joggled down the stairs. Molly arose with effort to stand at her friend's side, with Toya and Greesha nearing, as well.

"I wish we weren't needed at camp," was all Starbrill's sister said, staring longingly after her sibling.

Molly stared, too, willing him luck. And life.

When Greesha broke away and followed toward the stairwell, no one objected.

Molly said, "I should go with her," and she brushed aside Heather and Toya's restraining hands, along with their animated remonstrations.

Overhearing, Greesha momentarily retreated, blocking Molly's path. Sternly, she drew in on her. "I'm ill-equipped enough, girl. But at least I've killed. You, you can serve with better purpose by staying here and being useful in the fight, although in a different battle and in a different role, a quiet one at that. Go down there, and you'll be eaten first thing by that thorny monster, whereby I'll make my way and do my harm, at least for the while. But you, you stay here. Understand? Sometimes you need more than a weapon to fight. Your time will come, and you'll be better suited for it."

Molly tried to stop her knees from trembling. Her words were soft, slow. "I can't tell you why, but if it's Heather's fight, it has to be my fight, too. And if you go down there, then I should go down there, as well. I just can't watch you and everyone else—Starbrill, Sedgwar, Mastow, and all those people down in the street—risk their lives and fight for what they believe in while I just stand here and watch…and do nothing except feel sick and afraid.

"Some of those people that are my age…some of them will die…some *have* died…" Molly shook her head. "…they're gone, because they believed in a cause, in a place in their hearts. So, I can't just stand here. I can't. Not if I want to be…be *alive* in my skin. You, Heather, Starbrill, Toya—all of you—you're so brave. Do you see?"

Greesha wanted to laugh aloud at the girl's outrageousness, a child who could barely watch the fighting let alone raise a sword to participate. And yet, the woman wouldn't dare. Not on a dearth. She felt that there was something heroic, even noble, in the girl's simple bravery that deserved her respect, no matter how naive. The pair continued their faceoff, each determined in the staredown. Then, on impulse, on a sudden realization, Molly hugged her—just hugged her, hugged her, hugged her. She wouldn't let go, Greesha finally peeling her off, Molly now aware, knowing.

"Girl, what are you doing?"

"What are *you* doing? I mean, I *know* what you're doing. I know…I know. So, why, then, *why,* when you won't let *me…?"* Molly threw up a hand, gave a headshake.

There hung a dizzy silence between them, the clamors of war

serving as their backdrop.

"I have to. I'm bound to, proud to. It's my time…my duty." The woman's eyes held her mood. She whispered, "You're young yet, girl. So young." She laid her palm against Molly's cheek. "When it happens, let the moment's reward be for the both of us. For something greater." Molly glimpsed the hint of joy that found the woman's face. "For the Four."

"For Evermore." Molly's words barely came out, the girl holding her gaze, thankful for Greesha's gift.

They backed and let each other go, Greesha toward the stairs and most assuredly her death, Molly to stand near Heather in silent observance. Locked in the fastness, in the fierceness of the moment, she had no tears.

Meanwhile, Heather was doing battle with her patience. Thinking it her place to be a part of the fight in the street also, she bided her time and said nothing. She felt Aria was currently orchestrating the proceedings and needed the view from above to be thoroughly effective, and so saw her role minimized from active participant to that of a bystander. For how long she couldn't say, the girl certain Aria was aware of her restlessness.

Soon, crudely-armed or with fists, citizens in the area were pouring out of every possible access to join in the fray, the soldiers now on the defensive. Yet, ill-equipped, more losses were incurred by the locals of TiaraReign, the fighting now in full aggressive brawl and sprawl on the main avenue and down its adjoining roadways.

"Maybe it's time to use up your reserves, Aria. I mean, now that the soldiers on our side are real people, and they're losing, you might want to do something more."

"As you wish. I'll have very little left. Just in case."

"In case of what?"

"In case of dire, dire need."

"I think we're kind of dire now, don't you? Look at those guys."

"Their souls bled and depleted on behalf of the KA, it doesn't help that the citizens are fighting with only partial resolve, exerting half a will in the effort."

"So, doesn't that make things dire?"

"Trust me, Heather. Circumstances can get much more alarming."

Lyricying, Aria conjured up more Ozmonds, and they swiftly enmeshed themselves in the struggle, engaging both the RedSuits and the Crown soldiers. It wouldn't be long before they began to seize the advantage, swinging the momentum of the conflict their way.

"That, I think, should do for a while," said Aria. "Toya and Molly, I believe this could very well be the perfect time for the two of you to leave and return to camp."

Below the overgrown railing, they were able to observe their three companions fighting alongside some of the TiaraReigners, Mastow and the citizens having claimed weapons from among the many slain. Molly looked for Greesha, but couldn't find her in the commotion.

Where it was obvious to the balcony onlookers that Starbrill and Mastow were competent fighters and fended well for themselves, all could see Sedgwar's skill, knowledge, and courage taking him to an entirely superior level. He was like a buzz saw through the heart of the fighting, inflicting damage as he went, simply, precisely, cleanly, with notably efficient ease.

Throughout the conflict, Råd°Emitters, °Concussors, and Hemorrhage°Rays occasionally spit out with a beam, but due to the thickness of the fighting, the wielders were usually felled immediately thereafter, from a blindside or behind. The soldiers' stolen Vigen°Darr weaponry, when not turned openly on the Dark forces there on the spot, were secretly making their way into the hands of the TiaraReign citizenry, to be cached for future use.

Her eyes on the fury of warfare taking place before her, Heather was surprised to turn and see Molly standing beside her, awaiting her attention.

"I'm going now," she said. Molly wanted to touch and hold Heather, feeling an urgent need. She refrained.

Heather thought her friend appeared frail, deeply shaken, at war with herself to simply maintain. An aura scan confirmed as much.

Molly said, "Your Maiden clothes, I laid them over there near the corner, against the wall. I'll see you back at camp, all right?"

At a flash of brilliant light, Heather grabbed Molly, pulling her lower and into a crouch. There, she shielded her body with her own. Above them, siding on the building had exploded, raining down in bits. Heather waited, and then reared in separation, still ahold of Molly at the shoulders.

"Yeah. I'll see you guys soon, okay. If you run into Archie, tell him I'll be down in a little bit."

Molly was biting her lip, nodding. Her eyes were pleading, attempting to comprehend and accept the inconceivable that surrounded her.

Toya called, "Molly?"

Molly waved without a look.

In the low bleed of light, she saw Aria resume possession, Heather's eye color changing green to amber. With the SoulSylph finding her feet, returning her attention to the clamor and chaos in the streets, Molly arose and backed. Stumbling around the captive RedSuit, she followed after Toya. Swallowed up by darkness, she gave a lasting glance over her shoulder. It lingered on her friend. Just in case.

"Oh, where in Evermore's name is that sister of mine!" S'ilKuSheere snapped her fingers closed on the handheld 'Flame in a sweeping snatch of frustration.

Fixated, the Majestic Sorceress refocused on the battle unfolding on her WallScreen. She was not pleased at the turn of events. Standing rigidly upright, unable to restrain her impatience, she switched views to see her moths fluttering across the nighttime skies, the lights of TiaraReign CityHeights glowingly in the distance.

"Will this force be enough? Can we afford to take that chance?" she mumbled.

Switching views back to the larger swarm, unwilling to wait any longer, she instructed a second wave to break free and follow after the first.

Now, head inclined, eyes intent, arms tightly crossed, her lips pressed firmly together, she followed the course of her army's main thrust, those moths still headed for the quiet of TreeLoft.

"Soon, my Tertiary Charge," said S'ilKuSheere, "after your transformation to full form, I'll be needing you and your airborne unit to make a slight detour in your journey—but only for a moment. You see, there's a location up ahead…"

The Majestic Sorceress informed her lead of a particular spot located not far from their route where they'll be expected to land. Once there, they were to load up with Absorption°Spheres that Rendskorra had made available from a LapisStar CityHeights armory.

"Now," she continued, speaking directly into the mind of her Turlakk moth, " at this point, we've diverted more than half our force. Let's just see if we can't wipe out TreeLoft and its inhabitants in a single wave of surprise bombings. Or, if not on the first go round, perhaps a wholly devastating second, or perhaps even a thoroughly obliterating third. But wipe them out we shall. Completely. Utterly. And, need I say," she brought up a malevolent smirk, "Darkly."

"Okay, Aria. I think it's time we got involved in the fighting, don't you?"

"Yes, Heather, I do. However, in as much as we can, we need to keep an eye on the proceedings as we go. Unfortunately, we will no longer have this more advantageous view when locked in battle down on the street."

Heather began hurriedly stuffing her discarded Maiden clothing into her BodyTote, impatiently awaiting the absorption of one item before adding additional others. She decided not to store her cloak, and instead wrapped it in place over her shoulders, partially covering the sleeker Adaption°Suit.

"Get ready, Fallasha," she murmured to her brooch, "because now you're coming with me." Chin up, her hands were busy with buttons at the neck. "You, me, and Aria, together we're fighting for Evermore."

Heather strapped on her Maiden dagger. Unsheathing her blade, the youngling sprinted the length of the balcony and galloped down the stairs, following after the men and Greesha before her.

Leaping off the bottom steps, Heather had to pull her weapon in tight, angling her body past those running from the scene of escalating turmoil. Most were mothers with young children, glancing fearfully back over their shoulders, screaming, crying, running for shelter between buildings. Older folk who were frail and unable to fight made their way as well, some falling, trampled and injured in the tussle of bodies.

Heather approached the edge of the fray. Claiming bodily possession along with a sword thrown to her from a sleek and magical Heather lookalike, Aria said, "Heather, if you wouldn't mind, I'd like to be the first of us to engage."

"I don't mind, Aria. Just do *something,* okay? I need to be a part of this."

Immediately involved in the embroilment, in and among her iMagiNaciale Ozmonds Aria fought, utilizing long sword and dagger in a stunning display of swordsmanship.

"Wow, Aria, where did you—?"

"I learned to fight this way in my youth. And I'm not the only one. All my sisters have amazing athletic abilities, as do Maidens, *and,* of course…" Feinting with her dagger, she hammered her aggressive RedSuit counterpart with the butt of her sword, "…as do you." She slashed her attacker with finality across the chest.

In a wicked flurry, Aria took on another. She parried and lunged, briskly dispensing with the RedSuit, this time a woman. Furiously, she confronted a third. "Remember, Heather," the SoulSylph said, battling, "I have the history of the MaidenHood on my side, stored in my mental and physical memory." Knocking aside his shield, she locked swords at the hilt with her combatant. "And there in that memory, however *rusty,"* she grimaced and shoved off, her amazing strength casting the much larger man rearward, "is the best of the best in sword fighting technique. And as you can see…" she stabbed the RedSuit straight through the sternum, freeing up her weapon with a tug, "…I'm sharing that with you."

Turning quickly, she was once more engaged, this time finding herself entangled with a soldier of the Crown. When she pointedly drove him into retreat, he tripped over a fallen tin woodsman, and losing his balance, Aria ended his life as he wavered, striving to remain upright.

"Man, Aria, you're *lightning* with that sword!"

Aria ignored her, features locked in ire, looking to locate another opponent.

"Over there, Aria! Look, Starbrill's in trouble," said Heather. She ducked the swoosh of a RazorSlicer whipping her way. "He's cornered by three soldiers!"

Heather feigned with her sword, and, spinning, used her dagger to score with a lash across the neck of her adversary.

"Heather, there's not a whole lot of power left to draw on—"

"Aria, *please!"*

"As you wish."

Beginning to Lyricy, Aria was set upon by another RedSuit. She did all she could to haltingly HandFashion and finish off the spell while protecting herself, backpedaling on the defensive. Finished, she resumed the fight.

With a stride and a leap over a bush at the side of the avenue, the freewheeling Starbrill turned to reengage his three assailants who had him on the defensive. Adeptly, he held off his attackers, now backing them up with a series of aggressive parries—metal fiercely flashing and clanging on metal. In turn, they pressured him into retreat, forcing the young dashing figure up some stairs leading onto a porch with a doorway, the enclosure covered and protected by a low roof. Still, Starbrill managed to hold them at bay, the trio bunched in chinking, flickering swordplay at the bottom.

Suddenly, in an explosion of brilliant orange smoke on the shingles above him, the sorceress Rendskorra appeared for all to see, dressed in black attire and wearing a tall, pointed hat.

"My RedSuits, stop! Stop this fighting *immediately!*" commanded the sorceress, now hunched and peering, her arms spread, one hand emphatically clutching a straw broom.

Recognizing the voice of their Mistress, confused, some RedSuits paused long enough to be the recipients of a blade or spiky ball.

"Heather, you wanted a witch…" said Aria, backing in an exchange of steel, "…well, now…" she deflected a shield and stepped in closer, "I've given you one." She scored a fatal blow, and then another when immediately beset in opposition.

"You made her up? Who the heck is *that?* That's not the witch I know…from the movie, I mean. The one I know has a green face."

With an annoyed look, along with a murmur and an offhand dagger-wave, Aria gave her one. "Approve?"

Heather had scant opportunity to appraise the change. The pair undertook another challenger, the clashing of swordplay ringing out.

"From afar, I'd like you to meet my lovely sister…" Aria lunged and plunged, her steely point finding its mortal target, "…the now green-faced Rendskorra. Something tells me she would have applauded the additional color."

Meanwhile, assisted by the conjured distraction of smoke and witch, Starbrill's sword ably disposed of two of his three attackers. Then, dramatically leaping over the porch's rail, he gallantly reengaged the third and highhandedly made quick work of the soldier, clink, clink…*whick.* Swiftly withdrawing his quivering blade, he was once more on the hunt.

The grave battle increased in tempo, in fierceness and in bloodshed, more RedSuits and Crown soldiers falling at every turn. Casualties were not minimal on either side, but the advantage had clearly turned in favor of the Light, Aria's iMagiNaciale army employing proven tactics and swordplay many, many generations old. It didn't hurt that most the spectators on hand had joined ranks against the Dahklarr, using their discarded weaponry against them.

S'ilKuSheere peered at the WallScreen more closely, having flipped from the sight of moths flying over SpringShootorian forest to once more observing the TiaraReign CityHeights battle in full pitch.

"Rendskorra? What's she doing there? And where did she get that loathsome costume? That's not her! That *can't* be her. That sister of mine is just too colorful. Even at funerals, she'd never be caught *dead* dressed only in black!"

Trying to rouse Rendskorra via TeleFlame, the effort of the Majestic Sorceress proved futile, her sister fast asleep and unrousable at the urging of her own self-prescribed deviant potion.

S'ilKuSheere's brows dropped in an emphatic V. She snarled, "That sister of mine. At her next funeral, I'll see to it she dresses in black, all right. Because if Rendskorra's not careful, the next burial could very well be her own."

SightSharing, she contacted her lead warrior onscreen, exclaiming, "Time to transfigure." She watched as the moths on all sides found distance from one another, growing and reshaping into winged, screeching Turlakks. Then, throwing her empty glass at their images, she screamed, "And get rid of that stupid witch!"

Currently knotted in battle with a RedSuit, Heather said, "Way to go, Aria! With your help Starbrill escaped those guys." With a grunt and sneer, she shoved her opponent away and reengaged, clink, clink, clank.

"And in the process…" Aria crossed swords in quivering stalemate, thrusting her dagger home in an upper cut at close range, "…you were able to have your wicked witch. Now let's see…" With a grimace, she jerked her weapon loose, the figure tumbling at her feet. "…if we can't come up with a happy ending…" She glared downward, "…much happier than this poor deviate's."

"Hey!" Slammed unexpectedly from behind by another locked in battle, Heather sprawled to the ground, hitting her head before rolling. Managing to keep hold of her weapons, swift to reclaim her feet, she was ready to reenter the fracas.

Sword poised, she glanced about. "Rendskorra is still on the roof up there." The cloaked Maiden Portent leapt over an attacker's low swipe, allowing Aria to retake possession midair in time to deftly counter a thrust, and then hurriedly put an end to the Crown soldier. "I see that."

Unexpectedly, a dagger thrown from out of the night found Rendskorra's chest. Hand clutched to her heart, she twisted in pain. "You cursèd brat. Look what you've done. I'm melting…melting!" She collapsed back against the high wall of the building.

Pausing long enough to notice, Heather rolled her eyes. "Aria, that's *not…* " the youngling parried, deflecting several lunges, "…that's *not* how it's supposed to happen." She sliced at the side of her opponent, the RedSuit falling to the ground, writhing in agony.

When a scarecrow and Crown soldier—the pair wildly facing off, swinging their weapons on an upper stairway—crashed into a planter box, a large pail broke free and fell on the downed witch, dousing her with water. In a last gasp of exaggeration, the fallen Rendskorra rose up like a cyclone and stopped mid-twirl, the conjured witch dramatically clutching her chest, proclaiming, "Who would have thought an ugly little Turlakk like you could destroy my beautiful wickedness…"

Then she crumpled once more, eventually falling off the roof and onto the ground in a heap. There, she liquefied, leaving her hat and clothing behind near the overturned bucket.

"That better?"

"Yeah, Aria," said Heather with a parry and emphatic thrust to the heart. "That's better." The RedSuit sagged and dropped at her feet. "Hey, Aria, Rendskorra said 'Turlakk.' There aren't any—"

An eerie shrieking shook the air. Heather recognized the sound immediately. More daggers were thrown. Ozmonds and TiaraReigners around Heather reared and keeled, toppling to the ground.

"Above us, Aria! A whole *bunch* of Turlakks."

Appearing in great numbers from out of the sky, the grotesque creatures of the Ravaged Heavens descended on the scene of the battle. Just when it seemed that the pace of the conflict had begun to slacken as those battling for the Light seized the upper hand, with the infusion of Turlakk reinforcements, the fighting once more intensified.

Too, the less serious and more optimistic mood that had overcome Heather as victory seemed imminent now turned grim once more. All banter ceased. Several opponents later, despite her youthful Maiden strength and endurance, she could feel herself and Aria beginning to flag. Nevertheless, the Maiden and SoulSylph slogged onward in the fight, ignoring the muscles of their shared body that craved respite. Around them, more allies were succumbing at the hands of the crafty Turlakk reinforcements, uniting on the cluttered floor of the battlefield with those that had fallen previously in death and disablement.

"They have the advantage, Heather. The Turlakks, by using their wings and flying above us, they carefully select their targets. Then they dive in to surprise us while we're locked in swordfights here on the ground. Distracted that way, we don't know where they're coming from or when they'll strike next, whether to look up or concentrate fully on our opponents in front of us. The tactic is working. We're being overpowered, and quickly at that."

They could see that a few confiscated Vigen°Darr weapons were being used on the flying Turlakks, the beams flashing out until moments later when the shooters were quickly subdued.

"Come on, Aria. We have to keep going. We can take them."

"We'll never do it, Heather. Against these odds, we can never win. They're airborne. We can't match it."

"With what you have left in reserve, can't you do anything?"

"I can, but I can't assure it will be enough. And the effort will leave us vulnerable, without further iMagiNaciale power to effectively create new spells until we've had a chance to rest, to replenish and regain our strength."

"Do it, Aria. Just do it."

Vanquishing her Turlakk opponent after a much-heated exchange, Aria stepped over some corpses, the SoulSylph attempting to find room to Lyricy. Interrupted by a RedSuit, she engaged her combatant with heightened aggressiveness, dispatching the soldier in abrupt and perhaps overly brutal fashion, her intention to finish up her conjuration.

The Lyrica completed, the bright lights above them having temporarily dimmed with the effort, Aria threw herself once more into the fracas. Heather, meanwhile, had grown too tired and gloomy to be amused by Aria's final flourishes on the matter.

Flooding from the fringes of the site, scores of small black terriers dashed out of hiding to bite and grip the ankles of those Turlakks engrossed in battle on the ground. Once locked on and refusing to budge, the animals turned to stone. With the emaciated Turlakks' legs cemented firmly in place, their ability to maneuver became limited, preventing them from rising up and out of harm's reach. Restricted this way, they were slain as they stood.

From above, stylized flying monkeys swooped down to join in the battle, materializing out of the darkness, attacking with deadly skill those Turlakks hovering in air, waiting to pounce. Proving effective, Aria's latest spell caused the battle to once more swing in favor of the

Allies of the Light. Sadly, the advantage wasn't at all to last, Aria's iMagiNaciale lighting continuing to fade and lose power.

"Ah, but Lunaria and the latest Maiden Portent are strong in their use of ancient magic. Formidably strong. But with the dimming of the iMagiNacial lights, I sense her power is nearing its end. So lamentable, that. I may just sob uncontrollably."

S'ilKuSheere changed views on the WallScreen. Her face became animated in the soft light of the room, her eyes alive with mischief.

"Well, now, isn't this just exceptional? Let's see, shall we, how the Maiden Portent deals with another wave of my Turlakks now that they're about to descend on the CityHeights, *especially,* when she has no more iMagiNacia—oh, no, none whatsoever, poor thing—left to Lyricy.

"So, goodbye, little Maiden child. I hope you don't mind, but despite such creative storybook showmanship, this is where you so merrily meet your end."

When initially stealing away from the CityHeights, Molly had observed the inbound hoard of Turlakks flying overhead, the sound of their shrieking giving her goose bumps, making her feel the overwhelming Influence of Darkness.

And, now, from much farther away, hearing the sounds once again, she stopped and turned her attention back toward TiaraReign. She couldn't shake her sense of foreboding. "It doesn't sound encouraging, does it?"

Having extinguished her LuminTorch, Toya was at her shoulder on the summit of the hill. "No, it doesn't. But you'd be surprised. Starbrill is resourceful, and Heather and Aria much more so. They'll pull through this. You'll see."

Molly had no words, not wanting to counter Toya's optimism. Let her believe.

Meanwhile, Molly, herself, wasn't feeling good about the battle. Not in the least. She remembered what Heather had told her about Absorption°Spheres, how the Turlakks had dropped them near the grove and the cave of the Bantaar—on the forest all around—and how they left in their wake nothing but scorched and barren ground.

Molly tried hard not to think about it, wanting to disperse the dread that was continuing to creep over her, causing headache and nausea. To think she would never see Heather, Starbrill, or the others ever again was simply too much to bear. And to be left on her own in Evermore…

She turned away and took to the trail once more, before having to witness what she feared could very well be, at any given moment, Absorption°Sphere explosions.

Toya said, "What's that noise?"

"What noise?" In a fright, Molly whirled, focusing on the far off TiaraReign, expecting the worst. Seeing no eruptions of light, she let go in relief, in a grateful expulsion of breath, wiping away sudden tears. She managed, "I don't hear anything."

"Listen…"

Molly strained her ears. It was then she could hear it, like a distant roar of thunder growing all the louder. "What do you suppose that is?"

"On the road, it sounds like riders of some sort. I only hope if they're on their way to TiaraReign, that they're fighting on the side of the Light."

Molly returned her gaze to the far off CityHeights. Faintly, she could hear the Turlakk cries carrying on the night air.

"Yes," she murmured, "please be on the side of the Light. And for the sake of our friends, hurry…please, hurry."

At the sound of more vitriolic shrieking from above, Aria grimly looked over her shoulder and up to the sky, witnessing wave upon wave of descending Turlakks. Turning away to once again immerse herself in the fight, stubbornly increasing the ferocity of her attack against her RedSuited opponent, she said, "More Turlakks, Heather. More!" She dodged, parried, and slashed the battle-weary woman into submission. "This is not good in the least. Not good at all."

Spinning, she knocked an assailing Turlakk's weapon loose from his hand. Aria hacked down hard with her sword, and unable to evade the streaking arc, the cringing soldier completely suffered the blade.

All around her, the SoulSylph could hear the piercing, tormenting cries of the Turlakks as more flew onto the CityHeights battlefield, sworn to devote and forfeit their lives to slay and conquer on behalf of the Dahklarr Herth.

"Heather, I fear I'm going to have to leave you. If you're to...*go,* as you know, I can't allow myself to go with you."

Dipping her head, Aria avoided a thrown knife, hearing it embed itself thickly in the back of someone fighting behind her.

"I know," yelled Heather, over the clamor and skreighs.

Sword in one hand, dagger in another, Heather squared up face-to-face with a Turlakk. The youngling feinted one way and whirled another, resulting in an unobstructed path to her opponent's heart. She plunged her dagger home. Then she ripped and withdrew, saying, "Go ahead, Aria. Go. I'll take it from here." She kicked the sagging soldier away.

She could see the luminescent Turlakks above her ganging up on the flying monkeys, overwhelming them simply by the sheer force of their numbers. The pesky primates on wing were being besieged, outmaneuvered, falling around Heather in clumps of moist dark fur, sometimes quivering to the last.

Backing, then disposing of a Crown swordsman, the youngling caught sight of Sedgwar, the man an ongoing force despite the lengthy battle, still taking Turlakks expeditiously out of play both above and around him. He was working his way toward her.

Engaged in rigorous swordplay once more, when Heather was tripped up by a downed Turlakk, Aria took command and, plunging first with her dagger, killed the fallen soldier before rising to dispense with the advancing RedSuit.

Heather scanned the battlefield. She could see there weren't a lot of Ozmonds and TiaraReigners left in comparison to the vast amount of Turlakks, never mind the RedSuits and Crown soldiers still invested in the fight. Yet, there was nothing more to do other than wage war and battle onward. The thought of fleeing to live and fight another day never entered her mind.

Encountering a limping RedSuit, Heather dodged a thrust and responded with one of her own, quickly dismissing the idea of having an unfair advantage. Rather, she welcomed the superior position it presented. Swift to slice him open, sidestepping, she took on the next comer.

"It's been great getting to know you, Aria." There was no remorse whatsoever in Heather's voice. Only acceptance. "No matter how this ends, we've put up a real good fight, haven't we?"

Heather deflected a bladed lunge and drove a hafted fist into a soldier's throat. Then, slicing downward, she cut him with the edge of her steel, the fighting man reeling in pain, covering up. She moved on.

"So, see you, Aria."

"I'm not gone yet.

"Well, you shouldn't wait too much longer." Heather engaged another attacker.

Feeling disheartened at what seemed to be the arrival of ever increasing numbers of Turlakks, she quickly disregarded the sight, doggedly immersing herself in the fray.

Reclaiming possession with a quick swipe and deadly thrust, Aria said, "I'll assist until I can't wait any longer, thank you." She pulled her weapon free.

"What if I get hit from behind? You'll die with me. No, you better get out of here now." The youngling turned on the closest Turlakk.

"Remember how I'm getting to be more like you?" Aria finished off S'ilKuSheere's elite soldier. Another landed bare-bladed in confrontation.

"Yeah?"

"Well, then, call me a little too hardheaded," the SoulSylph parried, "too impractical," she dodged, "too impulsive," she lunged, "and not yet ready to concede my favorite Maiden Portent to date." Aria retreated, the Turlakk aggressively driving her rearward. Another descended alongside the first, joining in uneven swordplay against her.

"Aria, you better get out of here, while I still have time to do anything." Heather sidestepped a blow—barely—and then, driving upward from on low, made a thrust for the kill. "Get out of here, Aria. Now!" Using the dead Turlakk as a momentary shield, she turned her steel on the other in wicked fashion, slash, slash, slash! Then she stuck him: *whick.*

On the instant, Heather sensed when Aria left her, able to feel the sudden loss and resulting emptiness within at her departure. She was alone. The young Maiden glanced at the lights above. They had dimmed considerably, the chances of victory seemingly diminishing with them. And as the shadows drew deeper, the girl didn't want to think about it, her inevitable isolation and defeat and what that ultimately meant, and so she engaged: *whick;* engaged: *whick;* engaged: *whick!*

In what might very well prove to be her short-lived career as the green-eyed Maiden, Heather was determined to go down battling, on behalf of what had become her given purpose, on behalf of Evermore, its people, and the Light, until she had no more to give—or until someone took from her the little that remained.

One way or other, she would be glad to leave TiaraReign, wishing she and Molly could have seen it in a better day, thankful that her best friend had been able to depart when she had. And on the moment, Heather gave swift thought to Grandma Dawn, bringing her image to mind before leaving it alone to drift and fade in obscurity.

Over a shoulder, she could glimpse and hear her friend Sedgwar engrossed in battle, taking on three Turlakks, and now only two. She backed and stumbled, before righting herself. Noticing she was sagging from fatigue, she forced herself to stand all the taller.

Confronting another aggressor, Heather couldn't afford to step lightly, the ground around her heavily littered, soaked with seeping pools, strewn with bodies: Ozmonds, Crown soldiers, RedSuits, Turlakks, and TiaraReigners, all of them whole or in pieces, always bleeding, bleeding out. Some were felled in piles. Time and again, she encountered her own young face shockingly staring up at her: neck exposed and mouth agape, eyes wide and glazed in death, Aria's iMagiNaciale lookalikes taken down in battle.

Surprised from behind, alertly dodging a thrust, Heather gasped as the harsh slice of steel found her shoulder, feeling the biting pinch of pain as it seared and grew. She put the flesh wound out of her mind. Instinctively swinging her sword in an aggressive spin, she decapitated the RedSuit, and then surprised by her own ferocity and brutality, exerted even more energy in an attempt to bury her hostility in dismissal, lashing out to slice at the knees of a hovering Turlakk. Suffering the score, the grotesque creature reared and spun away only to smash upon his landing, left to flap and flop on the TiaraReign flooring.

When a fallen Turlakk grabbed the tail of her cloak, Heather was jerked backward and partially to the ground. Evading the thrust of a long blade from above, she managed to overcome the RedSuit with a slash to the ankles before rolling aside, her wounded attacker collapsing onto the Turlakk like a felled tree. Rising from a knee, Heather staggered as S'ilKuSheere's warrior desperately attempted to wriggle out from under, but, recovering, Heather ended his life with a well-placed heave, two-handedly plunging her sword deep through the RedSuit's fallen body and into the Turlakk's torso beneath. She left the weapon embedded, quivering.

With effort, Heather grabbed for a sword, any sword—at this point, any weapon feeling far too weighty—and retrieving her dagger, climbed wearily to her feet. Bloody, positioned loosely at Sedgwar's back once more, Heather fought on.

Between opponents, from afar she caught sight of Greesha lying among some bodies. The woman's clothing was torn and bloodied, and she lay unmoving, loosely ahold of her long knife. Too drained to feel anything whatsoever, Heather took on another Turlakk. Backpedaling in the fight, tripping and falling, she picked up a nearby tin man's axe to hurl and bury in his skeletal chest. She clambered to her feet.

Sedgwar had now moved closer, and vastly outnumbered, almost touching back-to-back, they were fighting for what remained of their lives. With a dip, Heather once more reclaimed her dagger. Dripping and spattered with blood, burning with sweat, fatigued and fighting at the limit of her endurance, she fought off and downed another Turlakk. And still there were more, oh, so, many more.

At the passing of a large shadow over her in the ever-dimming light, Heather instinctively flinched. More shadows followed. The girl glimpsed skyward. Daring to shield her eyes for only a breath, she saw teems of giant Bantaar riders gliding out of the night sky on their BracchaBeasts, driving and breaking apart the flying Turlakks with cleaves and heaves of their bloodthirsty blades.

All around her, savage Maidens, their sweaty Archmounts left breathless and in a lather below the CityHeights, were swarming from enclosures and stairways, welling from secretive ClearWeave doorways and passages, slinging deftly their hellbent axes and deadly swords and knives. In the drear, their blazing blue SearEye shone out like piercing sparks of hostile intimidation for their enemies, and, for allies, like pinpoint beacons of promise for all that was hopeful, reassuring, and everlasting in the Light.

After bashing the head of a RedSuit and thrusting her onto a pile, Heather backed and looked to one side to witness a great mass of Evermorians, young and old, from all across TiaraReign, spread wide on the intersecting avenues, arriving to take up the cause. Walking briskly, now running, brandishing weapons held on high, they charged and flooded the skirmish.

"Sedgwar…hey, Sedgwar!" cried Heather over their roars. "Look! All around us!"

Backing alongside, the stoic warrior glanced about. Sharing eyes with Heather, he nodded and his grimy, sweat-soaked face mustered a grin. And though it was to disappear quickly, it was a handsomely masculine grin in a spirited flash of white, and one Heather couldn't recall having seen previously.

And so inspired, she and Sedgwar dug deep to recover lost energies, and displaying renewed vigor and a swelling of emboldened hearts, they once again fiercely took to their battles, each in their own way forever changed.

Unmoving, staring at the great paneled image in silent agony, S'ilKuSheere finally turned off the WallScreen and doused the candelabras, casting the room into utter blackness. And in that collusion of ink, she stood subdued, realizing it was too late, that it would do little good to arrive on the scene, knowing the battle to be lost—a majority of her prized Turlakks with it.

"Credit the Maiden Portent and her timely allies. We almost had them. Really, how was Rendskorra—or any of us—to know that the Vigen°Darr weaponry would be ineffective against iMagiNacia? But the Maiden Portent herself is not immune, nor any of her friends.

"Yes, it seems we'll need to make some necessary adjustments to defeat this difficult child. And, surely, the Great Sul doesn't need to learn of this little setback. It would only ruin his night…week…" she shrugged, "…all right, maybe even his month or year. So, let us see to it, shall we, that the Great One never finds out."

S'ilKuSheere beckoned to a candle and heard one wriggle loose and whoosh over from its stand. The lone taper afloat near her ear, she snapped her fingers and it slipped into very tall flame.

Nearby, silent as the tiny Evermorian rodent was, nevertheless, the teese running along the wall caught S'ilKuSheere's eye in the lowlight. Commanding the rodent near, she dennunciated and changed it to the size of a burping WallowBeast, making the creature barely able to fit through the doorway.

"I want you to go downstairs," she commanded. "Tell the servants that I'm not to be disturbed for *any* reason until further notice."

The giant teese, with its newfound power of speech, asked, "What if they won't listen to me? What if they run?"

"Then you have my permission to eat them."

With that, she waved the creature away.

Slipping quietly into camp, Molly and Toya crept between

recumbent, scattered newcomers. The pair hadn't spoken for some time, Molly's headache and nausea having dissipated somewhat over the course of the remaining distance, replaced with that of a dull and heavy heart. Leaving the others to their sleep, they found a place near the fire, Toya stoking it, adding more wood. Not caring to eat or wash, not caring for much of anything, the two just waited glumly in silence, grateful for one another's company.

When Toya said, "Hear that?"

Molly shook her head and sat up. Then, along with Toya, they searched the wall of surrounding, unrevealing darkness, but neither saw nor heard anyone or anything more.

"There it is again."

This time, Molly had heard the faint rustling. It was followed by a soft whistle.

Molly looked up. She gasped when the boughs above her shook and a creature lowered himself, hanging by his tail.

Whistle? Skree?

"Pallár!" Molly whispered, in a gush. "Am I ever glad to see you."

Letting go, he dropped and landed close by on a rock. Skittering over to her, sensing her mood, the monkey-like creature with the child's face quietly curled in her lap. Wrapping him in her arms, Molly gently rocked and held him near.

The fire crackled and flared. And the night grew that much older.

And now to endure.

Deep beyond exhaustive hours Heather and Sedgwar fought, the warrior ever near, keeping a close eye on her whenever possible. If he could have, he would have taken on all the girl's opponents in an effort to give the proud young warrior a breather and save her from harm. And, yet, he knew she would only resent such an action, seeing it as nothing less than an unwarranted intrusion, and so he kept to himself and his clashes.

Then it occurred to Sedgwar that he wasn't the only one feeling protective. He realized that a ring of Maidens had slowly closed ranks to loosely encircle Heather, confronting and taking on the combatants that came her way, with only a few managing to get inside of their defenses to confront their Maiden Portent.

And in the interval between opponents, able to attain marginal rest, the tall sixteen year old proved herself a worthy force with those enemies that she did encounter, the youngling being swift, accurate, instinctive, and strong. And, yet, despite her revitalized battle efforts, it was obvious that Heather was worn in every fiber of her sinew, now letting her attackers come to her, her dagger housed and at rest, the tip of her two-handed sword asleep on the ground until awakened for action.

Eventually, Aria's flood of light had waned in its effectiveness, the influence of night having grown intrusive upon it. The battlefield had thinned, and what Turlakks, RedSuits, and Crown soldiers remained were fighting for their lives all around, some in retreat. Idle, areas of the crowds had begun to mill, some of the Bantaar giants beginning to fly off or simply patrol the night skies, swooping in when necessary. At that point, under the direction of Maidens, the victors began to attend to the wounded and the dead, separating them by need and affliction.

Finally dispensing with her current assailant after protracted involvement, Heather took a moment to observe Sedgwar, wholly impressed with how his fighting seemed so direct, so straight to the point, with no wasted effort whatsoever. He simply knew what to do and how to do it. Currently, he was occupied with a couple of RedSuits—and then, on a blur and a blink, there was left only the one.

At the sound of someone at her back, Heather spun, her sword raised at the ready. She could see stumbling among the bodies in the deepening gloom was a RedSuit soldier. Then she watched as he tripped and fell.

Bloodied, haggard, wounded from having taken part in the battle, with effort the man picked himself off the ground. Bending to retrieve a half-broken sword, the warrior looked up to spy the cloaked Heather. Staggering, attempting to focus, he threaded and headed her way.

Warily, she looked around her and then back at the man. Something told the girl that this was the RedSuit leader. Perhaps it was his demeanor, the fact he was older, a little fuller though fit, his uniform different at the shoulders in its markings. His aura ebbed in a lowly drubbing of resolute, honorable golds.

Halting at a distance, confronting the girl, he sized her up from under a lowered brow. Solemnly, Heather faced him square on.

"Please don't make me do this," she said, under her breath. Shaking her head, she drew a determined breath, and then set her jaw.

Gathering speed, tromping headlong, raising his weapon, Soldier One screamed gutturally and rushed the girl for all he had left. Lowering her guard, Heather let him pass unmolested and watched as he stumbled impotently to the ground, his sword clanging free. Heather turned away, scanning the area for more dangerous opponents.

When she looked again, he had climbed to his feet. Bent over, head down and sword propping him up, the elder warrior was breathing heavily, garnering strength. Yet, his battered body gave way, and he fell once more.

Noticing, Sedgwar bedded his weapons. Walking over, he hoisted the older man to his feet, all the while the RedSuit leader was cursing him, objecting, trying to pull himself free. Sedgwar handed Soldier One his sword.

Then he stepped away and beckoned. When the commander rushed him, employing swift maneuver, Sedgwar disarmed him and laid the man to ground. Heather's observant eyes saw the small dagger that had found his RedSuit heart in the interim, Sedgwar's hand swift and sure.

"He needs to find rest," was all he said upon rising. He left him there and relocated closer to Heather.

Hours passed and the encounters thinned all the more, Heather feeling safe and protected in Sedgwar's presence. The youngling knew she was being cared for and didn't mind in the least. As a matter of fact, tired as she was, she welcomed his skilled and wily presence.

Yet, after a time, she found herself wandering on her own, walking among the bodies at the last traces of Aria's once brilliant light, the SoulSylph's influence having little effect on the battle scene. At pace with its declination, she saw that the Ozmonds were deflating and becoming transparent, the scattered piles of defeated warriors settling all the more at their gradual withering and eventual disappearance.

In the low glow of the streetlamps, Heather spotted Starbrill in the distance, his sword still in motion.

"Heather! Over here!" It was Sedgwar.

Whirling, seeing the robed warrior handling two RedSuits, she scurried to intercept an onrushing third—more, even!—the fighting force for the Dahklarr making a final surge from high on the avenue, beyond the thriftshop.

She wasn't going to let anything happen to Sedgwar, not now, not when the battle had nearly reached its end—not ever, if she had any say in the matter.

Hastily angling over in her approach, she stepped between the

RedSuit and Sedgwar, before slipping on some unloosed entrails, sliding to the ground. She ducked a blade. *Whoosh!* Swiftly to her feet, she dodged another swipe, and then charged her aggressor, feinting one direction before twirling another: *whick!* Wounded, he dropped his weapon, his shield long gone.

"Incoming," said Sedgwar, and Heather looked to see more soldiers permeating the outer perimeter of warriors.

Finishing her opponent with a slice, she rushed to Sedgwar's side and took on two more RedSuits in succession, the youngling so impressively quick, at times a blur of body and limb. Glazed, standing unsteadily on her feet—yet, ready for more—she turned to see Sedgwar vanquish a RedSuit in a brutal blow. He then backed a pace and looked around. When the warrior saw no one further to engage, he lowered his sword and turned to Heather. He was breathing heavily.

"That should do it."

At the words, chest heaving, Heather just leaned into the big man's sweaty, blood smeared clothing. For the longest time, they said nothing, the girl numb. Sedgwar hesitated, then brought a hand to her upper arm and gave her a light squeeze. There, her slight wound bit in pain, but, eyes closed, she kept her head buried and at rest.

"You did quite well in battle, youngling."

"I guess I did." Heather pulled away and smiled grimly. "I'm still here."

"Are you all right?"

"I don't know." In the cold moonlight, in the weak spill of lamplight, she gave herself the once over, noticing where her Adaption°Suit had healed, the area slightly bloody. "I think everything's still where it should be."

"I mean—"

"I know what you mean." Heather felt prickly, hot—coarse. "I'm fine." Riding what little remained of her adrenaline, she dragged a forearm across her runny brow, a knuckle across her cheek, wiping away the sweat that was burning her eyes. "You and Starbrill, you made it—last I saw of him, anyway. I have no idea where Mastow is." The girl tiredly smiled on Fallasha. Then she frowned at her cloak, noticing where it was sullied and torn. "I guess my Maiden cloak is kaput, though."

"Here. Take mine," said a commanding voice from behind her.

Heather spun. She looked at the group of Maidens that had gathered, more joining their ranks, their eyes smoldering with blue Light. Awestruck, she couldn't bring herself to mutter a word.

"Astille Lia Staleen DiYoh?" said the Maiden closest. She had removed her cloak, her arms out in presentation.

Allowing Sedgwar her sword, Heather took the offered garment and simply held it.

"Just a guess," said Sedgwar, "but I think this is where you say something."

Heather continued to gaze at her spellbinding peers, a band of steely, graven warriors, their fierce and sweaty, unpigmented faces displaying those characteristics indicative of all Evermorian races, originating at their source within the Pool of Reason. In their presence, Heather seemed to fill out and grow all the taller, evidently very much a part of this formidable collection.

"Hi," she managed. Her battle eyes, still fiery, still deadly serious, darted among them. She nodded. "I'm her. I'm the green-eyed Maiden." Her words were almost a challenge, daring anyone to deny them. Heather softened and, slowly unveiling her great grin, said, "Really glad you could make it."

chapter six

The Wake of Warring

Following her brief introduction to the Maidens, Heather was helped on with her new cloak, the others desiring a glimpse of their Maiden Portent before turning their attention to post-battle duties.

At her neck, Heather reattached Fallasha, wanting her brooch with her always, in accompaniment with her small wooden Maiden doll which she kept near in her BodyTote, or stuffed reassuringly in a pants pocket. Having in her possession the simplistic hand-carved figurine from childhood, she felt, served as both a reminder of Grandma Dawn and, as well, a good luck talisman signifying her Evermorian birth.

"My name is Galestielle," said the Maiden who had given the gift of her cloak.

Heather said, "I guess you know mine, already." She wiped her dripping temple, surprised to see the smear of red on her gloved hand. "I wish I had something to give *you,* Galestielle."

"Oh, but you have. And you've given it by appearing here this night. You've given that something to all of us, returning to us our purpose, our reason for being, allowing us to begin the slow process of regrouping, and rededicating our lives to the future of Evermore."

Very much humbled, Heather was at a momentary loss. "Really, we just fought because we had to…"

The Maiden said, matter-of-factly, "And may that always be the case."

In a change of subject, Heather said, "Can I ask you something?"

"Of course."

"Why did you guys come and help us fight? I mean, up to this point, Maidens have always stayed hidden."

"We are here for the cause, united under you. We had heard of your visits, your progress, and were alerted to your coming to TiaraReign. And I'd say if we were going to assist you on a battlefield this large, we'd definitely have to come out of hiding to do so, wouldn't you agree?" She was smiling. "That's no small force out there. Also, we were made to understand, via WhisperEye Mirror, that if we weren't here on your behalf, that the consequences for Evermore's future would be disastrous. So says the seer."

"The Matron?"

"You know, then, of whom I speak."

"Yeah—yes. I really like her."

"It seems she likes you, as well. And for good reason, I see. Disbanded as Evermore's guardians, roaming while hunted down, we as Maidens thought it best to remain on our own until absolutely necessary, awaiting an opportune time—a greater calling, if you would—should we reunite in accordance with the Prophecies. As it happens, this was the first sign that that long awaited moment had finally arrived."

"Look, how can I help?"

"As I said, you have already, Nearling—"

"I mean, here," said Heather. "With what you and the other Maidens are doing."

"We're continuing to sort the dead and injured. We've more than enough on hand to aid us. There isn't anything you need assist with should you wish to depart for more immediate concerns—"

"What if more Turlakks come?"

"Something tells me that whomever was going to take part in this battle has been on hand to do so already, and that includes Evermore's very own sorceresses."

Heather scanned and spotted Sedgwar, and to her relief, Starbrill. Pressed by nagging unease, she was unable to find Mastow. And, yet, the battlefield was vast, stretching down the avenue, through the marketplace, and up the adjoining streets. "Well, it's not really up to me. I came with other people. We've got a bunch more back in camp, and I have Archie—my Archmount—waiting for me down in the forest."

"I'm well acquainted with your Archie. When as riders we neared TiaraReign, he guided us to your location."

"Did he? He's so great."

"As is his very brave Mistress." Galestielle bowed her head. "And with that, I shall leave you to tend to our fellow Sisters and my awaiting duties." She added, in closing, "As is, and has been, my honor, Astille Lia." Yet, the woman lingered a moment longer, taking in Heather's countenance, before turning away.

So proud to be a Maiden, proud to have been given her new Maiden cloak, Heather watched the statuesque warrior walk away. Not knowing whether to dispense with her current sword or not, she walked over to Sedgwar who was disentangling from piles the many dead and stricken. Fetor in ripe whiffs of wind stung her nose.

"Are you through entertaining your devoted admirers?" he asked, a dead RedSuit hanging limply over his shoulder.

Heather responded, "Galestielle—the Maiden leader—said we could go when we wanted, that they would take care of all this. I said I would check with you guys."

Setting the lifeless soldier down alongside another, Sedgwar said, "There's Starbrill, over there. Perhaps you should ask him." Sedgwar dipped and, with a grunt, hoisted another dead RedSuit to his shoulders. "You'll find me hereabouts when you've need."

Heather looked over the vast battlefield littered with the unmoving. Everywhere. Everywhere. Strewn beneath the trees, slain in the arms of the avenues. She let her sword fall away and walked toward Starbrill, trying not to think. She heard mutterings, cries for help, with agonized moans all around as she passed—people pleading and drawing on their last breathes, enduring or beyond the throes of pain. Among them, Heather spotted some Bantaar warriors having fallen in armed conflict from above, their lines of life splattered and severed on the sprawl. And close by, unimpressive in death, she glimpsed a few dead RogueTags, a few dead Maidens. She felt compelled to turn away.

Instead, she concentrated on those Maidens who were very much alive, and how they competently set about their tasks, unflinchingly picking up a dead Sister, or dragging a dangerous, repulsive Turlakk to an appropriated spot, or gathering a RedSuit or Crown soldier whole or in pieces. Too, the TiaraReigners assisted Maidens in the aid and the sorting, along with the Bantaar giants who could be seen attending to their own, flying them off for further medical assistance or burial.

Walking by, Heather found herself the recipient of lingering looks, those in the vicinity pausing in their duties, taking stock of her passing.

"Astille Lia Staleen DiYoh?" The voice was deep.

Heather turned. It was then that Clossnoor, the Bantaar leader, looked up from a fallen comrade's side. He called over one of his men to finish his work and disengaged, making his way toward her.

"I've something to say."

Heather waited, the giant appearing ill at ease.

"Upon seeing you, I wanted to express that, that what you did that day beside the cave of Mákayesh, allowing us to break free of his misguided leadership…while pointing my Bantaar brethren not only in the direction of the Light, but also for suggesting to us the Undulant Valley as a new place to make our home, I…I simply wanted to say that meeting with you has proven to be a very fortuitous and agreeable circumstance indeed. Your involvement is why the Bantaar have chosen to come tonight. Many of my people have given their lives here in this battle for TiaraReign…"

Heather said, "I know, and I—"

"Yet, you see, it's a far worthier cause fighting this way, dying for Evermore and our honor, rather than simply fighting for our own selfish and insular existence. What I'm trying to say is that, as Evermorians, you've allowed us to once again take pride in ourselves, in who the Bantaar as a people really are. And, for that, we thank you with our loyalty and with our lives."

This was too much for the girl, feeling she had done none of it, that if anything *had* been done when assisting the Bantaar, it had been Aria's doing—or the Bantaar simply finding a way to help themselves.

Tired as she was, Heather kept her poise, looking up into the face of the much taller, wider-built man. She said, simply, "I'm so glad you and your brave soldiers could come and fight with us, Clossnoor. We needed you. So, thank you."

The young Maiden Portent nodded and moved on amid the carnage, wanting to tell the Bantaar leader how sorry she was that some of his people had died. Yet, she couldn't, not knowing where to start, fearing she would be unable to find suitable words if she had. And at the moment, this entire surreal nightscape, it all seemed so very, very overwhelming. Part of her wished Aria's brilliant lights would return to dispel the mood, part of her was glad she couldn't see things too clearly. She didn't dare take an aura scan.

In the grave and burdensome bustle going on about her, she had located Starbrill. He was carrying a fourteen-year-old boy, the child unmoving in his arms, a °Concussor pistol jiggling loosely in his grip. Heather stood waiting until he had laid aside the child's body and noticed her presence. Nevertheless, Starbrill took time to remove the weapon from the boy's entanglement of fingers, handing it off to a TiaraReigner for caching. Only then did he turn to acknowledge her.

"Sedgwar said to ask when you wanted to start for camp," she said. "The Maidens said they would finish up."

"If that's the case, we really should leave soon, get back to Toya and Molly, the people in camp." Starbrill's weariness was evident. "I haven't been able to find either Mastow or Greesha."

Heather hadn't the heart to respond. Dully, she awaited his decision.

"Greesha knows the ScatterPortals. She can lead Mastow to TreeLoft should they want to join us. They've been there before," he added, noticing Sedgwar among the people actively passing to and fro. "So, I suppose now is a good time to gather our friend, here, and set off for camp. No doubt, the others will eagerly be awaiting our return."

Heather looked through Starbrill, her eyes unable to meet his directly. "Starbrill, about Greesha…"

Elsewhere, in the skies above the moonlit canopy of SpringShootorian forest and headed in an entirely different direction than that of TiaraReign CityHeights, were the remaining swarm of S'ilKuSheere's moths. Tightly clustered, they began to spread apart in formation, not only in distance side-to-side, but in elevation, as well.

Fluttering aloft, they began to enlarge, pushing and bulging out, recomposing and realigning various elements beneath their skin. And in that expansion, they grew longer, bonier arms and legs, sprouting hands and feet from their previous moth-like appendages. One pair of limbs disappeared entirely, merging into the bony ribcage of the slowly emerging Turlakk torso, the ugly face and greenish skin all the more apparent following subsequent flappings of their newly shaped wings.

And, now, reminiscent of warplanes, the freshly formed Turlakks peeled off to drop out of the starry sky successively on an arc, the screeching humanlike creatures descending like a dark and frenetic blanket unraveling on the thread. Reassembling, skirting the treetops and then the crudely carved road, they approached the lone hangar-like depot enclosed in high, barbed wire fencing. It was here they would be greeted and reinforced with Absorption°Spheres to complete the final leg of their flight toward the defenseless target awaiting them.

And somewhere in the warm SpringShootorian nighttime, the sleeping TreeLoft structures lay innocently spread, hidden among the leafy heights and the forest floor, wholly vulnerable to the ruthless and devastating impact of the Turlakks' explosively powerful, Vigen°Darr weaponry of war.

Having pointed to the area where she last saw Greesha, Heather parted ways with Sedgwar and Starbrill in the CityHeights, leaving the pair to embark on a final attempt to locate the woman—and possibly her TrueMate—before leaving.

Finding her way speedily to the park and the statue, able to open the ClearWeave doors with her Matron-implanted MindKey, Heather entered the ScatterPortal to arrive at ground level. Once there, she eventually found the cave that would take her underground to be delivered into the rough of the CityHeights' outskirts.

Emerging from the cave's hidden mouth, Heather abruptly halted, saying grumpily, "Aria, I know you're there."

Heather's eyes changed color under the stars. "Do you, now?"

"Yes. Are you surprised we survived?"

"Surprised, maybe. Relieved, most assuredly."

"I've been thinking—"

"And why, exactly, would you want to do that?"

Heather ignored her. "Aria, I've been thinking that maybe we could have escaped without taking on those RedSuits like that. I mean, if we had just snuck out of the CityHeights, then those Crown soldiers and TiaraReigners wouldn't have gotten involved at all, and then *we* wouldn't have had to get involved—"

"And if, if, if. Have you forgotten that the RedSuits had mounted a search for us, that one soldier even found and surprised our companions there on the balcony? And weren't those RedSuits lying in wait for your arrival at the thriftshop? They were, weren't they?"

At the mention, Heather grew more sullen, thinking of how Greesha and Mastow had probably lost their lives despite her efforts to save them. "Yeah." The word barely sounded.

"And rest assured, young Heather, that S'ilKuSheere's Turlakks were sent to come to the RedSuits' aid in not one, but two enormous waves. Do you really possess any doubt whatsoever that, at the very least, they wanted to be certain that the green-eyed Maiden was eliminated, wiped out beyond a doubt?"

Heather shook her head.

"And if we hadn't engaged the Dahklarr in the CityHeights like we did, would you have wanted that entire fighting force combing the forest floor in pursuit of you and your companions?

"So, I ask you, Heather, where better to confront Rendskorra's RedSuit army than in the CityHeights and among its angry populace? No, I think it all went as well as could be hoped for, and that when all was said and done, you escaped with your life while creating quite the legendary stir. And the spectacle of that encounter won't die, believe me. The magnitude of that event will surely live on to become glorified legend, and it will no doubt find its way into the Chronicles of MaidenLore."

"If you say so."

Aria, attempting to overcome Heather's cheerlessness, added, "And, Heather, think about it. With your help, the Prophecies are coming to fruition, the Maidens are now beginning to regroup and reform, while drawing on what little Light Magic has already seeped back in to reclaim the Realm—it's evident in their Maiden SearEye, I'm sure! Did you not see it? Rest assured, so did the TiaraReigners—*and* the Influenced. And with the defeat of the RedSuit and Turlakk armies, the fantastic battle that took place in the TiaraReign CityHeights can't help but fly off tongues throughout the entirety of Evermore! Surely, the Realm will be abuzz with your astounding feats for weeks, months—no doubt even years!—alive with talk about the conjuration of your iMagiNaciale army and the timely arrival of the Maidens and the Bantaar to join in and save the day. It's decidedly an inspiration for our cause, a boon for the Light."

"Aria, if this SoulSylph thing doesn't work out for you, have you ever thought of a career in advertising?"

"Just so you know, it pays to never underestimate the power of propaganda. Just ask any politician."

"I will, if I ever see one fighting next to me."

"Heather, it has to happen."

"Politicians fighting—?"

"Death in wartime. It's heartrending to be sure, but an obvious and brutal consequence."

Heather sulkily nodded and resumed walking in the direction of the trail. She wanted to find Archie before Sedgwar and Starbrill appeared.

"Aria, why does it take fighting to win back the good, the Light in us? I mean, if fighting and killing are Dark, why do we have to go through the Dark to finally get to the Light? Know what I mean? It doesn't seem right, you know, that instead we have to become Dark ourselves in a way. Wouldn't it be better if we could kill someone with kindness, like Grandma Dawn says, or-or fight it out with smiles and gifts and telling someone how smart they are or how nice they look? Instead, we have to hurt them to make them understand. Pretty weird, huh?"

"Sometimes, Heather, it's not the language you yourself speak and appreciate, but the language your enemy understands. There are those who respect only force and see an act of kindness as weak, something to be manipulated to achieve their predisposed ends. And maybe when HumanKind degradation gets to be too much, when people have had enough, is when they'll be willing and open to changing for the better. After all, in war it's not only HumanKinders that are mercilessly destroyed. There's the very fabric of existence that's torn apart along with them, all the interwoven threads."

"Well, now that I've done it, I don't think killing and fighting is all that great a thing, what we do to each other. If it were up to me, I'd rather be a Candy Bomber the whole world over—over and over and over. Or defeat others playing soccer or baseball or chess or something. Heck, that way if you lose, at least you can hang around and give it another go."

There hung a heavy silence, before Aria offered, "Maybe the answer isn't to be found in this lifetime, Heather."

"What do you mean? Answer to what?"

"The answer to how we live our lives given the time, why we do what we do, what motivates us, why we gravitate toward different people and different walks of life, all driven by those underlying needs and desires that line our souls. Maybe the answer doesn't exist in our particular universe, and that we'll find out why we did what we did in the next life. Ironically enough, maybe we're all fighting to stay alive when there's something far better awaiting us on the other side of death."

"Aw, Aria, if the losers are really winners, then why are we even fighting?"

"Why indeed?"

Heather paused. "Then you're saying it's good that people die?"

"Perhaps."

"Come to think of it, maybe it's good to think that way."

"Oh?"

"Yeah. So, maybe I'll look at tonight's fight as not killing and hurting a bunch of people in a mean way, but as just getting them out of our world so we can shift to the Light, and at the same time, sending them to a better place to work out their Darkness."

Aria chuckled. "It's a thought. Use it if it helps. I think many have and do."

"So, then, maybe if you lose here, you'll learn what you did wrong and be able to get another try at the game there, wherever *there* is."

On that notion, Heather went quiet. Aria tried to take possession, but Heather held her off. She just wanted to be still for a while, untangling her unruly threads of thought.

Finally, she said, "Aria, what if *I* lose as the green-eyed Maiden, if I try to be her and don't succeed? What then? And after this world, what if there really *is* no answer, and we never find out why we're born like we are and do what we do, and never figure out why certain things happened to us like they did? I mean, what if a bunch of stuff happened to you and it wasn't fair this time around, and you don't end up getting another chance because life really isn't like a game? Aria?"

But Heather knew she had gone. On a half-breath, she muttered to her lapel, "Wow, Fallasha, if it really is like that, it sure seems like a lot of work and worry to find out our entire life, this whole stupid thing, will all be for nothing."

With the height of night laid out in slumbering doldrums, a great many bodies swarmed the forest floors in stealth, skillfully, lithely, silently mounting the rooted upsurge of massive trees. Flesh and fingered handholds a-grip of scruffy bark, toeholds wedged in boot and leathered bindings, rising, rising, rising, they conquered the woodland loftiness.

Swift on the hush, methodically lowering ropes and ladders to the awaiting force that stood below, the eager groundswell grabbed hold and made great haste, boldly hoisting themselves up the knotted danglings, treading up the staggered climbs, fanning out amid the low glow of lanterns, to cross the extensive planks of flooring and the trusted reach of bridge and walk.

TreeLoft.

Now kneeling on fervent knees, whispering hot the desperate

whispers, and urging so their urgent pleas, the friendly invaders wrested the dwellings awake, everyone and to a man, woman, and child. Wide-eyed, roused, and rumpled—bundling feverish and groused—orderly throughout, the inhabitants descended empty handed, making haste into the night. And the question paramount among them was whether time allowed for distance, and, if so, would enough distance come in time?

"Shh-h-h. Never you mind. Just hurry, now, hurry."

Archie?

I'm here, StaLia.

Archie emerged from the shushing, shaking greenery at a trot.

I tried to reach you more than once to check on your progress. I noticed that a great many Turlakks had arrived over TiaraReign, and, at that, more than once.

Heather waited for her Archmount, and then, staring as if lost, touched and caressed his soft, downy face, his thick mane.

And the battle?

Heather was slow to respond. *Believe it or not, we defeated them. The Turlakks, the RedSuits, everyone. The Maidens and the Bantaar, along with the people of TiaraReign, are up there finishing, cleaning up…*

Heather couldn't rid her ears of the clashing, clear her nostrils of the stench in aftermath, the warm sickly sweat among the bodies, the urination and defecation…

*Sedgwar, Starbrill, those guys were amazing. And the men, women, the young people, they were great, too. All of us, we fought together. It was a lot, a lot of…*work*…*

I can't help but see it as a waste.

"The fighting? I know, but it has to get done or change for the better won't ever happen, right?"

No, I mean to wage war and risk your life for HumanKinders, when they seem so utterly undeserving.

Heather pulled back and turned away. She searched the sky and found the moon.

It's not just for HumanKinders, Archie. It's for Maidens, too. It's for Evermore, the people, animals, everything. It's for you and all the Archmounts everywhere. That's why were fighting.

I was going stir crazy and actually tried to figure out a way to reach you, sniffing around TiaraReign's lifts and garages. But, then, the other Archmounts contacted me—

The Maidens' Archmounts? Where are they?

There are great numbers at rest in the forest, awaiting the return of their Mistresses. They rode for a very long time to get here. They mentioned there were even more Archmounts to begin with, with more Maiden riders still, and that they were headed to a completely different location here in SpringShoot Green.

Where?

I didn't ask. We spoke of other concerns, those more immediate. For instance, they said their Mistresses knew of your previous interaction with the Bantaar, and so requested that those tribes join in the battle—what in MaidenLore the Maidens claimed would become known as the Battle of the TiaraReign CityHeights.

Seems like the right name for it.

The Maidens were saying on OpenMind, the MindSpeake wavelength we all share, that the Bantaar said they wouldn't miss fighting at your side for all the worlds. Their leader, Clossnoor, said your monument in Light caused the Bantaar to come to their senses on behalf of the Realm.

Heather became irritated, openly hostile. She reined it in. "Honestly, that really wasn't my monument." She felt the need and so changed the subject. *The Bantaar, the Maidens, they were both…really great, really wow. Without them, we would have lost the battle for sure. Archie, you know, for a while…* She chuckled softly, shaking her head. "For a while, there, I thought…" Heather didn't finish, didn't want to.

She let the night absorb the runaway words, the meaning behind them, the images flashing to mind. And, now, head thrust back, eyes closed and lips slightly parted, heaving a sigh, Heather tried, but was unable to rid herself of the turbulent clashes, their sounds, the enemy falling at her feet one to the next, *whick!, whick!, whick!,* her decapitation of the RedSuit. She was surprised to feel her hands beginning to tremble, and so dug them deep into the pockets of her Adaption°Suit. Wrapped in her cloak, the girl wandered away, heading off the trail and out of the glow of moonlight.

Yet, Archie would have none of her withdrawal. Angling directly in front of Heather, he blocked her path, forcing his Mistress to stop. In the jungle darkness, she reached out to her AniMate, again soft to the touch.

You were worried.

I was. I'm very glad to see you, StaLia, so glad that you returned to me. He nuzzled her, able to feel her trembling against him.

Hey, Archie, I made it, didn't I? I'm okay. Everything's all right. So, there's nothing to worry about, right? Nothing.

You're victorious, StaLia, but unhappy.

Really, Archie, I don't know what I am. It's just everything…everything that happened, everything that's bouncing around in my head, that's all.

Heather tried to break away. Archie wouldn't let her pass. On a sigh, she leaned into him, gently stroking his furry mane. She buried her cheek. The two were quiet. They stood together.

"Heather?" It was Sedgwar.

The girl wasn't ready for him. Not yet. She wasn't ready for anyone. Only Archie. Maybe.

I'm over— She tried again. "I'm over here."

A rustling moment later, parting plants revealed Sedgwar and Starbrill.

"I see you found Archie."

"More like he found me." She waited. "No Greesha? Mastow?"

The lack of response gave Heather her answer. In the bounce of light provided by Starbrill's LuminTorch, she couldn't help but notice the great, broad shouldered bulk of Sedgwar as he turned his attention to her. His brown fatigued aura broke free in proud oranges, yellows, and reds, respectful blues and greens.

"I don't know about the two of you, but I'm bone cold weary," said Starbrill. "And as soon as this battle rush slows, I'm going to want to sleep, at least for a short while, most probably longer. I say let's hurry and return to camp."

Heather asked, "Is that running water I hear?"

"There's a river not far from here," said the young man, pointing with his LuminTorch. The dark body of liquid became vaguely discernable just beyond the trees. "It's at the bottom of this slope. See it?" He wiggled the beam. "Eventually, it winds its way and passes under TiaraReign. Heather? Heather, wait. What the—? Heather, where are you going?"

Her back to them, the young Maiden was walking away, headed down the grassy incline, moonlight lining her head and shoulders. Archie followed.

"Heather?"

"What?" Annoyance.

"What are you doing?"

"Walking."

"That I can see. But where are you going?"

"In the water, all right? I'm going in the water."

Raising reasonable objections, Starbrill started to follow. Sedgwar held out his hand, blocking his path. Minutely, the robed warrior shook his head.

Starbrill angrily met his gaze, and then relaxed on a realization. In consideration, nodding his understanding, he lowered himself to the grass.

"Take all the time you need, Heather," said the young man, stretching out. Under his breath, he added, "And in Evermore's name, whatever you do, stick to the shallows."

Arms folded, worn and so craving rest, Sedgwar remained standing like a granite pillar above him, ever vigilant in the Evermorian darkness.

chapter seven

Culling of the Hours

The people of TreeLoft were herded and hurried through the growth of forest, at times a wide and silent wave, at others, a clotting, snaking mass. Some began to stall due to age and exertion.

Whispered one of the Maiden rescuers to another, "The elderly, we can only push them so hard. Their progress is too sluggish, slowing everyone down. At this pace, we'll never get ourselves and the others safely out of range."

"Can they be carried?"

"Some for a short while and, yet, surely, not the length of the entire journey. They're elderly and frail. And necessity forces us to move swiftly and continuously."

Pled an old man forced to rest on a stone, "You can leave us. Take the others, save yourselves. Hurry! Go!"

He was ignored—although some of the elderly would eventually choose to remain behind, nevertheless.

"The Archmounts," said one of the Maiden leaders to another. "On OpenMind, call the Archmounts. Paired or wild, let us call them here this instant."

"Doing so, we'll risk their deaths as well as our own."

"They'll have the choice. They always do. But we must request they come and quickly."

Archmounts were beckoned and ropes were slung and knotted and the elderly were held fast, securely in place for the ride of their lives. Pregnant women and young children were safely lashed atop majestic beasts, too. And although the exodus resumed, the effort had taken time. And time was short.

Heather shed her weaponry and boots, her BodyTote and Adaption°Suit, leaving them with Archie at rest upon the silt. Walking ponderously to the river's edge, she gazed up at the vast and mysterious expanse of moon and stars that soared across the heavens in unspeakable majesty. Before her, amid the currents and eddies, the glittering waves robbed the sky of moonglow, stealing in bits and pieces the jewels of its opulent splendor. She released and let fall her Maiden cloak billowing on the breeze, and it swelled and swept to shore.

Then the youngling waded into the cool dark wetness of the river, the liquid rushing to embrace her, to welcome her, slowly rising up past her knees, her waist, her shoulders. There, tilting back her head, closing her eyes and ears to the world this night, she stood in place and drifted, giving it all away to the waters, letting it bleed all the way away.

All time had slowed. Starbrill could hear no sound save the steady rush of the wind. Soaring high above in the emptiness, he was able to observe the moonlit bodies and thin-skinned wings of the flying Turlakks in formation below him. As they released their Absorption°Spheres, he watched in horror as the bombs rained down upon TreeLoft, watching them disappear beneath the permeable lining of forest that hid the interlocking network of manmade structures.

All the while, in differing views, he was able to see the Turlakks' ugly faces clenched in cluster-toothed grimace, their hate-soaked eyes, and their veined, gnarled hands as they released the red-centered °Spheres.

Peering more closely still, the Evermorian Seer followed after the heavy globes, feeling the sensation in his gut as they plummeted slowly in freefall from the creatures' emaciated clutches, feeling it in his head as they spun dizzily Realmward through the night air, the merciless firepower of the Dark turned loose to wreak havoc upon the unsuspecting inhabitants below.

Then Starbrill became stricken at the sight of the explosive tide unleashed upon impact, the Absorption°Spheres firing forth their hurricane desolation in wide ripping circles, only to inhale the destruction inflicted, making all things disappear at their absorbent centers. Steadily advancing, the circular explosions rocked the forest for many miles, the °Spheres leaving nothing in their path but desolate ground.

And still he heard only the rush of the wind.

"No!" Starbrill screamed. "No! There are children down there, there are mothers and fathers, LoreParents, believers in the cause. There are precious lives…beautiful lives…forest animals…my Savages…children to be shunneled…help them…someone, please, help them…" He was crying. "You've got to help them…"

"Starbrill, wake up!" It was Sedgwar, shaking the young man as he slept. The warrior roused him again, this time with greater force. "Come, now. Awaken."

Unleashed like a bolt of lightning, Starbrill sat up. He shook his head in an emphatic sweep to clear it. Towering above in blackness against the starry sky, he looked to see a freshly dressed Heather in Maiden clothing, her face dripping river water in dots and rivulets upon him. On a knee, Sedgwar was at his side.

"You were asleep, your dreaming beset with nightmare."

Utterly destroyed, Starbrill glanced from Heather to Sedgwar. "If only it were a dream, only a nightmare…but it wasn't."

"What do you mean?" asked the girl.

"The people of TreeLoft, their sanctuary and freedom, everything we worked for, strived for, lived for…all of it is no more."

The geetalvasse curled in sleep at her side, Molly heard Pallár murmur in bitty chirps and squeaks. Her voice kept low, she asked, "How long do you think it will take them?"

"To arrive back at camp?" Toya shook her head in the yellow-orange glow of firelight. "I don't know. It'll be dawn, here, before we know it."

Molly reflected on the sounds of fighting that had raged above when first descending the CityHeights, and then, afterward, how she and Toya swiftly hid among the bush and shrubbery upon hearing the first of the Turlakks' hideous shrieks overhead. She was thankful when, in the darkest darks of forest, Toya had finally turned on her LuminTorch fulltime rather than periodically. Yet, by then, they had walked for quite a lengthy distance. All along, she entertained the suspicion that they were being followed, although, if there had been another, or others, no one ever revealed themselves.

And now, having settled near to the fire, Molly noticed the blaze had ebbed and so rose to retrieve another log. Careful to not wake Pallár when passing, she sank to a knee, releasing the wood to drop quietly among the flames. With a stick, she stirred the embers, and then threw the meager piece in afterward.

They could hear their compatriots spread around them, some shifting, others breathing heavily, constantly. No one snored. Fighting her lingering sense of doom, Molly refused to leave the fireside, where what remained of hope continued to burn, igniting for a time and then dimming. Time and thoughts drifted, infiltrated with sounds of the rainforest night. The fire crackled and eventually faded. Toya arose to fetch another log.

"Toya, what do we—?"

"Shh," she said, a warning hand out to her side.

Noticing, Pallár had awakened; Molly silently found her feet. She whispered. "What did you hear?"

Toya just shook her head. Stationary, they listened.

Emerging from the surrounding greenery before them stepped a great, shadowy beast, lined in blue against the blackness.

Pallár squealed and retreated, and Molly gasped. Sleepers stirred.

Then another form appeared, this one tall and shapely. And afterward, two more, all the taller still.

"Well, don't just stand there, you guys. Welcome us back."

"Heather!"

"There can be no doubt, my Mistress," said the lead Turlakk, "that the rebels' forested refuge has been wiped completely from the face of the planet, the inhabitants vanishing along with it. Our bombing was not only accurate, but widespread and intensive in its obliteration."

"And if having received word of your secretive raid beforehand?"

"Even if forewarned, there could have been no escape. We were certain to cover the distance if given a partial-day's journey beforehand, and then some."

"That is good news indeed, my beauty," said S'ilKuSheere to the reactivated WallScreen. "Due to your thoroughness and reliability, Ghurlurr, I would love nothing more than to make you my exquisitely handsome lead warrior, my Primary Charge."

"Thank you, My Loveliness," said the hollow-cheeked Turlakk, delirious with the rush of pained pleasure, his Mark of the Ravaged Heavens aglow on his temple. "I'm greatly honored."

And you should be, thought the Majestic Sorceress. Just see to it that you continue to perform flawlessly. "Now, your first assignment as my Primary is to dress in the white and gray of Battlefield Custodians and take your troops benignly to TiaraReign. Once there, you are to collect the bodies of your fallen comrades—and that includes your slain predecessor. When you've returned with their corpses, place them near the Barebone Cliffs to be picked clean by the birds in preparation for burial."

"Yes, your Comeliness."

Turning her back, S'ilKuSheere signed off curtly.

Oh, how I hate funerals and weddings, she thought. Just hate them.

Hugs were dispensed enthusiastically all around with most the sleepers waking, some rising in welcome before drifting groggily off to bed once more—any stories could wait until morning. Toya was crying tears of joy, Molly, too, and in turn more hugs were lavished on the returning party. The second time around, the shy Molly stood awkwardly before Starbrill, finally embracing him with heartfelt zeal, but only after he initiated the exchange.

Looking muddled, his presence heavy and worn, Sedgwar broke away to go to the river, wanting to bathe before sleep.

"Where are Mastow and Greesha?" asked Toya.

"I don't know." Starbrill shifted uneasily. "We searched after the battle, but were unable to find either one of them."

Toya's eyes roamed her brother's strained face, sensing something else amiss, something of greater consequence. "What? What is it?"

Starbrill avoided her eyes.

"Starbrill?"

Aware, Molly was riveted.

"Here, let's sit." Starbrill lowered himself and motioned the girls to do the same, Heather joining them.

Her anxiety rising, Toya waited.

"I, uh…I don't know how…how to begin—" Starbrill choked up and, pausing, collected himself.

Molly found herself shaken, not having witnessed this side of the seemingly carefree and unflappable Starbrill.

His handsome features deeply agitated, he looked to the ground, saying in a somber half tone, "We've nothing left to us now, nowhere to go. Our beautiful home of TreeLoft, it no longer exists."

Confusion whirled about them, Molly distractedly reaching for and pulling Pallár in close.

"What are you saying?" Toya was leaning intently, her brows angled high in imploration, her horror beginning to seep.

"I had a vision," said Starbrill. "TreeLoft, every*one* and every*thing*, they were completely wiped out in a Turlakk bombing raid."

In the stunned silence that engulfed them, the forest saw fit to fill the vacuum in restless agitation. No one moved.

Aggrieved, a hand haltingly finding her lips, Toya knew better than to ask, but asked just the same. "You're certain?"

Eyes flooding, she didn't wait for an answer, beginning to squeal, to sob. Starbrill moved to his sister's side, pulling her in, clumsily holding her as she heaved in pain-wracked gasps. Slowly, blindly, she reached for him.

"No…" she whispered, "please, no. Say it's not so…oh, my brother…all those wonderful people…the children…all those beautiful children…" Shoulders shaking, her agony rumbled within her. She let her arms fall away. "…hadn't…hadn't these worlds given them enough grief…?"

Neither Heather nor Molly could see Toya's face, but her wholehearted collapse in posture spoke her heart. Meanwhile, visible upon his sister's shoulder, Starbrill's face displayed his anguish. Speaking into her hair, her flesh of neck, his comforting words came out softly muffled, meant for Toya only.

Undone by the sight and its cause, Molly's tears were streaming, and she began wiping her cheeks, looking blurredly elsewhere although, all the while, nowhere at all. Sedately alongside, watching the proceedings unfold, Heather held her own. The girl had no words of sympathy or compassion, no words of encouragement. Nothing. In her need for distance, she had given the night away.

Leaving brother and sister to share in their grief, the girls withdrew from the fire. Heather removed Fallasha and set her nearby, beside her dagger, before spreading out and lying down on her cloak. For a while, she gazed at the forested ceiling, at a loss in her weariness. Something seemed to be missing, but the girl was unable to recognize the void, let alone her greater emptiness.

Hearing Archie return to camp and lower himself next to her, she blindly extended her arm, coming up with a handful of fur. She waggled her fingers in the soft silken fluff. *Archie.*

Sleep well, StaLia.

You, too. Her spirit heavy, Heather drifted. The surrounding darkness withdrawn for the while, she hoped its forested depths and seeping fogs would continue to remain at bay.

Chapter Eight

A Spy Is Discovered

Drifting in and out of a clash-filled, war torn sleep, awakened in the night by someone rising, Heather opened her eyes. She lay quiet, still. She could hear Archie's breathing, Molly's all the lighter.

The air had cooled, but retained its warmth, the forest muttering ceaselessly its thin and hollow rasp.

And, now, Heather could hear a nightwalker diligently navigating between the slumbering bodies, avoiding the figures haphazardly nestled around the dormant campfires. Heather tossed, and unable to fall back to sleep, decided instead to rise. Surprised to find herself covered in a blanket, uncertain of its benefactor or time of delivery, she laid the soft fabric aside and donned her Maiden cloak. To it she pinned her brooch, wanting to take Fallasha with her into the darkness.

Everything all right, StaLia?

Yes, Archie. Please stay and sleep.

She saw his eyes droop and close in the darkness.

Truly, Heather wasn't at all concerned with the night's riser, as it seemed an appropriate thing to do if one considered all factors. Yet, when she couldn't find Sedgwar, just an empty spot where he had bedded down only a short while ago, on a whim she headed for the river. And it was there that she found the robed warrior.

Sitting alongside a sequence of small, trickling falls, he was bathed in moonglow, its circular source before him, low in the sky. Silvery, the light vaguely defined his features, his torso, his arms and legs at rest. And although Sedgwar's eyes were closed, Heather knew he was aware of her presence, his calm, meditative aura suddenly surging with red-orange fondness.

In front of him, he had piled a small tower of five weighty rocks that diminished in size, the largest at the bottom. Curious as to why, Heather didn't interrupt to ask, leaving Sedgwar to his ritual.

Awakening near Toya and the campfire, not seeing Heather, Molly climbed to her feet and tiptoed effectively among the sleepers, teetering once on a misstep, but never losing her balance to completely falter and topple. Inadvertently heading in a direction opposite to her friend's, she meandered through the trees until they thinned, emerging on a slow roll of hillside.

With the horizon above the distant treetops blushing slightly with impending dawn, Molly navigated away from the forest and toward an outcropping of several boulders half-buried in the ground. There, she encountered a lone figure sitting with his back to her. Even in the dark, Molly thought she recognized the familiar form.

"Starbrill?" she called, softly.

He turned and waited on her approach, before saying, "You're not sleeping."

"It seems I'm not the only one. Mind if I sit?"

"Here. Do." His face awash with harsh shadow, he made room.

Molly could well imagine that Starbrill was hurting, having lost his people, his home, and along with them, his purpose—or some greater portion of it. She wondered just how much he blamed himself for having gone to TiaraReign, while not being present at HomeBase to somehow defend and fight off the Turlakk attackers—or at least die in the trying. True or not, that's how she saw him, how Molly wanted to perceive the young man and his noble intentions.

"I, um, I'm sorry, Starbrill," she began. "I can't imagine…I can't imagine your loss…your grief…how you must feel right now…" Unable to find more words in the moment, she closed with, "I'm just truly, truly sorry."

He nodded, vaguely.

There hung a longing silence, and, yet, neither one cared or dared to breach its interposing layers. Molly desperately wanted to ask him what he was going to do now that he was free of TreeLoft responsibility, but hadn't the heart. And yet, she wasn't sure she truly wanted to know, either, the girl wondering whether Starbrill would even be around when she and Heather returned to Evermore in the future. After all, with the daring life he led, and with his involvement in the cause, who knew where happenstance would take him?

Would he even be alive? Molly pushed the ugly thought away, instead muttering, "He should have been a pirate."

"What's that?"

"Nothing. I'm," she emitted a light, embarrassed skitter, "I'm just mumbling to myself, that's all."

The skyline continued to lighten in preparation for the emerging face of dawn. It was from that distant point that Molly traced the course of the vault's deepening gradation overhead, following until the stars lost themselves behind the trees. Feeling lost herself, filled with vague uncertainties, she drew up her knees and hugged them.

Eventually, her interest found its way over to the young man's profile in study, and when Starbrill sensed her looking, he met her gaze. It lingered, Molly feeling slightly light-headed, hotly blushing, overwhelmed at the sudden surge of emotions—uncomfortable because of them. Not knowing what else to do, she lowered her legs to once more let her feet dangle over the rock face. Her hands found her lap.

Starbrill mused, "Not much company, I'm afraid."

"Me?"

"No!" he rushed. Then even softer, "No…no, of course, not. I was referring to me, to myself."

"You're fine, Starbrill. Really, you are." Molly was concentrating on the slope of hill that lay beyond them. "If you don't mind my saying, I'm happy just to sit here with you."

"No, I don't mind…" Silence. "…In fact, I'm glad you came…glad you found me."

She could feel his grieving eyes upon her and withdrew sedately under their persistence—and could have sworn she knew exactly the moment his attention shifted. When Starbrill offered nothing further, Molly hadn't any objections or, for that matter, any interjections. No observations.

And, so, the pair sat quietly side-by-side, the sun on the other side of the world pushing ever so slowly to make an appearance, to eventually set its influence loose in full measure upon the ever-lightening land, and to emblazon the course of day with its willful presence, come what may.

Rising, irritable, heavy of heart and head, Toya looked for Starbrill and then Molly—any of her companions. They'd all gone, even Archie. And however unreasonable, she became all the more piqued realizing that they had elected to disperse without her.

Bypassing some of the campers waking, some of the newcomers busy reigniting their fires for a hot cup of jerpa and breakfast, she walked glumly down to the stream to wash up—really, just to be alone with her thoughts. Passing some of those readily up and about, she put on a small rigid smile, unable to decorate her face amiably or muster any congenial words. Attention focused mostly before her, she threaded her way between trees to the water's edge.

When she spotted Sedgwar, he was rising and arranging his robes, intentionally kicking over and destroying the small stone pillar he had erected before him. Toya cared little for what he was doing. She went to her knees, splashing water on her puffy, grief-lined face.

She found herself starting to cry, shedding tears for the people of TreeLoft bombed into nothingness, for Evermore and their unrealized efforts to rescue its spirit, and for her brother, Starbrill, whom she knew was utterly devastated over the loss.

So, what next? she asked herself. What are Starbrill and I to do to resurrect the cause, to rebuild TreeLoft, and reestablish arteries to shunnel children, families, and slaves—and where should we start? And when feeling this way, where do we find the lost inspiration to begin again, to regroup and overcome our defeat?

I'm empty, cried Toya silently to her agitated, rippling reflection, her tears spilling to mix with the waters. So empty.

Molly and Starbrill squinted into the harshness of a newborn sun growing whole, the fiery orb slipping ever higher past the lip of the horizon.

He broke the self-inflicted silence, saying, "Toya and I, we're going to have to start over, you know, Molly, finding builders, engineers, organizers to join in with us, like we did before."

"Only if you want to—want to continue doing the same thing, I mean."

"What else is there, if not fighting for our cause, for freedom in the Realm, freedom from the KA?"

Molly shrugged, saying softly, "I don't know. Nothing, it sounds like."

Starbrill ran his hand over his downturned head, gathering his hair roughly before setting it free. And now, for the moment, he was challenging the sun, returning its glare, his face glowingly orangish-red. "I can't imagine what those poor souls must've gone through, what they were thinking, how they must have felt when those bombs began falling. Were they running, hiding, trembling…crying?" His voice dropped in volume, his words no longer directed at Molly. His eyes were downcast. "For all of those people, everyone…I, uh, I just…" He slowly shook his head. "…I'm just not sure…" Bringing up his hands, unable to grasp thoughts and thus emphasize them, he ended by gesturing in profound exasperation. "…I don't know." They collapsed heavily into his lap.

In her absorbent silence, Molly pondered, before offering, "Starbrill, I hope I'm not speaking out of turn, perhaps saying something hurtful or awful or-or horribly *silly* after what's happened. But if it's any consolation, I'm sure your friends knew that if you could have, you would have been there until the end, fighting and helping them to escape. How could they not after all you've done?

"And—and this probably *does* sound horribly silly—at the very least, the TreeLofters can be thankful to have known you, to have been touched by your-your goodness, your kindness…your bravery when fighting with them, for them. The TreeLofters, your Wild Savages, you cheered them up, cheered them on, fortified them, while giving them all your heart.

"I, um, I know this," Molly swallowed, "because in the short time that I've been here, I've felt it, too. And I'm sure they knew just how much you wanted good things for them, fighting, risking your own life to build them a better one. So, if you can, if it helps you, maybe see if you can't let those very special things be enough."

Molly was directing her gaze downward, hoping she hadn't offended, when she felt Starbrill's presence lean her way, felt him near, felt him kiss her gently on the forehead. She closed her eyes.

Molly heard a quiet rustle as he straightened and stood, his eyes to the horizon. "We best be getting back to the others. It's morning, and they'll be looking for us."

Having earlier left Sedgwar at the stream and its falls, Heather was wandering the dim forest, entertaining no purpose whatsoever other than, perhaps, constant movement and distraction. When she approached several small trees and bushes growing closely together, she heard a voice. The words faint at first, they became all the more distinct as she neared.

"My Mistress? You must answer. This may be the only time I have to slip away from the others and get this message to you. Are you there?"

In her usual soundless manner, Heather crept in close, concealing herself against a large tree bordering a small, intimate clearing. Secluded within was a person speaking to his Mistress—whomever that Mistress happened to be.

At a glance, Heather could see a silver light illuminating the leafy limbs close by and, to a lesser degree, some of the surrounding shrubbery. Although she had no qualms about listening in on the proceedings, for the young Maiden, such an act simply wasn't enough. And so, on the sly, she edged her way around the tree for a more informative view.

Even with his back to her, Heather recognized the freed slave and rescued newcomer, Kaggal, and only because of the distorted arrangement of his lopsided ears. She wanted to laugh aloud at the odd sight, how easy it was to identify him because of his unique characteristics, but the girl more than understood the seriousness of her situation and the danger it presented.

Vying for an unobstructed view of his upturned palm before him, she silently progressed and edged her way, and was ultimately rewarded, able to see clearly the silver flame that rested upon it. When a small face suddenly appeared within its midst, Heather recognized the wicked witch from the battle at TiaraReign, the familiar features belonging to Aria's sister, the Sorceress Rendskorra.

"My Mistress," said a relieved Kaggal, "there you are!"

But the face didn't respond directly. Rather, rotely, Rendskorra's likeness stared straight away and launched into speech, her tone casual: "Rendskorra, here, official Sorceress of SpringShoot Green, in the enchanted Realm of Evermore. I'm sorry I'm unable to come to the TeleFlame right now, but if you leave your face and a brief message, I'll return your call if I decide I want to.

"If you'd like to leave a message for my sister, the Majestic Sorceress, S'ilKuSheere, just push my nose. To leave a message for any of my other sisters, just poke me in the eye." Rendskorra chuckled deadpan, adding, "Seriously, do that and I'll roast you where you stand. Besides, they can field their own calls.

"So, if you do leave a message, it had better be worth my time, or trust me, I might just kill you. Or, worse yet, turn you into a worthless WhiffleMorr. Remember: I'm a sorceress. We kill simply because our new shoes are too tight or we don't like the color of your socks." Then, cheerily, "Don't make me angry."

Whooph! The flame soared for an instant, and when Rendskorra reappeared within, her head was cocked with one hand propped behind her ear.

"My Most Colorful Exalted One, this is Kaggal..." The spy and former slave slowed his words. Distracted, he added, "If you would, My Mistress, allow me to reestablish our connection in short order..." He closed his hand on the flame.

Standing before him was Heather.

Earlier, when Archie had awakened in camp, he scanned his surroundings looking for Heather. Not seeing his AniMate, he remembered she had risen previously. Sensing nothing amiss, the Archmount stood and stretched his impressive, muscular framework, his head low and tail high, his extended front legs before him on the quiver. Ever so haltingly, he dragged them in close while on the rise, gathering his swelling, rippling body in bulk. Afterward, he yawned noisily, drawing attention but caring little. Then he left the campsite and headed into the thick of forest, looking to kill his morning meal.

"You know," said Heather, "I never thought I'd meet a spy, let alone some guy who talked into his hand."

"I guess you don't get around much."

"Yeah, because people talking to their hands are all over the place."

Kaggal's eyes were busy, covering Heather's face, sizing her up, checking out her sheathed dagger. Casually, he put his hands in the pockets of his patched and baggy trousers.

Wary all the while, Heather kept watch.

"Who else knows you're a spy, I mean, other than Rendskorra?

Do any others here know you're a spy? Are there more spies?"

"Oh, please. As if I would answer your questions." Kaggal laughed. "What's it to you, youngling? What if I'm not the only one? What do you intend to do?"

"So, what are you trying to sneak away and tell your Mistress, anyway, Kaggal? Where we are? Where we're planning on going once we break camp? I mean, why would she even care about us, anyway?"

"You tell me. Why would she care about a traitor and wanted rebel named Starbrill? Or a young Maiden, quite possibly *the* Maiden Portent of the Prophecies? Have you forgotten, I watched you fight by the Maiden temple. Unlike your very deadly warrior friend, you're raw, but able, youngling. And, to top it off, you're a youngling with her very own Archmount."

"Archie."

"And how winsome is that? An Archmount named Archie. So sickly *sweet.*" His features grew heavy. "I notice a lot, youngling, and I'm not a fool—"

"You're not?"

"No…but, I fear, to your detriment, you must be and so are not destined to live for much longer. But don't worry, your death won't happen right away. What I mean is, first you'll be kindly and humanely tortured."

His smile smug, Kaggal seemed to be enjoying himself. From his loose clothing, the lanky man produced a swoopy handgun and leveled it on Heather.

"Råd°Emitter pistol. Standard issue."

Heather pointed. "Fallasha. A brooch who's not."

"What do you suppose would be my Mistress's reward for a possible Maiden Portent prisoner and all her secrets, especially after she's survived the trap we laid for her at TiaraReign?"

"I don't know. A new, bright and shiny medal? Maybe a date with a Turlakk…?"

Kaggal saw Heather's eyes wander to a location behind him.

He said, "Don't even try it."

"Try what?"

"Your little trick of having me think there's someone coming up on my back."

"Why would you think that?" Her amusement evident in the filtering light of the new day, Heather said, "Nah, I wouldn't bother to look, if I were you. There's no one coming, no one walking our way this very minute. No-o-o person at all..."

Her eyes flicked away for an instant and then back again to his face. She saw his aura aglow in distrustful and anxious greens.

"Besides, I don't think it's Sedgwar you need to worry about." Heather focused past Kaggal's shoulder. "Right, Archie?"

When his aura flinched coal gray with doubt, Heather acted, her body a vicious whirl, Kaggal choosing just the wrong moment to glance over his shoulder for a possible Archmount attack. It proved to be all the time Heather needed, her whipping kick knocking free the only thing within reach: the spy's Råd°Emitter. It flew harmlessly to one side, throwing up dirt and leaves.

Heather said, "I guess you're a fool after all."

She launched into another kick, Kaggal just managing to evade it.

Circling in a fighting stance, obviously trained in technique, the lanky spy didn't panic.

Relaxed, smooth, Heather stayed with him, shadowing his hands, aware of his feet. She wasn't thinking, just reacting, flowing in the moment.

Kaggal lashed out, Heather easily blocking his fists, letting the punches come to her before deflecting them, casting aside the errant blows. He threw others, pokes which Heather straightforwardly countered, bloodying his face. He missed with a kick.

"You're way slow," she said.

"You talk too much."

Heather sidestepped a punch and unleashed one of her own, managing to punish the side of Kaggal's jaw, staggering the man.

"Tell me, a young Maiden like you," he said, recovering, looking for a hook, an edge with teeth, "are you an only child?"

Heather didn't answer, but Kaggal noticed the temporary lapse in concentration.

"An abandoned child?" He jabbed Heather in the face and scored.

"Where do you come from, youngling?" Another jab. "An orphanage?" Jab. "Were you an abandoned child, left to fend on your own?" Jab.

Heather was getting angry, frustrated. She tried not to show it. She unleashed a punch and missed wildly.

"What was the orphanage like?"

Jab.

"Did they beat you there?"

Jab.

Kaggal's head was weaving, his shoulders swaying, his punches connecting. He was getting in close. "Orphan." Jab. He grinned with superiority. For effect, he even chuckled, despite the realization that the child was resilient, able to absorb punishment. He watched her give ground, watched his blows land just off their mark, lessening their impact.

Heather was blinking, her lip and nose slightly bloodied. Concentrate, she told herself. Flow.

"What's wrong, little Maiden orphan. No longer in a joking mood?"

Heather blocked his jab, his swift second scoring an indirect hit.

Flow, she told herself. Ignore him.

They circled.

When his next series of punches glanced off the side of her head, her cheek, her chin, causing her to stumble in retreat, Heather no longer told herself anything. She simply glided. In an instant, she reacted to an opening and flew into a spin, her foot scoring heavily to Kaggal's ribcage, viciously knocking him to the ground, the man crying out, squirming in pain. Suddenly upright on his knees, he lunged for the pistol. Heather dived on top to stop him.

The pair tumbled, wrestling, the Råd°Emitter shooting beams here, there, recklessly all over, small explosions throwing debris in the air all around. Kaggal was surprised at Heather's strength, how the slippery youth rolled him over to gain the advantage, wresting the weapon from his grip.

Still ahold of her wrist, he grappled from beneath, able to roll her once more onto her back while seizing her dagger from its sheath. Commandingly on top, he had the girl pinned firmly beneath him. With one hand sliding free, he pushed at her face while swiftly rearing up with the blade, now plunging it directly toward her heart.

That was when Heather blindly blasted Kaggal with his own Råd°Emitter, the power of the beam throwing him rearward, the dagger hurtling up and over his head. For several moments, she could see his skeletal underpinnings within his wavering, bulging form. Finally, Heather released the trigger, worried that if she didn't, Kaggal would explode like one of the tortured Maidens in Mustiffaire. She watched as the spy immediately went limp, collapsing to the ground just beyond her sprawl of legs, his head slamming against the base of a tree. Smoke could be seen arising from his body.

Heather sprang to her feet. Unwaveringly, she kept her weapon trained on the motionless spy and retrieved her dagger. She kicked Kaggal lightly to see if anything stirred, then chose to shoot him once more for certainty. Shoving the Råd°Emitter beneath her belt, Heather grabbed the man by the ankles and dragged him to the side of the small clearing. There, the girl laid his hands neatly over his chest. On a whim, within reach, she plucked loose a daisy-like flower and threaded it among his fingers.

"There. Talk about sickly sweet."

Heather took a brief inventory, dabbing her nose and lip with a gloved knuckle, looking herself over. Discovering nothing worthy of concern, she went sprinting back to camp, asking of her brooch, "You okay, Fallasha?" Then, her form smaller and farther away: "Think we can be done with the killing, already?"

Chapter Nine

Race for the PortalDoor

"Heather, there you are! Have you eaten?"

"Molly, there's no time." Heather was breathless. "Where's Starbrill?"

"He's over there. See him? He's talking to Toya."

"Thanks!"

The young Maiden started to disengage, when Molly noticed the bulge in her belt. "Where did you get that fancy gun?"

"A spy. Can you believe it? We had a spy in our camp." Heather held up her hand. "Don't even ask." She regarded her friend's half-eaten plate of food. "I hate to say it, but you're probably going to want to hurry with your breakfast."

"What—? *Why?*"

"Our stupid spy. I'll fill you in later."

On a skip, Heather broke into an uptempo gait, headed toward the brother and sister team huddled along the fringes of their encampment, their breakfasts barely touched. Looking up at her approach, they halted conversation.

"Starbrill, Toya, I think you should know. I just discovered a spy in camp—"

"I knew it!" said Toya, turning to Starbrill. "See? That's how they knew we were on our way to the CityHeights."

"Yeah, Kaggal, the guy with the cockeyed ears. Just now, he was trying to reach the Sorceress Rendskorra by talking to a flame in his hand. Anyway, he pulled his gun on me, and when we wrestled for it, the thing went off, shooting all over the place—"

"They'll trace it."

"That's what I thought," said Heather. "How, though? I mean—"

"The Vigen°Darr weaponry utilizes magic," Toya saw fit to interject. "It's traceable, resonating with the Sorceress's MagicAwareness, in most cases allowing her to sense distance and direction."

"Where's the spy now?" asked Starbrill.

"Dead." Heather momentarily looked away. "Dead in the forest, sorry to say. He didn't give me much of a choice. I should have just smacked him over the head from behind, only I wanted to find out some things, what exactly he knew and what he was up to."

All business, Starbrill ingested the information. "All right. Find Sedgwar. He was here just a minute ago. Let him know what's happened."

"Got it."

"Meanwhile, we'll round up the others, get them ready to leave first thing without inciting panic." With a nod, Starbrill dismissed Toya to do exactly that.

"Does the Dahklarr check it out every time one of their Vigen°Darr guns go off?"

"No, not all the time, Heather. Just in the odd instances. And, unfortunately, I think this happens to be one of them, with multiple rounds fired here in the forest—and not all that far from the site of last night's battle. If Rendskorra is interested, she'll first send her scouts to fly in and check on us. Then, if she feels the incident warrants further action, she'll send her RedSuits or S'ilKuSheere's Turlakks. Sometimes both."

Heather spotted Sedgwar. She began backpedaling. "Then I better hurry."

Archie had finished his meal, a young, but good-sized scurrant. The dark-furred, pugnacious forest dweller had put up a good fight, almost escaping due to its quickness, but in the end was no match for the Archmount's decisive pounce.

His appetite sated for the time being, Archie was heading back to camp. On the wind, he caught Heather's scent and, along with it, one very important other smell: that of a Råd˚Emitter having been fired.

StaLia?

Leaping into action, the Archmount altered direction, galloping briskly through the forest, the scents growing stronger on the breeze. In short order he came upon the dead spy lying tidily in the clearing, a dainty flower at rest upon his chest. Instinctively, Archie thought he recognized the handiwork.

StaLia.

An orangish TeleFlame abruptly bloomed in front of Brutessa. The scowling face centered within the flames found the sorceress painting in her Castle Grimmivid studio, a large dark canvas propped upon her easel. Gloppy brush in hand, Brutessa was leaning over her palette, her concentration on mixing color, and so paid her sister half a mind.

"S'ilKuSheere," she said, offhand, "how many times do I have to tell you, don't materialize too close to the turpentine. It's flammable."

The Majestic Sorceress was in no mood. "Shut up and wake Rendskorra. Now."

Walking alongside his AniMate on the trail, Archie said to her, *You had me worried for a moment there, StaLia.*

Something tells me you better get used to it. Heather was grinning. *Man, Archie, a spy. Who would have thought that would happen to me? You know, sometimes my life here in Evermore just doesn't seem real.*

Yes, and something tells me ***you*** *better get used to* ***that.***

Several paces in front of them, Sedgwar turned to Starbrill, "So, what's the plan?"

"We're going to SummersBreath Still by way of Greesha's recommended HiddenPortal. The problem is that we're not exactly sure where this Portal is located, and so might not make it there without first being spotted and attacked."

"I see you've recovered your pack."

"Yes, having ditched her own, Toya brought the larger of the two back with her from TiaraReign."

"Question," said Sedgwar. "How will we know when we've found the HiddenPortal and its whereabouts?"

"There are supposed to be two ancient arylites—old trees—that stand out above all others. And they crisscross one another in a very recognizable 'X' when viewed from the trail. As well, nearby is a sharply pointed rock tower, called SteepleRock. Hidden below, disguised in the adjoining cliff face, is where we'll find the Portal to SummersBreath Still."

Sedgwar said nothing in response. He was squinting through the boughs above him. "Have you looked to the sky lately?"

Starbrill turned his gaze upward and noticed dark feathered gliders occasionally passing through gaps in the tree cover.

"I see the scouts are searching for us. *That* certainly didn't take long."

Directly ahead, several of those same ominous birds took off from a branch overhanging the trail. They flew headlong at the travelers, so much so, some in the party screamed and cowered while others dove out of their paths, Starbrill included. Archie leapt and intercepted one of the scouts, slapping it between his front paws, voraciously ripping it apart with his teeth.

"If I'm not mistaken," said Sedgwar, offering Starbrill a hand up, "something tells me we've just been spotted."

Encompassed snuggly within the confines of soft down, Rendskorra lamented on a moan, "Wha-a-a-t?" Still in bed, the sorceress was stretching luxuriously, yawning, her multicolored hair swimming in untamed strokes upon the pillow. "Why must you disturb me in the middle of a sweet night's sleep?"

"Maybe," said Brutessa, "because it just happens to be mid-morning."

"Ah, but *that* depends on where you reside on the planet," her sister mumbled. "For instance, me? I'm residing in the Sweet Night time zone, undisturbed by time and you." Rendskorra pulled the coverlet up and turned on her side, fully intending to drift off once more. Her protruding hand waved. "This is where you go away."

Brutessa interlaced her arms. "It's S'ilKuSheere. She's been trying to reach you."

"Tell her everything is in hand."

"I think, dear Sister, she's trying to inform you that quite the opposite is true."

Head in profile upon her pillow, Rendskorra suddenly focused. "What are you saying?" She sat up, propped by an arm. "And this better be good."

"Actually, that depends on your point of view, I'm afraid. It seems that your RedSuits were soundly trounced last night in TiaraReign. So were the Crown soldiers along with a great many Turlakks."

"What! That can't be!" Indignantly, Rendskorra was throwing off the covers, swinging her legs out of bed. Jiggling freshly naked, she held out her hand. "S'ilKuSheere!"

Instantly, silver flames appeared on her upturned palm, the Majestic Sorceress's face deadly serious within them.

"There you are," S'ilKuSheere seethed. "Finally. Newsflash, sleeping beauty. Last night's death trap went awry, and this despite my added precautions. Lunaria, the Maidens, the Bantaar, and the TiaraReigners, they completely wiped out our armies in the CityHeights."

"I don't believe it!"

"As of this moment, you'd better start. Your Soldiers One and Two won't be around to fill you in on all the ugly details, either, I'm afraid, dear Sister. They, too, became casualties of the conflict."

Off balance, Rendskorra was attempting to swiftly dress using her free hand, the TeleFlame pitching side-to-side in the open other.

"Will you stop that!" snapped S'ilKuSheere. "Stand still, already! You're making me feel as though I'm in a storm at sea."

Rushed and feeling harried, Rendskorra tripped and almost fell over her skirts. "What else do I need to know?"

"The Vigen°Darr weaponry is ineffective against anything iMagiNacially conjured, and the power of the Light is growing stronger in the Realm. If we don't curtail its spread, we'll soon be having a revolution on our hands, with all of us and the Dahklarr ousted from power and cast into the null."

"You're sounding like a NewsBarker. Any good news?"

"Yes. You're finally out of bed."

"Anything else?"

"Fail again, and I might just see fit to kill you."

"S'ilKuSheere!"

"Yes. All right, then, there's this: my MagicAwareness detected the unusual use of a Råd°Emitter in a forest not far from TiaraReign, so, I sent your scouts to investigate. They've recently returned to your Castle Dravalian where I've made myself available to greet them in your absence. And they've just confirmed to me a very important sighting, a very important sighting, indeed. Now, I'm headed to Densearling this very moment where I'll *eagerly* be awaiting your arrival at my castle in the not too distant future."

The implied threat wasn't lost on Rendskorra. "Hold tight, Sis," she said, the sorceress hurrying all the more, almost catching a sleeve on fire as she tried to slip the handheld TeleFlame through the garment's loose opening without success. It was then that a prudent idea popped to mind. In a reach and gesture, she released the 'Flame to hover. Her hands now free, she returned to dressing in haste.

"S'ilKuSheere?"

"What?"

"You're staring."

The Majestic Sorceress frowned. "I'm *thinking.*" She continued, "You see, from Densearling, I plan on coordinating a little attack of sorts, and I'd like you to be there to witness it firsthand. That sighting I mentioned? Your scouts, they've informed me that our most sought after gang of Starbrill, the Maiden Portent, and their freed slaves have been spotted on a trail near the OpalineCascade CityHeights. Your funny-eared spy, I'm sorry to report, was not among them."

"No doubt discovered."

"No doubt killed. Now, I suggest you get on that flying beast of yours and ride a breakneck current. I'm sending my Turlakks after Starbrill and the Maiden Portent. As we speak, my elite soldiers are on their way to pick up more Absorption°Spheres. With any luck, we can still dispose of that entire gang before they enter what I assume will be their escape Portal."

"Escape Portal? How do you know—?"

"We're pursuing them, aren't we? I'm sure they've noticed. Count on it, they'll be on the run. Besides, if they haven't done so already, at some point they'll discover they've no home, Rendskorra, dear. I saw to that bit of mischief-making last night in a surprise Turlakk raid, making certain that their hidden base in the woods was bombed into nothingness. Poof. All gone…"

Rendskorra stopped dressing, regarding with admiration the hovering S'ilKuSheere in the TeleFlame. "I like that."

"You should. I've ridded your kingdom of its biggest nest of thorny pests. Now, dear Sister, are you going to get those lovely rainbow brows of yours over to my castle, or am I going to have to blast you out of the sky for arriving late?"

Resuming movement, reaching into her wardrobe closet to retrieve a free-flowing belt, Rendskorra was vexed. "S'ilKuSheere, I'm dressing, all right, doing the best I can under the circumstances."

"Dear Sister of mine, when in a hurry to dress, have you ever thought of simply using a spell?"

"And so, Heather," said Sedgwar, "to prove themselves supreme, that they were the superior race, the people allowed their leaders to drag them into yet another full scale war."

"Did they win?"

"No. Together with the Maiden alliance, we stopped them at great cost to both sides—but mostly to theirs, *and* their planetary pride."

Since being spotted by scouts, the party's movement along the trail had become more than brisk. For many, especially the older travelers, the greater pace proved extremely taxing. Periodically, while seeking to maintain the increased tempo, the former slaves would pass other refugees resigned to the path, alone or in groups, mostly hooded and in rags. Tired children rode their parents' shoulders or were carried in their arms.

"Sedgwar, if war is so horrible, why do people keep doing it?"

"It's a question, Heather, that has been asked many, many times since the Ancient Archannites first configured Evermore. I'm not sure there's any one answer, because people take up arms for many reasons, or are pulled into conflict for a multitude of others. Having fought my share of battles, I think the problem with wars one-to-the-next is that, in the interim, we forget how we die."

With barely a nod, Heather's gaze dropped to the stride of her boots. A moment later, her eyes found Sedgwar once again as she waited for more, but he just shook his head. Heather didn't pursue the topic.

From the moment the party had been discovered, try as he might to the contrary, the warrior had become ill-tempered, brusquely sharp-edged. Both he and the girl could *sense* the unrealized battle that was taking shape, the forces mounting in Darkness against them. Meanwhile, Heather kept her mind occupied with conversation, Sedgwar steeling himself for the inevitable showdown, slowly securing his battle face.

With every step taken, the warrior felt with growing dread that they were never going to make the HiddenPortal in time to avoid engagement. And against the superior forces of the Dahklarr, by his determination, there was simply no chance of survival with this scraggly, ill-prepared bunch, none whatsoever. It would be a slaughter.

Sedgwar looked over his shoulder, watching the animated Starbrill as he urged on the children and older adults to increase their step even more, the young man being met with gloomy stares, exasperation, and bitter complaints and objections—even though his intent was to ultimately save their lives.

Nevertheless, he encouraged them onward, cajoling, "Cloider, Goyntuss, you keep pace, and I'll buy you both a new pair of shoes that walk *themselves* once we reach the Portal for SummersBreath Still."

More grumbles. A few jokes and laughs.

In a surly search for patience, Sedgwar turned his attention to the road and sky. Secretly, he wondered if Heather's Aria would appear on the scene to once more unleash her timely magic in an effort to save them. And would such an effort be enough?

"Took you long enough," said Rendskorra smugly, clapping closed her hand on a small face and head mid-sentence, cutting short her skimming of TeleFlame messages. Arms crossed and leaning against a table, she stood triumphantly, awaiting her sister in front of the immense WallScreen in the Castle Densearling.

Newly arrived on the bustle, S'ilKuSheere didn't smile. "You *do* realize the gravity of the situation." With a flick of her fingers, the drapes began to close.

"I do."

Another flick and the candelabras sprang to life.

"Then I advise you act like it."

S'ilKuSheere dismissed her inquiring servant.

"Now, let us see if we can't redeem our heavy losses." In the semi-darkness, she waved her WallScreen to life. On it, the sorceress sisters were able to witness the freshly armed Turlakks rising on wing above the depot, their newly acquired Absorption°Spheres clasped firmly to their chests. Aligning in formation, they headed toward their target on the trail miles away.

The Majestic Sorceress switched views, and now the 'Screen

was SightSharing with Rendskorra's airborne scouts. Below, strands of people were wading through a meadow, nervously glancing to the sky, intent on finding swift shelter beneath the trees once more. One in particular stood out, her hand aglow with magical residue, visible through the scout's eyes.

"There they are, with Starbrill and the Maiden Portent toward the front of the pack."

"Well, then," said Rendskorra, waving a sure fist, "we mustn't let them escape!"

S'ilKuSheere heaved a sigh. "Brilliant tactical contribution, Sister. Just brilliant."

Momentarily disconcerted, Rendskorra glanced sidelong at S'ilKuSheere. She brightened. "Thank you."

"Oh, Mastow, there's no TreeLoft anymore," said a stunned Greesha to her TrueMate, the pair having exited the ScatterPortal. "Nothing's left."

"Freshly bombed, by the looks of it," he said, surveying the huge swath of scorched soil cutting irregularly through the forest. "And for a great distance. You're sure this is the right location for TreeLoft, hey, and that we've taken the same ScatterPortal we've always used in the past?"

"Have I ever been mistaken before?"

Mastow's eyes wandered to the bandages wrapping his TrueMaite's head injury, the result of a sword-butt on the TiaraReign battlefield. Her face swollen and bruised, the woman was wearing a sling, her left arm and shoulder injured when tussling soldiers had landed on her while she lay unconscious.

"Mastow, I know what you're thinking. And this head wound may have knocked me into the next kingdom and back, but it didn't rearrange the parts. They're still in working order. We took the correct Portal, all right, the same one we've always taken to get here."

Venturing closer to the vaporized destruction, Greesha grimaced and covered her nose and mouth with her hand. Mastow spit. The pair could still smell and taste the acrid residue of the exploded Absorption°Spheres on the site once sheltering the many TreeLofters in hiding.

"What now?" said a misty-eyed Greesha, the woman turning and walking away. "We were supposed to meet Starbrill and Toya here at HomeBase after the battle."

"If I remember rightly, they were going to stop first at the HiddenPortal to drop off any slaves that wanted to travel to SummersBreath Still. The rest they were going to bring back with them to TreeLoft."

"They must learn of TreeLoft's destruction, Mastow. We must tell them there's no longer anyone here, nothing to come home to, that there's simply no HomeBase."

"How, hey? Starbrill could be anywhere in that forest, 'suming they made it out of that battle alive."

"And you!" said Greesha, abruptly turning on her 'Mate. "Shame on you for up and leaving the fight early. You should have fought on! You should have!"

"I had to get you out of there, didn't I? Your head was a sight, hey. In that pile of bodies, I had to dig you out. I couldn't just leave you bleeding to your end. I couldn't."

"Fighting for the greater cause of Evermore is worth more than my life, more than any one person's."

"To some, hey. Don't hold it against me that I think you're worth more than Evermore, more than a million Realms like it."

"In the future, you're to leave me; you're to fight for Evermore, Mastow, for the Four. Understand? *For the Four!* We're ClearWeave, remember?" She softened on a breath. "Right, then. We've not had much sleep between us, now, have we? And these wounds leave me aching.

"So, all things considered," the woman continued, "here's what I propose we do. I know of a ScatterPortal nearby that will take us very close to the HiddenPortal that Starbrill and his lot are going to be using. Once we arrive, we can wait for him there on the spot at the PortalDoor, or look to meet up with him. After all, it's obvious we can no longer return to the CityHeights."

"This HiddenPortal you speak of, hey, is it far from where we'll be arriving?"

"No. Just the other side of SteepleRock. To one side of the rock is the small ScatterPortal, on the other, the HiddenPortal to SummersBreath Still."

"I only bring it up, because you're not in the best of health, hey, dollop, with those injuries you've got there. Rightly, you should be resting, eh?"

Greesha thrust out her chin. "Now, don't you start fretting on my account. I made it here, didn't I? I'll make it wher*ever* we need to go."

"If we have to look for Starbrill, just so you know, we'll be making slow time. And chances are slim we'll ever find him, hey."

"We'll figure a way."

"You're sure, then, set on this stubborn course of yours?"

"Sure as you're my annoying TrueMate." Amusement played across her features.

"And you're sure they'll be heading to that very Portal, right?"

"Enough that Starbrill confirmed its location with me when we met on the balcony steps last night."

"Then go there we will, my 'Maite, and with Evermore in mind."

"What *now?*" groaned one of the elderly. "Tarn't any way the sheer lot of us gonna be crawling over *that* thing, truly and for sure, golla."

Having shed his pack, hands on hips, Starbrill examined the enormous toppled tree that angled across the trail, blocking their path. Brush and branches pushing out from all sides, he walked along its girth, inspecting where the arylite's rounded bulk rested heavily on the forest floor.

With rising friction evident among the walkers, Starbrill signaled for a meeting under cover, away from the meadow. He was conscious of the scouts flying above, at times roaming through the forest, peering about menacingly while gliding on their great stretch of wings. He could see how the frequent sightings agitated his people all the more.

"Look, I've a plan—"

He was interrupted, a woman saying, "Why don't we just head into the forest and hide until those ugly birds go away?"

Maintaining patience, Starbrill replied, "There's food sure enough, but we can't guarantee the scouts won't follow us. And if the Turlakks or RedSuits get involved, they'll be hunting us down. By now, I'm sure they know we're here."

At the mention, chaos ensued, all parties speaking at once. Starbrill calmed them. Then he said, "Toya, Heather, Molly, Sedgwar, why don't you take the children and any others that want to go along at a much faster clip and make certain you find that Portal. And those who join you can assist by keeping a sharp lookout for it as you walk."

He briefly described the cross of trees and Steeple Rock. "Now, as for the rest of you, I'll wait here until we're ready, and then lead you to the HiddenPortal once you've had sufficient time to recover your strength—"

"No, you're not doing that," said Toya, her head shaking adamantly. "No."

Her brother ignored her. "Now, I've spotted a place where we can slip under the bulk of this fallen tree, where the ground is sunken, creating a hollow, a gap. It'll be a tight fit, but we can do it. The alternatives are to try going around the tree's busted base, but by doing so, we stand a chance of being spotted in the open and possibly hemmed in by those cliffs. The other is to climb directly over this immense trunk, but that would take more time, and high on the tree that way, you stand a greater risk of being exposed—and exposing the rest of us—while being vulnerable if attacked."

Said one woman, "Either way, with the RedSuits or Turlakks coming, it looks like there isn't a lot of hope, Starbrill, as much as I hate to say it. Just go! Go on! Go with them! See if you can make it safely with the greater part of our group. The rest of us will try to find you once we've regained our strength."

"Yes, why not?" said another.

"Why not?" exclaimed a sour man. "I'll tell you why not! If we don't make it, we'll either get recaptured as slaves, killed by soldiers, or be left behind to survive on our own—"

"They'll want us captured," chimed a gentleman in rags, "not killed. Let's be honest. Most of the adults here, we're Loyalists. And most of us possess Loyalist secrets. The KA, they'll want to torture us in a KAmp, find out who and what we know—*and* find out the location of the Portal we seek. And only the Universe knows what they'll do to these children…"

"You heard Starbrill. The KA, they're already on their way. We're not going to make it to *that* Portal or any Portal! Starbrill, you go on ahead—"

When more arguing ensued, finally able to get the upper hand, Starbrill said, "We're wasting time, here. Toya, take to the trail, swiftly, now." Starbrill could see Sedgwar was already directing the children under the great girth of fallen tree. "We'll follow first chance."

"Starbrill, are you sure—?"

He shot Toya a challenging look that told her he was.

Striding to a spot alongside the arylite, Starbrill had reassumed command, once more asserting himself, signaling for Sedgwar to crawl under and assist from the other side. He began directing others. "Let's go! Everyone who's able, who's ready to move quickly, now is the time to take to the path! Come along. That's it." More of the young were sliding hurriedly below its bulk. "Let's go. Watch your head...good...keep moving."

Molly, torn, turned and said to Heather, "Would you mind terribly if I stayed here to help Starbrill and the others?"

Heather gave her friend a brief and knowing hug, and afterward slipped beneath the rough bark, holding her cloak close so as not to entangle it.

Starbrill looked around for Molly, and spotting her, insisted she follow her friend. When she defiantly refused, he confided, "Molly, please trust me. You want to go now."

Looking at him, Molly suspected Starbrill didn't want to tell her the chances were slim that the slower walkers would ever make it to the Portal without first having to engage the forces of the Dahklarr. She also suspected that, after the TreeLoft bombings, he wanted to be on hand and fight for them should the need arise. It was the only hope they had—and as it stood, in her heart, she knew it was scarce hope at that.

Her eyes wandering to the more tired of the stragglers, truthfully, Molly had no idea how they were going to make it to the other side of the tree, let alone to any Portal. With a final glance at Starbrill, committing his image, she crawled beneath the overbearing weight of the once colossal evergreen.

Toya followed, Starbrill instructing as she passed, "When you spot the HiddenPortal, be evasive when sneaking into it. You don't want the Dark to follow."

"Starbrill, this is such a waste—"

"Toya." He took his sister by the shoulders. "Do me a favor?"

"Yes."

"Find safety."

Her face tense, her eyes clouding, she nodded and left her brother to himself and his folly.

Chapter Ten

Tangling with the Darkness

Mastow crawled from the ScatterPortal low on the cliff face, located in the shadow of SteepleRock. Greesha, at a disadvantage with her wounds, followed clumsily, haltingly. She was dizzy, craving rest, and her sore shoulder made most any movement limited and painful. Nevertheless, the woman didn't complain, spurning all Mastow's attempts to assist her. Certain there was no one near, they walked out from behind the rock and into the open to stand in front of the ever-narrowing, towering slab of stone.

"It's overgrown," said Greesha, throwing her head back with a wince.

"What's that, hey?" Mastow followed her gaze. "What're you saying?"

"SteepleRock, I can no longer see the top of it. I've not visited this Portal for quite some time, and it's become overgrown, blocked by foliage from below. And look, Mastow! There's only one large arylite where there used to be the two crossing in a gigantic and very noticeable 'X.'" Crestfallen, the normally honey-skinned woman paled all the more.

"What do you propose we do?"

"I have to say, I'm at a loss. There's no way Starbrill and his bunch can ever hope to find their way to the escape Portal without first catching sight of the landmark clues."

Seeing Toya slide and disappear under the tree, Starbrill turned to the people who remained, feeling the need to calm and reassure them. "When we've rested long enough and are again on the trail, if you tire, just do the best you can to keep up. I'll assist you. Truly, who can say if the forces of the KA will discover us before we reach the Portal? And exactly how long it will take them to get organized and begin their search, we don't know. We still might make it without incident. But just in case..."

Sifting through his pack, Starbrill produced some Vigen°Darr weapons. One he set aside for himself, another he kept hidden.

"I've three extra guns here, a °Concussor and two Hemorrhage°Rays. Who has had experience handling and firing a pistol?"

Handing them out, he said, "As much as possible, our goal is to shoot and distract the scouts from spotting our friends that have just gone ahead of us on the trail. And, later, should they ever arrive on the scene, we want to prevent the Turlakks or RedSuits from discovering them, as well. If the enemy does show, I've thought up a diversion that will allow us to eventually sneak away. Any questions?" He waited. "Everyone without a weapon, relax and recover your strength. We'll soon be back on the trail. Those of you with pistols, follow me. Now, let's position ourselves at points along the clearing," he indicated, "and then follow my lead."

Starting to edge their way out from under the forest overhang to achieve an unobstructed view of the circling, feathered gliders, one of the gunmen whispered, "Won't shooting these Vigen°Darr weapons tell the KA exactly where we are?"

"You forget, my friend, they already know where to find us. The trick here is to make certain we hold their interest."

Finding a spot to his liking, seeing that the others had settled into theirs, Starbrill took aim with his °Concussor. With the scout's majestic spread of wings in his sight, he squeezed the trigger.

"Oh!"

"What's happened? Rendskorra, what just happened to your scout?"

"I-I don't know."

While SightSharing on the WallScreen, the picture had suddenly become hazy, shaking convulsively in a burst of loose feathers. The image before them, displayed from the scout's perspective, dimmed and went dark.

"We've been shot!" S'ilKuSheere switched the WallScreen's view to that of another bird. And, now, from their new vantage point high in the air, she could see beams shooting skyward from the clearing.

"Looks like the Maiden and her friends are armed and intend on making a stand against our armies. If need be, we can have the scouts transfigure—"

"Wait!" said Rendskorra, looking perplexed. "How do you know? Maybe it's a ruse."

"A ruse? Care to explain?"

"Well, we don't see the Maiden Portent, do we? And there's no iMagiNacia being performed, is there?"

"After last night's performance, maybe she has nothing left for an encore."

"Still," insisted Rendskorra, "I'm not so sure. Suppose the Maiden and everyone else are sneaking off to their escape Portal while these, these *few* keep us distracted."

S'ilKuSheere stared sternly at her sister.

Suddenly on the defensive, her voice timid, Rendskorra said, "What?"

Headshake. "Nothing."

"S'ilKuSheere, *what?*"

"It's just that sometimes you surprise me, that's all—*especially* when you make such brilliant sense."

Rendskorra regarded her sister with mild indignation. "Thank you?"

At S'ilKuSheere's suggestion, Rendskorra directed her scout to fly in low. The sorceress sisters watched as the view from the meadow and beneath the branches revealed only a small portion of Starbrill's group remaining. When a yellow and violet beam spurted out from behind a concealing bush, the WallScreen went dark, but not before the image became blurred and a redness started seeping, discoloring the frame.

"Must be a Hemorrhage°Ray."

"So, my dear Sister," pondered S'ilKuSheere, "it seems we can see Starbrill and a few of his compatriots, but there's no indication of the others, including a particular young Maiden most troublesome."

"What do you suggest?"

"What do I suggest?" She turned on her sibling in full. *"What do I suggest?* I suggest we find and kill the Maiden Portent, that's what I *suggest!* And we'll bomb that entire stretch of forest until we do! The Maiden Portent, Starbrill, the slaves, I want them *all!*"

"Here it is," said Greesha. "This is it."

"This is what?"

"This fallen tree, here, it's one leg of the 'X' I was telling you about. Being old, the arylite must have broken loose in a storm, been hit by lightning, or just rotted through with age or disease. Who knows?"

"Sure is huge, this trunk, hey. And its stump, too. Enormous."

The pair were walking along the tree's length, approaching a meadow, when they heard gunfire.

"Get down!"

Greesha hunkered, but not without gasping in agony. Head lowered, she balled in pain.

Alarmed, her 'Mate asked, "You're not hit—?"

"No, it's…it's these injuries…" Slowly, she uncoiled, looking dazed.

"You're all right?"

"Fine…I'm fine. Let's go." Impatiently, she waved her TrueMate onward.

"Why don't you wait here," said Mastow, drawing his sword, "while I find out who's shooting and why."

At a crouch, shoulder skimming alongside the leveled trunk, he advanced. Greesha, defying his order, arose and followed.

When across the clearing a young man popped up from behind a bramble to fire a °Concussor and knock a scout out of the sky, Greesha said, under her breath, "Well, blush my pale cheeks blue. Starbrill!"

Startled by the sound of his TrueMaite's voice, Mastow confronted her on a half-turn. "I told you to stay put."

"And it wouldn't be the first time, now would it? Where's Toya? I don't see Toya."

"I'm sure the girl's around here somewhere." He sheathed his sword, his countenance brightening. "That pair always has a way of surprising, don't they, hey?"

More gunfire broke out, another scout falling from the sky,

landing with a shushing *whump!* amid the knee-high fernery.

"Mastow, best show ourselves to our young friend and his troop. We need to find out what's happening here. There's a reason he's shooting at scouts that way with Vigen°Darr weapons. I've a sneaking suspicion our Starbrill knows he's been found out."

"Something tells me you're right."

"And something tells me if we don't lead his people to the HiddenPortal as quickly as possible, we'll be the recipients of a whole lot of unwanted company in the not too distant future."

"My guess? They're shooting at scouts, drawing attention to themselves and away from us," said Sedgwar. He was backpedaling for several steps, looking to catch a glimpse, before righting himself on the trail. "At least, I hope that's the case."

"That means we probably don't want to use our guns unless we have to."

"Right, Heather. From here on out, unless absolutely necessary, stick to the use of your dagger."

The girl regarded the swell of people behind them, mostly children and younglings, a peppering of adult Evermorians, with Molly and Toya drawing up the rear. In the distance, through the intrusive leaves and dimness of forest, she could barely make out the toppled arylite.

Around her, the day had grown muggy, the sky beginning to cloud up, the penetrating sun losing its intensity. The faded blue-grays added a mood of oppressiveness to the atmosphere, dullness to the trail.

Heather took a look at Molly, the girl preoccupied with keeping an eye on the children. She appeared spiritless, ill at ease. At the sound of any shrill forest utterance or report of gunfire, she would hastily turn her attention upward past intermittent gaps in the forest canopy and toward the sky. Her aura glowed lowly in desperate greens and fretful blues.

Heather caught her eye and waved. She saw Molly's aura lighten at the acknowledgement, although the next instant had her retreating once more into her thoughts.

Heather did the same, pulling up her hood.

Stationed stiffly before the WallScreen, S'ilKuSheere was speaking directly into the mind of her lead warrior. As the magical display zoomed in, she and Rendskorra could see the Turlakk in ever-increasing close up from above. Moving past his translucent flap of wing and along his bony shoulder, the 'Screen came to rest on a sharpened view of his bald and craggy head, his glowing temple Mark and pointed ear. A vein throbbed.

Discarding the usual sultry, seductive pretense, the words of the Majestic Sorceress were measured, succinct.

"Ghurlurr, I want you to begin dropping your Absorption°Spheres north to south along the WheppingSkogg Trail, lighting up the forest, while making sure not a single tree is left standing nor a single soul surviving. I want this Maiden Portent obliterated—*no!* I want her blasted *beyond* obliteration, beyond any hope of future life." Her beautiful face transforming, turning monstrous, S'ilKuSheere seethed in a deep, unearthly voice, *"Blast them all."*

Reconfiguring, she cast a glance at her starkly silent sister alongside, before readdressing the WallScreen. "I hope I've made myself clear."

"Mastow! Greesha! I-I thought for sure…" Starbrill enthusiastically waved them toward the shelter of trees, where he swiftly joined them. "After the battle, we couldn't find you, either one of you. Heather thought she had seen Greesha, but when we looked—"

"One of us," said Greesha, "disobeyed the order of the land." She cast a sharp eye at her TrueMate, placing a fond hand upon his arm. "Stupid thing, he took me away and cared for me."

"I suppose I shouldn't say this," said Starbrill, amused, "but I'm glad he did." The young man's features suddenly darkened. He looked from one to the other. "You've something to tell me."

"You won't like the news we've to share, I'm afraid, Starbrill."

He searched Greesha's bruised and bandaged face. "TreeLoft?"

"You know, then."

He nodded; his voice was low. "I do. And, yet, the time to fully grieve will have to wait." In a flash, his seer's insight told him, come the appropriate hour, there would be even more to mourn. The unsettling moment hung, and the next instant, in an abrupt turnabout, his spirit seemed to rise up, his posture to inflate, his eyes reigniting to brim with fire. His words came quickly: "Greesha, can you lead these people to the HiddenPortal without being seen by the scouts? They're circling above, observing us as we speak."

"I don't see why not."

"Mastow," Starbrill offered his °Concussor, "I want you to join the other shooters and keep those scouts busy, distracting them, letting them think the entire group is still in hiding here by the meadow."

"Your gun, hey, you won't need it?"

"I've a backup."

"Then happy to oblige." Mastow took the pistol and broke away to secure an advantageous spot in the meadow.

"Now, I'm going to leave you for a time, Greesha. I have to hurry and fetch the others before they've gone too far up the trail. I've sent them off in the hopes of finding the Portal before the enemy finds us. You say the HiddenPortal is just beyond the meadow, against those cliffs?"

"Not far at all, Starbrill, to this side of the SteepleRock. It's disguised and not easy to sight, but just follow your nose, and you'll run directly into it. Better yet, follow this old spent arylite. Even in death it points the way."

"I can't thank you two enough for coming." Starbrill excitedly held Greesha's gaze. "Aren't you *ever* the greatest?"

She reddened. "Go on with you, for Evermore's sake. Get going before I have my TrueMate put that gun up your nose and blow your soggy wits to Winterspire."

"You can begin your bombing run," said S'ilKuSheere, her voice a harsh whisper in the room's lowlight. "It's not necessary to confine your °Spheres to the trail, going wide on either side. After you dispense with your bombs, I want your armed soldiers to reorganize at the front in an advancing line, ridding the forest of anyone or anything that moves, offering cover to protect our bombers from any ground fire while they finish up behind you."

"We've our Råd°Emitters and long daggers, My Mistress." The words were spoken softly on the wind, emanating distinctly from the WallScreen. "I'll let the troops know."

"Do."

"Halloa! Everyone! *Wait!*"

At Starbrill's command, the entire party turned. Several faces became animated at the sight of him, most notably the two young females trailing the pack.

"Hurry!" he said. "The Portal is back this way! Come on, now! *Run!*"

Stopping short of the group, putting his entire body into the gesture, Starbrill began waving them rearward, to hurry back down the trail and toward the fallen tree.

The very next instant, when a bright light strobed the sky, the ground trembled, and the canopy of forest blanched momentarily. Several children were thrown to the path. Some began crying, the adults scooping them up, taking them in their arms while dashing in retreat.

On the run, Sedgwar was glancing over his shoulder and toward the brooding gray of cloud cover. Between breaths, he murmured in ominous undertone, "Here they come."

The caustic screeching of the Turlakks, although distant, was growing louder. The ground shook once more, and then again. Each time, the sky streaked white through the foliage, while a great storm of wind violently shook the trees before going deathly calm. Frantic, people were being tossed to the ground, tripping over the fallen, picking themselves up, hurriedly helping their comrades to their feet.

Sedgwar grasped a stumbling child at the waist when passing, tucking her under his arm. After several paces, with a hitch, he righted the girl against his chest. There, she clutched his robe and held tight in the jostle and sprint.

The group, continually disrupted and thrown off stride with each detonation, encouraged one another forward, forging their way down the shaking, foliage-strewn path. Heather was reminded of a disturbed and confused trail of ants running around mindlessly, looking to regroup.

Knocking aside bits of greenery falling from above, racing alongside Sedgwar, she was making certain no one fell behind. The footing was tenuous, the earth beneath them steady one moment, shuddering the next. They could hear the bombs dropping closer, the resulting winds more intense, the trees bending in furious rages, their weighty branches snapping and falling in whumps and clumps around them.

From within the leafy trailside denseness, forest animals broke cover, scurrying and bounding by, seeking safe haven elsewhere. Above, birds abandoned their lofty perches to take to the wing in flurries, their shrill cries echoing amid the raucousness.

With another round of the ground's sudden quaking, Heather tumbled, her hood falling to her shoulders, the supremely athletic girl rolling to find her feet on the run. Her hands reaching to grip beneath the arms of a fallen child, she hoisted him up in stride before slowing to set him free.

"Let's go!" she hollered. "You can do it!" She saw to it he didn't lag.

The approaching blasts of the Absorption°Spheres were guttural, concussively deafening, tramping ever closer like a giant's overbearing footfalls. Periodically, Heather would join Sedgwar in glimpsing behind them, witnessing entire trees as they shook free of their rooted moorings. Twisting, they tumbled and bashed into swaying others, eventually flopping over the path in branch-crackling expiration, the explosive whiteness beyond streaking harshly through the newly created rifts.

"Go on, Heather!" urged Sedgwar. "Go on! Hurry ahead! I'll cover our backs." His hands full of child, the big man staggered on the rollicking ground before catching himself. On a sudden thought, he yelled, "Where's Archie?"

"He comes and goes," she tried, above the uproar. "Like Aria. Archie says wherever I am, he'll always find me."

Whether or not he heard, Heather didn't linger to clarify. She sprinted onward, the immense broadside of the path's toppled arylite revealing itself before her. Alongside, she could see Starbrill directing some to crawl under its imposing roundness, others to stream along its flank, having them move through the confusion of brush, over the branches, and toward the cliffs—everyone toward the cliffs.

Desperate to escape the oncoming danger, people rushed only to bunch when reaching the obstructing tree. Forced to wait, the teens and adults were nervously biding their time toward the back of the pack, impatiently glancing around, eager to again be on the move. Some began to panic, to cry. When the ground shivered, they cast their arms outward, instinctively hoping and groping to brace themselves, swaying off-balance like wobbly bowling pins. Thrust sidelong, others skidded tersely to ground.

Near to Starbrill, Molly was helping to assist and guide the frantic crowd, attempting to keep them orderly, calm, and moving, always moving. There was no sign of Toya. Heather figured she must have positioned herself nearer the PortalDoor.

Within the gathering, a few screamed and pointed. Many ran for cover. Through an extensive opening in the forest canopy behind her, Heather turned to see a strand of flying Turlakks pressing forward in uneven progression over the far tree line. Having dispensed with their Absorption°Spheres, they now formed a frontal wave of armed attackers. In the distance, the sky continued to shout out in whiteness, the bombers letting loose their devastating payloads while following up the rear.

Swift to remove her Råd°Emitter, Heather began shooting, eventually knocking a Turlakk from the air amid the hollers, cries, and chaos surrounding her. She avoided several bolts in return, the forest floor spitting up at their fiery impact.

Placing his child to ground, directing her and others to seek shelter ahead, Sedgwar put to use the pistol he had obtained from the RedSuit on the TiaraReign balcony. The man was unsurprisingly accurate with his aim. To dodge incoming bolts of light, he threw himself into a roll, and then came to right on his elbows. There, he proceeded to counter the enemy's streaking shots. Once more on his feet, he ran toward the arylite, pausing only to return fire and herd any strays.

Emerging from the surrounding greenery, a straggle of incoherent trail dwellers appeared. More followed. And then more after that. Initially confused in their step, out of their minds with panic, they merged to join ranks with the party, all running in fear of their lives.

Unflinching amid the beam-bursts, Starbrill steadfastly directed traffic, periodically shooting off his weapon while stationed alongside the curvature of tree. When his escapees would thin, he'd call out for more or point to others in hiding, eagerly waving them forward from seclusion and in the direction of the Portal.

"Go, go, go, go, *go!*" he barked.

Breaking from their linear formation, a portion of Turlakks streamed and attacked, diving through the overhead opening and swooping in above the trail. At once, from points on the ground and in the air—spraying in all directions—vary-colored beams stabbed out. Some in Starbrill's group fell over dead in a smoking heap, with lifeless or wounded Turlakks tumbling recklessly through the clearing. Many of the winged creatures, after skimming, then cartwheeling, would find wicked rest in a splash of limbs.

In a fit of daring, Heather sprinted toward the great impediment of tree, firing as she went. With her momentum carrying her, she leapt and practically ran up the convex wall of its bark-covered side, her free hand swinging and clawing at times to afford her balance and drive. Fully exposed on the way up, she could feel bumps of something that felt like stones pelting the back of her Maiden cloak, only to turn and discover the garment repelling the thrown daggers and Råd°Emission shots of the Turlakk aggressors. All the while, blades struck and stuck to the wood to either side of the ascending girl, beams chipping up the bark.

Perching herself high atop the rounded trunk, crouched behind her cloak's protective covering, she increased the power discharge of her weapon, turning it up several notches to compensate for distance. Then she returned fire over her draped forearm. At times, she would dip her head behind the shielding garment, only to pop up and deliver more flak.

Mastow, crawling up from behind, soon joined her when taking on the diving, screaming creatures of the Ravaged Heavens. Heather did a double take.

"You're back!"

"Greesha and I both." His Råd°Emitter belched a terse streak. "Good news, hey, is we plan on enjoying your company for a longer interval this time round..." Now positioned alongside, he shot while on his belly, his sleek gun thrusting out its brilliant beam, giving slightly with the recoil and hum. "...and, in the process, escort this frightened lot safely to the PortalDoor."

"I like your plan—" she ducked a dagger, "—but I'm not so sure these creepy Turlakks will go along with it." Heather fired, her winged, evasive target diving out of sight.

"And I say, let's see if you and I..." Mastow took careful aim, "...can't change their minds." He fired and scored.

Together, they began picking off the Turlakks while the bark all around erupted in fervent sparks and cries, the hurled daggers whooshing and stabbing at the wood. Amid the unsteadiness caused by the ground-rocking detonations, the pair attempted to maintain balance while holding true their aim. And yet, the entire time, both shooters couldn't help but be mindful of the steady advance of the Turlakk bombers, the violent spate of winds, the gasping suction in return, and the harsh, explosive white intermittently bursting forth in air, starkly illuminating the surrounding forest growth, while causing them to wince and turn away.

Having guided the remainder of their party under the tree and toward safety, Sedgwar beckoned Heather and Mastow down from its crest and to follow in the direction of the Portal. On the opposite side,

Starbrill encouraged them to do likewise, before firing off several rounds at the attackers and disappearing into the brush.

"Go, Mastow! I'll cover you!" cried Heather.

Rising to her feet, cloak flowing freely behind her, the Nearling Maiden boldly faced off against the enemy. Bolts screaming by, blades whizzing past, she waited until a descending Turlakk fully revealed himself from behind a high, shielding bough. On rigid wing, he power-dived toward the girl with eyes bloody red, mouth wide and screeching, gun ablaze in streaking, errant strobes. Heather sighted the repulsive target and squeezed the trigger. Then she watched as the fearless Turlakk leader lit up in her beam, his skeletal form igniting in definition from within. Afterward, limply dropping his arms and weapon, his wings going lax, the scorched and smoldering creature whirled sickeningly off kilter before slamming headlong into the bark-lined flank below her. She didn't witness the gruesome collision, though could readily visualize the outcome, her imagination fueled by the sound of crunching bone and smacking flesh.

Drawing heavy fire, her upraised cloak acting as a shield, Heather retreated, lowering herself from sight, before jumping the remaining distance to the ground. Alongside Sedgwar and Mastow, they raced toward the cliff and PortalDoor, exchanging gunfire all the way.

Only moments before, with the spectacular vista of forest spread large and detailed upon S'ilKuSheere's WallScreen, she and Rendskorra watched in silence as the Turlakk's steady bombardment ripped open a gaping, crawling wound of disintegration. Drop by drop, chomp after chomp, destructive circle after destructive circle, the explosions chewed into the greenery in a devastating migration across SpringShootorian heartland. Satisfied at its progress, the Majestic Sorceress switched views.

Now SightSharing with her screaming, diving Primary Charge, Ghurlurr, they had tuned in just in time to be the surprise recipient of Heather's Råd°Emission beam fired from atop the log, the screen momentarily blinking white. From the creature's point of view, the sisters watched as the stunned and paralyzed Turlakk went into a death spiral, slamming headfirst into the flank of the tree. The 'Screen went dark.

"Ouch."

"What just happened?" asked S'ilKuSheere.

"I don't know," said Rendskorra. "But whatever it was, it sure looked like it hurt."

"Was that the Maiden Portent I saw? On top of that tree for just an instant—? Had to be! Where's my Secondary Charge?" In a flash, S'ilKuSheere remembered she hadn't had time to appoint one since the previous evening's battle. At random, she chose a Turlakk presence, one she felt strongest. "Harguluff!"

"Yes, my Mistress?"

The scene displayed before them changed. The WallScreen's point-of-view was now originating from above the forest canopy, the Absorption°Spheres falling away one-by-one, getting smaller before exploding in bright-white impact.

"You are now my Primary Charge. In or around the clearing just ahead lies our main target, the Maiden Portent. I want you to lead the remainder of your Turlakks in an all out assault, commencing this very moment. When finished, make certain the bombing in your wake is thorough and thoroughly cleansing. Clear?"

"Clear, My Mistress."

"Now, eliminate the Maiden Portent and her allies. And *don't disappoint.*"

The ground pitching, the blasts nearing, Greesha and Toya were stationed alongside an unsteady SteepleRock. There, the pair guided the sporadic flow of frightened comrades and newly gathered refugees into a discreet fissured opening in the cliff face. Once several steps inside, they disappeared in an instant, destined for the desert kingdom of SummersBreath Still.

In front of the anxious women, the sky flashed and the wind screamed, with debris driven in eye-shielding, head-turning, face-creasing gusts. Afterwards, they witnessed boughs falling, trees crashing, people stumbling and coughing, appearing out of the roiling dust.

Amid the confusion, dashing wildly around the massive stump of the fallen tree, Molly appeared first, Starbrill trailing, rallying the three children and four adults they had collected along the way.

"Where's Heather?" yelled Molly, her face momentarily displaying its pleasure at discovering Greesha.

Responding over the fierceness of wind, she said, "We haven't seen her. She must still be fighting the Turlakks."

At the very mention, two of S'ilKuSheere's winged soldiers

whooshed through the dust swells, diving at them in a skreigh from on high, their guns spurting brilliantly their piercing rays. The next moment, they were blasted out of the air, Starbrill quick to eliminate one, another beam finding its mark, fired from somewhere within the turmoil. One of the children running toward Greesha had been hit in the exchange, reeling backward and into the Portal to vanish. Toya quickly bade the others to follow, to seek help for the wounded boy upon arrival.

In the brief lull that followed the hurricane winds, while trading gunfire with a host of Turlakks, Heather, Sedgwar, and Mastow materialized through the drifting wall of dust, closing in on the Portal. Scrambling over forest debris, they were leading twelve to fifteen refugees they had discovered in hiding near the trail, the unfamiliar party desperate to escape the bombing.

Dashing across the clearing, several were gunned down or became recipients of a dagger's blade. Hemorrhage°Ray blazing, Starbrill raced to assist them, diving out of the way of a crashing tree. Now going to a knee behind its foliage, steadying himself above the earthen shiver, he shot from behind its leafy cover. Doing so, he blasted several hovering Turlakks in the process, their pale bodies blooming red with blood just below the skin before bursting.

With Heather and Sedgwar settling beside him, discharging their weapons, Starbrill saw his chance, rushing to help Mastow guide the refugees to safety. But he had other intentions, as well. Once they reached the HiddenPortal, under heavy gunfire, he directed Molly, Toya, Mastow, and Greesha into the fissure. When Mastow spotted more refugees dashing toward them under a deadly rain of Råd°Emission rays, he hurried to assist, firing on the run.

"The rest of you, go!" Starbrill shouted over the tumult. "Toya! Molly! Greesha! Off with you! Into the Portal! We'll follow shortly."

He ran off to rejoin the fray, his Hemorrhage° beams streaking with accuracy, dispensing life-ending cruelty. Still, more Turlakks arrived, darting over and around them, their pistols returning fire to further spark and stir the madness.

With the wind whipping and ground shifting, trying to see through the scatter and rubble, Molly hesitated in her Portal departure. Chirping beams scored the cliff side surrounding her, fracturing chunks of stone into flinty bits. Meanwhile, above Molly's head, the mammoth SpireRock incrementally tipped her way due to the ground's constant upheaval.

"Heather!" she cried. "Heather! We're going! Hurry!"

Engaged in the thickness of battle, with debris flying, trees groaning, and boughs snapping and falling, Heather couldn't hear her. Attacking Turlakks shrieked above, flitting in and out of view.

"Starbrill!" Molly tried. "Star—*oh!*"

Grabbed from behind, Molly felt Toya's sturdy arms encircle her. While struggling to break free of her companion's firm grip, Molly unsuccessfully called out to Heather, wanting her to hurry and follow, but was wrestled inside the mouth of the fissure. There, she and Toya disappeared in a blink and swallow of the TimeLight Bridge.

Meanwhile, ignoring Starbrill's order, having stepped away, Greesha continued to await her battling comrades—and her TrueMate. Fully exposed, she saw more Turlakks gathering in the sky, some settling to ground, with gunfire spattering in flickering yelps about her. In the confusion, she thought she saw Archmounts leaping to snare and tear the emaciated bodies of S'ilKuSheere's warriors in the drifting haze, but then they were lost. An arm shielding her bandaged head, the woman squinted and blinked into an upsurge of wind.

The steady bombardment closing in, the ground beneath her convulsing, she ran halfway to meet the group of onrushing refugees, receiving them in handoff from Mastow. With the party in tow, Greesha raced awkwardly to the Portal in her sling, waving them on with her good arm, spurring them inside amid the potshots.

As she did so, the ground heaved, the environment suddenly screaming in blistering whiteout, the resulting gale blasting the area just beyond the closest fringe of trees, their crowns crumbling in snaps and crackles, falling in heaps. The squall finding Greesha, she was slammed bodily against the cliff. Gasping, she hugged and held fast, her teeth clenched, her eyes squeezed tight as fists. More rubble crashed down, boulders bounding and pebbles hurling in cacophonous spillage and dustup. Caught in the howling wind shear, flying Turlakks were cast from view, slapping and snagging in the highest trees, tumbling to settle in contorted poses. Restlessly agitated, the soil boiled all the more.

Moments later, the atmosphere seized in suction, Greesha bracing herself, hanging on, feeling the pull toward the center of the nearby explosion. Hearing SteepleRock cry out in a deep, cavernous moan, she shrank in suddenness. She watched as it plummeted headlong towards her before slowing, dragging surface-to-surface against the cliff face, halting its slide at the top of the Portal's fissure. Suspended, angled just above her bandaged head, the weighty slab cast its threatening shadow upon her.

Making use of her good arm, Greesha pushed off and bolted.

Pain-racked, she dropped to a knee. Securing a Råd°Emitter from a fallen Turlakk, she began shooting, lending cover to the swiftly approaching Starbrill and Mastow, the pair firing on the resurgent enemy while in retreat.

"Hurry! The Portal could be sealed any moment!" Her words were lost in the bedlam.

Dodging and leaping, Heather and Sedgwar were on their way, rushing through the swarming, swirling layers of dust. Noticing a tree collapsing in their direction, Heather lunged and pushed Sedgwar out of harm's way, the girl falling forward in the process. Hitting hard, she rolled and scrambled, her cloak becoming enmeshed in the resulting crash and spill of branches. Swift to her feet, turning to grab hold of her garment in a gather, she heaved, but try as she might, the sturdy Maiden fabric refused to tear free.

"Take it off!" screamed Sedgwar above the burst of wind, the flash of sky. He was gesturing with his hand at his neck, urgently tugging downward.

But with Fallasha attached, Heather wouldn't hear of it. She kept trying to disentangle herself, pulling heartily from differing angles. Swift to her side, Sedgwar produced his sword, and with a decisive hack at the green, cut the cloak free of its clutch of branches. He pulled Heather after him, the girl with a presence of mind to scoop up her weapon and shoot a threatening Turlakk en route. The pair was at full sprint toward the Portal, catching up to Starbrill and Mastow along the way.

Spying more refugees near a thrown boulder, two children bending over their crushed Mother, Mastow broke away to help them.

"Don't! There's no time!" yelled Starbrill, but his voice was lost in the ever-nearing bombardment. "Mastow! Mastow!" He pointed to the sky. "The next one will be ours!" But the man wouldn't or couldn't hear him. Starbrill recommitted to his Portal charge, separating from his friend.

When Heather slowed, intending to assist Mastow with the children, Sedgwar grabbed her roughly by the shoulders, dragging her along, making her regain her speed. She looked at him in helplessness. He shook his head.

Reaching the Portal entrance, joining Greesha, they turned to see Mastow leading the girls. Fear-faced, the youngsters were crying, the man blithely urging the two forward. When a Turlakk warrior loomed above them, Sedgwar was quick to shoot him out of the sky, but it was too late. The creature's thrown dagger struck Mastow in the calf, causing him to skip and limp. Then to stumble and fall.

"Oh, you fool! You beautiful, beautiful fool!" cried Greesha. With a worrisome glance to the sky, casting aside her weapon, she ran to him.

Encouraging and guiding the girls into the Portal, Starbrill followed after them, but not without looking over his shoulder all the while until vanishing.

Catching sight of the escaping Starbrill, Archie came charging out of the gritty sweep of clouds. Muzzle soaked with red, his muscular body was rippling, surging, his bloodied paws plunging over ground.

"Time to go!" screamed Sedgwar, but the fierce warrior didn't move.

Neither did Heather. Both watched as Greesha reached her 'Mate. They didn't hear Mastow when he looked up at her and said, "For the Four."

Greesha, draping herself protectively over him, whispered, "For Evermore." She lowered her head.

Above the clearing, the Turlakk released his Absorption°Sphere.

Archie galloped past. *StaLia! Now!* He leapt to find the fissure.

Swiftly, Sedgwar wrapped his arms around Heather, and they staggered backward into the Portal. The last thing he recalled feeling was the immense eruption of ground below his feet. The last thing he saw was SteepleRock falling before him, sealing the Portal shut, the blinding white of exploding light seeping from its fringes.

Then all was calm.

Chapter Eleven

In Evermorian Conclusion

"They're gone."

"All of them?"

"As you can see, Rendskorra, there's nothing and no one left."

"Did we kill them?"

"Hardly." With an offhand wave, S'ilKuSheere had Rendskorra's scout circle closer to the battle site, hanging on the breezes. "No, sadly, I think not."

She called for a Midnight Concoction, one of her dark beverages in the long stem glass. Then, on second thought, she doubled the order.

"Isn't it a bit early in the day to start drinking?" asked Rendskorra.

"You've forgotten. I work the nightshift." S'ilKuSheere stared at the WallScreen, at the bald ground wiped clean, the collapsed and singed SteepleRock. "First TiaraReign, now the WheppingSkogg Trail. Your RedSuits and my Turlakks, depleted." She paused in thought. "Lunaria and the Maiden Portent, together, they're quite the potent adversary, are they not?"

When her servant entered, the Majestic Sorceress went silent, collecting the two glasses from atop the tray presented. She turned to her sister, offering one of them. "Join me, Rendskorra?"

"Think I will."

They touched lips and then glasses.

"To Evermore," said Rendskorra, "and its sorceress sisters."

"Yes, to Evermore's Sisters of the Pool."

They sipped, and, afterward, glancing askance, S'ilKuSheere raised a brow to the 'Screen.

She murmured, "All but one."

The magical lady finished the beverage and called for another.

His prophetic dream interrupted upon his abrupt awakening by the river, Starbrill never fully realized how his vision would have played out. He never saw that the Maidens had been able to evacuate TreeLoft, the white-skinned, soldiering women taking his Savages and the remaining inhabitants with them, escaping safely through ScatterPortals and beyond the reach of the damage inflicted by the Absorption°Spheres.

And now, miles and miles away, climbing a steep, tree-lined hilltop overlooking the scarred forest that once sequestered their home of TreeLoft, Bremmis turned to Tremm.

"Think Starbrill, Toya, and all the rest were able to get away from last night's bombs?"

The dirt-smudged boy glumly shook his head. "They were supposed to come home, remember?" Pausing in his ascent, screwing up his face, he once more regarded the sight. On a dawning, he looked at Bremmis and began to nod. "Yes…" Then more emphatically, *"Yes!"* The boy perked up. "Yes, they got away, all right, Bremm. I'm sure of it!"

"You are? How—?"

Tremm laughed merrily. He pointed in all obviousness. "I'm wearing my lucky hat, aren't I?"

The sweet-faced girl beamed, able to smile, not wanting to dig too deep in the logic.

"Come, now," said the Maiden. "You mustn't tarry and fall behind the others."

Their step livelier, the two young refugees followed after the shepherding Maidens and their accompanying AniMates. And conquering the short rise of hill, falling in line with the other TreeLofters, they headed into the depths of the forest and toward their new home.

Last to mount the windblown summit, the trailing Maiden turned and paused upon her Archmount. Standing as one, bathed in the blood-red glow of the hour, the proud and dignified pair beheld the panoramic sweep of the valley come sunset. And then they were gone.

Chapter Twelve

A Third Floor Revelation

In the darkness, Heather didn't move—she didn't dare. Things felt different; things had changed.

Where am I? she wondered. What the heck just happened? And where *is* everyone, anyway?

Truth be known, Heather had expected to land somewhere in SummersBreath Still in a desert setting right out of Lawrence of Arabia, a movie she and Molly had watched countless times in the Art Deco theatre.

And, now, finding herself standing alone in the cool obscurity of some unfamiliar interior space, Heather keenly looked around, absorbing details.

Strange. She didn't see Sedgwar anywhere. She remembered that shortly after entering the Portal and the TimeLight Bridge, she had felt the intensity of his grip lessen and herself slip free, while losing touch with her pistol. It had happened in an instant, too. And, now, here she was, wherever 'here' happened to be.

It was so quiet.

Before her on both sides of the spacious corridor, she was able to distinguish shelves and shelves of books continuing onward in their slowly curving bookcases, occasional ladders leaning against them in the vagueness. There was also a spiral stairway leading up to lengths of narrow, railed walks, allowing access to another level of books entirely.

Far above, murkiness attached itself to a distant ceiling in retreat.

"Heather?" It was Molly, her voice far away.

Molly! thought Heather, relief flooding over her. She made it out of that craziness okay!

And as much as she wanted to cut loose in eager reply and let Molly know she was all right, Heather waited before answering. After all, there could be danger lurking. She took a scan of her confined surroundings and was glad to discover not a single aura, nothing that posed an immediate threat. And, so, despite her continued desire for caution, for some inexplicable reason, she felt at ease in her heart, that all was secure and safe.

"Are you here somewhere? Heather?"

"Molly, I'm over here."

Heather began to move, activating the lights directly above her and on the undersides of the finely finished walkways, the illumination itself limited to the confines of the corridor. When lit this way, she was surprised to discover she was once more occupying her twelve-year-old body.

Twelve again? That means we're probably back home in the Bristol House. At the thought, Heather pushed away her sudden confliction of emotions, realizing their fantastic Evermorian adventure, for the time being, had come to an end.

With her shoulder-length hair swinging loosely on either side of her face, she realized her MaidenBraid was gone, and that was disappointing. She wasn't wearing her gifted cloak, either, or any of her Maiden clothes. Doubly disappointing.

Heather was still in possession of her BodyTote, however, feeling the sleek, snug-fitting Maiden carrier beneath her clothes—those very same clothes she was wearing when she last left Noble through the PortalWindow. And she glimpsed her brooch in place below her chin, pinned to her sweatshirt, and found comfort in the fact.

"Well, Fallasha," she confided, "it looks like we made it back to the Bristol House, all right. Where in the Bristol House, though, only the Bristol House knows."

With her progress, the lights continued to go on above her, wink, wink, wink, tracing her course down the book-lined passageway. And with more of the curving corridor coming into view, she saw that the run of bookshelves ended on a much wider, intersecting aisle. She also noticed that, at Molly's advance, that aisle had become bathed in light from above, her best friend suddenly peering around the corner.

"Heather?" Molly's face lit up. "There you are!" She smiled her

Molly smile.

Heather couldn't help but laugh. It was so good to see her friend, no matter what their ages. The occasion seemed celebratory.

"What's so funny?"

"We're twelve again," said Heather. "I'm going to have to get used to this."

Molly giggled. "I know. Seems strange, doesn't it, after being older like we were." The girl momentarily looked away, her voice tinged with wistfulness. "I was just getting used to it, too, beginning to like being older."

"Don't worry," said Heather, maintaining her buoyancy, "If age works like it's supposed to, you'll get there again—and then some."

Molly brightened. "So, if we're twelve again, Heather, that means we must be home in the Bristol House."

"I was thinking that same exact thing."

The girls came together and hugged lightly, naturally, both just wanting to hang close. Each felt a vague sense of contentedness, of achievement in yet another shared adventure that brought them ever closer.

They disengaged.

"Anyone else around?"

"No, Heather, I ended up here alone. I called out, but no one answered until now. And look, I'm in my Noble clothes, the ones I thought I'd left in Evermore."

"You know, Molly, with everyone in our little gang no longer around us after all that's happened, and now that we're back home, it kinda makes our whole trip seem like a dream, doesn't it? The whole crazy thing."

"Yes."

"Well, all I can say is: *we better get used to it!*"

They shared the laugh before Molly mused, "They were all here just a minute ago, weren't they, our entire group? And we were running for our lives, with Turlakks and bombs falling all over the place." Gasping, Molly became suddenly serious, grim. "What happened after I left?" She hesitated, gazing intently at Heather, studying her eyes. She braced herself, the words, "Did he make it?" barely escaping her lips.

"Starbrill? Yeah, he made it." Heather flashed a grin. "Well, last I saw, anyway. He got into the Portal okay, taking two little girls with him. I don't have a clue where they ended up, though. And, I see, because you're *here,* neither do you." Chuckling, she watched as Molly's anxious green and gray aura softened, and began surging warmly in relieved oranges and hopeful yellows.

"And everyone else, did they—?"

"Boy, was it ever wild at the end, there, Molly! Whew," said Heather, cutting her off. "Everything, everything was just going crazy all *over* the place." Something caught the girl's eye, and she craned her neck. "Whoa." Over her friend's shoulder, along either side of the wide aisle, Heather could see corridor upon corridor of bookshelves disappearing gradually, succumbing to the shadows. "How big is this place? And where the heck are we, anyway? Another Bristol House library?"

"If it is, it's not like any of the sunny third floor libraries we're used to, is it? This one, it's so…so *obscure.*"

To distract from her discomfort, at random, Molly selected a book off the shelf nearest her and began flipping through its pages. Meanwhile, Heather started walking down the long throw of steps, the aisle gently sloping on the incline toward what looked to be an elevated circular stage.

"Holy Evermore, this place is amazing, Molly. Kinda mysterious, too. Sorta spooky-like." Heather bubbled forth a scary laugh, "Bwa-ha-ha-ha-a-a-a…"

"All right, you. Knock it off." Molly gave a swift, uneasy eye to the darkness that surrounded her.

Feeling suddenly goofy, giddy, Heather reached the bottom step, her gaze traveling up the draped leg of a remarkable statue of three stylized Maidens standing shoulder-to-shoulder, rising into the heights of the room's blackness.

Lit from below, their presence gave off a power Heather could never explain, only feel. And this was due to the statue's heightened emanation of drama, of significance and monumentality, of stability and everlastingness—perhaps, even, the power of righteous immortality.

"Wow. Molly, you've got to see this, these huge statues, here. They're a bunch of them all around. We must be in a Maiden Library."

"Or the Evermorian Library. Look, this book I picked out, it's about the Ancient Archannites."

"Then there must be a book on Portals around here, too—even though I have to say I learned a lot more about them on our trip."

"And had a lot of your questions answered?"

"Yeah." Heather reddened. "Yeah. 'Letting time give with time' helped."

"So, you're learning the MaidenWay, right?"

"Yeah, well, I'm working on it."

The girls laughed.

"So, what's this?" asked Heather, climbing up the small flight of stairs leading onto the circular platform. "Whoa, whoa, whoa, whoa, *whoa!* This is *awesome!* Look at *these* Maiden statues, Molly. So great!"

"So," said Molly, gazing about as she mounted the stairs, "this, this round *stage* looks to be at the center of the library—like a sun!—with all these aisles shooting out like sunbeams. And circling around and around us are endless corridors of books, as far as the eye can see. And then there are those colossal Maiden statues nearby, like sentries at the gate."

"Protecting and watching over us. How great is *that?* And look at these swoopy-doopy reading couches!"

Before the girls, positioned across from one another, were two high-backed sofas of swirling design. Centered between them was a wide-mouthed, light-emitting GlissenCauldron. Encircling it, four to a side, stood realistic life-sized Maiden statues, their heads bowed and arms linked before them, dressed in flowing robes. From under their hoods, their eyes were glowing a warm SearEye, helping to light the scene. There was more lighting from overhead and from smaller Maidens positioned to each side of the couches. Looking about them from their elevated vantage point, the girls couldn't help but feel they were in a predominantly lightless building of immeasurable proportions, although intimate in nature at the very same time.

"Oh, it's absolutely gorgeous, Heather. A truly mystical setting."

"Okay, Molly, choose a side. Which couch is yours?"

"You're the green-eyed Maiden. You choose."

"Well, then, I'll take this one," Heather chuckled, "and only because it's closest."

"Think we have time to sit for a while? We haven't been home for days. Mom might be worried."

"Molly, when's the last time the Bristol House made us late for dinner?"

"Or late for anything?"

"Yeah. I bet only an hour has passed since we left Noble. I mean, think about it. We're all spruced up, ready for anything: we're clean, our clothes are clean, and we don't even need to take a bath or shower or brush our teeth."

"That's good, because I just realized I left my toothbrush in Evermore."

Elated, the girls sat, Heather falling onto the couch with

enthusiasm. They looked excitedly across the GlissenCauldron at one another. Heather pushed on the cushion, feeling its give, saying, "Pretty comfortable, huh?"

"Yes, very. Very elegantly designed."

"Yeah, if you ask me, this place is all *very* everything." Heather's eyes kept wandering to the Maidens. Finally, she asked, "Feel different?"

Molly elicited a series of small eager nods. "Very."

The girls cracked up.

"Me, too. It's like we're too old inside to ever be us again."

Molly opened her book, her attention wandering over the pages. She murmured, "Geez, Heather, I hadn't noticed. This entire thing, it's all handwritten on parchment, with swirling hand-painted embellishments and illustrations. It's so intricate, so absolutely beautiful..." After a time, she asked, "So, how do you like being the green-eyed Maiden?"

Surprised Heather was taking so long to answer, Molly looked up from her book. And she was even more surprised to find Heather's cheerfulness had given way to somber reflection, the girl's face stained with her moodiness.

"Honestly, Molly, I'm trying hard not to think too much about it right now—you know, just trying to be happy that everything seemed to work out, and we got back okay. I'm not really sure why...but I'm kinda wanting to think about other stuff, trying to put all the bad things that happened away for now—like that's the Maiden shelf way over there in the Evermore closet, and right this minute we're sitting in the Noble dresser, inside a Bristol House drawer. Know what I mean?

"I mean, all those things I'm supposed to do, all the people that are trying to get me, with all the people I have to try and get before they do, it's a lot of...a lot of *stuff.* And even if they're super ugly, the Turlakks probably have friends like you, and families, their own Grandma Dawns, their own feelings about things they like and don't like...favorite comic books and movies. Same thing with the RedSuits."

"Heather, they were trying to kill you—to kill *us.* You know that, right? They're cruel and horrible people doing cruel and horrible things. You had to do what you did."

"Yeah. That's what's so crazy, I guess. I mean, I have to get used to it still. When I'm fighting, I don't even think about it. It's just that, you know, when it's over, and you see a bunch of bodies all over the place...some are crawling, some aren't moving at all...some are moaning and stuff, wanting someone to help them...I saw one Turlakk,

I think he was crying—*this mean ol' Turlakk!* He was looking up at me, too, real scared-like...and then he died. You could see it. You can tell. It's like they just burp up their life and go cold...they stop working." Heather's soulful eyes were traveling over the decorations on the large glowing 'Cauldron, her weariness suddenly evident. "It's weird. When they're hurt and can't hurt you anymore, things become different, Molly. I don't know why..." Heather's voice trailed off. She shrugged. "They all have faces, you know. It's hard."

Molly was alarmed. "You still want to be her, don't you?"

"The green-eyed Maiden? Yeah. Sure. I *have* to. A Realm is depending on me to help them." Heather paused. "But now I think I know why Sedgwar is so sick of this stuff. If you want to get to the Light, you have to go through the Darkness. But when you do, you have to become Dark yourself, and that's what you're trying to get rid of. It doesn't make sense, in a way."

Molly looked at her cheerless companion. Wanting to rush to her aid, she rallied up. "You know, don't you, Heather, that the initials for the green-eyed Maiden are g-e-m? And you *are* one and you shine for everyone in Evermore."

Heather wore her gloominess, her spirit rising through it. She gratefully looked at her friend. "I may be the green-eyed Maiden, Molly, but it's you, you're the g-e-m. You really are."

Having placed the freshly wrapped packages under the tree, Mrs. Pringle looked around her at the Bristol House so beautifully dressed for the Christmas holidays.

The girls will be thrilled with their gifts, she thought. What we lose in quantity, we make up for in quality. There *are* some very nice and original things here. As well, Sis will be thrilled with hers. Mr. Wilson Talbott? Who knows? Just a fun and thoughtful little knick-knack the girls and I will give to him over dinner Tuesday evening...

Mrs. Pringle lingered for a moment on the thought. Then she wandered upstairs to change into something a bit more casual and comfortable before heading to the kitchen for a nice glass of wine, end of day. There she'd plan dinner and await the girls.

"Hey!" declared Heather in sharp undertone, her attention

riveted.

"What?"

"Shh-h-h. Molly. Behind you. Look."

Quietly, Molly set down her book and, on her knees, peeked over the top of the couch. Both girls watched as a trail of lights flicked on along a distant corridor of the library, in and among the shelves. Whoever the visitor was swiftly made a path toward one of the main aisles.

Heather rose and motioned Molly to do likewise, and to hurry.

She shot on the low, "We can't be stuck up here if it turns out to be someone creepy."

Molly agreed.

Readily, the pair slinked down the short flight of stairs. Positioning themselves with their backs against a pedestal belonging to one of the monumental statues, they watched as the lights close by went on, flooding the intersecting aisle next to them with illumination. Slowly, Heather peered around the corner and then quickly withdrew into hiding. Her face was troubled.

"Oh, man, Molly," she whispered, hotly, "you're not going to believe who's coming."

Molly's eyes went wide. "Not one of the sorceresses?"

"Worse," replied Heather in the same heated undertone. "Get ready. There's no time to hide. We're going to have to jump him." She chanced another glimpse. "Ready?"

Swallowing, Molly nodded, steeling herself.

The next moment, Cary the Bristol House dog appeared from around the corner, powder puff tail wagging cheerily. He barked.

Molly exhaled sharply, bringing her hands to her hips. "Heather!"

Laughing and dropping to their knees next to the furry animal, both girls hugged and loved him up, Cary delighted to see them.

Cary happily led Heather and Molly from the Evermore Library, through a thick wooden door and into a wide cylindrical Bristol House turret. From there, they descended past the occasional small window and decorative hanging, brushing by a plainly planked attic entrance, the staircase continuing to hug the wall. Upon reaching a stretch of third floor hallway, the three passed a series of lofty doors, each unique unto itself. Unbeknownst to the girls, behind one that was formally and tastefully designed was a pair of frustrated Jagrulls.

"How do they do tha', eh, Lurz? I ken't seem te tie this thinger."

Still on their mandatory Bristol House vacation, the Jagrulls Lurz and Horvin were trying on finely tailored suits inside a contemporary men's clothing boutique. Fed up and done with it, Lurz had shed his new attire all over the floor near a full-length mirror, and had taken to redressing. Horvin was standing alongside a formally dressed mannequin, attempting to tie his necktie of choice in similar fashion. Irritated, collar up, he was pulling it loose once more, starting over.

"Ken yah not help me with this, already, Lurz?"

"Nah, not fer the likin', yah betcha I won't. Horvin, yah shop like my TrueMaite, only yah take a lot longer in the laggin'."

"Look a'this, will yah? A thin strip o' cloth, like a perty bloyder snake. A stupid HumanKinder fashion, if ever there was one, yea. I say, let's go back te tha' hat shop, Lurz, where we ken dilly-make our own."

Lurz was drearily looking out the shop's large front window, the sun low in the clouded sky.

"I think yah're getting a bit frilly 'bout the brain, juss like yur hats yah keep piled back there in the hall with all th'other souvenirs o' yurs. Me, I don't care fer fancy hats, I don't care fer walking sticks, or fer suits with their irritatin', snake-choking collars. I juss want te get home, already. I want te spend some time with my 'Maite and my brood."

Horvin drew up alongside, staring at the quaint small town street through the glass at the front of the shop. Spying his subtle reflection, he hoisted his chin and tightened his bowtie.

"What do yah think, now, o' me sportin' on the like?"

Lurz was impressed. "How'd yah manage to learn te tie tha' thinger?"

"I didn't. Juss took it off the stiff."

Lurz eyed the tieless, disheveled mannequin. "So yah did."

"Yah're lookin' blue as Lapis Lagoon, Lurz. Since we're plannin' te be on this lifelong vacation, wha' ken I do te help yah feel better righ' now? Just name it, 'grull."

"Know wha'? Like I tol' yah before, more than ever, I miss the hunt, Horvin, the kill, te trail the scent o' some un'spectin' prey. Right now, I'd fancy nothing more than te get my mouth sinking in on some HumanKinder flesh. Tha's what I'd like, right te flappin', and te lick clean them bones when I'm good and brimmin' fullup."

"And I'd love nothin' more than te help yah eat the juicy rascal. Yea, nothin' more."

"Then, let's see what we ken do about tha', scrumpin' on the hunt."

"But there's nothin' te be found nowheres, Lurz. Not another soul."

"Only 'cuz we've not found the right door, 'grull. Grab tha' flashy new coat o' yurs, will yah? Let's get. There's got te be some HumanKinders 'round here somewheres."

The girls rushed raucously down the stairs, spilling noisily into the kitchen, Cary on their heels. Mrs. Pringle looked up from her quiet glass of wine, Grandma Dawn's recipe books spread around her on the table.

"Hi, there, girls. Looks like you're having fun."

"We are, Mom," gushed Molly, giggling some more. She wiped her eyes.

"Were you out?" Mrs. Pringle asked.

"Kinda," said Heather. She and Molly exchanged a look and burst out laughing.

The woman shook her head. "And what's gotten the pair of you into such a silly state?"

Molly said, casually, "Oh, nothing." She paused. The girl glanced sidelong at Heather, and, sharing a twinkling, they broke into hearty laughter once more, Mrs. Pringle returning to the recipe books with a roll of her eyes.

When the uproar subsided, the woman added, "I was thinking of cooking something light tonight, something simple. It's been a long day, and I'm feeling somewhat pooped out."

"Mom, the visual on that—"

"Tuckered out."

The girls were sliding into their chairs, radiating seemingly boundless energy. Mrs. Pringle enjoyed the liveliness and was glad for their company.

"Whatever you'd like to eat for dinner, I'm okay with it, Mrs. Pringle," said Heather. "We can even cook it, if you'd like us to help. Right, Molly?"

"Shouldn't be that difficult, thank you, Heather. But you can certainly set and clear the table. I'll take care of the rest."

"Okay with me."

"Me, too, Mom."

Cary came to a rest on the floor, settling between the girls, Mrs. Pringle noticing without comment. Finally, she said, "You *are* providing your friendly stray with food and water, I hope."

"Cary? Yeah, he finds everything he needs on the third floor somewhere."

"He's the Bristol House dog, Mom. I think he watches over the place."

"Good," said Mrs. Pringle, turning her attention to Cary. "We can certainly use a good watchdog."

Following a sip of wine, her nose back in the pages of her book, she added, "I popped by earlier, and you weren't in your rooms. If you don't mind my saying, if not out and about, I'm guessing you both spent the better part of the afternoon exploring on the third floor."

Mrs. Pringle waited, the room suddenly losing its verve. Sensing the change, displaying mild curiosity, she turned her attention to the girls, her eyes sliding between them. Both were unforthcoming. Pursing her lips, the woman coolly returned to the page. "I see. So, I guess you *weren't* on the third floor, after all. And if not, may I ask where?" She waited. "Girls?" Neither offered. "All right, then—"

"We were in Evermore, Mrs. Pringle."

Molly shot a look of surprise at Heather.

"Well, why in heaven's name didn't you want to tell me?"

"Because it can be pretty—" Heather was going to conclude with the word *hairy,* but never got the chance.

"We didn't want to worry you, Mom," gushed Molly, running over her friend's words.

"Well, if it's so pretty, like Heather said, I don't see any need to withhold your traveling there from me."

"You're right. And I'm sorry."

"I understand, Molly, your want for privacy," said Mrs. Pringle, in mild rebuke. "But to you I have to play Mom, and to Heather, her guardian until her grandmother's return. I consider you both very responsible, but every magical Oz has its share of wicked witches."

"Funny, Mom, you should use that phrase—"

"We know that, Mrs. Pringle. We also know you have a lot on your mind, right now," said Heather, recalling Molly's words from the Shady House. "So, like Molly said, we don't want to worry you too much. We really don't."

Heather's sentiments seemed to mollify Mrs. Pringle. An

appreciative smile found her lips, gratitude lighting her eyes. She sipped her wine. "So, Evermore, what's it like?"

"Well," Heather briefly met Molly's gaze, "it can be very beautiful. The first time we went, there was this really, *really* great parade! Really super fantastic, huh, Molly?" Vigorous nods. "There was music and people all around, with everyone dressed up in costumes. And we got these crazy—really crazy!—treats, didn't we?" More nods. "A really fun kind of candy you eat like a game."

In all her Heather honesty, the youngster thought it high time to divulge all—both good and bad—even though she knew such a confession would place future Evermorian journeys in jeopardy. And, as tired as she was, she felt Mrs. Pringle was right, that as Molly's mother and her guardian, she needed to know everything. "And then things got *really* sorta hair—"

"Hold on a moment, if you would, Heather." The woman was sliding her chair away from the table. "Is that the telephone?" Mrs. Pringle rose. "I'm expecting a call from Molly's Aunt Liz. Excuse me, girls."

They watched her scurry out of the room, heard her footsteps hurrying down the hallway, now picking up speed in an effort to reach the phone before it stopped ringing.

"You were going to tell her, weren't you?"

Heather nodded. "Yeah."

"How much?"

"Pretty much all of it."

Quiet settled between them. Molly stifled a yawn. "It would have wrecked everything."

"I know, but she expects us to be responsible. She's your Mom. Besides, I couldn't just lie, even if it meant we wouldn't be allowed to go to Evermore anymore…and, you know, it kinda seems right, doesn't it, with all the stuff that's happened… I mean, she should know, right? Don't you think…? I mean…" Shrug. "…I mean, *you* know…" The girl threw out her hand, shaking her head in explanation. "I mean…I mean…" Frustrated, she slumped back in her chair. "Aw-w-w, I don't know *what* I mean." Then, on a sudden realization, Heather swiftly rose. "Come on, Molly, we have to get out of here."

"Why?"

"Just come on. You know the Bristol House, how it works. Hurry."

"What are you saying?"

Heather was racing out of the kitchen door, shuffling and

skidding into the hall, before mounting the stairs in twos and threes. Cary was scrambling on her heels, Molly trying to keep up with the both of them. Mrs. Pringle, meanwhile, could be seen down the hallway, headed back toward the kitchen.

"Where're you kiddos flying off to?"

"Upstairs." Molly dared to slow. "Was that Aunt Lizzie?"

"No. And whoever *was* on the phone never said a thing." The woman added, "Supper will be ready in an hour. Please see to it you're both on time."

chapter Thirteen

On the Wings of a MissivePlane

Dinner had been a quietly lethargic affair, Heather and Molly both sleepy, their exhaustion from their recent Evermorian experiences catching up to them. As a matter of fact, both were having trouble staying awake while sitting at the table.

"…and I hope you don't mind, but you see, I've thought about it, Mrs. Pringle. And I'd really be happy to tell you all about Evermore—" Heather couldn't help herself and yawned, covering her mouth. "Excuse me." Feeling dull, she tried to focus. "But I think it would only wreck it for you. You know, it's hard to describe Evermore's unbelievable…its unbelievable…"

"Ambiance?"

"Yeah, Molly, its ambiance and all that stuff. I mean, there's tons of ambiance all *over* the place there." Heather continued her verbal drift and slog. "So, really, I think you need to go and see all that unbelievable Evermore ambiance for yourself. I think you'll see that it's really…really…really *ambionic.* Don't you think so, Molly?"

"Yes."

"Yeah. Me, too."

Seeing how tired the girls were, the woman seemed satisfied and, for the present, saw no need to pursue the subject further.

"Get your shopping done?" asked Molly.

"I did. You'll be pleasantly surprised, I think, at what I bought you for Christmas. Heather, too. I really had fun picking out your gifts this year. Which reminds me, since Mr. Talbott will be joining us for dinner on Tuesday, I bought him a little something from all of us."

"Great. So, *that's* why you're looking through all those recipe books."

"True."

"What did you get him?"

"One second, Molly." Mrs. Pringle tapped her glass lightly with her spoon. "Heather, dear, if you don't wake up, your head is going to fall straight into your meal."

Heather shook herself awake, then reddened. "Sorry."

"I think that maybe you and Molly should wash up and head straight to bed after dinner. I'll take care of the cleanup."

"Are you sure?"

"As sure as you're about to become the first person since Dinosaur Dan to drown in their broccoli-beef stir-fry."

Cary growled low from the foot of the bed. The door opening on the half, brilliance streaked into Heather's room from the hallway.

"Heather, are you awake?"

"Yeah...yeah." Squinting, blinking, she reared her head. "Come on in." Heather rubbed her eyes in the thickness of night, her features lit softly by the spattering of Christmas lights adorning her room.

Clad in her pajamas, Molly closed the bedroom door and quietly approached the bed. Heather pulled back the covers, and her companion climbed in alongside her.

"Guess you can't sleep either," said Molly.

"I did for a while. I dreamt about a lot of weird stuff, but then I woke up. After that, I couldn't get back to sleep. What about you?"

"Like you, I slept for a while. Then I guess, after waking up, I started thinking too much."

Heather shifted and tugged on the covers, trying to get comfortable. Cary arose and, circling in place, resettled. He yawned with a squeak.

After a time, Molly said, "Mind if I ask what's keeping you awake?"

"Oh, you know, things about our trip, I guess, and how we just left Archie, Sedgwar, Starbrill, and all those guys wondering what the heck happened to us. I mean, they must have kept going, right, ending up in SummersBreath Still. Makes me wonder what they thought when we didn't show up."

"That all?"

"No. I've been thinking about a lot more."

Molly waited. She offered, lightly, "Like?"

"Stuff. Lots and lots of stuff." Heather drew a deep breath and lowered her voice to a whisper. "Stuff." The girl repositioned herself moodily. She noticed the moon, near full, shining through the windows of the turret room. "And, well, if you forget that I feel like I should be in Evermore right now, I'm also sorta wondering…Archie, Sedgwar, the Maidens, everyone else we met on our trip, will we ever see them again? That's some of it, anyway."

"You know, Heather, I'd like to say, 'Why wouldn't we see them again?' But I really can't when I'm thinking some of those very same thoughts."

The two lay quiet. Molly looked at the colorful Christmas lights throughout the room, lights that gave off a touch of cheer and comfort in the night. It added to the Bristol House coziness, lifting her spirits somewhat. When a fire suddenly swelled in the fireplace, appreciative, Molly was the only one who cared to take notice, focusing on the dance of flames.

"I wonder, Heather," she said, dreamily, "when we go back to Evermore again, how old will we be, how much time will have passed? What shape will Evermore be in? And will I see Starbrill? If I do, and we return too far into the future, will he have a girlfriend or TrueMaite by then? A family, even? And it's frustrating, because there's no way I can be around him right now other than to wait until we return, until the Bristol House allows us to go. And it's not like Starbrill and I can stay in touch by writing or with phone calls."

"Well, Molly," said Heather, turning to face her bedmate, propping her head on her bunched-up pillow. "You once told me not to think the worst. And I try, I really do, but as you can see, it's not an easy thing to do, is it?"

"No…no, it's not. Not at all. And I miss Pallár, Heather, and never really had a chance to say goodbye to him or to Starbrill, to Toya…or anyone."

Heather shrugged. "I think, Molly, this is just one of those really tough things, you know? I mean, like with Grandma Dawn, it's kinda hard not to think about her and not want to do something to be with her. But there's really nothing I can do except maybe let time give with time. Know what I mean?

"I guess, Molly, what I'm trying to say is, it sounds like you'll probably have to do the same with Starbrill. And maybe that means you can *hope* to see him again, and do your best to make it come true, but then kinda just let it all happen as it happens, because, really, we can't do anything else. And if we want things to hurry and be different, and go stomping around because they're not happening fast enough, it'll only make us miserable. Trust me. I know."

"Does that mean I shouldn't miss Starbrill, while ignoring any thoughts of him—just putting him completely out of my mind?"

"Heck, no. I think of Grandma Dawn a lot, and miss her all the time. Every day. Just know you'll see him when you can."

Before the quiet could settle comfortably between them, Heather said, "Hey, Molly, wasn't it you who told me this exact same thing once? Or something like it?" Not waiting for a reply, Heather ventured onward, "Anyway, if it makes you feel any better, I bet the Bristol House knows what'll happen, whether you'll see Starbrill again. But you know what? I also have a feeling its not going tell us a thing."

With a glance at the ceiling, Molly chuckled. "I have that feeling, too."

"You know what I think we need to do, Molly? I think we need to think about other things, and concentrate on Mr. Simpletripp instead. Until we go back."

"Mr. Simpletripp? But what about practicing the MaidenWay, Heather, about not putting yourself in danger?"

"Who says we'll be putting ourselves in danger? We'll just have to be careful, that's all."

"Oh-h-h, I don't know about this, Heather."

"I do."

"You sure?"

"Yeah. Positive."

"All right, then. Mr. Simpletripp it is. When do we start?"

"I already have. That's another reason I haven't been able to sleep. You? You start tomorrow."

From the foot of the bed, Cary came up to nestle between the girls. Molly draped her arm over him and snuggled closer. It wasn't long before she and the Bristol House dog fell asleep. Heather never did.

"You just missed her, Molly." Seated in the kitchen, Mrs. Pringle was looking up from her morning tea and paper. "Heather was only here for a second and said to tell you she'd be up in the library— Wait! Aren't you going to eat breakfast?"

Mrs. Pringle's answer came from the hallway. "I'll have it at lunch!"

Standing before a bookcase in the Evermore Library, Heather heard the large entry door slam. "Molly, I'm over here!" she shouted.

Out of breath from running past the circular stage and up an aisle, Molly trundled into the lighted corridor, the girl glancing at books high and low as she passed. It wasn't long before she spotted Heather, a large volume spread open in her hands.

"Don't you just love libraries?" asked Molly between huffs, collecting herself.

"Yeah, especially when I don't have to go hunting for books."

"What do you mean?"

"Well, I was walking in front of these shelves, you know, exploring, reading the titles of these guys as I went. When I got to this spot here, right where I'm standing, I said, 'Hey, I wish I could find some books on Portals.' So, when I looked at the shelf in front of me, suddenly there were a bunch of them, Portals galore!"

"Had they been there all along?"

"Nope. And check this out." Heather showed her the cover of the tome she was holding.

"*The LostPortals of Evermore.* I love the title. What's it about?"

Heather drew a lopsided grin. "The LostPortals of Evermore."

Molly giggled. "I know *that,* silly. But, briefly, what's the book about?"

"I don't know. I just pulled it off the shelf a second ago. Come on. Pick a book and let's go sit on the stage, on our couches."

"I think my book on the Ancient Archannites is still there. But just in case…" Molly turned to the bookshelf, saying, "I wish I could find some books on the Ancient Archannites of Evermore." For several moments, the books blurred and whirred past along the shelves—like a colorful game show wheel—before slowing to a climactic standstill. Molly's face lit up. "Wow! It works."

She made her selection and the girls found their way down the aisle and onto the stage.

Approaching her self-appointed reading couch, Heather said, "Hey, look, Molly."

Curious, they set aside their books. From the cushion, Heather retrieved and held up an envelope.

"Who do you think put it there?" Molly glanced at her couch, and was mildly disappointed to find it lacked a similar surprise.

"Beats the heck out of me. I guess it's just been sitting here the whole time we were busy looking at books. It has my name on it, too. And on the back, this wax seal has the greatest little picture stamped into it. Look! It's some kind of Evermorian symbol of a big bowl that has wings, with lines of magic-looking steam curling out."

"Here, let's see." Upon receiving the envelope, she studied the red circular seal. "Beautiful, Heather! I wonder what it means? Actually, come to think of it, it looks a lot like that big pot in the middle of the room. Don't you think? Here. Open it."

Letter in hand, Heather compared the image on the circular waxen stamp to that of the GlissenCauldron.

"Hey, Molly, you know, I think you're right."

She ran her finger over the seal and then pressed on it, like a button. It clicked, and the envelope suddenly changed shape.

"Whoa."

Molly giggled. "It turned into a paper airplane. So, what now?"

The girls looked excitedly at one another: "Throw it!"

Heather gave the Missive a flick of the wrist and they watched as the paper plane with the red seal on its fuselage circled lazily above, before descending in an elegant swoop directly toward the wide-open mouth of the GlissenCauldron.

"Uh-oh!" Lunging, Heather tried to catch the Missive as it glided past, but the crafty craft swerved to elude her fingertips and continue its course.

"Drat!"

Plunging nose-first into the great 'Cauldron, the 'Plane disappeared from view.

"Heather," said Molly, drawing closer. "Look at the pot…"

The GlissenCauldron's light was intensifying, surging, becoming appreciably brighter. The girls stood captivated, their faces full of anticipation, full of the glow.

Molly shrieked and shrank away as, from within the large vessel, a blinding light flashed and dimmed.

"Molly…?"

"What?"

"Look."

The cringing girl dared to open her eyes.

There, in front of the pair, looming large—far larger than life—above the lip of the GlissenCauldron floated a beautiful face in a paper-thin veneer of golden light.

Overcome with awe, Heather said, simply, “Grandma Dawn.”

The impressive vision wavered, fading and strengthening against the blackness of the room. She faced the girls.

“Heather Nighborne?”

“It’s me, Grandma Dawn. I’m right here.”

“Yes.” Grandma Dawn paused. And then: “Dearest Heather, I hope my magical MissivePlane finds you well and in good spirits. I’ve been meaning to contact you right along, to send you greetings and information from Evermore, but unfortunately until this moment, I have found it unsafe to do so, for so many lines of communication have been compromised. And even then, I’m not so sure this message will find its way solely into your hands, and so trust you will forgive me if I’m spare of detail.

“Nevertheless, I wanted to let you know that I am well, and that though it took some time, I’ve completely recovered from the wounds I suffered during my encounter with the TimeLight Assassin. So, you mustn’t worry on that account. As well, I was able to do as planned afterward, seeing to it his body was safely moved to be discovered elsewhere, averting further danger from our home. Avella, I’m pleased to say, has completely healed also, though most unfortunately has lost an arm where she was struck in your defense.

“But you must not let this news be burdensome upon your conscience, young One. She is proud, Heather, and could be no prouder to have sacrificed in your honor, in an effort to sustain your life, that of our Astille Lia Staleen DiYoh. This she has done for the good of the MaidenHood and, more importantly, the Light in the Realm. After all, here in Evermore such is a Maiden’s purpose; such is the MaidenWay. She is a fearless warrior having served in fulfillment of her duty, and, for that, we owe her a great debt of gratitude. Among us, she is held in high esteem.”

The floating face paused, and her look grew pensive. “Young Heather, I do wish I could see you now, this very moment, and hear you speak of your latest thoughts and plans, and watch as you go about your daily routines…” Her voice softened, “…to see your lovely face, see you laugh again…” Momentarily quiet, adrift, Grandma Dawn’s next words regained their stoic assertiveness. “However, I realize such an extravagant request is simply too much to ask for in these difficult and turbulent times, and so trust it will wait for a more opportune moment, on a far brighter day.

"And my duties that hold me here in Evermore will continue to fill my days from sunup till sundown, and most often into the night. Please do remember, not a day goes by that I do not think of you, and that you are always with me, always in my heart. And I've no doubt that I am there with you, too."

"You are, Grandma Dawn, you are…" Heather's eyes brimmed, her silent tears finding their course. She bit her trembling lip, watching as her grandmother's fluctuating apparition continued to hold forth.

"I cannot tell you much more, though know that Evermorian preparation for your eventual return has us constantly on the move. And although I know where we are going, how we intend to arrive there I cannot say. To do so would expose far too much to risk. All I know is that we in Evermore, here, are lost, and it's looking like we'll become even more lost by the time all is said and done. At that, I'm so very glad you are the One chosen to eventually find us.

"I have heard stories of your battle at TiaraReign CityHeights, for they are sung with high praise here among the Maidens and shared in secrecy between hopeful citizens in all the Realm. Such bravery!" The woman's great face shone with pride, with a smile. It soon faded.

"Sadly, in the course of your most recent journey you have come to witness firsthand the current state of our once beautiful Realm. It now desperately awaits its green-eyed Maiden of the Evermore Portent, and with her its Golden Reclamation.

"Perhaps it will be on one of your upcoming visits that we will see each other again, and, if so, may the Universe allow this meeting to take place soon. Do take care and be well. And please try not to worry for my sake. Have a Merry Christmas with Molly and Mrs. Pringle, and be sure to give them my regards. I will communicate when time and opportunity allows. Until I see you again…all my love, my beautiful, beautiful girl, my precious Heather." The words grew fainter. "All my love…all my love to all…"

The image flickered and dimmed, before dissolving into shiny bits, the sprinkling of colorful dust disappearing into the mouth of the GlissenCauldron. From within, the golden light swelled anew as if prompted by a sigh. Emerging shortly thereafter was the MissivePlane, flying once around overhead to land as a sealed envelope upon the couch nearest Heather. There it sat until a wistful Heather picked it up and slipped it inside her back pocket, to be deposited later into her BodyTote, in a flap located nearest her heart.

chapter fourteen

On Christmas Vacation

"What's today, Molly?"

"It's Monday morning."

"Already?"

Heather sat up in bed, blinking irritably at the sunlight through her turret room windows. Unbeknownst to Molly, she had returned home just before sunup. Restless and unable to sleep, she had spent a good portion of the night wandering the neighborhood streets, spying on Mr. Simpletripp at one point, and then heading up to the Evermore Library to replay the spectacular message from Grandma Dawn.

It had been her routine for several nights now.

During the daylight hours, she and Molly had been spending a majority of their time together, Christmas shopping on the festive courthouse square, exploring and ice skating on the third floor of the Bristol House, and clandestinely watching Mr. Simpletripp for short intervals when they could find him. Today promised to be no different.

"Missed you at breakfast." said Molly, sitting on the edge of the bed, eliciting a slight bounce upon landing. Already dressed, she was fresh and full of the morning. "I looked in earlier, and you were still asleep, so I didn't wake you."

"Great. Thanks."

"Mom's excited. Mr. Talbott's coming to dinner tomorrow

night."

"Oh, yeah," said Heather, unenthusiastically, "Mr. Talbott." She scratched her head.

"She was going on and on about it this morning—not a lot, but a lot for her, if you know what I mean."

"Yeah, I know what you mean." Heather threw off the covers.

Grumpy and disheveled, without a glance for the Christmas décor, she moped toward the turret room in her pajamas. Finding place at its westernmost window, she gazed down the hill at the Simpletripp house. Molly followed and sat on a chair nearby. She picked up a magazine.

"You don't like him much, do you?"

"It's hard to, Molly. He's such a creepy guy."

"Mr. Talbott?"

"Oh…sorry. I thought you were talking about Mr. Simpletripp. He had his basement door open again late last night, you know. The light was on. He was doing something in there, Molly, I just couldn't see what. But then, after a while, he started loading up that old junk car of his. And after that, he drove off, before coming back to unload some stuff. Later, it looked like he loaded it all back up again."

"Where do you think he was going?"

Heather pulled a face, never turning from the window. "No clue."

"What was he loading into the car?"

"I watched him for a while. When he came back the first time, I tried, but I couldn't see what he was doing in the basement *or* carrying back and forth to the car. So, it's a mystery to be solved."

Heather withheld that she had actually sneaked up to the partially open basement door, able to glimpse only a portion of his open freezer against the far wall, behind a table. When she heard Mr. Simpletripp approaching, she withdrew and disappeared into the night.

"So, you couldn't sleep again?"

"Nope."

"Are you sure you shouldn't tell Mom? Maybe she can think of something that'll help."

"That's all right, Molly. Thanks, anyway. Really. I'll be okay in a little bit. I think I just need to play Grandma Dawn's message every night before bedtime."

"Why?"

"I don't know. It just feels good, I guess."

"You know, you could always come and wake me. And if you go

out, I'd love to go with you. It's Christmas vacation, so I don't have to worry about school."

"I actually thought about it. And I'd really like you to come, too, but you should probably get as much sleep as you can."

Heather didn't mention that without Molly there, she could take more chances and be more daring should any situation arise that required stealth. She also didn't confide that several times when she had been walking, Heather thought she was being followed, but was unable to spot an aura.

Once or twice, she saw the familiar boxy green car, too. And that was weird, that the funny little car had a way of seeming to find her, to pass by when she was on some deserted little road somewhere or walking by a bunch of gloomy houses. She never could see past the car's darkened windows, either, to get a glimpse of who was driving or how many passengers were inside.

No, when she roamed at night like that, it was just too dangerous, and Heather figured it best she did it alone.

She flashed on an idea, a compromise of sorts. "How about tonight, after your mom goes to bed, we sneak out to the treehouse and spy on Mr. Simpletripp? Without December's normal ice or snow, it shouldn't be too dangerous climbing up there, and, heck, with the warm weather, it'll be a lot of fun."

Molly was up for it. "I'll bring the snacks."

"And I'll make sure not to forget the spyglass. Should be a full moon, too, so that'll help light the way."

"All right. That's settled, then," said Molly. "And that leaves all of today. So, let's see... All our Christmas shopping is finished, the packages are wrapped and under the tree, so there's nothing left that has to get done. Mom will be off to work soon, so we pretty much can do whatever we want all day long."

Heather eyed Molly. "What do *you* want to do?"

"It's going to be warm again today. Doesn't seem too Christmassy for Noble, does it?"

"This weather is so weird, Molly. No rain, no snow—no clouds. But at least it's not too cold when I go out late. Actually, it's been kinda warm these last few nights."

"Well, I have an idea. How about a Christmas movie in the Art Deco Theatre this morning? That'll get us in the mood."

"Our favorite?" Heather was getting excited. "The one we watch every year?"

"Absolutely."

"Hello, Bedford Falls!" Enthusiastic, Heather danced away from the windows in a twirl. She jogged into her room and began to hurriedly dress, slipping into her pants. "Molly, I can smell the popcorn this very minute!"

Lana Pringle was at the front counter of the library, working through her shift, a shift that seemed interminably long.

Another slow day, she thought, preferring instead to lose track of herself and her working hours in a slur of busyness.

She had assumed there would be more students catching up on their homework over the holidays, but as it turned out, such was not the case.

And who can blame them, she mused. They're probably out shopping and horsing around, taking advantage of this beautiful weather. If I were young again, I know I'd be.

Mrs. Pringle gave thought to spending Christmas with Heather and Molly. We'll have a great time, she told herself. The magical Bristol House sure has a way of lifting everyone's spirits. And no Ned this year—the greatest Christmas gift of all.

She chuckled and, bored, looking for busywork, began to wipe down the counter.

"Lana, are we still on for Tuesday night?"

Mrs. Pringle jumped.

"Oh! Hi, Wilson. You startled me. I-I didn't see you walk up."

"My apologies. I certainly didn't mean to give you a fright," he lied. Having arrived before her shift, he'd been watching Lana Pringle from between the racks, seeing how she moved, where she went, wondering what she was thinking. It hadn't been the first time.

Talbott felt a supreme sense of power when spying on an individual, when they hadn't the slightest clue in the world that he was hidden nearby, observing their every uninhibited movement. He also felt that same sense of power when frightening someone like he just had, able to walk up at exactly the right moment and catch them unawares, to completely disrupt the reigning calm in their world.

"You're not working today?"

"Actually, Lana, I took the day off."

Talbott could still feel his body aching from his fall off the Bristol House staircase. His stitched and swollen calf continued to smart, as well. It didn't help that he had stubbornly resumed delivering upon his mail route despite the injuries, only serving to aggravate them all the more.

"Anything wrong?"

"No. No, nothing," said Talbott. "I just thought it a good day to relax, browse the books, take some time to myself."

"I see. Well, I hope you're not expecting too much tomorrow night. The dinner won't be extravagant in any way—"

"Don't you worry yourself on that account," he chuckled, stepping aside, making room for a patron. "Remember, I'm a bachelor…" catching her eye, he let the words linger just long enough, "…and can't be too picky. If I were, you can rest assured I'd never be invited out to dinner."

"And, may I ask," said Mrs. Pringle, playfully, as she finished wiping the counter, "when's the last time an eligible bachelor such as yourself *was* invited to dinner?" She set aside the cloth.

"Well, funny you should inquire, really. There was an older gentleman along my mail route, a man named Thaddeus Levine. He'd recently lost his wife, you see, and, so, we began to chat more and more frequently. We became fast friends and would have dinner quite often. We grew close." Talbott's empty grin seemed to free-float on his face, as if it were part of a mobile suspended on a string from his nose. And like a heatless fire, it lacked warmth and existed for the pure pleasure of display only—much like the lighting of his attractive blue eyes, heartless, perceptive, startling blue eyes, deceptive eyes that shielded other thoughts entirely.

He glimpsed the woman impatiently awaiting Lana Pringle's attention. The man chuckled. "I see I should go, now," he said with a wink. "Things to do. People to see. An entire day to embrace. And just think, not a single envelope to deliver." Full of good humor, he began edging away toward the set of entry doors across the lobby.

"Goodbye, Wilson," she said, turning to greet Mrs. Downcladd-Rumpleskirt, the woman sliding several books her way across the squeaky clean counter. Giving a final glance toward the departing Talbott, she noted with surprise that he was limping.

With the splash of light from the large screen in the Art Deco Theatre illuminating her face, Molly murmured, "Mary is so nice, so pretty, George would be an absolute *dope* not to marry her. Besides, she may be a small town girl, and might not have traveled the world, but I bet she's smart, has a broad vocabulary, and has read a lot of books on most every subject. Don't you think she's exceptional…?"

When Molly didn't get a response, she turned to the seat next to her. Eyes closed, head tilted slightly, Heather had fallen asleep.

Molly gazed upon her friend's open countenance, her lovely features influenced by the screen's soft play of dancing light. Molly couldn't help but think that when she was older, Heather would definitely be as beautiful as Mary. Even more beautiful, if such a thing were possible.

Heather shifted, some of her popcorn spilling into her lap, trickling onto the floor. Molly gently removed the tall, red-striped bag from her relaxed hands, ever so careful not to wake her.

In the back room of the Clay Pigeon Gallery, Mr. Simpletripp was admiring the sculptures he had recently removed from the kiln. Each in turn, he held them up or crouched before their faces, loving the way the glaze had dripped and run between their features.

"Like kiln-inspired blood…"

And all perfect likenesses, he thought, studying the last of his hollowed-out creations. Now I only have to fill and seal them.

He heard the front door chime, indicating someone had entered the gallery. Hoping for a holiday sale, he almost pounced out of the back room and onto the sales floor, aggressive as he was, only to discover his visitor was Sheriff Dane. Mr. Simpletripp eyed the slender black man with undisguised annoyance.

"What can I do for you, Sheriff? Christmas is just around the corner. Finally decide to make that long awaited purchase for the wife?"

Dane ignored the question, not bothering to mention that he had already done so, but elsewhere.

"Busy?" The sheriff was looking around the art gallery, looking past Mr. Simpletripp, before focusing on the closed door leading to the backroom.

"It's Christmas. What do *you* think?"

"I think I don't see anyone," said the Sheriff, genially. "A lot of work stored in the back?" Curious, he wouldn't mind having a peek behind the scenes, although he doubted Simpletripp was stupid enough to have anything incriminating on hand. And yet, the big bully liked to tease, liked to push limits and challenge authority. He could be reckless that way.

"Yeah. There's a lot back here." Simpletripp was snide, cocky. "A *lot.*"

He stood in standoff at a distance, an imposing and rabid defender stationed between the sheriff and the back room door.

"Then you wouldn't mind if I had a look."

"Not at all, you show me your search warrant."

Pleasant and unperturbed, Dane was again glancing around, this time at the art, saying, "I've been checking on your neighbor, Mr. Thaddeus Levine. I was at his house earlier, and there's still no sign of him."

"Have you thought of putting out an All Points Bulletin, Sheriff?"

Dane managed a wrinkle of amusement at the remark. He concentrated on the display case close by, full of the same jewelry he'd seen upon his last visit. "Since you have so few visitors, I was sure that if Mr. Levine *had* come in here, you'd remember the exact time and day."

Simpletripp's great bulk settled stone still, his dead eyes resting heavily upon the sheriff. The silence hung leadenly between them, like a weighty powder keg awaiting the spark of greater friction.

The big man finally snarled, "If he stops by with Elvis, Sheriff, I'll be sure and let you know."

"I'd be obliged."

Vera Simpletripp was engrossed, her small fingers on her small hand guiding the tiny pair of scissors, the childlike shears cutting painstakingly through the heart of the red construction paper. Slowly the metal blades advanced, squeezing, sliding, and edging their way to create the curved lips that she would paste into place upon his pink oval face.

Such a sweet and handsome face it was, too!

The colors of her artistic creation were basic, and the shapes were crude, but the thought was simple and pure, deeply felt and held. And the smiles were happy ones, the round cheeks ever so rosy, and the eyes ever so clear in this fanciful world of the mind.

She decided to add v-shaped birds to the sky and, so, picking up her black paper began to cut.

Earlier, after her husband had barged and blustered off to work, Mrs. Simpletripp had fully intended on going Christmas shopping. And, yet, when she left the house to do so, something happened when she passed The Gilded Brush and Palette on the square. Compelled to venture inside, she had picked up a pad of assorted colored papers and a jar of paste. She also bought a small pair of grade school scissors—even though she had in her possession some very fine dressmaking shears at home. Horace would never approve of the unnecessary expenditure, this she knew. Nevertheless, on that very thought, she added to the mix a small box of crayons.

And now, in the sublime sanctuary of her kitchen, the scissors sounded annoyingly loud each time she set them down with a clack. And she wasn't so clean with the paste, either, making a small sticky mess when she applied the adhesive, getting it on the tabletop. But she was almost finished, and the essentials of her vision almost complete.

Next, Mrs. Simpletripp cut two small circles. They didn't quite look like freshly baked cookies when glued in place—they hardly looked like circles!—but she knew what they were and, to her, that's all that mattered.

Spreading the crayons on the table, using them to add the final flourishes throughout, she lost herself in her work for an hour or more. In the throes of concentration, her tongue sometimes found its way to actively curl in a corner of her mouth and, later, unconsciously sweep along her lips. She completely skipped lunch.

And when she used an indigo crayon to make her gray eyes brighter, she was thoroughly satisfied.

"There," she said with finality, sitting back, admiring the finished product.

Pasty fingertips squeezing her lower lip, she scrutinized her small attempt at art, thinking the arc of the rainbow not quite symmetrical enough, and the house that sat high upon it too misshapen, and the few clouds on either side too puffy. Was the yellow sun large and bright enough?

"Doesn't matter," she concluded. The two people eating cookies on the porch were perfect. And her creation brought her closer to the dream.

Setting the picture preciously aside, Vera Simpletripp put everything away, hiding her morning's purchases at the bottom of her sewing box before wiping down the table. When the doorbell rang, she jumped, but ignored it, knowing in her heart it wasn't that someone special. It could never be him. And then afterward, dismissing the interruption, for the longest time she sat and stared at her artwork.

Glancing at the clock, she was startled at the time, realizing

Horace could very well walk in any moment after the noon hour traffic had waned at the gallery—if the Clay Pigeon had had any. He'd done it before. Walking her creation hurriedly—but carefully—to the fireplace, laying it down tenderly on the ash-filled hearth, she struck a flame to one corner. And then she watched her perfect world burn away.

The afternoon was wearing gratingly on Mr. Simpletripp and, disturbingly enough, doing so with very few customers. Worse still, there were no sales. Not a one. Mr. Simpletripp had never seen the Clay Pigeon gallery so dead, so in need of buyers amid the usual bustle of the holiday season. And to think he used to brag about the Pigeon being unable to survive without his guidance.

It didn't help that he had gotten rid of his best-selling artists, forcing them to leave by ripping them off in some fashion, including shortchanging them on the percentage due from their sales—or by needlessly bashing heads with them, spreading malicious lies, or *misplacing* their artwork. So difficult and stubborn was the man that, each time, their disagreements ended in verbal abuse coupled with the threat of physical harm—and sometimes a period of overt stalking.

After all, Horace Simpletripp saw himself as bad news, as the rough and tumble enforcer, the supreme leader, the one who held total and complete reign over his gallery till death do you part. So watch your foolish step.

Restless in the back room, the big man struggled to stay confined to the gallery, looking at the beautiful creations he had sculpted in a variety of sizes, small to large, each corresponding in likeness to the animals he had mutilated. It was their contents that he kept stored in the basement freezer, each bag carefully marked and numbered for identification, to be matched to its ceramic mate.

If he had his way, this very minute, he would just close up the gallery early like he had been doing these past few nights. And then he could rush home to unload and begin filling his empty sculptures with what remained of his victims—including their once beating hearts—in a masterful artistic endeavor if ever there was one. He'd even signed and numbered their vessels.

But, when completed, their sculptured coffins weren't kept here at the gallery, no, sir. And they'd never be offered for sale ever. And why? Because they belonged next to the hidden pond, that's why, in his greatest creation to date: his artistic cemetery. And it was growing, expanding—just like the Noble suburbs! *Simpletripp's Graveyard,* that's what he called his latest exhibition, although not a solitary soul would ever be permitted to see it. Not a one. Just him. And as with all great art these days, the public wasn't invited. And that's because the simpleminded fools of Noble would never understand. They couldn't. His masterful art was above them—as was the man, himself!

Mr. Simpletripp hoped that one day he'd die in a manner just as artistic, just as memorable. He deserved nothing less. And those animals owed him; they should thank him. After all, they were being immortalized, their lives living on long after they did, just like the pharaohs, like the great busts and sculptures you see in museums all over the world. His art was that good, his concept that original.

Yeah, that Horace Simpletripp, they'd say in the years to come, he was a genius, that man. Pure genius. An original. And a real bad boy—like Caravaggio.

And the world just *loves* bad boys.

For the gloating Simpletripp, much like his sculpting, killing animals had become a raging compulsion, an overwhelming desire that had consumed him since he could remember. Only back then, he hadn't always acted on it. But now, agitated this way, he found he was unable to restrain himself. And once the tension built up, feverishly escalating to the breaking point, it just had to find release. It just had to. There really wasn't a choice. If he didn't do something, his head would ache so severely, pound so hellishly, he truly felt as if it were about to explode.

Even now, his palms were nervously moist at the thought of his next victim, soon to be kidnapped and helpless under his hand.

Yes…soon, he thought, soon. Kindling that very spark of thought, he rode its comforting, feel-good heat.

It was at that moment that the gallery's door chime rang out. Swift to wipe his hands on his pants, he emerged from the back room with lumbering joviality.

"Can I help you?" he said, approaching the elderly woman and her granddaughter. In her arms, the young girl carried a small dog.

"Do you mind if we bring our puppy inside with us?" asked the woman.

"Not at all. I just *love* animals. All kinds." Simpletripp didn't try to be friendly by reaching out to the small black and brown creature. He knew better, recognizing long ago that animals simply didn't like him. The realization never sat well.

As a boy, he had killed both dogs he owned, burying their

dismembered remains in the woods, telling his mother they had run away. And when his eldest sister had left her Irish setter, Angel, in his care for the afternoon, the young Horace Simpletripp stood in front of their house, calling the dog's name, while he could hear him getting mauled by a pack of vicious predators within the tangle of hillside trees below. He never saw exactly what animals had attacked his sister's dog that day, yet, enthralled at the sounds of the conflict, imagining the destruction being inflicted to the silky strands of his mahogany coat, he did nothing to intercede.

Horace just kept calling, "Angel! Angel, come home!" until the snarling, barking, and yelping ceased. Only then did he retrieve a baseball bat from the garage and begin a search for him.

The dog almost died, costing his sister dearly in vet bills. Horace told his mother that Angel had somehow escaped their fenced-in yard, when in fact young Simpletripp had held the gate, encouraging the animal to run free, knowing full well the danger of doing so.

And, now, if asked, Mr. Simpletripp would tell you exactly how Angel had found his way out by digging under the fence, the big man fully believing his fabricated version of the story.

Yet, like so much of his misspent youth, the incident took place in Mr. Simpletripp's fully rationalized and reinvented past. And as such, all those incidents, all those dubious events, well, that was then, wasn't it, and not at all in the here and now. So, why bother to open the memory vault? In his view, there was absolutely no reason whatsoever to expose to the light those old tarnished recollections so brightly repainted and safely locked away—things like the death of his first wife.

"Welcome to the Clay Pigeon." The burly owner was gruff, but charming. "I'm the owner, Horace Simpletripp."

"Thank you. I'm Jennifer Wimple and this is Pauline. And the little one with her is Wilbur." Her eyes wandered the room. "This is our first time in your gallery."

"Are you new in town?"

"We are," said the woman, readdressing Simpletripp. "My granddaughter and I moved into the old Stanton place."

"On Scarlett Drive?"

"Yes."

"I know it well. Maybe I can interest you in some art for your new home?"

"Well, we don't have much time today, I'm afraid, but just wanted to stop in and have a look around. Do you mind?"

Mr. Simpletripp's demeanor darkened slightly in

disappointment, his manner becoming a bit more pointed. "Feel free." The words were cold.

"Grandma?"

"What Pauline?"

Disgusted, the girl had set the puppy down, her hands and arm loosely soiled, the floor all the more.

"Oh, Mr. Simpletripp," said the woman, "I'm so sorry, but little Wilbur has messed. And he's been so good, too. Can we bother you for some towels?"

Hard and heartless, without a word, Mr. Simpletripp turned and stalked away to procure some rags. Reaching the back room, he heard the front door chime and knew the pair had gone, taking their vile little creature with them—and leaving him to clean the mess.

Forehead pimpled with sweat, Wilson Talbott unlocked the front door and hobbled to a seat in his living room. Once there, he put up his foot, resting the weight on his heel. His calf was throbbing, killing him.

In hindsight, he should have stayed off it, taken the necessary time to let it heal properly. As for his hip and ribs, he undoubtedly should have done the same.

But whatever, he thought. Too late for self-recriminations.

Leaning back with a wince, Talbott swore under his breath, trying unsuccessfully to get comfortable, determined to ignore the stabbing pain.

So, he wondered, what to do with the pretty and soon to be divorced Lana Pringle, a woman he was beginning to find very much to his liking—and more than ever intended? Use her, that's what. Just use her. Exactly like all those other women in his life, only this time as something more than merely a tool for his own satisfaction and validation. Yes, use her to access Scarbone's treasure, as planned.

And where exactly does one begin a search for treasure in the Bristol House? Ah, well, he'd find the answer to that question tomorrow night at dinner. There'll be plenty of useful information to glean if one asks the right questions and stays keenly aware of the small things disclosed inadvertently, the casual embellishment, the comment within the comment.

Of the three hosts, Talbott felt Molly to be the most susceptible, the one most easily manipulated. Honest. Open. Trusting.

The perfect mark.

And, yet, if Scarbone's treasure did exist indoors, chances are Heather would be the one who knew where it was. But she seemed cagy, distrustful, and not at all inclined to share. However, there's a good chance she might have confided in Molly, which again pointed to the Pringle child as the key.

Too, Wilson Talbott realized that when it came to Heather, as a Nearling Maiden and possible Maiden Portent, she could very well pose a dangerous threat, so he had better tread cautiously for the time being. And, later, if things went as planned with Lana, maybe then he could find a way to get Heather forever out of the picture, making certain she met with an unfortunate accident—say, like a loose ladder rung on her treehouse hideaway giving way, or maybe a patch of unattached bark slipping free on the tree bridging the creek. Only this time, making certain such an exercise proved fatal to the girl's well-being.

As for Lana Pringle, the woman seems clueless about most everything. Even about me, about my motives.

Talbott wondered briefly why he had told Lana about Thaddeus Levine. Could it be he instinctively found her trustworthy? That meant he might possibly allow himself to get too close to the woman. For her, such a thing would be unhealthy, so unhealthy indeed. But, then again, it wasn't *his* health.

Yes, when people did get close to Wilson Talbott, things had a way of ending badly. Just ask Thaddeus Levine—if anyone can find him.

See? Talbott concluded, It just happens. It wasn't *his* fault Levine went bye-bye.

The scheming man realized a big question would be whether or not Scarbones, in his reincarnation as the house, would let him inside unmolested come Tuesday evening. But Talbott felt he would, and only because he had been invited and would be supervised during his stay.

So, let us see, shall we, what information is served up over dinner? Maybe after everyone has gone to sleep, I can find a way back inside and do some late night treasure hunting. And you better believe I'll be on the watch for an opening, *any* opening.

So, dinner, then. Six sharp. The perfect occasion for setting in motion *any* brilliantly conceived, wholly unscrupulous plan.

Chapter Fifteen

View from the Basement, View from the Treehouse, a Matter of Perspectives

"Think your Mom is asleep yet?" Heather was at the turret window, looking out on the starry night, the waxing of the full moon.

"Yes. We've given her plenty of time, don't you think?"

"Yeah. Unless she's still up worrying about tomorrow night's dinner with Mr. Talbott."

"She didn't talk about him when we were eating tonight, so that's a good sign."

"You like him, Molly?" Heather tried to sound casual, noncommittal with the question, wondering if her friend's opinion had changed.

"Mom does, I suppose." Molly shrugged, trying to hide her concern. "It makes her happy."

"Yeah. Yeah, I guess." Treading once more over delicate ground like she was, Heather didn't know what else to add, if anything. She let the topic go.

In preparation for their treehouse visit, the girls were wriggling into their light jackets, buttoning or zipping them up. Both of their backpacks were stuffed and ready to go, Heather's with the spyglass and her latest mystery book, and Molly's with goodies and some fashion magazines. Their flashlights they considered a treehouse essential, and so along with them, each had stowed extra batteries.

Heather had been tempted to bring the *Book of LostPortals,* but knew the oversized text would prove cumbersome. And besides, she and Molly had decided it was best they read all books from the Evermore Library while there and nowhere else. The beautifully bound volumes just seemed special, sacred in their way, and the girls wouldn't want anything to happen to them should they chance to bring them downstairs.

"Think Mr. Simpletripp is home?"

"It's too early yet, Molly. He'll get home in a couple of hours when the Clay Pigeon closes. Maybe sooner. I guess it depends how busy the gallery is tonight."

"Or if he just decides he wants to leave."

"Yeah, he has a way of coming and going whenever he wants, doesn't he?"

"When we've gone by the Clay Pigeon during the day, he sure doesn't look very busy in there. Even at Christmastime. Not like the other shops on the square."

"Can you blame people, Molly? I mean, who wants a bunch of sculptures that are supposed to be someone else, but they all look like him?"

"Mrs. Dentspire told Mom that there was a sculpture in his gallery of two girls that resembled you and me."

"Oh, yeah, great. Our clothes and hair with Mr. Simpletripp's face."

"Can you imagine?"

"Only if it's Halloween and we're out trick-or-treating."

Molly giggled. "Ready?"

"Yeah, let's go."

Vera Simpletripp hung up the phone, delicately placing the receiver in its cradle, gently putting an end to her one-sided conversation with Horace. She wasn't surprised that he would be working late at the gallery, leaving her home to eat alone. And it wouldn't be the first time, either, that, while patiently awaiting his tardy arrival, the dinner she had so diligently prepared had grown cold, having sat out on the table for several hours. Now, aware of her welling resentment, she found herself not at all hungry, while at the same time feeling so utterly, utterly starved.

Vera only wished she hadn't destroyed her paper and glue painting so soon after creating it, that she had waited and taken the time to really relish and treasure her vision come to life.

As she shuffled moodily about the kitchen wrapping and putting dinner away in the fridge, feeling isolated and frozen out of her world—or some *other* world elsewhere—she had been gripped several times with the impulse to stop and look out the window in the hope of seeing a light burning at Thaddeus's house, wanting desperately to exalt in the fact that he had returned safely home. But each time she had stopped herself from doing so—and not just tonight, but many times since learning of his unforeseen departure. And, yet, from the very first, instinct told her he was never coming back, that he couldn't if he wanted to, and so there wasn't any reason to bother ever.

As a result, everyday, she resolved to simply keep busy, trying not to think about her neighbor. Instead, she concentrated on cleaning house to make Horace happy—even though he would comment only when things appeared messy, dusty, or out of place, asking why she had been so sloppy in her duties. For a change, she wished her husband would tell her when he liked something, or when she did something well. Yet, she knew it just wasn't in his nature, no more than it was in his nature to throw her a surprise party, or ask what movie she'd like to see, or where she'd like to go for dinner.

Nevertheless, Mrs. Simpletripp took what she could from him, reminding herself that she should be happy with the little she was given, that in many, many ways it was only what she deserved. After all, hadn't she asked for such treatment when agreeing to marry the man?

But it could have been different, very, very different. She just didn't know it. Not then. So, consequently, she had decided she would forever tolerate him in the now. It wasn't Horace's fault she had awakened.

And these days, she knew her husband was worried, though he would never tell her that. He was worried about their mounting debts, the gallery and its woeful sales, worried about *her* and why his little Vera-pet had become so suddenly unmanageable, behaving like she did. And Mrs. Simpletripp knew he wanted to stop her, wanting to calm his mind by putting an end to her small rebellion, her clash and flash of independence, to shake and pound her brutally back into submission—to stuff her into the outgrown mold of the submissive wife.

And, really, as strange as it might seem, she wanted to be able to be that person again, blindly subservient, appreciative of the crumbs he offered now and then. But only in a small way did she want that—inasmuch as there was a naïve contentment in being her, in feeling undeserving without expectation, in not thinking too much while setting aside her inner pain, as well as ignoring the hurt from the outer violations that caused her to constantly suffer it. And put up with it. And wither from it.

And yet, Vera Simpletripp knew full well she could never again be that version of herself. Never. It would be like un-baking a cake. It was done. Feeling like Thaddeus made her feel, her insides had suddenly swelled, filling out into something wholly delectable, more than just a mixture of the everyday blandness she had come to know. Now her feelings were beautiful to behold, and she looked good and felt good—*so, so good!*—even aspiring to be something better, deserving to be better—deserving to be *someone special.* And to be special to someone. Imagine. Imagine *her* feeling like *that.* But she had.

At least that's how she saw it.

But now it was gone. All gone. Like a beautiful dream realized only in stardust. Like it never truly existed at all.

Despite herself, Mrs. Simpletripp wandered over to sneak a peek out of the kitchen window.

The house nextdoor remained dark.

Locking up the Clay Pigeon early, Mr. Simpletripp had made several trips to load up his car with the last of the sculptures. Conveniently, he had taken the time to pull up and park just outside the back door, in the dimness of the alley at night.

Like most evenings recently, he found himself unable stay calm as a prisoner locked within his failing gallery's walls. It was unbearable, hanging around in the stillness, the emptiness, waiting for the front door to chime, only to watch the crowds walk casually by—as if the front of his shop didn't have windows and a door!

To him, it was like watching himself waste away, awaiting his own death, while forced to be on hand to attend the funeral afterwards. And, meanwhile, having to suffer the indignity of having died so pathetically.

There's something wrong here! he told himself. There's something wrong! I shouldn't be treated this way! This art deserves attention! *I* deserve attention!

Mr. Simpletripp knew that it couldn't be his fault that holiday sales were lousy, that his artists had up and left him for other galleries in town or to form their own. So what if they looked to be doing a worthwhile business? It was only because they took *his* business, *that's* what it was. And they talked dirt about him—obviously making up stories—*lies, lies, all of it!* It kept people away. Why else wouldn't they come in?

Those artists! If they hadn't been so damned *pigheaded,* so *pushy* while sticking their noses where they didn't belong, if they had just listened to what *he,* Horace Simpletripp, had to say about gallery operations, he wouldn't be so strapped this way, wouldn't be in this predicament. He wouldn't be so angry, so edgy—so *pent-up.*

Gunning his car to coughingly get it started, Mr. Simpletripp stomped on the gas to make it go. Only afterwards did he turn on his headlights. Now he was rumbling down the narrow alleyway, swerving at the last possible instant so as to avoid hitting a couple walking to one side.

With a glimpse in the rearview mirror, he knew they were cursing him, but who cares? They hadn't stopped by the gallery, had they? They deserved it, then.

Turning onto the street with a jolt and a bounce, his tires barking, his headlights slashing across the pavement before him, he headed home to another uncontrollable nightmare. His wife.

Uneasy at being out after dark, Vera Simpletripp came inside from the porch to stand in the relative safety of the entryway light. Involuntarily, she shuddered, unable to pull herself away and close the door completely.

Earlier, after the dinner cleanup had been completed, she had worked up the nerve to venture over to the fence that separated the Simpletripp property from that of Thaddeus Levine. There, mired with a sense of helplessness, of longing, the woman had taken to simply staring at his house. She hadn't expected to see anything whatsoever other than its shut up lifelessness, but at the sight she made an important wish, nevertheless. It wasn't for herself. Once upon a time she would have said a prayer, but she didn't care to do that anymore.

Now retreating, attempting to shut out the night, Vera closed the front door louder than intended. Walking with determination through the living room, she avoided looking at the fireplace and headed straight for the basement stairs.

Why not? Horace wasn't going to be home until later.

Mrs. Simpletripp wasn't sure exactly why she was misty-eyed, on the verge of crying. All she knew is that she felt lost between worlds, both collapsing, both unable to offer comfort or safe refuge.

Why am I always afraid? she asked herself. Afraid of the night, afraid of living alone, afraid of ending up alone—afraid of Horace—afraid of who he really is and what he might have done. And afraid he did it because of me.

In Vera Simpletripp's life, as of this moment, nothing seemed to matter, to be worthy of concern. She had determined that her world was made of beeswax, its walls pliant, uncertain and apt to change, and always ready to melt or cave in around her—sometimes softly in the let down, sometimes with all the weight and suddenness of falling space debris.

Turning on the staircase light, seemingly in a daze, the diminutive Mrs. Simpletripp descended the basement stairs. Reaching the bottom, she strayed into the void of blackness, a place that, to her, suddenly felt safe.

Hearing a car turn into the drive, she tensed.

It was Horace. He was home.

Sitting in his car, Mr. Simpletripp didn't want to turn off the motor, didn't want to go inside the house. He just didn't feel ready to face the other big problem currently confronting him. Not yet, anyway. He remembered the last time he had felt this pent-up, and how as a result he had slapped Vera silly.

She was different now. If he went in there, the end result might not be pretty, the outcome unintended, undesired. God help Horace Simpletripp if Vera walked away. And God help her if she tried to.

Frustrated, backing recklessly into the street, he braked to a lurching halt before jamming the transmission into forward gear. Behind him, one of the animal urns tumbled off the seat, colliding loudly with others. If any busted, it didn't matter. Mr. Simpletripp just wanted to keep moving.

Flooring the accelerator, the heavy vehicle didn't gain traction right away, but when it did, the squealing car shot off like a bolt. He ignored the stop sign at the corner, continuing toward the outskirts of town. Snarling, savage, he pounded the steering wheel, once, twice. Gripping it fiercely, he wanted to strangle it, and now tear it loose.

He drove.

It was way too early to go to the pond.

On a whim, he decided to pay a visit to the home of the woman who came by the gallery with her granddaughter earlier that afternoon. And the dog—that stupid, stupid loose-bowelled dog.

The old Stanton house, huh? On Scarlett Drive. Yeah, I know it. I know it well.

Hearing her husband's car noisily race off, Mrs. Simpletripp again came to life. She felt her entire body relax, her head drooping momentarily in release. Heart pounding, she began to breathe again. Having previously raced up the stairs to extinguish the light, she now made an abrupt turnabout and descended once more into the basement's blackness, thankful to be swallowed up and consumed for the moment. Invisible. Just footsteps on the floor.

She wondered why she had always been so afraid of the dark, when in fact it was a sheltering cocoon where she could be anyone, really. Anyone. Anytime. Anywhere. All she really needed to do was set her imagination loose to roam freely.

Vera had a thought: Maybe death is like this, only without a floor. And when you're in that place, there aren't any obstacles to bump into, real or imagined, and there's no one around to do you harm. How can they? You can't get any more dead than dead, right? Inside or out.

Eventually feeling about her, finding the light switch, she didn't turn it on right away. She didn't need to. She knew everything, all those ceramic pieces she'd seen that her husband had been working on—whatever they were—had gone.

A flick of the switch confirmed it.

And, yet, Mrs. Simpletripp wasn't disappointed. How could she be? Even though she still didn't know what her husband had been doing, or any more about who exactly he was, she couldn't help but feel she had learned a little more about herself. And, at the moment, maybe such a discovery was far more significant.

She shut off the light.

There. Better. Now she was able to see more clearly.

Nearing the vicinity of the old Stanton place, Mr. Simpletripp braked to slow the car, cruising by on the prowl. Glimpsing the house, he noticed there were lights still burning in a few of the windows, with one illuminating the porch. The large front yard was predominantly full of shadow, full of the night. He liked that.

Turning onto a smaller lane, he parked his beater beneath a bare-boned tree. Emerging, the hefty figure quietly closed the door while sticking to the shadows, proceeding down the tree-lined sidewalk. Rounding the corner, coming upon the length of white pickets that fenced the Stanton yard, he stood against a hedge, staying well outside the streetlamp's influence.

Unmoving, Mr. Simpletripp remained there for the longest time, simply observing. He really didn't expect to find the puppy running freely in the yard. But the man felt he was up to something rewarding, gathering and storing information for a future visit, reacquainting himself with details of the house and yard. Plus, he just liked to watch, to stare, knowing of his power, and what that devastating power could unleash.

And when Mr. O'Malley walked by late on his evening stroll, puffing on his cigar, the distinguished gray-haired banker didn't even notice the big man hugging the shadow, although he passed within a hair's breath of him.

Mr. Simpletripp gloated. How slick was that?

And wasn't this one of his favorite endeavors when singling out his victims, taking his time to get to know them a little better before making the snatch? Oh, it was. It really, really was. He was reliably personal that way. In fact, on his next visit, he intended to get even more personal.

In the distance, Mr. Simpletripp heard the clock towers in the town throw off their late-night bells. It was getting on towards the witching hour. He still had more work to do in the basement.

When he felt enough time had passed, satisfied, Mr. Simpletripp made his way back to the car, avoiding headlights and streetlamps along the way. And, then, settling his bulk into the driver's seat, he started his junker and drove off, with no one the wiser.

"So, Greesha and Mastow didn't make it?"

"No."

Sitting, Molly was in tears, Heather kneeling next to her, both girls on the treehouse floor. The hour was late, the pair high off the ground in the old Oak Triplets, beneath the spread of stars.

Heather's words were gentle, apologetic. "And I'm sorry I didn't tell you sooner, Molly, but I just couldn't. I don't know why. I guess I didn't want to think about it, and I knew it would make you…make you feel like *this,* that it was sad. But since you asked me what happened there at the Portal after you left, well, I had to let you know."

"Those two, they seemed so loyal to the ClearWeave and to Evermore. And Greesha was so brave, Heather. I'll always remember her bravery. And even though I hardly knew her…she really saved my life, you know, stopping me from going down and trying to fight, saying I could fight for Evermore in a better way. She saved me…she did, she did…"

With her words, Molly started sobbing in full, although for more things Evermorian than were uppermost in her mind. Heather put an arm over her friend's shoulders, gently holding her.

"Maybe I shouldn't have told you."

"No," Molly's face was grief-stricken, "I would have wanted you to." She wiped her eyes, before breaking into quiet sobs once more, her petite body lightly tremulous under her thinness of jacket. Her weeping lasted for a brief interval, before slowly subsiding. "I'd want to know something like that. Promise you'll always tell me." She took a deep breath, her eyes downcast. "Promise?"

Heather released Molly's shoulders, moving her face closer, trying to glimpse her friend's downturned head in the small patch of moonlight. "I promise. Okay?"

A small nod. Molly began to wipe her cheeks with her sleeve, slowly composing herself. She sniffed and swallowed, then wiped some more. "Thank you," she added, her saturated words stronger.

At the sound of an approaching vehicle on Lone Oak Avenue, Heather scrambled to her feet, staring between branches at the dark rectangle coursing up the sloping road, its headlights leading the way. From her backpack, she produced Scarbone's spyglass and extended the scope. Raising it to her eye, she pointed the instrument to sight on Mr. Simpletripp's car, watching its route in closeup until it eventually turned into his drive. When the vehicle temporarily disappeared from view, she focused near to the basement door, waiting to see the rotund man turn the corner, exposed briefly in the revealing light of the full moon.

They heard the car door slam, listened on his footsteps.

"An-n-n-n-d," muttered Heather, eye to the spyglass, her face askew, "ladies and gentlemen, here he is...the one...the only..." she paused, waiting, "...Mr. Creepy Pants."

Unloading the last of his ceramic vessels from the car, Mr. Simpletripp left the basement door ajar upon entering, the room's cool fluorescent light escaping into the warm night air. He glanced toward the dim stairwell, uncertainty overtaking him.

Would he hear his wife's meek voice call out from the top of the stairs? Realizing he would like nothing more, he quickly quashed the thought, and with it any sign of its wimpy weakness.

In the past, he couldn't be bothered to climb those stairs to say *anything* to Vera—no hello, not a word. Only an afterthought, his wife deserved nothing more. And now?

Something told him he should.

With a scowl, he turned from the stairs and lumbered toward the freezer. He had work to do.

Heather and Molly were standing side-by-side on the treehouse planking, the moonlight shining through the twisted limbs in fragments, the girls making sure to avoid their revealing glow.

"You know, Heather, because Mr. Simpletripp turned off the basement light, I can't tell what he's carrying back and forth to the car."

"He's sure being sneaky, isn't he, turning the thing off like that, running around in the dark?"

Molly lowered the small telescope, handing it back to her friend.

Hoisting it, Heather straightened and peered. "I'll tell you one thing I *can* see, and that is Mr. Simpletripp's shine. He's got one of the creepiest shines I've ever seen on the guy. It's big time creepy, Molly—'haunted house meets crazy forest fire' kind of creepy."

"Mistraya creepy?"

"Almost."

"I just wonder, Heather, how in the world can he see what he's doing there in the dark?"

"I think there's a small light he keeps on when he's loading all those things up, like a desk lamp. It's on one of the tables near the sink."

"Oh, really? And just how do you know that?"

Heather shrugged, keeping the spyglass glued to her eye. "Oh, you know…"

Molly was keen for more.

Heather sensed it, and confided, "Well, I, um, I kinda snuck up and saw it once." She cleared her throat, Molly shooting her a look. "Long time ago. You know, way back when I wasn't being responsible and practicing the MaidenWay and stuff."

"Oh-h-h-h, all the way back then, huh?"

"Oh, yeah, way, *way-y-y-y* back, Molly, back when Scarbones played on the Bristol House swings."

Molly stifled a giggle. "Here, let me look." She took up the relinquished instrument. "I guess that's the last of it, then. It looks like he's locking up the basement."

"Too bad the moon isn't lighting up his backyard, huh? We'd've seen more. You know, Molly, I know I should be practicing the MaidenWay and stuff, but I'm thinking this needs further investigation. Don't you?"

"Yes, you're right. It sure does—but carefully."

"It *is* a great ol' mystery to be solved, isn't it?" Heather received the spyglass in handoff. She raised it on the squint. "I mean, where is he taking all this stuff? Why is he going in and out of the basement that way? And just what the *heck* is he up to? You know, there's a reason he's not turning all those basement lights on when he's loading up."

"He doesn't want to be seen by anyone, none of the neighbors, not even Mrs. Simpletripp. They might get a little too curious."

"Yep. Just like us. And what's he carrying, anyway, that makes his shine so, so…"

"Menacing? Sinister? Threatening? Ominous? Devilishly evil?"

"Oh, yeah, all of those things, Molly, all of them stuck together. You know, I think this definitely calls for a much closer inspection."

"But they're all loaded up, Heather. Whatever those things are, he'll be taking them away any second now."

"Doesn't have to be tonight," said Heather, her eye still fastened to the lens.

"You think there'll be more, then?"

Heather nodded. She knew Mr. Simpletripp was up to something with big time creep, and, determined, the girl was going to find out exactly what it was, MaidenWay or not.

On that thought, Heather decided to sneak out after dinner the following evening, checking to see if Mr. Simpletripp didn't come back with another carload of whatever it was he was trying to hide. And since she would need to get in close with the possibility of being exposed in the moonlight, that meant it might be ultra-dangerous, so it would be best if she did it alone.

She lowered the scope, but continued to stare. They heard Mr. Simpletripp's car door slam and his vehicle start up with a rasp, a gasp, and a rumble. Afterward, the girls watched its red-tailed, yellow-beamed progress as it headed back down Lone Oak Avenue and eventually out of sight, lost to obstructing homes and trees.

Collapsing the antique spyglass, in contemplation, Heather tapped the brass barrel against her palm.

Ol' Creepy Pants, she mused, so what are you trying to hide that's so, so secret? And what's going on, there, in your ugly basement dungeon?

Lost to thought, little did Heather realize that, standing alongside and studying her nocturnal-blue features, Molly knew she was formulating a plan. And knowing Heather as she did, Molly harbored little doubt that she would carry out her newly devised scheme sooner than later. And most probably the very next night.

chapter sixteen

Mr. Wilson Talbott and His Bristol House Dinner

"So, Lana, do you feel like you've finally settled in here at the Bristol House?"

Mrs. Pringle looked up from her meal and across the greater stretch of table, focusing on their genial and charming guest, Wilson Talbott. Poised in hand, her utensils remained stationary, expectant.

The woman hesitated. "Well, I have decidedly mixed feelings, really." She glanced at Molly and then Heather, the girls sitting between her and Talbott, one to a side. "This house is so beautiful, it never fails to surprise—"

"I bet."

"Yes. On the other hand, at times, it can be quite overwhelming really, especially when I think about the-the *scope* of this place. It takes some getting used to. And, yet, despite its large size, the Bristol House has a way of feeling cozy, too—and oddly enough, welcoming and caring!—I can't explain it, really. And it's just full of colorful arrangements and such tasteful décor. It's all very sumptuous, very plush, and that makes me feel comfortable. So, in some ways I feel settled, in others, not so much."

"I suppose, with Dawn's having been away, you've had to learn a few of the ropes when managing such a large household on your own.

And keeping the rooms clean and tidy must almost be a full time job—”

“We help her out, Mr. Talbott,” said Heather, uncomfortable with the subtle line of questioning and where it could lead.

“The girls are so good about it, too,” added Mrs. Pringle. “But Dawn has cleaning people that come in and out, and they’re usually done so quickly, we really don’t notice that they’ve come until they’re actually gone.”

Heather and Molly nodded in amused agreement.

“I see.”

Both the youngsters had been fairly quiet throughout the meal, occasionally exchanging glances, the adults making small talk about Noble and their time in it, the people they knew, the acquaintances held in common.

Eliciting a contented sigh, Talbott conclusively set down his fork and knife, the fine silverware chiming on his plate. “This has been a most splendid dinner, Lana. The roasted chicken and all your fixings have been nothing, if not delicious.”

Mrs. Pringle beamed, reddening slightly. “Thank you, Wilson. I’m glad you enjoyed it. But we’re not finished yet. There’s still dessert to come, and I think you’re going to enjoy what the girls prepared.”

“Oh, really?” Talbott turned his attention on Molly, instinctively aware that Heather hadn’t bothered to look his way. “And what may I ask—?”

“Oh, it’s not a big deal, really, Mr. Talbott. Heather and I just made a devil’s food cake. It was Heather’s idea, really, but we did it together. The ice cream Mom bought at the store.”

“Wonderful.” Talbott glimpsed sidelong to see Heather still hadn’t looked up, absently rolling a pea around on her plate with her fork. Brat! he thought. *Devil’s* food cake, my hindquarters. I see I’ll have to be very careful with this one. “So, Lana, these rooms have been decorated so beautifully. Is the entire house done up this way?”

“Sort of, Mr. Talbott,” said Heather, before Mrs. Pringle could get into specifics. “It’s really great. Every Christmas it’s kinda like this.”

“Superb. Well, then, maybe after dinner, you can give me a tour of your Bristol House winter wonderland.”

“Oh. I, um, I really can’t tonight, Mr. Talbott. I’ve got a bunch of stuff to do—”

“Well, maybe Lana and Molly are up to it, then.”

Her attention having returned to her pea, Heather looked up sharply.

"Actually, Wilson," said Mrs. Pringle, "I know this is hard to believe, but I've not seen the entire house, myself. I think it would be best for Heather to be on hand and give us both the tour. Molly, too. Perhaps we'll arrange something at some point, maybe after the New Year sometime."

Mrs. Pringle purposely left it vague, understanding Heather's desire to keep the magical house free of visitors who may not quite understand its peculiar brand of uniqueness. She felt the policy would serve them well for the time being, anyway, until they had come to know Wilson Talbott better.

Feeling rebuffed, however gently, Talbott fumed. And his finely tuned sense of manipulation told him that it would be foolhardy to push the subject.

"Well, then, another time, perhaps." The man's thin and patient smile stretched wide across his face, icy-cold and frozen in place. Stiffly, he took a sip of wine.

And, still, Heather refused to look at him.

Perhaps it was a bit too much Christmas cheer. Perhaps it was sheer, unendurable boredom and, in it, the inspired notion of stirring up some rowdy holiday mischief. And just maybe it was all of that and more.

Whatever the case, tired of hanging out on the courthouse square, a group of festive Noble teens dredged up an idea for having a bit of fun. Hopping into several cars, they sped off, headed toward the outskirts of town, toward their science professor's house, a man with the given name of a certain color blue. More specifically, they decided on a whim to once again hijack his flying machine, and take the much-maligned contraption for a spin.

Mrs. Pringle and Wilson Talbott were alone, conversing easily across the table. For the moment, the girls had left the room, the pair having gone off to the kitchen after clearing away the dishes.

"But I think, Wilson, that with Heather's help, Molly has been able to navigate her way through the turbulent waters, so to speak. The worst is behind her. She loves it here in the Bristol House. And despite my minor reservations, *I* love it here. We've been very lucky."

"Well," said Talbott, "I'm certainly pleased you've decided to stay here. Molly, too. And I hope you plan on sticking around for a while."

Mrs. Pringle was touched by what she saw as the man's earnest sentiments. "Molly told me that after living here, she doesn't know how she can possibly live anywhere else."

"Why would anyone want to? The house is a virtual playland. I assume all the rooms are furnished, too, even the ones on the third floor?"

"Oh, the third floor is really something else entirely. I haven't spent a lot of time up there, but fully intend to at some point. The girls rave about it—"

"We're back," declared Molly.

Cheerily, she and Heather entered the dining room in a tremulous, methodical advance. In each hand rested a plate of chocolate cake and ice cream carefully portioned out beforehand in the kitchen.

"Honey, it looks absolutely delicious. Wilson, I hope you don't mind, but we're a bit informal around here—"

Displaying good humor, Talbott waved away any possible issue with an air of nonchalance, while secretly hiding his irritation at the untimely entrance of the girls. "Not at all. It's perfectly fine, Lana."

"I hope the slices aren't too big," said Molly in concentration, treading slowly and cautiously, balancing the two plates along with their apt-to-slide spoons, "...or the scoops too large. Heather has Mom's dish, and, Mr. Talbott, this one is for...*you.*" Molly said the last word brightly, setting the dessert down in front of him.

Stepping away, she placed her own dish to rest and—acquiring a lively, go-ahead nod from her mother—hurried to the small, adorned tree atop a nearby hutch. From under it, she selected a package. "And this is for you, too," she said in a burbled rush, if not a bit shyly, "from all of us." The gift box sat before Mr. Talbott, its bow large and red.

The man truly looked surprised, actually sitting up all the straighter.

"What's this, then? What's *this?* For me?"

"Merry Christmas, Mr. Talbott." Molly was going to add a hug, but an imperceptible something held her back. "Open it."

"Yes, open it, Wilson."

A big grin slapped silly upon his face, their guest made quick work of the wrappings, unveiling the product box.

He laughed. "What the—?"

"Take it out, Mr. Talbott." It was Heather, the girl curious, this being the first time she had seen the gift.

"Yes, show us."

Opening the box and removing the snow globe, he shook it and then held the swirling wintry sphere in front of him for all to see.

"Wilson, I know it's a silly gift, but when I saw it, I thought, 'We just *have* to get this for Wilson.' It's so reminiscent of the Bristol House, don't you think? It's got the pirate inside the globe with the open treasure chest next to him—you know that Scarbones Bristol, the builder of this house, was a pirate, right? And that supposedly there's some hidden treasure of his buried somewhere on the grounds? So, you can see, behind the pirate and his treasure you've got the house, there, in the trees on a hill, along with his tiny sailing ship in the cove. It's perfect."

Talbott was beaming. "It *is* perfect, Lana. Thank you, all." And, really, the scheming man thought, you could never know just *how* perfect.

Wilson Talbott reared back and, for the first time that night, genuinely laughed.

On the back roads of Noble, parking their cars quite a distance away from Professor Periwinkle's house, the dozen or so teens walked for what seemed like a country mile. But they didn't let the lengthy distance dampen their enthusiasm—rather just the opposite, the rambunctious kids goofing, chiding, and laughing all the way.

The houses and yards giving way to pastureland and orchards, the spirited party shushed and shoved one another as they turned down Wild Hyde Avenue, the homes on the long stretch of road becoming more densely packed.

"There it is!"

"Hey, keep it down!"

"Don't tell *me* to shut up, man!"

"Well, then, Megaphone Mouth, keep your voice down."

"Go sell your mother."

"Darrin, stop it, will ya? Just chill out."

"I'm not doin' anything, all right? You're the one who can't shut up."

"Knock it off, or you're gonna wreck it for everybody."

"Look, I told ya. I'm not doin' *anything.*"

"Right. Are you guys done, yet? Are we done arguing, here? Good. Okay, so how do you want to do this?"

The group huddled loosely, and a whispering frenzy ensued that included a few pushes and several "No way's," "Get outta here's," and "You gotta be out of your friggin' mind's." Reaching consensus, the group went on the sneak, approaching Professor Periwinkle's house on the crouch and stumble.

Opening the gate, the rowdy bunch stole into the moonlit yard and cut the craft loose from its moorings. Shuffling and bumbling, taking up positions around the flying machine's perimeter, on a signal from the school's star athlete, they hoisted it into the air. Then, like a drunken centipede, it crawled slowly out of the yard, one kid at the front almost getting trampled when he tripped and fell in the dark.

Reaching the road, they didn't set the machine down immediately, but carried it a safe enough distance from the Periwinkle house, before sounding out with manmade engine noises to accompany its handheld flight. Nearing Farmer Annandale's orchard, they lowered the winged and rotor-bladed contrivance to a shrill and boisterous landing at the side of the pavement.

And, there, after a few admonishments for loudness, a sharp 'Shut yourself up' and 'Go away, Your Highness,' using a bicycle pump, they stupidly checked and inflated the tires. Only then did they feel the professor's invention to be adequately primed and ready for takeoff.

"It's been a marvelous evening, Lana. I'd like to thank you so much." The dinner guest humbly gestured with his gift. "This was great, too."

"Oh, Wilson, it was our pleasure. Really, it was."

The girls stayed at the door while Mrs. Pringle walked Talbott to the end of the porch.

"Thanks again, Lana." He reached out and took her hand. Mrs. Pringle expected him to shake it. Instead, Talbott leaned over and kissed her on the cheek.

Slightly flustered, Mrs. Pringle recovered quickly, her smile wavering. "Goodnight, Wilson."

"Lana."

Mrs. Pringle watched Talbott as he descended the steps and walked away, his limp barely noticeable. At one point, she waved, expecting him to turn and do likewise before disappearing down the path. But he didn't. The calculating man only stopped and turned when he was safely out of sight. And when he saw the porch light go dark, he cleverly retraced his steps back toward the house.

In the Bristol House kitchen, Mrs. Pringle was hand-washing the heirloom china while Molly dried. Ranging here and rushing there, Heather was seeing to it that the dinner items were properly and safely stowed away. Waiting for Molly to finish up with another dinner plate, Heather suppressed a yawn.

Noticing, Molly's towel briefly stopped its motion. The girl eyed her companion, assuming correctly that for yet another night Heather hadn't gotten much sleep. Her lips pressed firmly together, Molly set her drying cloth to work all the more vigorously before handing off the plate.

"Tired?" It was Mrs. Pringle, her forearms submerged and searching in the sudsy sink water.

"Yeah," said Heather, "I am," adding the proffered plate to the stack, and then hoisting the cylindrical pile carefully. "When I'm done here, I think I'll go up to bed, if you don't mind."

"Not at all. I'll wager it's been a long day for all of us."

Molly nodded, but kept quiet. The girl knew Heather had plans. Yet, what Heather never suspected is that Molly fully intended on making herself a part of them.

Hidden in the sheltering shadows of the Bristol House vegetable garden, Wilson Talbott willed the warm yellow illumination filling the kitchen windows to shut down.

He stood watching, waiting on the ongoing light until blackness finally leapt to claim the panes.

"About time," he said, under his breath.

Lingering all the longer, finally feeling certain the lights wouldn't again burst to life in afterthought, Talbott set off for the front porch, knowing from information gleaned over dinner to avoid the heavily trafficked rear staircase whenever able.

When the covered porch came into view, its chairs and tables at one with the vagueness, Talbott settled in the trees for the moment and made himself comfortable. In a patch of moonshine, he decided to play around with his newly acquired gift before stashing it. He wanted to give everyone in the house plenty of opportunity to get ready for bed. Hopefully, they'd fall asleep immediately.

Removing it from the box, he lightly stirred the globe, the snowbound world now awhirl, infused with the soft blue hue of moonlight.

"That Lana..." He roused a smile and shook his head at her thoughtfulness. Then his face completely dropped expression. "Oh, make no mistake. This doesn't change things. I still want to do her harm." Agitating the globe into furious flurry, with relish he watched the resulting moonlit madness. "But only in a *nice* way."

Seeing the girls off to their rooms, throwing herself down in the comfort of her bedroom's reading chair, Mrs. Pringle heaved a contented sigh. She picked up her current novel, intending to relax and read for a while.

Her mind drifted, however, and soon she found herself appraising the evening's activities.

Dinner went well, she surmised, and Wilson seemed to enjoy himself. He's a nice man: older, well dressed and groomed, intelligent, articulate—quite distinguished, really. Tonight Heather seemed a bit sulky, true enough, but only because the poor thing was tired, I'm sure. Molly held up well, was attentive throughout, and so, all in all, everyone seemed to have a good time.

And didn't that pirate snow globe go over big? That thing was a smash, it really was. Couldn't have been better.

Glancing at the ceiling, she thought, And I bet even Scarbones would have approved.

With her approach, Heather lit up at the sight of the full moon. As always, she felt an affinity with the Earth's lone satellite, that the heavenly body was her companion and silently watched over her.

The girl was standing before the turret room's center window. The sash was open, and she could feel the breeze, noticing how it caused the drapery to fill, to curl and roll.

Warm night. It felt good. And, yet, somehow it still didn't feel *right.* Not for Noble at Christmastime. And *definitely* not for winter.

She tried to dismiss her shifting sense of discomfort, urging her attention elsewhere.

Across Whisper Creek, Heather found herself disappointed to discover there was no activity whatsoever taking place at the Simpletripp house—no light, no movement, nothing to incite her interest.

And, yet, as if in magical fulfillment of unspoken expectation, it was then that Heather noticed a pair of headlights crawling up Lone Oak Avenue. She lost sight of them when they turned into the Simpletripp drive.

"Well," murmured Heather, withdrawing from the window to snatch up her jacket, "what the heck took you so long?"

Like Heather, Molly had undressed, but only to change into more comfortable, casual clothing—preferably dark, mind you—apparel better suited for anything that might prove to be rough and tumble. Her light out and bedroom door ajar on the sliver, she had her eye pressed to the opening, waiting for Heather on the walk-by.

Moments later, Molly was surprised when Heather actually did come into view, and only because she was so soundless in her stealth.

How does Heather move like that?

Molly determined she must know where not to step, which floorboards creaked. But the rest of her movements were quiet, too. In ways, watching Heather was like watching a real life silent movie.

Molly afforded her plenty of time to get down the hall, determining Heather would choose to go out the kitchen's Dutch door, as was usual by past accounts.

When she felt enough time had passed, Molly followed after her, attempting to avoid those areas in the hall where she knew the floorboards were apt to cry out and give her away. And though she could never compete on a par with Heather, Molly was becoming quite proficient when implementing her spy skills, as Heather liked to call them—so much so, Heather herself had recently thought to compliment them!

Reaching the end of the hall, slinking ever so slowly down the stairs, Molly decided she would most likely find Heather in the treehouse—at least initially. And whatever her partner-in-crime had planned for Mr. Simpletripp, Heather must have assumed it was going to involve a certain amount of risk and danger, or she would have invited Molly along.

But within reason, Molly felt up to the task, whatever it involved. After all, she'd been through more dangerous situations in Evermore, hadn't she, and survived those? And tonight, she was resolved to surprise even Heather, and do it in a way that would make her and Greesha proud. Starbrill, too.

Surreptitiously mounting the stairs, crossing the reclusive porch, Wilson Talbott approached the front door of the Bristol House. Uneasy, the man looked around, unsure of what to expect. Talbott felt for his knife, a sharp-bladed, slash-and-stab of a Christmas present he brought along for protection—a gift for an overaggressive, unsuspecting watchdog, should the need arise.

"Please be unlocked," whispered Talbott, trying his hand at the darkened door. When it opened without a hitch, he said in undertone, "Oh, thank you, Lana. You're more generous than you know."

Treading softly, he slipped inside.

Cary the Bristol House dog was trotting amiably down the upstairs' hallway, breezing towards Heather's room. Picking up the girl's fresh scent, he continued on and followed after her, down the rear staircase.

Coming to a dead end in the kitchen, Cary sniffed heatedly about the Dutch door. The fact that it was closed didn't deter the animal in the least. Although the Bristol House took its time in allowing it, Cary eventually found his way outside. And shortly after that, he was able to rediscover Heather's scent. Molly's, too.

Mrs. Pringle set down her book. She had been unable to read anyway, unable to relax and keep her mind from entertaining some very *un*entertaining thoughts. And now flashing on one of them in particular, she was on her way down the hall toward Molly's room, remembering that Ned had modified the plans he had originally proposed for the weekend, possibly affecting their upcoming holiday.

Oh, and wasn't that so Ned! she smoldered.

Mrs. Pringle tried not to become too worked up at the thought of him, at their ongoing feud, especially before bedtime. Since their separation, he had been haunting her dreams far too often as it was.

However, while fresh in her mind and before it slipped free, Mrs. Pringle wanted to inform her daughter of the change, knowing Molly would calmly work through it to acceptance. For such a young girl, Mrs. Pringle believed her to be graciously gifted that way.

She knocked lightly on the open door and stuck her head inside. "Molly?" She flipped on the lights. Amid the Christmas finery, the room was empty, Molly's pajamas folded neatly on the chair alongside her bed.

Hmm.

Assuming the girls to be talking in Heather's room, Mrs. Pringle angled across the hallway.

"Heather? Molly?"

She was leaning against the jamb, peering in past Heather's partially open door. She could see the room was enveloped in darkness, the Christmas lights blinking and gleaming in colorful pinpoints all around. Mrs. Pringle flicked on the overhead chandeliers. Having done so, her eyes immediately went to the immense snow statue of Michelangelo's David, the icy white representation wearing the same silly hand-me-down beanie and propeller above his Santa suit.

"Anyone here?" Walking through the heart of Heather's room, Mrs. Pringle spied beneath the arch. "Anyone?"

She thought, Those girls. They're probably on the third floor somewhere, playing a late night game of tennis or ping-pong.

When Mrs. Pringle recognized the open Book of Autumnsloe left out on the end table, she scanned the room once more. Not spotting Cary, the protective Bristol House dog, she backtracked and closed the door, intending to keep the pet away. Returning to the turret room, she picked up the oversized book, and sitting in one of the upholstered chairs, brought it to rest upon her lap.

"Now," she said, with a bounce or two, making herself more comfortable, "let's have a look and see what this secretive book is all about."

Having crossed lower bridge, the toppled tree spanning Whisper Creek, Heather soon found herself nearing the base of the old Oak Triplets. About to mount the snarl of low-lying branches in an effort to reach the treehouse, Heather froze when she noticed the lights in Mr. Simpletripp's basement shut down.

Moments afterward, in the vagueness of night, she saw her neighbor quietly emerge and close the door. His aura screaming in deadly blue-violets and thrashing magentas, the big-bellied figure made his way down to the banks of Whisper Creek. From there, she watched as he paralleled its watery course downstream, avoiding moonlight whenever possible, passing through the brush, grass, trees, and rocky terrain.

About to follow, Heather halted when she spied another indistinct form detaching from the shadows of the Simpletripp house to begin trailing the ponderous bully, this one smaller in stature. Her night vision acute, Heather waited for confirmation, until the person passed near.

Yep, it's definitely her, all right.

Admittedly, Heather was surprised to discover Mr. Simpletripp's late night pursuer was none other than his very own wife.

After tailing Heather across Whisper Creek, Molly was startled to discover her companion noiselessly reversing course and coming directly at her, the girl's slender body defined by the blue-green shades of moon glow. To Molly, the entire soft-edged scene appeared eerie and surreal, and yet at the same time wildly intriguing, watching as Heather skillfully and clandestinely maneuvered in pursuit of her prey.

Going completely still, her heart thumping, Molly looked on while Heather surprisingly overlooked her and her sufficiently hidden form. Instead, head up and poised, her attention raptly focused downstream, the motionless girl monitored the progress of the moonlit Mr. and Mrs. Simpletripp.

And when Heather came out of hiding to steal after them, Molly patiently waited and then followed, wherever such dangerous and unpredictable adventures led.

Wilson Talbott harbored no illusions. If caught, he'd be hard-pressed to come up with any wholly believable explanation as to why he had been discovered inside the confines of the Bristol House. And, he realized, a ski mask would no longer disguise him—if ever it really could.

No, this straightforward intrusion of his was all a gamble—a breathtaking, dangerously exciting, adrenaline-pumping gamble of the kind that stimulated his otherwise muted emotional system. And although the sensation of sneaking through people's houses while they slept was hardly a new experience for the daredevil intruder, he relished the rush it provided nonetheless, each and every time.

Trustily at his side, open-bladed in his hand, his knife was poised at the ready to ward off any canine surprises. In their brief encounter, he had had more than enough of that mangy, Bristol House mutt.

And now, when carefully crossing the foyer in its still and darkened state, Talbott paid no mind to the room's décor. He wasn't in the least bit interested in the multicolored lights, in the long strands of indistinct garland which held the indiscernible ribbons, bows, and candy canes, or how the entire ensemble conspired with shadow to present this mysterious and dramatic mood, the magnificence of the Bristol House afterhours.

No, in these things he displayed no interest whatsoever. It was in getting to the third floor undetected that consumed him, the need to begin his hunt. Now, *these* were fixations worthy of his character and of his time remaining, time that was constantly and irrevocably counting down lest he discover that much anticipated and longed for Bristol House plunder.

Oh, and how that would change his life forever—literally!

Reaching the end of the foyer, the tall upright form furtively approached the decorated staircase, knowing for certain that the third floor stairway he sought was located at the far end of the hallway directly above him.

Over dinner, it was a tantalizing *something* Lana Pringle had mentioned that piqued Talbott's interest, the woman saying that the third floor was *something else,* as she put it. Something else? Well, if *that* wasn't invitation enough as to where to begin his search, there never existed a one!

And, now, having attained a better viewing angle from the base of the stairs, Talbott focused his attention upward, only to find that the second floor hallway lights were still on! Did that mean they were still awake?

Maybe.

Frustrated for the moment, Talbott thought it best that he be patient and give the occupants more time to settle in and find sleep. He reassured himself there was no need to rush. He'd have the greater part of the night to search the house.

Stowing his knife, slinking under the arch and into the obscurity of the living room, Talbott lowered himself into a chair. Unintentionally, he had chosen to sit beneath the large, life-sized portrait of Scarbones Bristol that hung over the mantel.

One can only wonder if Wilson Talbott would have found it so surprising, would have found it so far-fetched, would have found it so uproariously entertaining, if someone told him that the portrait of the frisky pirate captain had been observing his every move—and was enjoying every moment.

The volume blaring, Professor Anders Periwinkle was watching television in his den, a film documentary presented by none other than the Science Research Institute for Astronomical Studies. Intent, absently flossing his teeth while seated on the sofa, the eccentric, wiry, and bespectacled man was positively captivated by the idea of black holes and multiple universes.

When the program cut to commercial, setting down his floss, he was taken aback to discover his wife had been standing over him, cuddling one of their Siamese cats beneath her chin. When he muted the sound, the professor could hear the animal purring.

"Anders," she said, "it seems some of your students have been at it again."

He sat up, excitedly. "Have they?"

"Yes."

"And the flying machine, Bertha, is it gone?"

The woman nodded.

"Again, then! Superb! Fascinating! I have to say, knowing what we know these days about aeronautics, anyone can make a plane fly. But to make *my* flying machine take flight, *that* would take more, wouldn't it? Those are young minds out there, Bertha, the fresh minds of an entirely new generation. Maybe *they* can get it to fly!"

"Not *those* young minds, I'm afraid."

The professor seemed to deflate in disappointment. "You're certain?"

"They could very well hurt themselves, much like the last time. If you remember, they tried to get your machine up to speed while towing it on the interstate. Before that, they used it like a tank to chase

Old Man Posner into his barn on a busted leg."

"True. Never heard the end of that, did we, from Dr. Sedentary?" At the thought, his eye held a certain gleam. "Well, then, if I must, let me bother the good sheriff with a phone call." Bracing his hands on the chair arms, about to rise, he paused and resettled, once more looking up at his wife. "No chance, then, the youngsters will get it to fly?"

She spoke playfully, but with finality, into the face of her cat. "None."

Heather had tailed the husband and wife alongside the gurgling meanderings of Whisper Creek to a point somewhere before the Dairy Street Bridge, and from there they veered sharply away from the water. Coming out by the Pedagogy Instructional Academy, they set a course for the outskirts of town, Heather allowing herself to lag behind on the open landscape as she followed Mrs. Simpletripp, the woman still in unflagging pursuit of her mate.

Despite the long straight stretches of roadway, the girl found it easy to steal along undetected by wading into the old farming fields, hiding tree to fencepost to shrubbery and ditch. And rarely did they encounter an outlying streetlamp or oncoming car.

Finding herself on the backside of Farmer Annandale's orchard, it suddenly occurred to Heather where Mr. Simpletripp was going—although she had no idea of the actual destination itself. But intuition told her it had to be the same exact place he was headed when she spotted him from her lone perch high in the orchard tree. And she remembered that his wife just happened to be following him that day, as well.

Way too weird.

Okay, so whatever this guy's up to has something to do with what's been going on in his basement. It has to. So, what the heck is it, then?

Heather was getting excited, feeling all tingly inside. The girl couldn't help but sense she was on the verge of making this really amazing discovery.

"It's no wonder the girls love Evermore!" Mrs. Pringle gushed.

"Look at these pictures. They're absolutely breathtaking!"

Dreamy, the woman slowly closed the Book of Autumnsloe, not realizing the images she had been viewing were not the same as those available to Heather and Molly, the magical RepliGraphs of their visits. What Mrs. Pringle saw instead were picture postcards of Autumnsloe before the Bloodlet Overthrow, courtesy of that Intergalactic Tourist Organization commonly referred to as the Bristol House.

Looking around Heather's bedroom, the woman couldn't help but wish she and her sister had grown up in a Bristol House of their very own. Rising, she replaced the magical tome and then headed towards the hall, deciding to look for the girls upstairs, on the third floor.

The Bristol House, what a truly extraordinary place! What a truly extraordinary *experience!*

Having initially climbed the front staircase to take refuge in one of the many parlor rooms located throughout the second floor, Wilson Talbott began to slowly and cautiously advance down the hall, sneaking room to room. Upon entry, he wasn't bothering to discover what was in each, what lay spread out before him in the festive, light-blinking darkness. He only lingered near the doorway, out of range of the hallway light until he thought it safe to proceed.

If he found a door to be closed, he didn't bother with it, but instead flitted past, going swiftly to the next available entryway. In this fashion, he had nearly progressed to the end of the corridor.

About to emerge from a sitting room, he halted wide-eyed, and suddenly dipped back inside. Then, while losing himself to the shadows, he watched as Lana Pringle walked by.

Whew! He exhaled softly in relief. Close shave!

Idling patiently, allowing for time and distance, he finally inched his head out, enough so that he could see her striding figure turn from sight at the hallway's end. Then, exiting the room on his subtle limp, he edged his way in pursuit, sneaking ever closer. Daring to peer around the corner, he could see Mrs. Pringle heading up the stairs and towards the third floor.

So, she didn't visit the third floor much, eh? Did the woman have a secret she was hiding? If so, he'd certainly find out what it was!

When Talbott thought he had loitered long enough, he deftly followed.

Sheriff Dane was annoyed. Tired, he knew better than to take the call. But working late to catch up on paperwork, he had just finished exiting his computer when the phone rang. And looking to extend a holiday hand, with Deputy Foley out on a domestic dispute, and the new kid, Ramsey, dealing with a retching drunk in one of the holding cells, he found himself stuck behind the wheel of his agèd pickup truck. Headlights piercing the rush of night, he was heading to Noble's back roads in search of Periwinkle's purloined flying machine.

Of all things.

Despite his aggravation, the sheriff chuckled. If he were young again and partying with the fellas, they'd try and make that old, beat up contraption fly, too. And whether he and his buddies got the thing off the ground or not, they'd have a hell of a good time doing it—so long as his dad didn't catch him at it. If that happened, he'd be the one flying—flying to get out of the house before the old man got ahold of him.

One thing the fellas wouldn't do? For sure, they wouldn't take that flying scrapheap on the freeway. Those idiots almost got killed.

As for stealing Periwinkle's machine, let that be the worst thing that happens in Noble during the holidays.

Not superstitious in the least, Sheriff Dane knocked on the dashboard for good luck, anyway.

So far it had been a relatively quiet Christmas. Let's hope it stayed that way.

Loosely gathered along the roadway, the Noble teens were jesting, some guffawing.

"Drive much, Darrin?"

"This thing's hard to peddle and get up to speed, mommy's boy. *You* try it."

"Fire up that engine; I'll give it a shot. Otherwise, it can sit here and rot for all I care."

Having pushed it around and around, again trying to get the rotor blades spinning and the wings to flap, the brash abductors had pretty much worn themselves out. And so finally ditching it on the side of the road, some of the more exuberant pushers threw themselves down in the dirt from exhaustion, while in twos and threes, others began to wander down the road and back towards town.

"Where you guys goin'?"

"To the car."

"Hey, when you get there, come back and pick us up."

"Right."

"Aw, come on!"

"Yeah, we'll come back, all right…'bout the same time you and your best wishes get that thing to fly."

Snickers, barbs, and brays ensued. Shirts open to the warm night air, some teens brushing their sweaty locks out of their faces, everyone eventually flowed to the open road, leaving the flying machine at rest, alone and to itself.

Okay, where the heck did she go?

With an aura scan, Heather couldn't detect anyone in the orchard. It seemed she had given Mrs. Simpletripp too great a lead, and once she and her husband disappeared among the trees, they proved hard to spot again.

Although she was relatively unfamiliar with the wide-ranging orchard, having visited just the once, Heather pressed on, nevertheless. Yet, she was prudent, not wanting to hurry in pursuit of her quarry lest she inadvertently stumble into them.

And that was sorta MaidenWay-ish, wasn't it? thought Heather, being extra safe that way? After all, it wasn't like she was stomping around all over the place, honking on a tuba and stuff, while taking stupid chances. Right? Maidens, they take chances all the time. Lots of them. The thing is, they just make sure they don't get caught. Now, *that's* the MaidenWay.

When getting this close to Mr. Simpletripp and whatever he was doing, Heather knew she was treading on very dangerous ground. The man may look big and blubbery, but he was full of ugliness—total creepiness—that much was for certain. And if she were caught spying, who knew what that crazy guy would do to her?

Good thing she hadn't brought Molly along. Now, that would have been really *un*-MaidenWay-ish.

Ahead through the trees, moonlight filtered through the bare-knuckled branches, illuminating the soil below in velvety patches of bluish light. Several steps later, Heather was fortunate enough to rediscover Mrs. Simpletripp's aura, the woman plodding many rows ahead and to one side. Swiftly and silently the girl navigated the darkened maze of trees in an attempt to close the gap. Try as she might, however, she couldn't see Mr. Simpletripp anywhere.

Before her, Heather noticed a seeping glow of yellowish light, and with the moonlight brightening, she knew she was approaching the outer fringe of the orchard. Coming to a standstill well within the grove's shadows, the overly cautious girl took her time surveying the area.

Wow. Look at that.

Not far from Heather, over a scrubby patch of ground, down a walled embankment, and across a wide rim of uneven shoreline was a large pond fed by underground springs. Surrounding it were mud, boulders, grass, and an assortment of trees that were very tall and different from those comprising the orchard. Vying for sunlight, some rose to hang over the smooth, dark body of water. Once past the steep bank at the far end, the orchards sprang up again to encircle the pond, thick in their denseness.

There's no way people know about this place, thought Heather. How could they, hidden like this?

She regarded the neglected orchard above and behind her.

And there's no way Farmer Annandale's been down here for a while, that's for sure. Or he'd've seen whatever Mr. Simpletripp was doing—*and* he would have put an end to it.

Heather looked around for Mrs. Simpletripp. Having again lost sight of her, she assumed the woman had gone into hiding. The girl didn't need to take an aura scan to recognize Mr. Simpletripp just beyond some boulders, standing below the edge of the brush-lined embankment. His form lit by lantern light, she could only see his head and shoulders, unable to tell exactly what the man was doing on the other side of a huge, intervening rock.

After another aura scan taken for good measure, Heather slinked to the last in the row of orchard trees. Once there, she went into a crouch. Combing the area, she spotted a tree to her liking that she felt was safe enough to climb. And the way it hung over the water, Heather reasoned that if she climbed high enough, she would be able to attain a clear view of whatever lay between the sheer bank and the water's edge. That meant she could see exactly what Mr. Simpletripp was up to—what he had been up to all this time.

Accomplished as she was when climbing trees and moving in silence, and as far away as she and the tree were from Mr. Simpletripp, Heather felt certain it was 'MaidenWay safe' to proceed.

No problem, right? she thought. What could possibly go wrong?

Upon reaching the third floor, choosing to enter the first room encountered at the top of the stairs, Mrs. Pringle couldn't believe her eyes.

"This must be some kind of room of board games."

Looking around her, the walls were of flashing neon, of moving scenarios, glimpses of people and places game-related, fading and zooming, shifting and merging, transitioning into the very next image.

There were tables set up throughout the large room, and between were shelves and shelves of board games in their boxes, available for the choosing from floating racks or from spare, open-faced cabinets lining the walls.

Walking over an internally lighted floor amid carpets comprised of board designs, passing close by the tables, Mrs. Pringle thought she recognized some of the games from her childhood—at least their names were familiar.

Yet, now they appeared vastly different, set up in multilevel holographic layouts with, for instance, realistic hotels rising up in flashy modernity, and swanky areas of the game board displaying wealth and glitz, compared with other areas that were more mundane and low rent. And the incidental people occupying the game boards actually bustled about on all tiers, conversing with one another in lively gesture, or quietly and resolutely making their way past the hotels and storefronts—at times pausing before a display window, pushing past a cluttered doorway, or stepping to the curb to hail a taxi. They were tall, short, fat, and thin, dressed fashionably or feebly, and constantly in motion on the streets and sidewalks of the cities or in the adjoining neighborhoods.

Other complex game boards on other tables displayed battlefields populated with invading armies, great ships of war either firing guns or being sunk, knights laying siege to castles, detectives solving crimes in mansions, soldiers battling across enemy terrain to capture kings or flags, all taking place on many levels, in closeup and at a distance, in cross-sections, side, and overhead views. And until contestants sat down to actually play, the oversized game boards competed solely on their own, playing themselves to glorious victory while, at the same time, ignominious defeat.

"Where would one start?" Mrs. Pringle asked, very impressed. "The girls would know, I'm sure."

Making her way out the door, she entered a much quieter environment. The woman slowed her pace, her eyes traveling the room. The space was smaller though sizeable, with a vast array of scarves throughout.

Lovely! she thought. A shop of scarves.

In one corner, the scarves were arranged by color, in another area by pattern, or by length, warmth, fabric, style and weave. There were floor tables and shelves filled with scarves, and mirrors all around where browsers could try them on.

I wonder if Molly has been here?

Reaching the door, Mrs. Pringle stopped, thinking she had heard someone else in the shop. Surveying the room, she jumped at the sight of her face in a mirror.

"Gads…" She chuckled with relief, at what she felt was her silliness.

Unable to detect another soul, she exited into a great hallway with many doors to one side, the starry night gazing in through the overhead glass.

The wallpaper around her pictured bare trees, but before her eyes they slowly filled with leaves, and then blooms and fruits, before losing their leaves altogether to go barren once more. Relative to the season, wallpaper birds flew in and out, perched or built nests, while insects fluttered or buzzed past on the wall's flatness. Some of the trees, she noticed with amusement, became lit and decorated for Christmas before transitioning.

"Simply remarkable."

Walking down the hall, discovering no sign of the girls, Mrs. Pringle selected a door to her liking. She thought, Why not? Maybe they're in here.

The woman turned the handle and stepped inside a dimly lit room, closing the door after her. Unsure, she hesitated as she leaned in and looked around, her hand resting lightly on the knob.

"Hello?" she queried on the quiet. "Anyone here?"

Wilson Talbott opened the door a crack. Then wider. Not seeing Mrs. Pringle in the great hallway, he waited to be certain it was safe to proceed and then exited the shop of scarves. As was typical, he was unconcerned with any of the magical décor—with any décor whatsoever.

That said, he was astounded with what he found inside the rooms on the third floor of the Bristol House. From the little he had seen so far, Lana was right. The third floor was indeed something else, something else entirely. What made him wary, however, was how much it very much resembled the Bristol House of his nightmarish dream, with its many hallways and doors—and this despite the fact that he had never laid eyes on the place before. And, yet, at the same time the uncanny familiarity only heightened his curiosity, exciting his interest all the more. His senses alive on all counts, he welcomed the resulting exhilaration, and with it, the promise of supreme discovery.

Along one wall, Talbott glanced over the doors, each of a differing design. He began his approach, his brow lowered in serious contemplation.

So, which one did Lana choose?

He had no idea, and wasn't sure where to begin.

Well, I'll just pick one, then. If it's not the right one, I'll just leave and try another, no harm done.

On a nearby door, he saw a doorknob jiggle and start to turn. Caught unawares, Talbott quickly backed, not knowing what to do. His aim was to pursue, but not to be discovered in the process. And yet, if Lana Pringle knew something, something of value, he needed to know which door she had entered, so he could follow discreetly after her and find out what she was doing. In the process, perhaps he could stumble onto some vital piece of information related to the whereabouts of Scarbone's treasure—or, better yet, find the very treasure itself!

Now, his back pressed against the wall, Talbott waited, distrustfully observing the knob. When it remained stationary for an extended period of time, he decided he'd give the room a try. And why not, right? It had to be Lana inside. Or the girls.

Soundlessly turning the knob, he opened the door and stuck his head in, angling it this way and that.

What's this? On the third floor of the Bristol House? I don't believe it.

With no sign of Mrs. Pringle within his immediate view, Talbott stepped over the threshold. Moments later, he found himself walking out of a small darkened novelty shop and onto a rainy street, the door closing behind him. It was nighttime, the streetlamps lighting the quaint shops up and down the lane, the rainwater pooling in areas.

Why, it's England, thought Talbott, and the village where I first lived when coming to Earth from Evermore! Though it's changed quite a bit, I must say. He eyed the new, unfamiliar shops. "But this is it, all right. I'd know Lesserwood Downs anywhere! There's the pub over there on the corner, just so, and the bakery, and-and the cobbler's and the chemist's. Superb!"

Talbott spied a figure down the lane and across the street, under an awning near the old haberdashery. The individual was browsing, looking in a shop window, though its lights were out.

Is that Lana? Had to be. Hard to tell, though, through the rain.

Talbott turned up the collar on his trim jacket, his mind racing.

Surely, by his presence, Lana wouldn't suspect that he'd sneaked back into the Bristol House—why would she?—or have any clue whatsoever as to why he suddenly turned up on this particular street. By the very fact that they were standing in his hometown meant that Talbott really wouldn't have need to explain himself away—although he would. And when he invented a big fat fanciful lie to sway her, his explanation would sound perfectly plausible under the circumstances.

After all, this entire scenario, it *was* magic, wasn't it? Why, that stupid old pirate Bristol saw fit to bring him home, to inadvertently bring he and Lana together this way! What a dolt! What a dunderheaded thing to do! Surely, he, Talbott, would be able to manipulate this occasion to further advance his romantic agenda. Suddenly, he wanted to laugh and sing. What fortunate happenstance!

Ha-*ha!*

Inspired, leaping joyously off the curb and over a puddle, the tall upright Talbott dashed across the street despite the shouting pain from his wounded calf.

"Hey, there! Lana!" He waved. "Lana! Welcome to my beautiful hometown of Lesserwood. If you'd care to join me for a cup of tea or maybe a glass of wine, I'd be forever…" His words trailed off. "…grateful…" He slowed to a limp.

That wasn't Lana.

And now, walking out through the nearest door to join the shorter figure on the walk was a much taller man—if you could call him that. He was dressed in an open coat, a suit and tie.

"Well, surprise, surprise. If'n I'm not lookin' square at th'answer te a dream, yea. Horvin, will yah look at tha'."

"By all rights te shakin', looks te me te be a HumanKinder. How 'bout yah?"

"Oh, I'd likes te think I'd know me a HumanKinder any-a-wheres, 'grull. Hungry?"

"Famished te bedlam."

The pair stepped out from under the awning, off the curb and into the swirl of mist and rain.

Talbott backed while fishing in his pocket for his knife. Fumbling while removing it, his hands slick with wetness, the weapon fell uselessly to the ground, to be lost in a puddle. And there was no time to drop and look after it, no time to search.

Talbott emitted a little laugh. Ignoring the aggravated aching of his leg and side, he spun and began a sprint back towards the opposite side of the street, in the direction of the hallway door.

Which shop was it?

He realized he had never really looked. While glimpsing over his shoulder at his pursuers, he tripped over the curb, spilling to the ground. Staggering to his feet amid the screaming, soaring pain of his hip and ribs, he began desperately trying the handles on the shop doors, one to the next. All were locked.

Edged with dangerous purpose, the Jagrulls closed in, approaching through the rain, stepping over the curb of sidewalk.

"Someone!" yelled Talbott to the night, to the upper storied windows. "Hey, someone help me here!" He swallowed, madly glancing left, right. "Is there anyone here? Lana…?" He directed his attention to the nearest door and began pulling at the knob. "Come on, you!" he screamed. *"Give!"*

He pounded and kicked frantically. Now the Jagrulls were only footfalls away. Wilson Talbott could hear them, the rustle of their fabric, their breathing—their *stench.* He spun and retreated until he could retreat no longer. His back pressed against a stone storefront, his face was gripped with terror.

The Jagrulls closed the distance. One was displaying a sharp-toothed sneer.

"Horvin, I juss hates te see yah get tha' shiny new suit o' yurs spotted and dirty."

"Fer this'n? It'll be worth it, 'grull. I promise."

Having tentatively made her way inside, Mrs. Pringle found herself in a very comfortable octagonal room with the lights on low. The few walls were of white, with plush sofas and vista windows all around.

"How lovely."

Seeming to almost glide through the open glass doors and onto a balcony, she could see she was on the side of a hill, above the treetops, with the sun setting in the distance. The wide wandering river below held captive the vivid sky in muted colors still bright, and the lantern-lilies afloat all along the water's edge glowed in delicate hues of orange and yellow, red and blue, purple and green. Fragrantly, the wind whispered its phrases, end of day.

Welcome, Lana Pringle read the simple, embossed note card left upon a small circular table. It sat next to the wine that had been poured into an elegant glass, its rim catching sun. Mrs. Pringle picked up the goblet and, drifting to the rail, took in the view.

"So, this must be Evermore..."

chapter seventeen

End of a Journey

Stealing silently like a shadow, Heather left the concealment of the orchard and moved diligently overground, surpassing grass and bush to eventually encounter her desired climbing tree. Once there, she stood motionless, waiting to see if Mr. Simpletripp possessed any unforeseen inclination to come her way. Still preoccupied, he hadn't bothered to look up, his aura pulsing obsessively in dark and sinister blues. Meanwhile, Heather didn't have a good feeling about what lay beyond the embankment, of what Mr. Simpletripp was doing in that sunken area out of view.

Carefully securing what seemed to be a solid hand and foothold, Heather began her climb up the thick rough trunk. Along the way, she avoided grabbing any of the small shoot-like branches for assistance. The girl knew from experience that to do so would prove disastrous, as they would only bust loose with a sharp *snap!,* drawing Mr. Simpletripp's unwanted attention, bringing him charging at her in what would most likely be a rage.

Swiftly reaching a plateau of sorts among the branches, a junction of thick secondary limbs, Heather chose neither the lowest nor the highest, but settled on one that offered support and just a bit of cover. With that, she began to edge her way out over the embankment and towards the water. Sure-footed, she maneuvered, careful not to shake the branch or break loose any of its smaller appendages. She looked up at the confliction of limbs overhead and then at the moon and the starry sky beyond. On most any other night, under different circumstances, she would definitely enjoy her time in a tree like this. Not tonight, however.

As she advanced, Heather didn't dare to look down—and not because she was frightened. Far from it. She didn't look down because of her need to concentrate intensely on stealth, that to lose focus might cause her to become distracted and give her presence away in an unfortunate misstep.

And, now, balanced over the generous shoreline, feeling secured in place, Heather finally turned her attention below. At the sight, she wavered in recoil, stunned as she was.

Whoa… *Whoa!*

Revealed by moonlight and lantern glow was a series of ceramic animal coffins. Sculpted and looking somewhat crude in appearance, they were laid out in uneven rows stretching the length and breadth of the sunken shoreline. The majority were of small and medium size, but there were those, stationed near the center and toward the corners, that were extremely large and bulky. But that wasn't all. Scattered among them, a great many animal carcasses could be seen, their bare bones protruding, their woolly fleeces in various stages of decomposition.

In the midst of the lantern-lit grimness, next to a table-sized slab of stone, stood villainous Mr. Simpletripp. He was cutting deeply into his latest kidnap victim, a large sheep he had procured earlier that evening from the nearby town of Willard's Lamp. It was dead, laid to rest atop the rock, the kidnapper's hands darkly and viscously at work.

So, Mr. Simpletripp *was* the pet stalker, after all! I knew it! *I knew it!*

Enraged, her brow sharply furrowed and her eyes set afire, Heather began to breathe slowly and deeply, trying to calm herself—trying to practice the MaidenWay. Really, she just wanted to get out of there, away from the grisly scene. Mr. Simpletripp was proving to be a far, far sicker character than she could ever have imagined.

Trying to settle, trying to clear her head, Heather drew another deep breath.

She realized she would have to tell someone, that someone needed to know about this—though not Molly. Never Molly. Ever. Sheriff Dane. He'd do something about it.

Struggling with her rage, Heather wanted to do something herself, and do it right this very second. Yet, if she confronted Mr.

Simpletripp, never minding his size—and forget how whacked out the guy was—she truly feared she would do something horrible and very un-Maiden-like, something she would later regret. And this guy wasn't worth it. He just wasn't.

She continued to glare at the madman in the lantern light, concluding it was sad that a person like him was even alive.

People like Mr. Simpletripp didn't bring or give life to things, but instead took it away in a mean and ugly way. That can't be good for the world. And it's not right. Something like that *wasn't* the MaidenWay. When you hurt people and animals, how can you really feel good about yourself? *How?* Heather certainly never could.

On those thoughts, she began to descend the limb, never wanting to get away from a place so badly in her life—and never wanting to see or spy on this creepy, creepy guy ever again.

Truly, she just wanted to retreat somewhere and be alone with the moon.

Molly was lost in the orchard. In her pursuit of Heather, she had somehow become confused and off track, only to find herself wandering alone amid the orderly rows of trees. Moreover, it was extremely dark, too, and the girl was doing her best not to feel frightened.

Where can Heather possibly be?

Molly couldn't help but feel disappointed. Until just moments before, she had been doing so well. And, now, what's the use of practicing her spy skills, if there wasn't anyone to spy on? Besides, how could she hope to surprise Heather with her new and improved capabilities when she had no idea where to find her—and only because she had lost her trail?

Definitely *not* very impressive technique.

Well, then, it's probably time to give up the chase and head for home. But which way was it?

Deciding to follow the line of trees in an effort to find the street, it wasn't long before Molly spied the yellow lantern light in the clearing. Altering course, she began her secretive approach, bending low on the sneak to do so.

Now bravely advancing the remaining distance on hands and knees, she was surprised to discover the pond. And at the nearest end she spotted Mr. Simpletripp, his back and side to her. What was he doing?

And where was Heather?

Slinking in closer still, carefully mounting a large group of boulders embedded in the embankment, Molly kept herself close to the ground, all the while maneuvering to get a better glimpse, a better line of sight. Knowing Mr. Simpletripp to be absorbed for the time being, Molly realized if she simply stood and edged over a couple steps, she could achieve the precise view she desired.

So, very deliberately, she began to rise to her full height on the angled rock. And then she leaned—her arm shakily out for balance, her head atilt and her neck craned—until she beheld the gruesome sight. Slowly, on a dawning, Molly's mouth dropped as her eyes went wide, the girl shaking her head, bringing a hand to her parted lips. She watched in fascinated horror as Mr. Simpletripp stripped off the sheep's fur as if it were a wet blanket. Instinctively, she started backpedaling up the boulder's incline, and when she turned to flee, she glimpsed Vera Simpletripp behind her in the darkness, hiding near a tree.

Screaming at the unexpected sight, Molly cringed and lost her balance. Faltering, she fell over backward, tumbling down the rock face and over the sheer bank, landing in the mud and grass along the shoreline below.

"Hey! Who's over there?" It was the guttural voice of Simpletripp sounding out. Hands dripping at his sides, he was stepping away from the lantern's influence, glaring into the darkness and in Molly's direction.

Dazed and hurt from her fall, Molly tried to recover and swiftly find her feet. Finally clambering upright, exposed fully in the moonlight, she began running, finding the very act itself to be ungainly while traversing the uneven, unpredictable ground.

"Hey, you! *You!* Stop right there!" roared Simpletripp, the butcher having caught sight of her.

Molly screamed again.

Up in the tree, Heather was beside herself. Oh, no! Molly! What the heck? *What the heck!!!*

And now, Mr. Simpletripp was giving chase, racing to intercept the terrified Molly before she could escape up a gentle incline located in the corner below Heather, a place where she would be able to hurry out of the sunken area without hindrance.

For Heather, everything was unfolding far too quickly. She was trying to descend the tree as fast as possible, muttering to herself, "Come on, Molly. Get away, get into that orchard!"

And actually, Heather thought her friend had a pretty good chance of making it, too, given the fact that Mr. Simpletripp didn't appear to be in any great physical shape or moving all that swiftly. But then she watched as Molly caught her shoe among the squabble of shoreline brush and rock, tripping and falling, before hurriedly scrambling to regain her feet.

In her desperate attempt to reach the more accommodating corner, Molly was giving an all out effort, blindly and clumsily making headway—at times, stumbling and clawing. Meanwhile, lumbering toward her and closing ground in the process, Mr. Simpletripp was dodging between his tombstone sculptures, in his haste sometimes stomping on the strewn assortment of ribcages and skulls, snapping and kicking up shards of bone.

Realizing he was several steps in the lagging and that Molly would escape to expose his secret, in desperation, Simpletripp scooped up the thick end of a long, broken branch, and, whirling, whipped it viciously before him.

"Horace, no!" Mastering her fear, Mrs. Simpletripp had finally bolted from the shadows, running to assist the girl, to try and ward off her husband from inflicting any harm. But her effort came far too late, and from a distance far too far away.

Mr. Simpletripp's slashing flash of limb connected with a loud *thwack!*, smacking the youngster thickly on the side of the head. With the impact, Molly yelped, the rotted branch snapping and busting loose, the girl crumpling in a slender heap to the ground.

Heather gasped, pausing in stupefied distress. Hurry! she told herself. *Hurry, or he'll hit her again!* Instantly alive and once more in motion, Heather took to sliding recklessly in descent, freeing herself up from the confusion of limbs.

Yet, it wasn't long before the swiftly moving Heather realized Mr. Simpletripp had other, more malevolent intentions for his unwanted interloper, this intrusive witness to his most disturbing artistic creation. Bending to lift a large and weighty pet coffin into his arms, the big man tottered under the strain as he clomped in Molly's direction. Now, his hovering form only steps away, with a bounce and a face-contorting heave he hoisted the moonlit burden high overhead—its elongated shadow settling like an ominous cloud over Molly, darkening her face and torso. Heavily, his arms shaking under the strain, he blundered toward her.

"No-o-o-o!" At the yelling of the word, Heather leapt high from one branch to grab hold of another, and swinging out with her feet, she

touched down and launched herself from a third.

Hurtling through the air, she could only watch as, straightening, Simpletripp brought the ceramic piece down with great force. Managing to kick the coffin aside just enough to miss Molly—the heavy corner crashing down to bury itself in the earth—Heather landed awkwardly on Mr. Simpletripp's shoulders, his thick body giving with the force, stumbling with the impact. Then, as he righted himself, the scrabbling girl maneuvered and clamped onto his neck with her legs. From above and behind, she began hitting him with all the force she could muster, the man yelling in fits his muffled rage.

Staggering somewhat comically, Mr. Simpletripp tried to wedge the pummeling Heather from his shoulders—as if removing an irritating, hollow pumpkin attached snugly over his head. Yet, the slender girl seriously rode this bull of a man as they lurched about in the lantern light, Heather landing blow after blow, her fists raining down with amazing strength, Simpletripp's cringing head dodging this way and that, taking a thrashing.

In agony from his swollen mouth, the man cried out for her to stop, the thick slapping of fist to skin agitating the night air. And, still, amid the flurry, his slippery, fumbling hands doggedly tried to tear her loose—her crossed ankles holding her firmly in place, her thighs squeezing hard his barrel neck.

"How could you hurt Molly! *How could you?!*" she gasped at him through her savage tears, the fisted volley of wrecking balls having their way unimpeded. "You creep!" *Whap!* "You're a creep!" *Whack! Whack!* "You hear me?" *Whack!* "You punish people." *Whack!* "You hurt animals." *Whap!* "You're the kind who would kill lions and rhinos and elephants and-and Archmounts." *Whack! Whack!* "You *don't* kill animals! You don't. You listen to them. If we listen to animals, they talk to us. You hear me?" *Whack!* "They have their special way, and they talk to us. So, you *start* listening! Get it?" *Whap! Whap! Whap!* "*You start listening!*"

When Heather grabbed him under the chin, wrenching his face upward, she drove downward and scored with another fist to his mouth, dislodging some teeth. All Simpletripp could do was try to bring his forearms up to cover his face, but Heather continued her assault, her decisive punches landing on and around his ham hock defenses.

When the big man reeled, Heather's blows continued to find their mark ruthlessly and nevertheless, resulting in a fleshy, puffy façade smeared and splashed with dark liquid. And still she relentlessly rode the wounded bull.

"Why anyone would ever love you," Heather cried, "I don't know. I don't know! How could they? *How?!* You're so cruel…" *Whack!* "…so mean!" *Slap! Slap! Slap!* "You hurt things...you hurt these poor animals…" *Whack! Whack!* "…you hurt Molly! You're a mean…" *Whack!* "…mean…" *Whack!* "…ugly, killing creepball!" *Whap!*

"Heather…Heather stop," pleaded Mrs. Simpletripp, nervously milling alongside, maintaining her distance. "You'll kill him." But her soft voice refused to penetrate, the girl focused solely on the man.

Abstractly, Heather knew she was out of control. Faraway, she could hear Sedgwar's voice, calming her, soothing her, fighting for her to overcome her rampaging spirit, for her to tame her inner beast. She tried to get ahold of herself, of her stampeding emotions run amok, but, truly, she had no desire to do so. Legs still locking her firmly in place, in frustration, Heather threw back her head and cast up her arms. For all she felt for Molly, for all the love contained within her torn and devastated heart, she looked to the overseeing moon and let loose with a howl, a pain-wracked primal cry. Her plea cleaved the night.

With that, lest he be the recipient of more punishing madness, Mr. Simpletripp cowered below her. Dizzied, the burly man, his face ravaged and covered in blood, pitched forward on buckling knees, only to fall face first into the soft mud lining the water's edge. Heather, riding him to ground, tumbled upon impact, before slipping in an effort to gain her feet.

Mrs. Simpletripp ran to her husband and with great effort turned him over. Then resting back on her haunches, she gazed with relief, seeing he was still alive, his breathing labored, his mouth a gurgling sinkhole.

Having risen from her knees, Heather could only stare, her narrow chest heaving, the girl wanting to resume the assault, wanting to stomp Molly's assailant beyond recognition and straight into some horrid, furious kind of hell. Fiery tears streaming down her cheeks, she was crying openly, her sobs riding her gasps in waves, her smarting fists balled at her sides, ready for more.

"She wasn't supposed to come!" Heather yelled at the castigated man. "You hear me? *She wasn't supposed to be here!*"

The girl whirled. In challenge, she glared into Mrs. Simpletripp's shadowed features, the woman now dumbly returning her gaze. Full of unbridled rage, Heather wanted to scream at her for the man she had married, for the man who assaulted her friend, but instead broke away to run to the strewn-limbed Molly. Slapping down hard on her knees, plowing up the soil, she brushed her friend's gloppy hair aside, revealing in full Molly's bloodied face.

Was she breathing? Heather couldn't tell, and so lowered her ear close to the girl's mouth. She couldn't hear her draw, couldn't feel her breath.

"Molly?" She shook her gently. "Oh, Molly, please...please, talk to me."

Molly remained slack, unmoving, her head wound bleeding profusely.

Heather was trembling. "Oh, Molly...please, don't go...okay? Please." She screamed out to the empty night, "Someone help!" Then looking at the lifeless Molly through a swim of wetness, she whispered, "Please, help."

The night was quiet, the wind still. Heather attempted an aura scan on Molly, but everything ran wetly together, and so she scrambled, her fingers to the side of her friend's neck, feeling for a pulse. Heather was impatient, clumsy, her fingers frantically feeling, feeling...

"Heather, why don't you come away, now. Come."

"No!" Heather shook her shoulders loose from the gentle touch. "This is Molly! You stop it! Just stop!"

"Here, Heather, move aside, child." Heather looked over in surprise at the compassionate words, her cheeks glazed with moon glow. It was the Maiden from the Shady House garden going to a knee beside her. Uncomprehending, Heather made room, watching as the woman felt for a pulse on Molly's neck, before briefly inspecting her head wound. Then, sliding her arms beneath the recumbent girl, the Maiden lifted her easily while rising to her feet.

"We'll take care of her."

Still on her knees, dazed, Heather watched as the tall, darkened form walked away from her, Molly limply in her arms. Against the moonlight shimmering off the water, the woman stood momentarily stationary. Then, as the Maiden strode towards the pond, the framework of an arched, translucent doorway remarkably appeared before her. And in the very next instant, in the dire pounding of an Evermorian heartbeat, she and Molly entered only to disappear from sight. Shortly afterward, the Portal dimmed, before fading altogether.

Heather continued to look on as if in a dream, as if trying to come to terms with what had just happened, attempting to recognize the entire scene for what it was and, by doing so, bring it into some form of acceptable reality. No longer crying, blinking in its aftermath, she worked to make the series of events whole and real.

"Well, *that* certainly was a shocker, wasn't it?" said a familiar voice at her ear. "You can't help but love an unexpected, but entirely happy ending."

Heather didn't respond. Awakening from her stupor, the girl climbed to her feet. She glimpsed LoviL flying at eye level beside her, but then returned her attention to the vicinity of the pond.

"Molly being hurt that way is nothing to joke about." The girl's words were low, perhaps menacing. "And I don't see how you could ever call anything like that a happy ending."

"Oh, but it *is,* as happy as one can have under the circumstances. She's a Maiden taking Molly to be cared for by Maidens. It gets no better."

"You think so?" The girl still wore her serious, dangerous edge.

"I do."

Turning, Heather gazed openly in his direction, and in all her naked vulnerably, asked the Nefflyn, "LoviL, really? Is Molly really going to be all right?"

LoviL slowed so he was momentarily visible. "I thought I just said so. Heather, she *will* be. She's going to be cared for by the best."

Taking a moment to absorb the information, Heather's ire suddenly surfaced.

"So, then, where were *you,* huh? How come you didn't just magically stop Molly from getting hurt?"

"As always, I had business to attend to. I'm sorry. I only just arrived—"

"Right."

Although Heather could no longer see LoviL directly, she could sense him flying all the closer, scrutinizing her. She waved him off.

"What's wrong? Heather, there's no reason to feel downhearted that way when Molly—"

The girl turned her back on him, longing to push away the world, craving distance. Not wanting to get near Mr. Simpletripp, in fear of herself, she abruptly veered to wander in a different direction. Still, she was trying to think clearly, needing to formulate a plan. Meanwhile, the Nefflyn hovered.

Shaking her head, Heather muttered: "I lost it, LoviL. I lost my temper and the war against myself. I'm a Maiden, right? I'm supposed to be a Maiden, a responsible Maiden practicing the MaidenWay, only fighting when I need to. And look at me…" Heather regarded her bloodied hands, "…I almost became a Simpletripp."

"Heather, you're still young, still learning, and Molly is your best friend. It's understandable—"

"Sedgwar…he'd…he'd be super disappointed in me right now. I'll have to tell him, too…" Heather was trying to once more calm her overwhelming storm of emotions, the rage of her conflicted seas. And, yet, when she glanced at Mr. Simpletripp, just the revulsion that immediately arose in her made her want to pummel him some more. The Nefflyn noticed.

"Aw, forget that loveless man, dear girl." LoviL's tone was consoling. "Stars like you, you encounter people like your neighbor all the time in the biz—small people who want to be big, people who need to best others in an effort to feel themselves supremely important, and only because they feel inadequate and truly loathe themselves. They're insecure, jealous, and petty, and they spend their lives trying to climb and plant a flag on everyone else's mountain, when they should really be climbing to conquer their own."

Adrift in thought, Heather awoke from her trance and regarded the Nefflyn with mild irritation. "LoviL, what the *heck* are you talking about?"

Having come up with a plan, the girl started backing. She was surprised to find Vera Simpletripp staring at her. A quick scan revealed her confused aura in muddled grays, interspersed with the dawning of lighter colors.

"Come on, then," said Heather, in a hurry to depart the scene, heading into the trees and towards the street. "We need to go after Molly and the Maiden. Do you know if there's a Portal around here?"

"Well, actually, I do. I'm a Nefflyn. We know of these things, these venues, how to leave the stage quickly if ever we need to run for the wings and the nearest exit—"

"Okay, okay. Come on, then. Follow me." Heather ducked below some branches, her night vision called upon once again as she sped through the moonlight-dappled orchard. "Remember the stage at the Small Thyme Theatre?"

"How can I forget? A command performance, if ever there was one. Among my best."

"Well, then, we need to get some LoviL-magic working right here, right now. Just like you did that night. Can you do it?"

"Can I do it? *Of course, I can do it!* I'm a Nefflyn, remember? We're blazing the trail of *history in the making!*"

"Yeah, yeah, yeah, whatever…"

Up to speed in an all out sprint, Heather was tearing through the orchard and toward the street, LoviL close behind, sometimes at her ear. Emerging breathless, spotting the abandoned flying machine, Heather was surprised to see it so conveniently parked before her, the girl fully intending to run down to the Professor's house to retrieve it.

Hands on knees, she spoke while riding her harsh exhalations. "See Professor Periwinkle's flying machine over there?" She pointed with her chin.

"Yes. A cantankerous configuration if ever there was one—"

"Can we make it fly?"

Heather didn't wait for an answer, but started running toward it, LoviL breezing alongside.

"Can we make it fly?" The Nefflyn scoffed. "Piece of cake, as they say."

"Thought so."

In the soft shine provided by the moon, Heather was climbing aboard, gripping the grips on the handlebars, quickly moving them this way and that, getting the feel of the pedals beneath her red sneakers. She glanced sidelong at LoviL.

"Ready?"

He nodded eagerly. "When am I never?"

"Well, for one, when you're leaning against my bedroom wall asleep. But never mind. Come on, let's get this thing *moving!*" She lowered her chin. "Hold on, Fallasha, because here we go!"

Abruptly standing, her weight and muscle pushing foot to pedal, foot to pedal, urgh!, urgh!, urgh!, urgh!, *urgh!,* Heather put her extraordinary strength to work, getting the flying machine swiftly up to speed, its wheels at a smooth blur gliding over the pavement. Cloth wings flapping, propeller blades above her pumping and spinning clackity-clack, Heather pointed the whacky contraption down the long reach of roadway. First passing Sheriff Dane's pickup truck parked so neatly, now passing the mysterious boxy green car abandoned at an harried angle, Heather drove the professor's invention forcefully onward—for Molly, for her grandmother, for herself and all her worlds—the machine wobbling frantically side-to-side beneath her seat.

At the sound of barking, Heather glanced sidelong and slowed. Racing out into the road, appearing as if by magic, was Cary the Bristol House dog. With a leap, the pet slammed into her tummy—"Hey!"—before settling in her lap. Temporarily thrown off stride, pausing to collect herself, the next instant had Heather peddling furiously once more.

Behind her, LoviL had taken the opportunity to arrange himself comfortably on the back seat, harp in hand. Feeling the drawn-out bounce and skim of the many wheels beneath him, the Nefflyn proclaimed, "Set your sights on the stars, young lady, because here we *go!*"

A *Bling!* rang out, and the machine started to rise, the smear of moonlit asphalt falling away below, their shadow parting company with the road. Cary jumped into the large storage basket just over the handlebars and behind the fuel tanks, the hair on his protruding head and shoulders blowing with the wind.

Turning the handlebars while pushing down gently on the grips caused some fins at the sides and rear of the craft to angle differently, and gaining altitude, the machine banked and headed over the orchard. In the distance, the town of Noble became slowly visible beyond the trees, lit festively for Christmas.

The machine's wings still a-flap, its rotors whirring in a blur, Heather continued to pedal. Peering down over the treetops, she saw the clearing and its small body of water, and, alongside, the dotting of the ceramic caskets containing the dead. She recognized the recumbent body of Mr. Simpletripp, with Mrs. Simpletripp standing over him. The girl thought she waved.

Before turning away, a brief aura scan revealed her creepy neighbor emanating in bruised and blackened violets amid stable browns, while his wife gave off shades of disconcerted, disconsolate greens.

Aiming the preposterous aircraft toward the large circle of moon—where else?—Heather asked, "Hey, LoviL, can I stop peddling yet?"

"Anytime. I'll take it from here."

"You mean—?"

"I do. I mean that, up to this point, this hunk of trash was flying on Heather power in an outstanding, athletic performance by my rising young star."

"Really?" Heather chuckled.

"Of course, I admit, as we Nefflyns are prone to do, getting this entire production off the ground, I did help you there at the start."

Easing in her effort, Heather continued to peddle, nevertheless. It just seemed the natural thing to do when moseying across the sky. Cary took a brash moment to hop out of the basket, climb over Heather, and deposit himself on the backseat.

"Hey!" she exclaimed, peeling him off, now assisting him. Then, laughing, she added, "You goofy dog."

Settling on his haunches, mouth open, tongue hanging, Cary relished the onrushing air. The displaced LoviL took to the wing, zipping his way up and alongside Heather.

In awe of the great lunar sphere before them, the girl herself aglow, she remarked, "Gotta love that moon!" and, then, more seriously, "So, where are we headed?"

"SkyPortal."

"Is that like a WindowPortal in the sky?"

"Can be."

Heather gave her head a shake, freeing some strands of windblown hair from her face. "Where does it lead?"

"I'm not sure. Some Evermorian venue where you'll no doubt be asked to perform in your award winning role as the green-eyed Maiden."

"Will you hang around and watch the show?"

"Oh, you know. But I'll certainly wish you well and beg that you break a leg."

"Whatever *that* means. Hey, do you think wherever the Maiden took Molly, that's where I'll find Grandma Dawn and Avella?"

"Perhaps."

"And you're sure Molly is going to be all right?"

"The Maiden said the MaidenHood would take care of her, didn't she?"

"Yep!" And like a young Maiden practicing the MaidenWay, Heather trusted in the words, taking them in to the deepest part of her, while allowing time to give with time.

Daring to reach and give Cary's hair a tousle midflight, she asked LoviL, "Think we'll be back in time for Christmas?"

Yet, before the Nefflyn could respond, content in the zany, carefree moment and under the gaze of her glorious moon, Heather Nighborne was certain she knew the answer.

On the ground far below, having doused both her husband's lanterns, Mrs. Simpletripp stood feeling isolated in the blue-green spill of moonlight. Nevertheless, she didn't move. Longingly, the woman watched the progress of the winged and rotored flying machine, wishing she were on it, wishing she were far away, so far away.

She continued to stare, unable to pull her eyes from the chattering, bobbing contrivance with the venturesome girl at the controls. Unknowingly, the child was defying the very gravity that kept Vera Simpletripp planted so firmly in Noble, planted for a calcified lifetime with a husband she didn't know, never knew, and certainly didn't love.

What Heather had said to him only a short while ago, the girl was right. And now, having sorted it out for herself, surrounded by such irrefutable and repulsive evidence, Mrs. Simpletripp was unafraid to acknowledge that Horace Simpletripp was a horrible, despicable man, someone with whom Vera realized she could no longer bring herself to live. And that certainly changed things.

At her feet, Mr. Simpletripp moaned, but didn't move. His wife heard him mutter, and paid his utterance little heed. She didn't want to look down any longer.

Instead, she kept her vision riveted high overhead where, glazed in constant contrast against the full circle of moon, rode the lively-spirited Heather, an amazing, strong-willed girl full of youth, vigor, and passion—full of *life.*

And Vera Simpletripp couldn't help but find herself envying that. At this moment, here, she wanted to reel in time so badly, and knowing everything around her could be so different, wished to start her life over again for all she imagined that was absolutely possible.

Still staring, she heard a murmur of words adrift on air, Heather's words floating down to her. She waved in desperation, wanting to scream out, "Take me with you!" but, stuck for a lifetime being Vera Simpletripp, she couldn't bring herself to do so. Perhaps it was too late for that. And, yet, she had waved, hadn't she? So, maybe that was a start.

When the clatter suddenly ceased, she searched the sky only to find the image of the rickety aircraft had all but disappeared, leaving her irrevocably alone with her life. It was then that Mrs. Simpletripp heard the trees rustle and felt a wintry breeze. She shivered. The woman, determined to be no one's fool ever again, knew the weather was changing.

Her eyes roamed once more over the sickening pond-side scenery, over the decaying skeletal remains of the exposed animals, as well as the many containers clumsily depicting the various pets killed, dismembered, and entombed by her wicked husband.

And that's when she noticed the large, handmade coffin half-buried in the mud. On its lid, in the vague bluish light, she recognized her husband's sculpted likeness of their neighbor, the missing Thaddeus Levine. Ironically, for once, Horace's attempt at a life-sized face was remarkably well done. Walking over to it, she knelt and placed her hand tentatively, delicately, against his cool ceramic cheek. At rest, she left it there to linger, at least knowing she had loved.

Slightly bent over, Professor Anders Periwinkle pulled his eye away from his tripod telescope. He stood up straight, blinking while replacing his glasses, his gaze still absently lifted toward the heavens.

Earlier, when searching the nighttime sky to spot a meteor shower, he had inadvertently come across a young girl and her dog puttering before the stars and the moon in his very own flying machine.

"Well, I'll be…"

Having observed the pair until they abruptly disappeared, now walking distractedly back toward the house, he soon picked up speed. Then, eliciting a small hop, he clicked his heels before mounting the stairs to the porch with a spring and a bound.

"Bertha?" he called. "Bertha, you're never going to believe this…"

Entering the Periwinkle household, he slammed the front door behind him. With the impact, the porch light buzzed and sputtered, and then went dark, leaving the secretive face of night to conspire, hidden beneath its alluring veil of moon glow.

Endsong

Allowing Sleeping Dogs to Lie

Sheriff Dane was moody, surly even.

His mouth pressed tight one moment, he shook his head the next, muttering, "Yessir. Delivered for all the hell in the here and hereafter."

Driving home in his pickup truck, Dane found himself mulling over justice, karma, and the differences between the two, concluding that justice didn't need a courtroom when karma was on hand to deliver the ultimate verdict and even out the score. And when that happened, if left alone—if left untouched, immaculate, and pristinely played out—the world was a better place for it.

Earlier that evening, upon discovering the whereabouts of Periwinkle's stolen machine, Dane had been drawn towards the shouting and, subsequently, the lantern light. From his remote and advantageous spot within the orchard trees, the sheriff had arrived in time to observe the young Heather Nighborne riding Simpletripp's beefy shoulders roughshod to the ground. Hustling to intervene, he suddenly held off, watching with fascination when a strangely dressed woman stepped forward to spirit the injured Molly Pringle away.

Damned unreal, that.

And, afterward, he was himself an eyewitness to the Nighborne girl and the dog when they rode off in Periwinkle's flying machine. Even now, he could recall their figures riding in that rickety, bumbling contraption, framed against the large moon above, their images reflected on the pond below. Here one minute, they were gone the next.

Who in town would believe his report and not think Dane delusional?

And, then, in yet another stupefying stretch of the imagination, the sheriff found himself positioned perfectly to confirm his suspicions about the murderer Horace Simpletripp. Stationed closer to the scene, Dane couldn't help but overhear the one-sided conversation that transpired, Mrs. Simpletripp talking gently and lovingly to what looked like a crude ceramic coffin, amid the revelation that it was Thaddeus Levine's burial site.

Mindboggling.

And finally, about to step in and offer assistance to what appeared to be a distressed Vera Simpletripp, the lawman further restrained himself. Simply on a notion. Continuing to observe from his hidden vantage point, he watched her pick up her husband's shovel—no doubt, he thought, to begin burying what remained of the man's latest Pet Stalker victim, a stripped and gutted sheep there in the makeshift graveyard.

Yet, Sheriff Dane was surprised to see her instead walk calmly over to the idle figure of Horace Simpletripp, face up in the mud, and lifting the shovel to the extreme, bring it hurtling down to deliver a wicked blow to his head. And still, Dane didn't move. Not a muscle. He continued to grimly observe, bearing witness as the small woman brought up the shovel for yet another time and then down again in dull, bell-ringing fashion. And, afterwards, once more in a gruesome shock of finality.

That was when Dane turned away. He'd seen enough—more than enough. The sheriff decided he would return later to recover Simpletripp's lifeless body after the rains set in. Or not.

Acknowledgements

Having given life to *Maiden of a Darkness Shining,* I wish to thank my TrueSisters Leila and Tracy; my First and Final Draft Readers, Chris Medrea, Lyn Hawkins, Pat Jackson, Cathleen Cherry, and Joanna Hawthorne; as well as the delicate and indelible web of family, students, and friends that I left behind in Prescott, Arizona, upon my departure. At times of dusky reflection, they surprisingly emerge to inhabit the ever-expansive playgrounds of my imagination.

A very important thank you goes to my brother George Aleco-Sima who sat and shared with me the many warrior ways. And special thanks, as well, to his alter ego Michael who first learned them.

I'd like to thank my cousins Vito and Teresa Saccheri for entrusting me to reside on their ten acre property in Santa Rosa, California for a year-and-a-half while writing the first drafts of Parts Two and Three of *Maiden*, as the area wove itself finely into the living texture of the story, creating a broader landscape, a greater quilt.

And not to be left out or ever forgotten for his generosity, many thanks to my boyhood friend from the 'ideal family' of memory, Gregory Kopta, who granted me the freedom to stay and have the run of the entire downstairs in his home in Seattle, Washington. It was there that I untangled and smoothed out the many wrinkles of my final draft, while coming full circle with Mazie and Carrie, reacquainting myself with the insightful Elise, and fending off spiders the size of Manhattan.

Also, I'd be remiss for not mentioning those who have lent support to my lovely and creative *Maiden* along the way in the form of advice, patience, and steadfast encouragement: Doug Chiang and Shirley Glasshoff, Brad Hamer and Stella Sutherland. Undeniably, the world is a better place with them in it.

I'd also like to extend my gratitude to the Prescott Police Department and Alameda County Sheriffs Department for their valuable time when relating invaluable information in reference to parts of the story.

As to my dear friend, Wendy, who has been there for me several times over, may she live on in real time. And, too, for young Heather, may she thrive as she strives to make a place for herself in the world.

Meanwhile I must include a shout-out to my own personal Nefflyn who has existed in a state of self-imposed exile. Do put in an appearance soon, will you? Like darling Brutessa, I can't take much more of this.

And, finally, a tip of the hat must be given to the lonely boy who continually haunts and intrigues.

About the Author

David Saccheri—traditionally-trained studio draughtsman and painter, digital artist of film and game, author, illustrator, instructor, nurturer of roses, pursuer of the Greater Creative, a scattered philosopher and dreamer renowned—wisely remains in hiding until the world reclaims a modicum of its sanity. He was last seen doing something somewhere, although this cannot be confirmed.

www.GoldenHourArt.com

www.ingramcontent.com/pod-product-compliance
Lightning Source LLC
LaVergne TN
LVHW050510100826
845148LV00002B/290

* 9 7 8 0 6 9 2 8 2 4 8 7 0 *